The SHAPE of SNAKES

Also by

M I N E T T E   W A L T E R S

The Breaker   •

The Echo   •

The Dark Room   •

The Scold's Bridle   •

The Sculptress   •

The Ice House   •

The SHAPE of SNAKES

MINETTE WALTERS

G. P. PUTNAM'S SONS
NEW YORK

Photographs for Chapter Six by Michael Trevillion, The Trevillion Picture Library. Reproduced by permission of Macmillan General Books, London.

G. P. Putnam's Sons
Publishers Since 1838
a member of
Penguin Putnam Inc.
375 Hudson Street
New York, NY 10014

Library of Congress Cataloging-in-Publication Data

Walters, Minette.
   The shape of snakes / Minette Walters.
      p.   cm.
   ISBN 0-399-14733-0
      1. West Indians—England—Fiction.   2. Women cat owners—Fiction.
3. London (England)—Fiction.   4. Women, Black—Fiction.   I. Title.

PR6073.A444 S48   2001   00-065319
823'.914—dc21

Printed in the United States of America

10   9   8   7   6   5   4   3   2   1

This book is printed on acid-free paper. ∞

BOOK DESIGN BY DEBORAH KERNER

For
John,
Henry
and Frank

Only pure White Christian people of non-jewish, non-negro, non-asian descent . . . can enter the Knights of the Ku Klux Klan

. . . The name Ku Klux Klan comes from the Greek word *Kuklos,* meaning circle . . . Kuklos thought about in this context simply means White Racial Brotherhood . . .

. . . The Klan symbol of the Blood Drop denotes: "the blood of Jesus Christ which was shed for the White Aryan Race" . . .

. . . The Fiery Cross "is used to rally the forces of Christianity against the ever increasing hordes of the anti-Christ and enemies of . . . the White Race" . . .

. . . "The Knights of the Ku Klux Klan does not consider itself the enemy of non-Whites . . . (but) . . . will oppose integration in all its manifestations" . . .

UNRESTRICTED KKK PROPAGANDA ON THE INTERNET

With thanks to:

Adrian, Alec, Andrew, Annika, Beverley, Caroline, James, Jane, Michael, Philippa, Richard, Sharon and Susanna.

And with special thanks to Nick Godwin, Allen Anscombe, Rachel Harris and Ruth Wild for their professional help and advice.

Tics are categorized as Motor or Vocal, Simple or Complex. . : . Complex symptoms include: Body jerking, Skipping, Hitting, Walking on toes, Talking to oneself, Yelling, Coprolalia—vocalizing obscene or other socially unacceptable words or phrases. . . . Tics increase as a result of tension or stress.

KANSAS CITY CHAPTER
OF THE TOURETTE
SYNDROME ASSOCIATION

Unhappiness has a habit of being passed around.

MARGARET ATWOOD,
BBC RADIO 4'S BOOK
CLUB, MAY 9, 1999

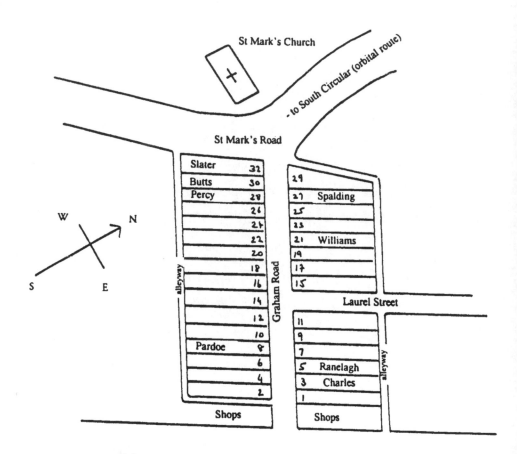

St Mark's Church

- to South Circular (orbital route)

St Mark's Road

Slater	32		29	
Butts	30		27	Spalding
Percy	28		25	
	26		23	
	24		21	Williams
	22		19	
	20		17	
	18		15	
	16			
	14			
	12			
	10			
Pardoe	8			
	6			
	4			
	2			

Graham Road

alleyway

Laurel Street

11	
9	
7	
5	Ranelagh
3	Charles
1	

alleyway

Shops

Shops

W   N

S   E

- to M3 & the South -   Lower Richmond Road (A316)   -   to London

LONDON BOROUGH OF
RICHMOND UPON THAMES

one

I could never decide whether "Mad Annie" was murdered because she was mad or because she was black. We were living in southwest London at the time and I remember my shock when I came home from work one wet November evening to find her collapsed in the gutter outside our house. It was 1978—the winter of discontent—when the government lost control of the trade unions, strikes were an everyday occurrence, hospitals ceased to cater to the sick and uncollected rubbish lay in heaps along the pavement. If I hadn't recognized her old plaid coat I might have ignored her, thinking the bundle in the gutter was a heap of discarded clothes.

Her real name was Ann Butts and she was the only black person in our road. She was a well-built woman with a closed expression and a strong aversion to social contact, who was known to enjoy a drink, particularly Caribbean rum, and was often to be found sitting on the pavement in the summer singing gospel hymns. She had acquired the "Mad" label because she made strange faces and muttered to herself as she scurried along in a bizarre dot-and-carry trot that suggested a child playing "Ride a cock horse to Banbury Cross."

Little was known about her circumstances except that she had inherited her house and a small independent income upon her mother's death and, apart from a menagerie of stray cats that had taken up residence with her, she lived alone. It was said that her mother had been madder than she was and that her father had abandoned them both because of it. One of the long-term residents of Graham Road swore blind that Mrs. Butts senior used to shout obscenities at passersby and twirl like a dervish when the mood was on her, but as Mrs. Butts had been dead some time the story had undoubtedly grown in the telling.

I didn't believe it any more than I believed the rumors that Annie kept live chickens inside her house, which she killed by boiling, feathers and all, for her own and her cats' supper. It was nonsense—she bought her meat, dead, at the local supermarket like everyone else— but her close neighbors talked about rats in her garden and a terrible smell coming from her kitchen, and the story of live chickens was born. I always said she couldn't have rats *and* cats, but no one wanted to hear the voice of reason.

The same neighbors made life difficult for her by reporting her regularly to the local council, the RSPCA and the police, but nothing came of their complaints because the council couldn't force her out of her own house, the cats were not ill-treated and she wasn't mad enough to be committed to an institution. Had there been family and friends to support her, she might have taken her harassers to court, but she was a solitary person who guarded her privacy jealously. At various times health visitors and social workers made unsuccessful attempts to persuade her into sheltered accommodations, and once a week the local vicar knocked on her door to make sure she was still alive. He was always cursed loudly for his trouble from an upstairs window, but he took it in stride, despite Annie's refusal to go anywhere near his church.

I knew her only by sight because we lived at the other end of the road but I never understood why the street took against her so strongly. My husband said it had to do with property values, but I couldn't agree with him. When we moved onto Graham Road in 1976 we had no illusions about why we could afford it. It had a Richmond postcode but it was very definitely "on the wrong side of the tracks." Built for laborers in the 1880s, it was a double row of two-up, two-down terraced housing off the A316 between Richmond and Mortlake, and no one who bought a house there expected to make a fortune overnight, particularly as council-owned properties were seeded among the privately owned ones. They were easily identified by their uniform yellow doors and were looked down on by those of us who'd bought our houses because at least two of them held problem families.

Personally, I thought the way the children treated Annie was a better barometer of the adults' feelings. They teased her mercilessly, calling her names and aping her dot-and-carry trot in a cruel demonstration of their right to feel superior, then ran away with squeals of fear if their pestering irritated her enough to make her raise her head and glare at them. It was a form of bearbaiting. They goaded her because they despised her, but they were also afraid of her.

In retrospect, of course, I wish I'd taken up cudgels on her behalf but, like everyone else who stayed silent, I assumed she could take care of herself. Certainly the children weren't alone in finding her intimidating. On the one occasion when I made an attempt to speak to her, she rounded on me angrily, calling me "honky," and I didn't have the courage to try again. Once in a while afterward I would come out of my front door to find her staring up at our house, but she scampered off the minute she saw me and my husband warned me not to antagonize her any further. I told him I thought she was trying to say "sorry," but he laughed and said I was naïve.

On the night she died a freezing rain was falling. The hunched trees that lined the pavements were black and sodden with water and made the street look very grim as I turned onto it from the main road. On the other side, a couple paused briefly under one of the few lampposts, then separated, the man to walk ahead, the woman to cross on a diagonal in front of me. I pulled up my coat collar to shield my face from the stabbing rain before stepping off the curb to run through sheets of water toward my house.

I found Annie lying on the edge of the yellow lamplight in a space between two parked cars and I remember wondering why the couple hadn't noticed her. Or perhaps they had chosen to ignore her, believing, as I did, that she was drunk. I stooped to rock her shoulder but the movement caused her to cry out and I stepped back immediately. She lay with her head cradled in her arms, her knees drawn up tight against her chin and I assumed she was protecting herself from the rain. She smelled powerfully of urine, and I guessed she'd had an accident, but I shrank from the responsibility of cleaning her up and told her instead that I was going home to call for an ambulance.

Did she think I wouldn't come back? Is that what persuaded her to uncradle her poor head and lift her pain-filled eyes to mine? I have no idea if that was the moment she died—they said afterward it probably was, because her skull was so badly fractured that any movement would have been dangerous—but I do know I will never experience such an intense intimacy with another human being again. I felt everything she felt—sorrow, anguish, despair, suffering—most poignantly, her complete bewilderment about why anyone would want to kill her. "Was I unlovable?" she seemed to be asking. "Was I unkind? Was I less deserving because I was different?"

Many hours later, the police questioned my incoherent ramblings. Did Miss Butts actually say these things? No. Did she accuse someone directly? No. Did she speak at all? No. Did you see anyone run away? No. So there's no evidence to support your assertion of murder other than a puzzled look in her eyes? No.

I couldn't blame them for being skeptical. As they pointed out, it was unlikely I could have interpreted Annie's look with any accuracy. Sudden death was always difficult to come to terms with because the emotions surrounding it are complex. They tried to convince me it was heightened imagination following my shock at finding her and offered me post-traumatic stress counseling to get over it. I refused. I was only interested in justice. As far as I was concerned, whatever residual shock I felt would vanish the minute Annie's murderer or murderers were caught and convicted.

They never were.

The coroner's verdict, based on the postmortem results and witness statements taken during a two-week police investigation, was death by misadventure. He painted a picture of a woman whose hold on reality was poor even when she was sober but who, on the night in question, had been drinking heavily. Her blood showed a high level of alcohol and she was seen staggering around the road by passing motorists and several neighbors. One said he had tried to persuade her to go home but gave up when she started swearing at him. Her injuries—in particular the fractures to her skull and broken left arm—were consistent with a glancing blow from a heavy vehicle, probably a truck, which had thrown her between the stationary cars and against the lamppost as it passed. Due to the heavy rainfall that night, it was unsurprising that no blood, hair or tissue traces were discovered on the lamppost.

The fact that no driver had come forward to admit liability was not considered significant either. It was dark, pouring with rain, parked vehicles restricted visibility and the street lighting was inadequate. With a critical reference to council officers who allowed badly lit streets in poorer areas to become rat-runs for heavy traffic, the coroner endorsed the police view that Miss Butts had stumbled off the pavement into the side of a passing truck without, in all probability, the driver being aware of the contact. It was impossible to establish when the accident occurred, although due to the seriousness of Miss Butts's injuries it was doubtful she could have survived more than fifteen to thirty minutes.

It was a sad case, the coroner said, which highlighted the need to have an element of compulsion in the treatment of vulnerable people in a modern society. There was clear evidence—the squalid state of her house when the police entered it the day after her death; her alcohol dependency—that she was unable to look after herself properly, and it was his opinion that if social services and health workers had been able to force Miss Butts to accept help, she would still be alive today. The witness who found Miss Butts's body had alleged a racist campaign against Miss Butts by her neighbors, but there was no evidence to support this and the coroner accepted that her neighbors' actions had been prompted only by concern for her welfare. In conclusion and despite the same witness's emotional insistence that Miss Butts had been deliberately pushed in front of an oncoming vehicle, the coroner's verdict was unequivocal. Death by misadventure. Case closed . . .

I fell ill shortly afterward and took to my bed for several days. I told the doctor who came to see me that I had the flu, but he diagnosed depression and prescribed tranquilizers, which I refused to take. I became frightened of the telephone; every sound from the road had me jumping out of my chair. My husband, Sam, was initially sympathetic but soon lost interest when I began sleeping in the spare room and talking about rats in the downstairs lavatory. Thereafter, I developed mild agoraphobia and found it harder and harder to go to work. I was a teacher at a local comprehensive school and my overburdened colleagues were even less sympathetic than Sam when I said I felt stifled by the way the children crowded around me in the corridor. After a few weeks I ceased going in altogether.

The whole episode—from Annie's death to the loss of my job—caused a rift between me and Sam, who walked delicately around me for weeks, then took to speaking to my mother for hours on the telephone. He was careful to close the door but I could still hear most of his conversation through the paper-thin walls on the rare occasions when I bothered to listen. The phrases repeated most often were "impossible to live with . . ." "having a nervous breakdown . . ." "got a thing about rats . . ." "stupid fuss over a bloody black woman . . ." and "divorce . . ."

Some time in February my parents drove up from Hampshire where they were then living. Sam had moved out three weeks previously to sleep on a friend's sofa, and our marriage was effectively over. Wisely, my father refused to get involved, but my mother couldn't resist taking Sam's part. She comes from that generation of women who believe that marriage is the key to a woman's happiness and she told me in no uncertain terms that if I was determined to reject Sam then I needn't look to her and my father for support. As she pointed out, I'd been deserted by my friends because my behavior was so peculiar. . . . I was rapidly becoming anorexic. . . . I had no job . . . worse, no prospect of a job while I remained firmly closeted in the house. What was I planning to do? Where was I planning to go?

I expressed only mild annoyance that she believed everything Sam told her, and suggested she question a man's honesty for once in her life. It was like a red flag to a bull. We couldn't talk about sex—or lack of it, Sam's real bone of contention with me—because it was a taboo subject between us, so instead she lectured me on the way I was letting myself go, my failure to cook proper meals for my hardworking husband, my lackluster approach to cleaning the house and inevitably my absurd obsession with the death of a colored person.

"There might be some sense in it if she'd been one of us," she finished tartly, "but she wasn't even English . . . just another wretched immigrant living off benefit and clogging up the health service with imported diseases. Why we ever let them in, I can't imagine, and for you to jeopardize your marriage—" She broke off abruptly. "Can't you see how ridiculous you're being?"

I couldn't, but it wasn't something I was prepared to discuss with her. Predictably, my silence persuaded her she'd won the argument when all she'd really achieved was to prove to me how little I cared about anyone's opinion but my own. In an odd way her complete lack of sympathy was more liberating than distressing because it made me realize that control rests with whomever worries least about being seen to exercise it, and with cold deliberation I agreed to mend fences with my husband if only to keep a roof over my head.

Three months later, Sam and I moved abroad.

CORONER'S COURT

Medical Report on Miss Ann Butts, submitted to Mr. Brian A. Hooper, coroner, on December 12, 1978, by Dr. Sheila Arnold, GP, FRCP, from the Howarth Clinic, Chicago, Illinois, U.S.A. (Formerly a partner in the Cromwell Street Surgery, Richmond, Surrey.)

(Dr. Arnold left for a twelve-month sabbatical in America on September 10, 1978, and was absent at the time of Miss Butts's death. Although Miss Butts had been assigned to one of Dr. Arnold's partners for the duration of the sabbatical, Miss Butts died before the partner had time to meet and assess her. It was therefore agreed that Dr. Arnold would submit the following report from America. A full set of medical notes relating to Miss Butts has been made available to the Coroner by the Cromwell Street Surgery.)

Ann Butts was my patient from June 1969 until my departure for America on September 10, 1978. She suffered from Tourette's syndrome, a neuropsychiatric disorder characterized by recurrent muscle tics and involuntary vocalizations. It was an inherited condition from her mother who had a complex form of the disorder, which manifested itself as *coprolalia,* a compulsion to utter obscenities. Ann, who cared for her mother for many years until her death in 1968, had a good understanding of Tourette's syndrome and had learned to manage her own condition successfully. Ann's most noticeable symptoms were 1) motor tics in the face and shoulders; 2) a compulsion to talk to herself; and 3) obsessive behavior, particularly in relation to home and personal security.

I referred her in December 1969 to Dr. Randreth Patel (Middlesex Hospital), who took a particular interest in Ann and was sympathetic toward her firmly held views against the taking of psychoactive drugs, which she felt had worsened her mother's condition rather than improved it. While no one has yet discovered a cure for Tourette's syndrome, the disorder tends to improve with age and Ann was no exception to this. My understanding is that her tics were a great deal more pronounced when she was a teenager (DOB—12.3.36). As a result, she suffered considerable teasing and unkindness from her peers and had few social skills following an early withdrawal from formal education. In recent years Ann's symptoms had been comparatively mild although she was inclined to exacerbate them from time to time through an overindulgence in alcohol. She had an average IQ and had no difficulty leading an independent life, although her obsession with home and personal security meant she shunned the company of others. I made a point of visiting her every six to eight weeks and on my last visit—September 8, 1978—she was in good health, both physical and mental.

Sheila Arnold

Sheila Arnold GP, FRCP

TWENTY
YEARS
LATER

CURRAN HOUSE
Whitehay Road
Torquay
Devon

Thursday, May 27, 1999

Darling,

I don't know why you always have to get so angry when someone questions your decisions. It's most unladylike to scream like a fishwife down the telephone, particularly when you're three thousand miles away. Of course Daddy and I will be pleased to have you home but you can't expect us to be thrilled about this silly idea to rent a farmhouse in Dorchester. It's over two hours' drive away, and your father will never be able to manage the double journey in a day. Also, it's hurtful. We've only seen our grandchildren twice in twenty years—each time on very expensive holidays—and we always hoped you'd bring them to live near us when you finally came back.

I can't help feeling it's not too late for me to find you something in Devon. We have a very good real estate agent here who has a list of reasonable properties to rent. Have you taken the trouble to have this farmhouse vetted? The description you gave was very vague, and frankly £650 a month sounds very expensive for a house in the middle of nowhere. You do realize, I suppose, that there are a lot of charlatans about and it's very easy to put an advertisement in the "Sunday Times" in the hopes of attracting foreigners to summer lets.

You know I <u>hate</u> to be critical, but I do wonder if Sam and the boys have been consulted about this move. As usual, I fear you have made a unilateral decision <u>and totally ignored the wishes of everyone else.</u> You say you're only renting the farmhouse for three or four months, but do please explain why Dorset is preferable to Devon. It's absurd to say you want to revisit the place where you spent your honeymoon. I thought you had more sense than to pursue holiday memories from 1976.

We're glad to hear that Sam is on the mend although we found Luke and Tom's flippant references to his "dodgy ticker" somewhat inappropriate, particularly as Sam was clearly listening to the phone call. I find it difficult to believe that they're now eighteen and nineteen. Frankly I'd have expected a little more maturity from boys of their age, and I fear you've been spoiling them.

I shall wait to hear re the real estate agent.

All my love,

Ma

PS Dear M, personally, thought the "dodgy ticker" was wonderful and loved to hear Sam laugh at the other end. <u>What a marvelous relationship you and he have with your boys</u> and what a blessing they've been these last few months. I'm much looking forward to sharing some of the Ranelagh Jr. fun, even if it means driving two hours to experience it! Tell Luke I have every intention of having at least one go on a surfboard even if I do go "arse over tit" in the process. I may be an old codger, but I'm not in my grave yet.

Dad

X X X

Cape Town

5 June

Dear Mother,

    Written in haste. Sorry about the screaming but the line was bad. I enclose a photocopy of the farmhouse details. I have taken up references and am reliably informed that £650 is a good price. It would be considerably more, apparently, if it weren't a property of "character," which appears to be real estate–agent shorthand for "somewhat dilapidated." However, Sam and the boys are looking forward to slumming it as much as I am. All being well we should be there by the first week in July and will expect you and Dad at the end of the month. I'll ring to confirm a weekend as soon as we're installed. We're all fine and send our love to you both.

N

Dorchester: 18th century stone farmhouse for short or long let. Character property in idyllic rural setting, 2 mls from town center, 5 bedrooms, 3 reception rooms, 2 bathrooms, large quarry-tiled kitchen. 1 acre garden, adjacent paddocks. Fully furnished, oil-fired c/h, Aga, garage. £650 p.c.m. Tel: 01305 231494

t w o

I recognized Dr. Arnold as soon as I opened the door to her, although there was no answering smile of recognition from her. I wasn't surprised. We were both twenty years older, and I had changed a great deal more than she had after two decades abroad. She was silver-haired and thinner, late fifties, I judged, but she still had the same rather searching gray eyes and air of unassailable competence. On the only other occasion I'd met her, I'd found her thoroughly intimidating, but today she gave me a sisterly pat on the arm when I told her my husband was complaining of chest pains.

"He says it's a pulled muscle," I said, leading the way up the stairs of our rented farmhouse, "but he had a coronary six months ago and I'm worried he's about to have another one."

In the event, Sam was right—it was a pulled muscle from too much digging in the garden the day before—and I concealed my total lack of surprise behind an apologetic smile. Dr. Arnold reproved him for scoffing at my concern. "You can't take chances," she told him, folding her stethoscope, "not when you've had one close shave already."

Sam, whose memory for faces was almost as bad as his memory for names, buttoned his shirt and cast an irritable glance in my direction. "It's a ridiculous fuss about nothing," he complained. "I said I'd go to the surgery but she wouldn't let me . . . just takes it into her head to start treating me like a blasted invalid."

"He's been biting my head off all morning," I told Dr. Arnold. "It's one of the reasons I thought it might be serious."

"Goddamit!" Sam snapped. "What's the matter with you? All I said was, I had a small twinge in my side . . . which isn't surprising in view of the number of weeds I hauled out yesterday. The garden's a mess, the house is falling down. What am I supposed to do? Sit on my hands all day?"

Dr. Arnold poured oil on troubled waters. "You should be grateful you have someone who still cares enough to make the phone call," she said with a laugh. "I had a patient once whose wife left him to writhe in agony on the kitchen floor while she downed half a bottle of gin to celebrate her imminent widowhood."

Sam wasn't the type to stay angry for long. "Did he survive?" he asked with a grin.

"Just about. The marriage didn't." She studied his face for a moment, then looked curiously toward me. "I feel I know you both but I can't think why."

"I recognized you when I opened the door," I said. "It's an extraordinary coincidence. You were our GP in Richmond. We lived in Graham Road from '76 to the beginning of '79. You came to our house once when Sam had a bout of bronchitis."

She nodded immediately. "Mrs. Ranelagh. I should have recognized the name. You're the one who found Annie Butts. I've often wondered where you went and what happened to you."

I looked casually from her to Sam, and was relieved to see surprised pleasure on both their faces, and no suspicion . . .

Sam landed a job as overseas sales director for a shipping company, which took us in turn to Hong Kong, Australia and South Africa. They were good times, and I came to understand why black sheep are so often sent abroad by their families to start again. It does wonders for the character to cut the emotional ties that bind you to places and people. We produced two sons who grew like saplings in the never-ending sunshine and soon towered over their parents, and I could always find teaching jobs in whichever school was educating them.

As one always does, we thought of ourselves as immortal, so Sam's coronary at the age of fifty-two came like a bolt from the blue. With doctors warning of another one being imminent if he didn't change a lifestyle that involved too much traveling, too much entertaining of clients and too little exercise, we returned to England in the summer of '99 with no employment and a couple of boys in their late teens who had never seen their homeland.

For no particular reason except that we'd spent our honeymoon in Dorset in '76, we decided to rent an old farmhouse near Dorchester, which I found among the property ads in the *Sunday Times* before we left Cape Town. The idea was to have an extended summer holiday while we looked around for somewhere more permanent to settle. Neither of us had connections with any particular part of England. My husband's parents were dead and my own parents had retired to the neighboring county of Devon and the balmy climate of Torquay. We enrolled the boys at college for the autumn and set out to rediscover our roots. We'd done well during our time abroad and there was no immediate hurry for either of us to find a job. Or so we imagined.

The reality was rather different. England had changed into New Labor's "Cool Britannia" during the time we'd been abroad, strikes were almost unknown, the pace of life had quickened dramatically and there was a new widespread affluence that hadn't existed in the '70s. We couldn't believe how expensive everything was, how crowded the roads were and how difficult it was to find a parking space now that "shopping" had become the Brits' favorite pastime. Hastily the boys abandoned us for their own age group. Garden fêtes and village cricket were for old people. Designer clothes and techno music were the order of the day, and clubs and theme pubs were the places to be seen, particularly those that stayed open into the early hours to show widescreen satellite feeds of world sporting fixtures.

"Do you get the feeling we've been left behind?" Sam asked glumly at the end of our first week as we sat like a couple of pensioners on the patio of our rented farmhouse, watching some horses graze in a nearby paddock.

"By the boys."

"No. Our peers. I was talking to Jock Williams on the phone to-day"—an old friend from our Richmond days—"and he told me he made a couple of million last year by selling off one of his businesses." He made a wry face. "So I asked him how many businesses he had left, and he said, only two but together they're worth ten million. He wanted to know what *I* was doing so I lied through my teeth."

I took time to wonder why it never seemed to occur to Sam that Jock was as big a fantasist as he was, particularly as Jock had been trum-peting "mega-buck sales" down the phone to him for years but had never managed to find the time—*or money?*—to fly out for a visit. "What did you say?"

"That we'd made a killing on the Hong Kong stock market before it reverted to China and could afford to take early retirement. I also said we were buying an eight-bedroom house and a hundred acres in Dorset."

"Mm." I used my foot to stir some clumps of grass growing be-tween the cracks in the patio, which were symptomatic of the air of tired neglect that pervaded the whole property. "A brick box in a mod-ern development more likely. I had a look in a real estate agent's win-dow yesterday and anything of any size is well outside our price range. Something like this would cost around £300,000 and that's not count-ing the money we'd need to spend doing it up. Let's just hope Jock doesn't decide to visit."

Sam's gloom deepened at the prospect. "If we'd had any sense we'd have hung on to the house on Graham Road. Jock says it's worth ten times what we paid for it in '76. We were mad to sell. You need to keep a stake in the property market if you want to trade up to something reasonable."

There were times when I despaired of my husband's memory. It was a peculiarly selective one that allowed him to remember the precise details of past negotiating triumphs but insisted he forgot where the cutlery was kept in every kitchen we'd ever had. It had its advantages—he was easily persuaded he was in the wrong—but once in a while it caught me on the raw. At the very least, he ought to have remembered the weeks of abuse that followed the inquest into Annie's death . . .

"It was *my* choice to leave," I said flatly, "and I don't care if we end up living in a caravan, it's one decision I'll never regret. You might have been able to stay on Graham Road. . . . I certainly couldn't . . . not once the phone calls started anyway."

He eyed me nervously. "I thought you'd forgotten all that."

"No."

The horses kicked up their heels for no apparent reason to canter to the other side of the field, and I wondered how good their hearing was and whether they could pick up vibrations of anger in a single word. We watched them in silence for a moment or two, and I put money on Sam backing away as usual from the period in our lives that had brought us to the brink of divorce. He chose to follow a tangent.

"In purely financial terms Jock's probably right, though," he said "If we'd kept the house and let it, we'd not only have had an income all these years but we'd have made a 1,000 percent increase on our capital to boot."

"We had a mortgage," I told him, "so the income would have gone straight into paying it off and we'd never have seen a penny of it."

"Except Jock says . . ."

I only half-listened to Jock's views on the beneficial effects to borrowers of the galloping inflation of the late '70s and early '80s and how the Thatcher revolution had freed up entrepreneurs to play roulette with other people's money. I hadn't had much time for him when we lived in London and, from Sam's reports of the conversations he'd had with him via the international phone network over the years, I could see no reason to change my opinion. Theirs was a competitive relationship, based on vainglorious self-promotion from Jock and ridiculous counterclaims from Sam, which anyone with an ounce of intelligence would see straight through.

I roused myself when Sam fell silent. "Jock Williams has been lying about money since the first time we met him," I murmured. "He latched on to us in the pub for the sole purpose of getting free drinks because he claimed he'd left his wallet at home. He said he'd pay us back but he never did. I didn't believe him then and I don't believe him now. If he's worth ten million"—I bared my teeth—"then I've got the body of a twenty-year-old."

I was doing Sam a kindness although he couldn't see it because it would never occur to him that I might know more about Jock than he did. How could I? Jock and I had had no contact since our strained farewells on the day Sam and I left London. Yet I knew exactly what Jock was worth, and I also knew that the only person likely to lose sleep over it was Jock himself when his braggadocio lies finally came home to roost.

Sam's gloom began to lift. "Oh, come on," he said. "Things aren't *that* bad. The old bum's spread a bit, admittedly, but the tits still hold their shape."

I gave him an affectionate cuff across the back of the head. "At least I've still got all my hair."

POLICE WITNESS STATEMENT

Date: 16.11.78

Time: 18:27

Officer in charge: PC Quentin, Richmond Police

Witness: Sam Ranelagh, 5 Graham Road, Richmond, Surrey

Incident: Death of Miss A. Butts in Graham Road on 14.11.78

On Tuesday, 14.11.78, I reached Richmond station at about 7:30. My friend, Jock Williams, who lives at 21 Graham Road, was on the same train and caught up with me as I passed through the ticket barrier. It was raining heavily, and Jock suggested we make a detour to the Hoop and Grapes in Kew Road for a pint. I was tired and invited him back to my house instead. My wife, a teacher, was at a parents' evening and was not due home until 9:30. The walk along the A316 takes approximately 15 minutes, and Jock and I turned into Graham Road at around 7:45.

I have lived in Graham Road for two years and knew Ann Butts well by sight. On several occasions in the last six months I have come across her outside our house, staring in through the windows. I have no idea why she did this although I believe she may have been trying to intimidate my wife, whom she called "honky." In view of the bad weather, I was surprised to see her there again on Tuesday night (14.11.78). She moved away as we rounded the corner. She was clearly drunk and when I pointed her out to Jock we both used the word "paralytic" to describe her. We were reluctant to approach her because she seemed to have a strong dislike of white people. We crossed the road behind her and let ourselves into my house.

Jock remained with me for approximately one-and-a-half hours, and we spent most of that time in the kitchen. The kitchen is at the back of the house and the door to the corridor was closed. At no point did we hear anything from the road that would suggest an accident had occurred. Jock left at approximately 9:15 and I accompanied him to the front door. I had completely forgotten seeing Ann Butts earlier and it did not occur to me to look for her again. I watched Jock turn right out of our gate toward his own house before going back inside.

I was shocked when my wife came rushing in fifteen minutes later to say Mad Annie had collapsed in the gutter and looked as if she was dying. I ran out with a torch and found her body between two parked cars outside number 1. It seemed obvious to me that she was already dead. Her eyes were open and there was no pulse in her neck or her wrist. I made an attempt at mouth-to-mouth resuscitation but gave up when there was no response. An ambulance arrived shortly afterward.

I regret now that I made no attempt to assist Ann Butts back to her house at 7:45, although I am convinced she would have rejected the offer.

Signed:
  Sam Ranelagh

In the presence of: *A. Quann*

39a Templeton Road
Southampton
Hampshire
UK

May 20, 1980

M'dear!

You could have knocked me down with a feather when your letter came through my door. And what great news about the baby. Seven months old, eh? Conceived in England and born in Hong Kong. Has to be lucky! Of course we must remain friends. God knows, I didn't spend hours listening to your heartache in the wake of Annie's death to abandon you the minute you move abroad. I'm just so glad you got in touch because the way things are—i.e., Jock and I aren't speaking. AT ALL!—I didn't know how to contact you. Of course I'll help you in any way I can, although I'm a little worried that your letter seems to imply Jock and Sam had a hand in Annie's death. Much as I loathe the two-timing maggot I married, I don't think he's vile enough to kill anyone and certainly not someone he hardly knew. As for Sam! Do me a favor!

Okay, so Sam got drunk one night and admitted they lied to the police about where they were and now refuses to have Annie's name mentioned. Well, trust me, sweetheart, I don't think you should read too much into it even if I do understand how angry you must feel. Sam had no business to lie for Jock however "good" the cause. Still, that's men for you. They stick to each other like glue, but cast off their women whenever it suits them!

Re your questions:

1) Did I tell the police that Jock had been with Sam? Yes. As you know, they started knocking on everyone's doors the day after the event, wanting to know if we'd seen or heard the accident. I said I'd been alone at home watching telly and hadn't heard a thing, so they promptly asked me what my husband had been doing and I said, "Having a drink with Sam Ranelagh at number 5."

2) Did Jock volunteer the information when he got home or did I ask for it? I asked him the night of the 14th. The little toerag came rolling in half-cut as usual and I said, "Where the hell have you been?" "Round at Sam's having a beer," he came back quick as a flash. I should have known he was lying! He always used Sam as a way out of a crisis.

3) What time did Jock get home that night? Nine-fifteenish. Can't recall exactly. I'm sure the nine o'clock news was still on.

4) Have I any idea when Jock spoke to Sam in order to concoct the alibi? Knowing Jock, he would have phoned Sam at work the next morning and told him he was on the spot and had to think up a lie on the spur of the moment. "If anyone asks, I was with you. So don't let me down, will you?" That kind of thing.

In passing, I doubt very much if Jock had been gambling again, whatever he may have told Sam. He had a floozy in Graham Road, a bleached vampire called Sharon Percy, who was little better than a prostitute. He claims he was having an affair with her but my solicitor forced him to produce his bank statements and it looks as if he was making regular payments to her every Tuesday in return for sex. He's denying the payments at the moment (but not the affair—he seems quite proud of that!) but my solicitor's confident we can drag the truth out of him if he refuses to make a reasonable settlement and we end up in court.

Anyway, the point is, Annie died on a Tuesday and I suspect Jock was rogering Sharon rather than gambling! For all I know it may have been the first time because he never bothered to explain his lateness on a Tuesday again. Or any other day for that matter! You're right. The prospect of imminent divorce is a great relief and I have every intention of taking him to the cleaners if I possibly can. He only produces documents after my solicitor applies thumbscrews, and he explains his purchase of a house in Alveston Road (v. swank £70,000 five-bedroom job within spitting distance of Richmond Park—complete with live-in blonde bimbo!) as a "long-term, heavily mortgaged investment." This, on the back of the paltry £10,000 he took as his 50 percent share of 21 Graham Road. Do me a favor! Do the sums add up, or do they? The best I could afford was this two-room flat in Southampton.

Feel free to ask for any help I can give you. It would never occur to me for a minute that talking about Annie might bring on "a fit of the vapors" and how very old-fashioned of Sam to come up with such an expression. No woman I know goes in for such idiocies, and I doubt if they ever did. It was yet another invention of man to undermine the onward march of female supremacy. Yes, I'm bitter, and . . . yes, the whole male sex can go fuck itself as far as I'm concerned . . . I've taken a leaf out of your book and have come to Southampton to train for a career in teaching. Dammit, girl, if you can make money tutoring Chinamen in Hong Kong, I can surely make money tutoring brats over here!

Love,

Libby

PS For purely selfish reasons, I'm glad you're not keen for Sam and Jock to know you're asking questions! My solicitor's warned me to stay mum about how much I already know about his shenanigans, otherwise he'll bury his assets in hidden accounts and I'll never get my fair share of the booty!

three

"It blew over very quickly," Sheila Arnold told me as we went downstairs, "except that Annie's house stood empty for about three years. She hadn't made a will and no one knew if there were any living relatives. In the end, everything was appropriated by the government and the property was released for sale. It was bought by a builder who renovated it before selling it to a young couple with two small children."

"A white couple presumably," I said with poorly veiled sarcasm.

She ignored the remark although her mouth lifted in a faint smile. "I visited the house soon after they moved in when the younger child fell ill," she went on, "and the place was unrecognizable. The builder had gutted the whole of the downstairs and redesigned it as one huge open-plan room with patio doors to the garden." There was reservation in her voice as if she wasn't sure that an open plan was an improvement.

"Didn't you like it?"

She paused by the door. "Oh, it was splendid enough, but I couldn't help remembering what it was like in Annie's day. Did you ever go inside while she was living there?" I shook my head. "It was like an Aladdin's cave. She and her mother were both hoarders. The front room was packed with West Indian and Central American artifacts, all brought back to England by Annie's father during the '40s and '50s. Some of them were quite valuable, particularly the gold pieces. I remember there was a little statuette on the mantelpiece which had emeralds for eyes and rubies for lips."

"I didn't know there was a Mr. Butts," I said in surprise. "I always assumed the mother had been left holding the baby."

"Good Lord, no. Her father died of lung cancer some time in the late '50s. I never knew him but one of my partners remembered him fondly. His name was George. He was a retired merchant seaman with a fund of anecdotes about his travels round the world. He married Annie's mother in Jamaica in the '30s and brought her and Annie home to live in Graham Road soon after the war." She smiled again. "He said he couldn't bring them back while his parents were alive because they wouldn't have approved of a black daughter-in-law."

I shook my head in amazement, realizing how many gaps there still were in my knowledge of a woman I had never spoken to. Did Annie's neighbors know she was half white? I wondered, and would it have made a difference if they had? I thought "no" to both questions. They had been even later arrivals to the street than Sam and I . . . and Annie had been too dark-skinned to pass as anything other than black. "I didn't know any of this," I told Sheila. "I certainly didn't know her father was a white man. Why didn't someone come forward to claim her estate? She must have had English relations, surely?"

"Apparently not. My colleague said George had a younger brother who was torpedoed in the North Atlantic, but other than that—" She broke off on a shrug. "It's tragic but not unusual. Whole families were wiped out during the two world wars, particularly those with sons and no daughters." She glanced reluctantly at her watch and stepped outside. "I really must go. I've two more patients to see." But she moved slowly as if she didn't want to break this link with the past. "Do you still think she was murdered?"

"I know she was."

"Why?"

I led the way down the path. "I can't explain it. I tried once, but everyone just thought I was as mad as she was. Now I don't bother."

"I meant, why would anyone have wanted to murder her?"

It was the great imponderable. "Because she was different," I suggested. "Perhaps they'd have left her alone if she'd been mad but not black . . . or black but not mad . . . Sometimes I think they despised her for her color, other times I think they were afraid of her."

We halted beside her car. "Meaning you think one of her neighbors killed her?"

I didn't say anything, just gave a small shrug which she could interpret as she liked.

She watched me for a moment, then opened the rear door of her car and put her bag on the backseat. "She wasn't mad," she said matter-of-factly. "She had Tourette's syndrome, which caused her to grimace and talk to herself, but she was as normal as you or I in every other respect."

"That's not the impression the coroner gave at the inquest."

Dr. Arnold nodded unhappily. "The man was an idiot. He knew nothing at all about TS and wasn't interested in finding out. I've always felt very badly about not giving evidence in person, but I left for a twelve-month sabbatical in the U.S. before she died and had no idea he would effectively ignore Annie's medical records." She saw the sudden hope in my face. "The verdict would have been the same," she said apologetically. "There was no evidence to suggest it was anything other than an accident but I was very angry afterward to discover how her reputation had been destroyed."

I thought cynically that the anguish I'd seen in Annie's dying eyes had had nothing to do with concern for her reputation. "Did you read the pathologist's report?"

She nodded. "I was sent a copy with the inquest verdict. It was very straightforward. She caught a glancing blow from a truck and was thrown against a lamppost. Frankly, it was a tragedy waiting to happen—they should never have let Graham Road be used as a shortcut—but I always thought a child would be hit, not someone as mindful of safety as Annie was."

I nodded. "She was wearing a dark coat the night she died, and the weather was frightful . . . rain like stair rods. I only saw her because I almost stepped on her as I was crossing the road." I put a hand on Dr. Arnold's arm as she prepared to open the driver's door. "You said you were angry about her reputation being destroyed. Did you follow that up?"

A faraway look crept into her eyes as if she were searching some distant horizon. "Not for three years. It may sound callous but I forgot all about her while I was in the States, and it wasn't until I saw what the builder had done to her house that it occurred to me to ask what had happened to the contents."

"Presumably they were sold off."

She went on as if she hadn't heard me. "People had a very false impression of Annie because of the way she dressed and the way she behaved, but she wasn't a poor woman by any manner of means. She once showed me a list of valuations that a dealer had put on some of the artifacts, and my recollection was that the total came to over £50,000. That was a fair sum in the 1970s."

"The police must know what happened to it all," I said. "Did you ask them?"

She gave a theatrical shudder. "Not *them*," she countered tartly, "just the one. A man by the name of Sergeant Drury—Joseph Stalin's younger, ruder and more aggressive brother. It was his case so I wasn't allowed access to anyone else."

I laughed. "I knew him. It's a good description."

"Yes . . . well, according to him, Annie was destitute. They took some RSPCA inspectors in the day after the accident in order to remove her cats, and Drury said there was nothing of value in the house. Worse, he described the conditions inside as little short of a cesspit."

I nodded again, remembering. "It was mentioned at the inquest. The Coroner said the RSPCA should have taken her animals away from her when the neighbors first complained about the smell."

"Except squalor was alien to her nature," said Dr. Arnold, folding herself behind the steering wheel. "I used to visit her regularly and it was a battle to stop her jumping up every ten minutes to wash her hands. She had a thing about germs—it's a common symptom of Tourette's syndrome—along with a compulsion to check the bolts on the front door hourly. Of course Drury didn't believe me. It was three years down the road and he decided I was confusing her house with someone else's." She reached out to shut her door, apparently under the impression that I understood what she was talking about.

I held it open. "What didn't he believe?"

She blinked in surprise. "Well . . . obviously . . . that Annie's house had been ransacked and everything of value stolen."

In the past, Sam had always shied away from discussions about Annie. I remember his embarrassment when I tackled a chief superintendent at a party in Hong Kong and pinned him to a wall with an hour-long diatribe on the inequities of the Richmond Police. Sam had hauled me away eventually and by the time we reached home his embarrassment had turned to fury. "Have you any idea how idiotic you sound when you start talking about that bloody woman?" he had demanded angrily. "You can't lecture total strangers on garbage about the eyes being the windows of the soul if you want to be taken seriously. You're my wife, for Christ's sake, and people are starting to avoid the pair of us because they think you're as mad as she was."

Two decades on, and once he'd ruminated at length on the bizarre coincidence of having Sheila Arnold as our GP for a second time—"You've got to admit, it's pretty damn spooky. . . . It's only a couple of days since Jock reminded me of Graham Road"—he was surprisingly interested in what Sheila and I had been talking about. I thought I knew why. He was never inclined to believe anything I said, but he rolled over to have his tummy scratched by doctors . . . particularly female ones.

"Does she agree with you? Does she think Annie was murdered?"

"I'm not sure," I answered. "All she said was the house had been ransacked."

He ruminated some more. "When? Before Annie died, or after?"

"What difference does it make?"

"If it happened afterward," he said reasonably, "then it means some-body knew she was lying in the gutter and grabbed the opportunity to break in." He gave his jaw a thoughtful scratch. "Which in turn means she was probably out there a damn sight longer than the coroner said she was."

"That's one way of looking at it," I agreed, before wandering off to the kitchen to prepare some lunch. Old habits die hard, I find, and the subject of Annie had been taboo for so long between us that she wasn't easily resurrected from her grave.

Sam pursued me. "And if it happened *before* she died," he went on, "that might explain why she drank herself into a stupor. It must have been a terrible shock to go home and find all her treasures gone. Poor woman, I've never understood why she did that. I mean, we saw her pretty tipsy on occasion but never so paralytic that she didn't know what she was doing." He flicked me an apologetic smile. "I've always had a problem believing one of her neighbors pushed her under a lorry. Okay, some of them were shits, and some of them made her life mis-erable by complaining about her, but that's a far cry from committing cold-blooded murder."

I opened the fridge door and wondered what sort of meal I could make out of half a can of tomatoes, some staggeringly old cheese and iceberg lettuce. "She was five-foot-nine-inches tall and weighed four-teen stone," I murmured, "and was exactly fifteen milligrams over the legal driving limit—the equivalent of five shots of spirits or five pints of lager. By any stretch of the imagination that does not amount to drinking herself into a stupor." I pulled out the tin and inspected it for mold. "In fact the chances were she wasn't even tipsy because she was a practiced drinker and could probably consume twice as much as the rest of us before showing any signs of drunkenness." I smiled at him. "Look at yourself, if you don't believe me. You're a stone lighter and two inches taller, and you can put away eight pints of lager before you become embarrassing."

He retreated into his shell immediately because it was one thing for him to introduce the subject, and quite another for me to challenge the facts from superior knowledge. "Everyone said she was paralytic," he said huffily.

"Even if she was," I went on, "what makes you think one of her neighbors didn't give in to a spur-of-the-moment temptation to shove her into the road? It was dark. . . . It was raining. . . . She was mad as a hatter . . . deeply irritating . . . the street was empty . . . and there was a truck coming. One quick shove and, hey presto, problem solved. No more blacks on the road and property values rise immediately." I lifted an amused eyebrow. "No one ever said her murder was planned, Sam."

Two or three days later, a folder of photocopied documents arrived in the post from Sheila Arnold with "Annie Butts" written on the front.

"Thought the enclosed might interest you," she wrote on a compliments slip. "It's not much, I'm afraid, because I gave up when I realized I was beating my head against a brick wall! PS How delightful to run into you both again."

By coincidence, it was the same day that Sam and I went for lunch in Weymouth, and Sam took against a man who seemed to be staring at me. We had chosen a pub overlooking the harbor, with tables outside, which allowed us to bathe in the sun and watch the yachts drift in and out of the marina every time the swing bridge lifted. It was a pretty place to while away a couple of hours, with eighteenth-century houses lining cobbled wharfs and battered trawlers unloading crates full of monkfish and crab, but Sam started bellyaching about the landlord who kept coming to the door to look at me, and my pleasure in the peaceful scene evaporated. I was wearing dark glasses and I studied the man secretly from behind my lenses. He was as lean and hungry as he had always been and undoubtedly as vicious. But he was better looking than Joseph Stalin . . . or Joseph Stalin's brother . . .

INCIDENT REPORT

Date: 15.11.78

Time: 11:15

Officer in charge: PS Drury, Richmond Police

Incident: Authorized entry to 30 Graham Road, Richmond, following the death of the owner, Miss Ann Butts. Neighbors had reported a number of cats trapped inside the property. No next of kin was available.

Officers attending: PS Drury, PC Andrew Quentin. Also in attendance: RSPCA Inspectors: John Howlett, Tony Barrett

Entry to the property was gained via the front door with a Yale key that Miss Butts was wearing on a string around her neck at the time of her death. The house was very cold with no central-heating provision. There were two gas fires in each of the downstairs rooms, but neither was lit at the time of entry. None of the windows was open, although a small casement in the back cloakroom was insecurely fastened due to a broken fixing.

The officers had been informed by neighbors that there were at least twenty cats inside the premises, and the smell of cats' urine in the front hallway was overpowering. The conditions inside the house were squalid and untidy—in particular the downstairs cloakroom and the upstairs bathroom where neither toilet had been flushed and soiled paper was lying on the floors. Human feces was found in the two downstairs rooms. Boxes of empty vodka bottles were stacked against the kitchen walls.

The smell of cats' urine in the kitchen was particularly bad. Litter from a tray had been scattered across the linoleum floor and used indiscriminately by the animals. The RSPCA inspectors expressed concern that Miss Butts had wedged a small chest of drawers against the cat flap, which she had agreed to install after a previous visit from them. Numerous food and water bowls lined the edges of the floor, but all were empty.

A search of the cupboards in the kitchen revealed inadequate provisions, both for Miss Butts herself and the colony of cats in her care. There was little in the way of tinned or boxed food, although there were fifteen pints of milk in her fridge and some raw meat, mostly chicken. "Reduced price" stickers suggested Miss Butts had acquired the goods cheaply, although subsequent inquiries at a local supermarket provided information that she picked over "binned" goods in order to obtain cat food free.

There were two downstairs rooms, excluding the kitchen and cloakroom, and the doors to both were open. These rooms had also been fouled by the animals, although to a lesser extent than the kitchen. In the front sitting room, three dead cats were found under a pile of cushions in a corner. In the opinion of John Howlett (RSPCA) all three had been dead for a minimum of four days. Two of them, both toms, had little or no fur on their faces and severe scratches to their bodies, and appeared to have died from untended wounds inflicted during a fight. The third, also a tom, had lost most of its fur and had died from a broken neck. Two more dead tomcats were discovered upstairs in Miss Butts's bedroom, wrapped in towels and placed in the wardrobe. Both were severely undernourished, shorn of fur and had broken necks.

The doors to all the upstairs rooms were closed. Five live cats, all toms, were found trapped in the back bedroom. The animals were in a distressed state, and had clearly been fouling the room for several days. All had bite and scratch wounds from fighting. There were bowls on the floor, which may have contained water or food, but were empty at the time of entry to the house. Apart from the dead toms in the wardrobe, the front bedroom contained four live queens and two neutered toms that were also in a distressed state.

The total number of cats removed from the premises by the RSPCA inspectors was twenty-one, five of which were dead.* Their full report (attached) concludes that the tomcats had suffered the worst neglect while the condition of the queens and neutered toms gave less cause for concern. It is their view that Miss Butts had been allowing the animals to foul the interior for some time—in particular the tomcats whose odor is powerful and distinctive. They also pointed to clear evidence of cruelty in the shorn fur, broken necks and apparent willingness to allow the animals to fight "to the death," and drew attention to the fact that it was the male animals that appeared to have been singled out for torture. The inadequate supplies in the kitchen and the estimated time of death of the dead cats suggests that Miss Butts had ceased to provide proper care and attention some five to seven days before her death.

A superficial search of the house produced nothing to indicate the names and/or addresses of Miss Butts's next of kin. A box of papers was removed from a cupboard in the front sitting room for later examination.**

The general impression received by those attending was that Miss Butts had been living in conditions of extreme poverty for some time. There were no carpets in either of the downstairs rooms, much of the furniture was broken and dilapidated and there were few adornments. The temperature in the house was cold, yet the gas supply in the cupboard under the stairs had been turned off. In addition, several fuses had been removed from the electrical circuits, although the main supply was still on. When an attempt was made to flush the toilets, it was discovered that the stopcock under the sink had also been turned off. One explanation is that Miss Butts had become worried about paying her utility bills. This may have been influenced by a dependence on alcohol.

* Veterinarian postmortems of the five dead cats concurred with John Howlett's assessment at the time of entry to the premises. Two had died of untreated wounds following a fight; three had died after having their necks broken. All showed clear evidence of cruelty, specifically: fur ripped from their faces—probably from the application of cellophane tape, parcel tape or carpet tape, which was then torn off. Also, two of the dead animals appeared to have had superglue applied to their lips and lids, residues of which remained on scraps of fur around their mouths and eyes. Estimated time of death: four to seven days prior to the bodies being found. Allowances were made for the cold conditions in the house, which had slowed decomposition.

** All the papers were official: various bills—some paid, some (gas and electricity) unpaid; a check book and bank statements; a building society book (Abbey National), showing £15,340.21 in an interest-bearing account; TV license; and tax and rate receipts. There was an envelope containing assorted photographs of a woman (black) and man (white) with "Mum" and "Dad" or "Elizabeth" and "George" written on the back, but nothing else of a personal nature. Subsequent inquiries at Miss Butts's bank produced the deeds to the house, various share certificates and a current bank-account statement showing £4,324.82 in credit. (NB: Miss Butts's bank manager said she was "regularly abusive toward the cashiers and had bees in her bonnet about them stealing her money." He also said it wouldn't surprise him if she was confused about whether she could afford to pay her bills because she wasn't "quite with it.")

Correspondence between Dr. Sheila Arnold and
Inspector John Howlett, of the RSPCA—dated 1983

39 LYVEDON AVENUE, RICHMOND, SURREY

Inspector John Howlett
RSPCA
Guardian House
Twickenham
Surrey

February 22, 1983

Dear Mr. Howlett,

I am making inquiries about a visit you and your colleague, Tony Barrett, made to 30 Graham Road, Richmond, just over three years ago on November 15, 1978. The house belonged to a woman called Ann Butts who died in a road accident, and you were asked to accompany the police to her house the following day in order to rescue her cats. I have a copy of the police report of the incident, but the report that you and your colleague made had been omitted. Do you still have a copy on file and, if so, would it be possible for me to read it?

I was Miss Butts's general practitioner for several years and I have a number of concerns relating to the way the police described her living conditions. "Squalid" and "living in conditions of extreme poverty" does not accord with my memories of Miss Butts and/or her house. With reference to her cats, my recollection is that they were always sleek, deeply loved and well cared for. In addition: my understanding is that, following complaints from Miss Butts's neighbors, you made several visits to 30 Graham Road in 1978, but that none of the complaints was upheld.

From your memory of those visits, can you describe any of the West Indian or Central American ornaments or artifacts that she had in her front room? I am puzzled that the police have no record of their existence, particularly as Ann was proud of them and often told me how valuable they were.

I should be most grateful for any information you can give me.

Yours sincerely,

Sheila Arnold

Dr. Sheila Arnold

White Cottage
Littlehampton
Nr Preston
Lancashire

Dr. Sheila Arnold
39 Lyvedon Avenue
Richmond
Surrey

March 7, 1983

Dear Dr. Arnold,

I regret to say that I retired from the RSPCA in June 1980, and, while my colleagues were kind enough to forward your letter to my new address in Lancashire, I no longer have access to files and cannot supply you with a copy of the report you requested. Nevertheless, I do recall the case quite well and am happy to pass on what I remember of Miss Butts.

In fact you're correct in saying I made several visits (four in total) to 30 Graham Road in the months prior to Miss Butts's death. You are also correct in saying that none of the neighbors' complaints was borne out by the evidence. Her cats were well looked after and in excellent condition. However, on none of those visits did I find more than seven cats in residence (six on the last occasion, following the death of one which affected Miss Butts deeply) nor was there any evidence to suggest there were more cats to find.

I made two recommendations on my first visit in March 1978: 1) that she install a cat flap in the kitchen door to allow the animals free access to and from the garden; 2) that she consider having her tomcats neutered in order to mitigate her neighbors' complaints of offensive odor. She followed both recommendations and, despite continued complaints against her, I had no reason to suspect her of neglect and/or cruelty to her animals. Indeed, I went further and suggested to the police that the complaints were malicious and would warrant investigation. However, I have no idea if anything was done about it.

What my colleague and I found in her house on November 15, 1978, was a different matter altogether. Between my last visit—some time in August '78—and that November morning she seemed to have acquired another fifteen cats. If you have a copy of the police incident report, you will know that we found five tomcats dead, and another five severely distressed and injured behind the closed door of the back bedroom. Not to put too fine a point on it, the dead ones had either killed each other or had their necks broken, and the live ones had been so badly tortured and neglected that they were skin and bone, and covered in scratch and bite marks from fighting each other. A decision was made to put three of them down immediately and the other two died within forty-eight hours. Of the remaining eleven cats, all were either neutered or queens, six of which I was able to identify as the cats I had seen on my previous visits.

In my opinion, the police description of the house as "squalid" was an understatement. In truth, it was disgusting. The cat flap in the kitchen had been blocked by a piece of furniture with the result that the animals had been fouling the interior for several days. Miss Butts's own sanitary arrangements were appalling with reeking unflushed toilets and dirty paper and feces on the floors. I cannot stress too highly that I was horrified by what we found, although I have no idea why her circumstances had deteriorated so badly between August and November. There was evidence that she had been drinking heavily—as I recall the police discovered in excess of fifty empty spirit bottles about the house—and this may have contributed to her decline.

I regret I cannot give any clear descriptions of West Indian or Central American ornaments from my previous visits. I do remember that Miss Butts had a number of interesting and colorful displays in her front room but I was never allowed to inspect them long enough to be precise about what they were. Sadly, she viewed me with suspicion because of my uniform and preferred to talk to me in the kitchen. I recall some vivid paintings on the wall opposite the sitting-room doorway and a display of peacock feathers in a brass artillery shell beside the front door; also, a pair of matching silhouette pictures in the hall which she told me represented her grandparents. However, the house was bare of ornamentation on November 15, and I assume she sold everything off to pay for her drinking habit.

With particular reference to the twenty-plus cats we found in the house, I can only speculate that she began to attract strays to the property following my last visit in August and panicked when the tomcats fought. It seems to me significant that: 1) there was evidence the toms' mouths had been taped, which implies she was trying to find a way to stop them from biting each other; 2) the cat flap was wedged closed with the intention, presumably, of trying to stop more strays from coming in, although why she chose to contain the ones already there remains a mystery. The male cats had received the worst treatment, which I found disturbing—evidence perhaps that Miss Butts had developed some sort of obsession against men in general?—and I do wonder if she chose to contain them for fear of giving her neighbors the proof of neglect and cruelty of which they habitually accused her.

In conclusion, I have always been sorry that her life ended in the way it did. She wasn't an easy woman to deal with as I'm sure you know. However, despite the official nature of my visits, I believe she looked on me as a friend and I'm saddened that she did not think to call me when my help might have made a difference.

Yours sincerely,

John Howlett

39 LYVEDON AVENUE, RICHMOND, SURREY

John Howlett, Esq.
White Cottage
Littlehampton
Nr Preston
Lancashire

March 23, 1983

Dear Mr. Howlett,

Thank you for your letter of March 7. I should tell you that I visited Annie in her house two months before she died and there was nothing then to indicate a deterioration in her circumstances. I am not a cat lover myself, so did not take particular notice of the ones I saw that day. However, had there been more than normal I'm sure I would have registered the fact. Certainly there was no question of the house smelling.

One of the reasons for my visit was to tell her that I was going away for twelve months. Annie became extremely agitated at the news, which I had been expecting. Sufferers from Tourette's syndrome dislike change, so I sat with her for an hour in her sitting room talking about the colleague who would be taking over in my absence. I had ample opportunity, therefore, to evaluate the room and what was in it. Before I left, she said she wanted to give me a going-away present and invited me to choose something. We spent a further fifteen minutes examining the many treasures she had—most of them quite small—and I can say with absolute certainty that, on that day—September 8—that room was full of ornaments.

Unfortunately I am having huge difficulty persuading the police that the most likely explanation for the house being "empty" nine weeks later is that she was robbed. I have shown your letter to Sergeant James Drury—one of the officers who accompanied you that day—and he tells me that unless I can find someone who saw the interior during the week before her death, he must conclude, as you did, that she sold her possessions herself in order to buy drink. This was his most helpful contribution! Rather less helpful was his suggestion that my memory is at fault or, worse, that I am deliberately lying in order to gloss over my failure to safeguard the health of a patient. Neither is true. I cannot repeat often enough that the last time I saw Annie she was in good mental and physical health. There was no indication that she was drinking more than usual and certainly no evidence of incontinence.

At the time of her death, I assumed that the only privileged knowledge I had about her was her medical history. However, I now realize I also had privileged information about the inside of her house because I was among the handful of people who were allowed beyond the front door. Even the vicar was made to stand on the doorstep because she mistrusted his perceived friendship with her neighbors. I have located a social worker who was shown into the sitting room in '77 but her description of it, although it accords with mine, has been ruled too out of date to be of value. Sergeant Drury dismisses your recollection of "vivid paintings," "peacock feathers" and "silhouette pictures" for the same reason—i.e., your last visit was in August '78—on the basis that three months was quite long enough for her to have disposed of the items herself.

I won't bore you with my extreme irritation (and anger!) at having both my memory and my professional expertise questioned by a policeman who is clearly reluctant to reopen an old case, but I do wonder if you could try to picture to yourself what was on the right-hand side of the mantelpiece in the sitting room. The going-away present that Annie gave me came from there and, as I still have it, it would be very helpful indeed if I could demonstrate to Sergeant Drury that in this respect at least I am not "imagining things." A positive and unprompted memory from one of her few "friends" would be invaluable.

It's only fair to tell you that I am extremely unimpressed by both Sergeant Drury and by the coroner, both of whom seem to have paid lip service to their responsibility for investigating Annie's death. While I wouldn't go so far as to say she was murdered—as I understand one of her neighbors did—I certainly believe she was reduced to a state of extreme anxiety by having her house invaded and her treasured possessions stolen. This, in turn, may have led to the deterioration in her circumstances and the overindulgence in alcohol, which was a contributory factor in her death.

Yours sincerely,

Sheila Arnold

<u>Dr. Sheila Arnold</u>

White Cottage
Littlehampton
Nr Preston
Lancashire

Dr. Sheila Arnold
39 Lyvedon Avenue
Richmond
Surrey

March 24, 1983

Dear Dr. Arnold,

I regret I cannot remember the mantelpiece at all, nor what was on it, but my wife has reminded me that one of the pictures in the sitting room was a framed mosaic of an Aztec god—Quetzalcoatl—otherwise known as the plumed serpent or feathered snake. My wife is a lover of D. H. Lawrence's work and apparently I told her after one of my visits to Graham Road that Miss Butts owned an extraordinary mosaic of "The Plumed Serpent." Sadly, I can barely remember either the picture or the conversation, but my wife is adamant that it was "the mad black woman with the cats" who had the Quetzalcoatl on her wall.

Trusting this will be of help,
Yours sincerely,

John Howlett

Correspondence between Dr. Sheila Arnold and Richmond Police—dated 1983

39 LYVEDON AVENUE, RICHMOND, SURREY

Sergeant J. Drury
Richmond Police Station
Richmond
Surrey

May 25, 1983

Dear Sergeant Drury,

Re Miss Ann Butts, 30 Graham Road, Richmond, Surrey

Following numerous conversations with you, both in person and on the telephone, I have become increasingly angry about your refusal to investigate the possible theft of property from Miss Ann Butts prior to her death on 14.11.78. In the absence of any other explanation, I am forced to conclude that Richmond Police are as indifferent to Miss Butts today as they clearly were at the time of her death.

It is unacceptable to say, as you did on the telephone this morning, that "anyone as mad as Mad Annie could easily have blown a fortune on drink over a nine-week period." As your own report from the time states, she had £4,000 in her bank account and £15,000 in a building society. Therefore there was no necessity for her to sell her prized possessions as you claim she must have done. Nor can I stress too strongly that Tourette's syndrome is not a form of insanity, but rather an inability to control certain motor functions, and the fact that Miss Butts made faces and muttered to herself in no way affected her intelligence.

I am now convinced that her extraordinarily rapid decline must have been due to her house being ransacked in the week before her death. I have said to you many times that an invasion of her property would have triggered extreme anxiety because of her compulsive—therefore uncontrollable—obsession with home and personal security, and it is pointless to keep arguing that she would have called the police if such an invasion had happened. All strangers worried her, including officials in uniform (c.f. John Howlett's letter, dated March 7, '83) and if you and your colleagues treated her while she was alive with the sort of indifference you seem to be demonstrating now, she would have had no reason to trust you. In this one respect—trusting strangers—Ann's behavior could be described as irrational but only because obsessive behavior is compulsive. In all other respects her behavior was normal.

I hesitate to say that your indifference amounts to contempt, although I am angry enough to believe that that is what it is. Yes, Ann suffered a neuropsychiatric disorder, and yes, she was black, but neither fact should influence your decision to pursue belated justice on her behalf.

Of course it's true—and I am quoting your own words—that the cost of pursuing her alleged robbers will far outweigh any benefit to the taxpayer from the recovery of her possessions, but since when did justice have anything to do with cost? Justice is, and should be, impartial, yet your remark suggests that the police are selective in how, when and for whom they enforce the law.

Yours sincerely,

Sheila Arnold

Dr. Sheila Arnold

c.c.   Police Superintendent Hathaway, Richmond Police
      Rt. Honourable William Whitelaw, home secretary

From the office of:

Police Superintendent A. P. Hathaway,

Metropolitan Police, Richmond

Dr. Sheila Arnold

39 Lyvedon Avenue

Richmond

Surrey

June 21, 1983

Ref: APH/VJ

Dear Dr. Arnold,

Re Miss Ann Butts, 30 Graham Road, Richmond

Thank you for the copy of your letter of May 25 to PS Drury, together
with photocopies of correspondence and notes of telephone
conversations, all of which I have read with interest. I have since
discussed the case at some length with Sergeant Drury and, while I
have some sympathy with your contention that Miss Butts was robbed
prior to her death, I also agree with Sergeant Drury that no purpose
would be served by investigating it.

Sergeant Drury admits that the inquiry in November 1978 did not
take into account the possibility of robbery, however he stresses that
at *no time* was it suggested to him that the situation found inside Miss
Butts's house was unusual. Quite the reverse. There was considerable
evidence, already on record following complaints from her neighbors,
that the house was overrun with cats; that there was a continuous
unpleasant smell from the premises; and that her living conditions

were unhygienic and squalid. In these circumstances I do not consider that Sergeant Drury was either indifferent or negligent in his handling of the case.

The incidence of theft and burglary in England and Wales is rising at over 15 percent per annum, with few successful convictions resulting from police investigations. These figures are a matter of public record, and politicians from all parties are now demanding tougher sentencing policies and increased funding for police forces in order to stem what has effectively become a crime epidemic.

In such a climate it would be unreasonable to order an investigation into a burglary that may or may not have happened five years ago; where the alleged victim is no longer alive to give evidence; where there is no accurate inventory of what was in her house; and where the chances of successful closure are zero. While I realize this is not what you want to hear, I hope you will understand the reasoning behind this decision. It would be different had there been any question marks over the manner of Miss Butts's death, but the inquest verdict was unequivocal.

In conclusion, let me assure you that Richmond Police take their responsibilities to all members of the public extremely seriously, irrespective of race, color, creed or disability.

Yours sincerely,

A. P. Hathaway

Police Superintendent A. P. Hathaway

four

"One of your letters to the RSPCA inspector mentions a going-away present that Annie gave you," I said to Sheila Arnold when she and her husband came to lunch the following Sunday. "What was it?"

She extended an arm. "A jade bracelet," she said, turning a pale green bangle on her slender wrist. "There was a set of them on her mantelpiece and she chose this one for me because she thought it suited my coloring. I had red hair in those days."

"I remember," I said.

Her husband, Larry, a tall, soft-spoken American, stirred in his seat. "In fact it's jadeite," he said, "which is the most expensive of the jades. We had it assessed in '83 so that Sheila could demonstrate to the police that she wasn't imagining the value of what was in Annie's house." He circled the bracelet with a finger and thumb. "It's of Mexican origin . . . probably eighteenth century . . . worth in excess of £200. Considering Sheila thinks there were ten in the set, it gives you some sort of starting point for estimating Annie's wealth."

Sam gave a low whistle. "No wonder you wanted the police to investigate."

Sheila sighed. "I still feel I should have pushed a bit harder . . . at the very least forced Drury to face a disciplinary hearing. He was appallingly negligent. Worse, a racist. He just assumed a black woman would be living in squalor."

Larry clicked his tongue impatiently. "That's twenty-twenty vision speaking. I agree the man was an asshole but he was correct about one thing . . . no one suggested there was anything odd about the house . . . even John Howlett, the RSPCA inspector, didn't challenge the conditions." He spoke with surprising firmness as if the subject were a touchy one between them. "And there weren't enough hours in the day for you to commit any more time to Annie's cause, not with your practice and two kids to bring up. Also," he went on, turning to us, "the Superintendent made sense when he talked about zero success rates. Sheila made a list of the things she remembered but it was very vague on detail and, as the police pointed out, there was no hope of a prosecution if she couldn't be more positive in her descriptions. In the end it seemed pointless to go on."

We were sitting outside on the terrace under the shade of a worn umbrella which had had most of its color bleached out by long summers of sunshine. The garden fell away at the back of the house and some sensible person in the distant past had had the foresight to construct a raised platform out of Portland stone, which gave a glorious view of the other side of the bowl-shaped valley in which we lived. It seemed strange to me how the English climate had changed during the years we'd been away. I had always thought of it as a green and luscious place, but the garden, paddocks and fields had turned brown in the heat, and the drought-starved flowers drooped their heads. Sheila and Larry were sporting matching panama hats and they made an elegant couple, she in a primrose-colored cotton dress, he in white shirt and chinos. I guessed him to be about ten years older than she was, and I wondered where they'd met and when they'd married, and whether the two children he'd mentioned were his or a previous husband's.

I leaned across the table to refill their wine glasses while I thought lazily about going inside to fetch lunch, a simple affair of cold meat, salad and French bread. "If it was one of her neighbors who robbed her," I said idly, "they might have kept some of the pieces, particularly if they weren't of any value. The peacock feathers in the artillery shell,

for example . . . the one John Howlett described. When I read his letter I couldn't help thinking they were the kind of things someone
would hang on to, if only because feathers could never be specifically
identified as Annie's."

Sheila eyed me curiously. "You seem to have quite a down on her
neighbors," she remarked. "Why is that?"

Sam answered for me. "The whole damn street took against her after she labeled them racists at the inquest. They plagued us for weeks
with abusive phone calls. It's the reason we left England."

Liar! I thought.

"No wonder you hate them," said Larry sympathetically.

It was a throwaway line, which Sheila, with a questioning lift of her
eyebrows, invited me to expand upon. Instead I stood up and said it was
time for lunch. I had learned to talk about threatening phone calls
without becoming strident . . .

. . . but *hate?* That was a different matter entirely.

Sheila and I walked down to the paddock after lunch and leaned on the
rail to watch the horses nibble halfheartedly at the withered vegetation.
"Larry and I always assumed it was professional thieves," she told me. "I
don't think it ever occurred to us that it might have been someone
closer to home."

"How would professionals know what was in the house?" I asked.
"You said yourself she never let anyone inside."

"That's equally true of her neighbors," she pointed out reasonably.
"She was more suspicious of them than she was of strangers."

"They used to look through her windows," I said, remembering
how I'd come across a gang of young thugs making faces at her through
the glass. "The children were the worst. They thought it was funny to
frighten her."

Sheila caught at the brim of her hat as a warm breeze blew across
the field. "Larry's convinced it was whoever did that valuation she
showed me. He thinks it was a scam—someone knocking on doors and

posing as an art or antiques expert in order to find out which houses were worth robbing."

It makes sense, I thought.

"But I don't agree with him," she went on. "I'm almost certain it was a Sotheby's valuation because I remember thinking that the figures must be right if a bona fide auction house had come up with them." She sighed. "And now I'm furious with myself that I didn't question it at the time. I mean, the whole episode was very odd. What prompted her to get a valuation? And how on earth did she gear herself up to letting a stranger loose on her treasures?" She shook her wrist and rattled the jade bracelet against her watch. "When she asked me to choose a present she wouldn't let me touch anything. I had to choose by sight, not by feel."

"When did she show you the valuation?"

"Sometime during the summer. I remember she was particularly difficult that day. One minute she wanted me to read it, the next she snatched it away as if she thought I was going to steal it. She used to get caught in mental loops that made her repeat the same words and actions over and over until something new pushed her on to another track. She could be very tiresome when she was in that sort of mood, which is probably why I didn't question what the valuation was for."

"An insurance condition?" I suggested. "No valuation, no insurance."

She gave an exasperated sigh. "That's what the police said and it made me boiling mad. 'You can't have it both ways,' I told them. Either she was a mindless cretin who let cats and drink destroy her life, or she was so switched on that she was able to organize insurance for herself. It might have helped if I could have talked to her bank manager but by the time I got around to thinking about it he was long gone. Someone told me he was working in Saudi Arabia but I never followed it up."

(*I* had, and I could remember the man's answer verbatim down a crackly line from Riyadh. "I can't help you, I'm afraid. Unfortunately Miss Butts decided I was stealing her money, so I passed her account to my deputy, who died five years ago.")

"Did you think of contacting Sotheby's to find out if they still had a copy of the valuation and why she wanted it?" I asked.

"No, but it wouldn't have made any difference if I had," she said with a dry laugh. "Larry started getting stroppy about the amount of time I was wasting so I put the husband and children first and let Annie go."

I thought about Sam's fury over the policeman in Hong Kong. "It's very irritating, isn't it?"

"What?"

"Doing your duty."

"Yes." She pulled a wry smile. "The worst is yet to come, though."

"How do you mean?"

"Larry's older than I am and he's here under sufferance until I reach pensionable age . . . and that's only two years away. Then we retire to his condo in Florida."

"Why?" I asked curiously.

"It's the bargain we made when he took on me and the children." She read my expression as criticism. "We don't have the same sort of marriage as you and Sam. The plan was to return to the States when Larry retired, but he agreed to wait after I was offered this job in Dorset. He said he could tolerate another few years as long we weren't in London." She sighed. "It's a long story . . . full of compromise."

"It sounds it," I said sympathetically. "Do you want to live in Florida?"

"No," she said honestly, "but I want lonely old age even less. I've seen too much of it to consider it as an option."

It was a salutary warning, coming from a doctor. "What makes you think Sam's and my marriage is any different?"

She shrugged. "He wouldn't abandon you if you gave him an ultimatum."

I was about to point out that Sam had done it once and there was no reason to imagine he wouldn't do it again. But I realized she was probably right. Somewhere along the line our roles had changed and it was Sam who feared ultimatums now. "He's more afraid of loneliness than I am," I said slowly, "which means I hold the cards in our relationship . . . just as Larry does in yours."

She glanced at me in surprise. "That's a very calculated way of looking at it."

"Born out of experience," I said lightly. "I think real loneliness is to be abandoned *inside* a relationship . . . to find yourself questioning your worth all the time. I know what that's like, and I know I can survive it. I imagine the same is true of Larry. He's been there, done it, got the T-shirt . . . and you haven't. Neither has Sam. It puts you both at a disadvantage."

"Larry wouldn't know what loneliness was if it smacked him in the face," she protested. "He's the most gregarious creature I know. It drives me to distraction sometimes. I'm constantly being hauled out to social functions when all I want to do is sleep because I'm dog-tired from pandering to the ill all day."

I smiled at her. "That's the whole point. You're leading a fulfilled existence and Larry isn't. He has to go outside to find a sense of purpose. Yours is so strong you just fall asleep and prepare for the next day's challenges."

She propped her arms on the fence and stared across the field. "Is this your way of telling me Annie was your sense of purpose?"

"Part of it."

"You had babies," she said. "Didn't they fill a gap?"

"Did yours?"

"No, but then I had a career. In any case I'm not remotely maternal. I can cope with my patients being totally dependent on me . . . but not my children. I expect my children to fend for themselves."

I wondered if she was listening to herself, and whether she'd asked Larry how he felt about the professional/private divide. "Mine just added to the general anxiety," I said, joining her at the fence. "My elder one did, anyway. We moved to Hong Kong while I was pregnant and a child was about the last thing I needed at that stage."

"How did Sam take it?"

"Blindly."

Sheila gave a snort of laughter. "What's that supposed to mean?"

"He had a son," I said dryly. "He was thrilled . . . just so long as someone else looked after it." We stood in companionable silence for a few moments, understanding each other. "Do you still have a copy of the list you made of Annie's possessions?" I asked her next.

"Isn't it in the file?"

"No."

She looked doubtful. "I'll have a look when I get home . . . the problem is we threw so much out when we moved down here seven years ago. The other thing that's missing is the correspondence I had with the social worker. I remember she wrote a long letter describing the interior of Annie's house, but none of it was in the file when I photocopied it for you. I'm afraid it must have come adrift during the move."

I wondered what else had come adrift and indulged in a few dark thoughts about Larry, who clearly wasn't above a little sabotage to ensure that his needs came first. *Shades of Sam?* "Could you make another list?"

"I can try. It won't be as detailed as the first. What do you expect to find?"

"Nothing valuable," I said. "Little things that someone might have kept."

"Like the peacock feathers?"

I nodded.

"They could never be used as evidence."

"I know but . . ." I hesitated, afraid of sounding ridiculous. "It's a stupid idea really but supposing you put on your list the peacock feathers, the silhouette pictures of her grandparents and . . . well, other things of little or no value . . . a wooden statue, say. . . ." I ran out of ideas. "I just thought that if I found someone with a similar combination in their house, I'd at least feel I was on the right track."

She threw me a startled glance. "Does that mean you're going to look?"

I shrugged self-consciously.

"But where would you start, for goodness' sake?"

"Graham Road? There must be someone left who was there in 1978. If I knock on a few doors I might come up with something." I spoke only to give her an answer, not because I had any intention of taking such a scattergun approach. I watched her expression change to one of skepticism.

"But why? It'll just be a lot of hard work for nothing. Larry was right when he said there'd be no prosecution."

"I wouldn't be looking for a prosecution for theft, Sheila; I'd be looking for a prosecution for murder. As the chief superintendent said in his letter to you, it would be different if there were question marks over Annie's death." I smiled. "Well, there are . . . and I intend to prove it."

She searched my face intently for a moment. "What really happened between you and Annie that night?" she asked abruptly. "Drury showed me your statement, but you said she never spoke to you."

"She didn't."

"Then . . . *why?*"

"I've got nothing better to do at the moment."

It wasn't much of an explanation but it seemed to satisfy her. "I doubt many of her neighbors will still be there," she warned. "Most of them had moved on even before we left."

"What about the vicar?" I asked. "He was always visiting people in Graham Road."

She pulled on the brim of her hat to shade her eyes from the sun. "I don't think he's there anymore."

I lifted one shoulder in a relaxed shrug. "His successor at St. Mark's ought to be able to tell me where he is. Do you know his name?"

"The new vicar? No."

"What about the one who knew Annie?"

She didn't answer immediately, and I turned to look at her. Her expression was impossible to read because her eyes were still in shade, but the set of her jaw was very grim. "Peter Stanhope," she said.

Southampton
October 3, 1982

Dear M,

Thought the enclosed might interest you. I went up to see some old friends in Richmond and happened upon the Rich & Twick by chance. Skullduggery abounds, it seems, and there won't be much love lost between cloth and stethoscope following the Rev's libelous remarks! I remember him from Annie's funeral—a fat little bloke with sweaty palms—but don't think I ever came across the doctor. Jock and I had a man with a huge mustache.

All goes well here. I'm into my final year and after numerous attempts—a girl has to do what a girl has to do if she isn't to make the same mistake again!—I have finally met a winner. Sweet guy by the name of Jim Garth. Watch this space, as they say!

Love,

Libby

Local doctor denies neglect

Dr. Sheila Arnold, 41, a partner at the Cromwell Street Surgery, Richmond, denies neglect after Frederick Potts, 87, was discovered close to death earlier this week in his flat in Channing Towers. Mr. Potts owes his life to his neighbor, Mrs. Gwen Roberts, 62. "I heard Fred banging on the party wall," she said, "so I phoned the police."

Police described Mr. Potts's condition as "shocking." He had been unable to get out of bed for several days and was in severe pain from untreated ulcers on his legs and back. He was also dehydrated and undernourished. Dr. Arnold was questioned by police following alleged claims from neighbors that she had refused to arrange nursing care for Mr. Potts because "he had been abusive to carers in the past." Dr. Arnold denies the claims.

Parallels are being drawn between this case and the case of Ann Butts, 42, an untreated alcoholic with a history of mental illness, who was also a patient of Dr. Arnold. Following Miss Butts's death in November 1978, the coroner described the conditions in which she had been living as "disgraceful." It is the responsibility of health and social workers to protect the most vulnerable members of our society," he said. Dr. Arnold denies that the coroner was referring to her, claiming she was in America when Miss Butts stumbled in front of a truck after a drinking spree and suffered fatal head injuries.

According to the Reverend Peter Stanhope, 45, vicar of St. Mark's church, Mr. Potts will be offered a flat in sheltered accommodation as soon as he's well enough to leave the hospital. "There's no excuse for this kind of neglect," the Reverend Stanhope said. "Lessons should have been learned following Ann Butts's death so that the same mistakes could not happen again."

Richmond & Twickenham Times—
Friday, June 18, 1982

Southampton

12 February 1983

Written in haste. This is the follow-up to the doctor/vicar saga.
2nd round to the Doc, I think, although the piece is so tiny I
doubt anyone bothered to read it!

Love,

Libby

Doctor cleared by BMA

Dr. Sheila Arnold, 42, of the Cromwell Road Surgery, Richmond, was cleared of neglect during a brief hearing at the British Medical Association yesterday. Written evidence was submitted to show that Mr. Potts, 87, was registered with another practice at the time of the alleged incident and had not been a patient of Dr. Arnold since May 1980.

Richmond & Twickenham Times—
Friday, January 28, 1983

five

An immediate pall fell over our little party when Sheila told Larry that I was planning to look up Peter Stanhope to see if he knew what had become of Annie's possessions. Neither of them seemed remotely interested that he had never been inside her house, and couldn't possibly know what possessions she had. His name alone spelled depression.

Larry didn't like the idea at all and watched me warily from behind his wine glass, while Sam flicked worried glances around the three of us, clearly wondering who Peter Stanhope was and why his name should cause Larry concern. Sam became rather loud as a result—he always hated finding himself at a disadvantage—and, in an unkind way, I took pleasure from his embarrassment. He had only himself to blame, after all, for it was he who had imposed a silence on the whole subject.

I spent half an hour that evening trying to locate the Reverend Peter Stanhope through directory inquiries, but no one of that name was listed in Richmond and the operator refused to look for Rev P. Stanhopes in other parts of England. Nor was there a listing for St. Mark's Church and, as I didn't know the name of the present vicar, I couldn't obtain the number of the vicarage either. It would all have been a great deal easier if Sam hadn't stood over me while I did it—I could have suggested the operator try Stanhopes in Exeter, but I wasn't ready to show my hand quite so blatantly. In the end, and half-jokingly, I suggested Sam phone Jock Williams, a confirmed atheist, and ask him to drive to St. Mark's Church from his house on the other side of Richmond to see if the new vicar's name was printed on the board outside. To my surprise he agreed.

"He wants to know what's up," Sam said on his return to the kitchen where I was doing the washing up.

"What did you tell him?"

"That the boss would have my guts for garters if I didn't help her track down 'Mad Annie's' missing valuables." He gave a quirky grin. "He thought you were 'round the bend twenty years ago. Now he thinks we've both lost it. He asked me why anyone would think an old tramp like Annie had valuables."

I propped a plate on the drain board. "What did you say?"

"Repeated what Larry told us about jadeite. It gave him a bit of a shock, as a matter of fact . . . said he didn't think Annie had two brass farthings to rub together."

"I expect he'd have been nicer to her if he'd known," I said tartly. "Jock always responds better to the chink of money."

"Mm, well, he's now advising me to put my huge gains from Hong Kong into some offshore fund he's operating out of the Isle of Man. He's got a wheeze for avoiding tax and he's prepared to cut me in on the deal if I'm interested."

"Knowing Jock, it'll be illegal."

"Unethical certainly," said Sam cheerfully, "but then he doesn't believe in a welfare state. Says it's against Darwin's theory of evolution. The sick, the lame and the poor are supposed to die. That's how natural selection works."

I held up a fork to examine the prongs. "He'll get his comeuppance one day," I said. "Arrogant, self-serving bastards always do. That's the *unwritten* law of natural selection—old bulls die painfully." I eyed him suspiciously. "I hope you told him where to stuff his tax wheeze."

"Not likely," he said. "The only reason he's driven off to St. Mark's on a Sunday evening is because he thinks I'm going to swell his coffers with megabucks." He straddled a chair. "How come you and Jock know each other so well? As I remember it, you used to avoid him as much as possible."

The question took me by surprise. "What kind of 'knowing' are we talking about?"

"I've no idea. That's why I'm asking."

I tried unsuccessfully to hide a smile. "Are you hinting at the biblical kind?"

"Maybe."

I snorted laughter through my nose. "That's funny."

"Why?"

"He's a boring little squirt with a power complex," I said. "Even his wife didn't fancy him, so I don't know what makes you think I would."

"It was just a question," he said huffily.

"What brought it on?"

"He wasn't surprised when I told him you'd taken up Annie's cause again. He said he'd been expecting it."

"So?" I asked curiously.

"He seems to know you better than I do. I thought you'd forgotten all about her. You haven't mentioned her name in twenty years."

"You asked me not to."

"Did I?" he said with a puzzled frown. "I don't remember."

I wasn't sure how genuine the frown was, so I changed the subject. "You shouldn't believe everything Jock tells you," I said. "He's needling you, just as he's needling you about how much money he has. He enjoys making you squirm."

"Why?"

I shook my head at his naïveté. The trouble with my husband, I sometimes thought, was that he was too ready to take people at face value. It should have been a disadvantage to him in his career, but oddly enough it worked the other way because people responded positively to his easy acceptance of the image they wanted to present. When I first knew him, I thought he was using a peculiarly sophisticated form of reverse psychology but, as time passed, I came to understand that he genuinely had no conception of the sides that exist in most people's natures. It was his most attractive quality. . . . It was also the most irritating. . . .

"Jock's a stirrer," I said lightly. "He resents other people's happiness . . . particularly where relationships are concerned. He's only ever known disasters . . . divorced parents . . . a brother who killed himself . . . a failed marriage . . . no children." I pointed a pan scourer at Sam's heart. "He wouldn't be needling you at all if you'd told him about your coronary and hadn't lied about how much money you've made. As far as he's concerned you've got everything. Health. Wealth. Happiness. Early retirement. A faithful wife. *And* sons."

Sam laced his fingers behind his head and stared at the ceiling. "He never got over his brother's death," he said.

"So you always say, but you never explain why."

"I didn't want you jumping to conclusions."

I frowned at him. "How did the brother kill himself?"

"Hanged himself from a tree one day. There was no suicide note so the police thought it was murder and most of the suspicion fell on Jock because he took some money from the kid's bedroom after he was dead. In the end the coroner accepted that the boy had been depressed about his parents' divorce and came down on the side of suicide, but it wrecked the entire family, according to Jock. They all ended up blaming each other."

"That's sad," I said, meaning it. "How old was he?"

"Sixteen. Three years younger than Jock."

"God, that really *is* sad. What happened to the parents?"

"Jock lost all contact with them after the divorce. I don't think he even knows where they are anymore . . . whether they're alive . . . or whether they still care about him. He claims it doesn't worry him, then spends every waking hour trying to prove he's a man to be reckoned with." Sam lowered his eyes to look at me. "It doesn't stop him being an arrogant, self-serving bastard but it probably explains the reasons behind it."

It explained a lot, I thought, as I promised to make a point of being pleasant when Jock came back with the name of St. Mark's vicar. What it didn't explain was where Jock had found the extra money that had allowed him to trade up his share in 21 Graham Road for a more impressive, and expensive, property near Richmond Park.

It was Wednesday before I was able to speak to Peter Stanhope in person. My previous calls had been answered by a recorded message and it seemed unreasonable to fill his tape with long explanations of who I was and why I wanted to talk to him. His new parish was in Exeter, about sixty miles west of Dorchester, and I was about to begin a letter to him when he answered the phone on Wednesday morning.

I had spoken to him only once when we lived in Richmond, and I wasn't confident that he'd remember me as well as I remembered him. I gave him my name and said I wanted to talk to him about Annie Butts, "the black woman who was run over by a truck."

There was a long pause and I had time to recall Libby's description of him as "a fat little bloke with sweaty palms." I was beginning to wonder if the reason for the silence was because the phone had slipped from his hand, when he suddenly barked, "Did you say Ranelagh? Any connection with the woman who claimed Annie was murdered?"

"That's who I am," I said. "I didn't realize the name would mean anything to you."

"Oh, goodness me, yes! You were quite famous for a while."

"For all of fifteen minutes," I agreed dryly. "They weren't the most pleasant fifteen minutes of my life."

"No, I don't suppose they were." A pause. "You had quite a tough time of it afterward."

"Yes."

He clearly didn't like one-word answers and sought for a change of subject. "Someone told me you and your husband went abroad. Did that work out all right?"

I guessed it was his polite way of asking me if I was still married, so

I assured him I was, gave him a thumbnail sketch of our twenty years away, mentioned my two boys, then asked him if I might pay him a visit. "To talk about Annie's neighbors," I explained, wishing I could put a little more enthusiasm into my voice at the prospect of seeing him again. I was relying on his sense of duty to agree to the meeting, but I didn't believe he had any more relish for it than I did.

A more noticeably guarded edge crept into his voice. "Is that wise?" he asked. "Twenty years is a long time, and you seem to have done so well for yourselves . . . stayed together . . . made a family . . . put the unpleasantness behind you."

"You remember our little chat then?" I murmured. "I didn't think you would."

"I remember it well," he said.

"Then you'll understand why I want to talk about Annie's neighbors."

I heard his sigh down the wire. "What good will it do to rake over dead ashes?"

"It depends what you find," I said. "My father put a log on the fire once and a gold sovereign dropped out of it as it burnt. Someone had obviously hidden it in the tree and a couple of centuries later my father reaped the reward."

Another pause. "I think you're making a mistake, Mrs. Ranelagh, but I'm free on Friday afternoon. You're welcome to come any time after two o'clock."

"Thank you." It was my turn to pause. "Why am I making a mistake?"

"Revenge is an unworthy ambition."

I stared into a gilt-edged mirror that was hanging on the wall in front of me. It was old and cracked and, standing where I was then, it produced a lengthened image that made my face look thin and cruel. "It's not revenge I'm after," I said with studied lightness. "It's justice."

The vicar gave an unexpected laugh. "I don't think so, Mrs. Ranelagh."

I had no intention of taking Sam to Exeter so I told him it was pointless for the pair of us to go when the lawn needed mowing and the flower beds tidying. He seemed happy enough although I caught him looking at me rather strangely over breakfast. "What's the matter?" I asked.

"I was just wondering why everyone seems to be moving to the west country," he said.

Peter Stanhope's parish was in the St. David's area of Exeter. I arrived too early and sat at the end of the road for an hour, watching the world go by through my windshield. I was on the edge of the university campus, and most of the pedestrian traffic seemed to be students—groups of boys and girls carrying books, or young couples clamped at the hip and shoulder like Siamese twins. I found myself envying them, particularly the skimpily clad girls in bottom-hugging skirts and crop tops, who swung along in the sunshine and radiated the sort of confidence I had never had.

The original vicarage was an impressive Victorian mansion, hidden behind high hedges, with a real estate agent's board outside, advertising a "desirable penthouse flat" for sale. The new vicarage was a cheaply constructed cube, across the road from the church, lacking both charm and character. As I parked outside at exactly two o'clock, I was beginning to wish I'd had the sense to spend the last hour in a pub. Dutch courage would have been better than no courage at all. A part of me thought about driving away with my tail between my legs, but I noticed a net curtain twitch in a downstairs window and knew I'd been seen. Pride is always a stronger motivator than courage.

The door was opened by a tall, cadaverous-looking woman with a beak of a nose, shoulder-length grey hair and the speed of delivery of a machine gun. "You must be Mrs. Ranelagh," she said, taking my hand and drawing me inside. "I'm Wendy Stanhope. Peter's running late. It's his morning at the shelter. Battered wives, poor souls. Come into the kitchen. He told me you were driving from Dorchester. Are you hungry? What about a drink? Chardonnay, do you?"

I followed her across the tiny hall. "Thank you." I looked around the white melamine kitchen which was mind-numbingly uniform and hardly big enough to swing a cat. "This is nice."

She thrust a glass into my hand with long, bony fingers. "Do you think so?" she asked in surprise. "I can't stand it myself. I much preferred the one we had in Richmond. The church doesn't give you much choice, you see. You have to make do with whatever pokey little kitchen they give you." She took a breath. "But there you go," she went on cheerfully, "I've only myself to blame. No one forced me to marry a vicar."

"Has it been a good life?"

She filled her own glass and tapped it against mine. "Oh, yes, I don't have many regrets. I wonder sometimes what it might have been like to be a lap dancer, but I try not to dwell on it." Her eyes twinkled mischievously. "What about you, my dear?"

"I don't think I've got the body for it," I said.

She laughed happily. "I meant, has life been good to you? You're looking well, so I assume it must have been."

"It has," I said.

She waited for me to go on and, when I didn't, she said brightly, "Peter tells me you've been living abroad. Was that exciting? And you've two boys, I believe?"

There was so much blatant curiosity in her over-thin face that I took pity on her—it wasn't her fault that her husband was late—and talked enthusiastically about our years abroad and our children. She studied me over the rim of her glass while I spoke, and there was a shrewd glint in her eyes that I didn't much like. I wasn't used to having people see straight through me, not after so many years of growing an impenetrable skin.

"We've been lucky," I finished lamely.

She looked amused. "You're almost as good a liar as I am," she said matter-of-factly. "Most of the time I can contain my frustration, but every so often I drive to a wide-open space, usually a cliff top, and scream my head off. Peter knows nothing about it, of course, because if he did he'd think I was mad and I simply couldn't bear to have him fussing round me." She shook her Lear-like locks in grotesque parody of a lap dancer. "It's quite absurd. We've been married forty years, we have three children and seven grandchildren, yet he has no idea how much I resent the utter futility of my existence. I'd have made an excellent vicar, but my only choice was to play second fiddle to a man."

"Is that why you scream?"

She refilled my glass. "It's more fun than having a hangover," she said.

QUEEN VICTORIA HOSPITAL

Hong Kong

Dept. of Psychiatry

A consultation was requested for Mrs. M. Ranelagh of 12 Greenhough Lane, Pokfulam, Hong Kong, by her general practitioner, Dr. J. Tang, querying postpartum depression after the birth of her son, Luke (DOB 20.10.79). According to her husband, she has been suffering from depression for some time. She refuses all medication. Mrs. Ranelagh had a two-hour consultation with Dr. Joseph Elias on December 19, 1979.

(The following extracts are taken from Dr. Elias's report, which was released to Mrs. Ranelagh in February 1999.)

. . . Mrs. Ranelagh was a difficult patient. She insisted on making it clear from the outset that her only reason for attending was to prove once and for all that she wasn't suffering from depression. She was uncooperative and angry. She expressed considerable hostility toward "men in authority" and "people who throw their weight about," and referred to "coercion," "bullying" and "intimidation" on a number of occasions. When I suggested to her that, far from persuading me to give her a clean bill of health, such statements were leading me to question the existence of a paranoid disorder, she agreed to cooperate.

. . . She admits to feelings of emotional turmoil following various events that happened at the end of last year and the beginning of this in London. She refused to discuss these in any detail for fear of confirming my suspicion of paranoia, however, she touched on three—two of a highly personal nature—to explain her "anger." She produced a number of newspaper clippings as evidence that the first incident had occurred—the death of a black woman—but was unable to support her other allegations. Without independent confirmation, I cannot say whether the subsequent incidents a) happened or b) are a construct to validate her sense of injustice re the black woman's death.

. . . The main focuses of her resentment are her husband (resident with her in Hong Kong) and mother (resident in England), whom, for various reasons, she feels betrayed her. This has resulted in a "coldness" toward them, which she "needs time to overcome." She describes her pregnancy as "ill-conceived"—(pun intentional?)—pointing to the difficulties of starting a new life abroad while carrying a baby to term. She talks lovingly about the child, calling it "my baby," while blaming her husband for "exposing her to an unplanned pregnancy." She retains a close bond with her father (resident in England), whom she contacts regularly by telephone and who is her only confidant. In addition, she listed a number of related problems: a dislike of being touched; feelings of insecurity when alone in her house; an obsession with hygiene; dislike of certain sounds—i.e. doorbells, London accents, rats scratching(?).

. . . I advised her against forging alliances—particularly with her father, who is "conducting some research" for her—which her husband will almost certainly see as betrayal if he finds out. I also pointed to the potential danger of making an ally of her son as he matures. She concurred on both counts, but remains adamant that her marriage will end tomorrow if she forces another confrontation with her husband. This is not what she wants. She rejected my offer of a joint session with herself and Mr. Ranelagh, as she believes that neither of them would be able to talk honestly without causing the immediate separation referred to above. Her feelings for her husband are confused. She seems to retain a close bond with him despite her resentment and believes her decision earlier this year to stay in the marriage was the right one. Nevertheless she is intent on punishing him for sins of "omission and commission."

. . . Mrs. Ranelagh presents herself as an intelligent, self-aware woman who is trying to come to terms with some extremely unpleasant, and as yet unresolved, issues in her life. Once satisfied that she had persuaded me she was not a "depressive"—a view I encouraged—she talked at length about her intention to seek "closure," although she is clearly ambivalent about what sort of closure she wants. In simple terms, she prefers the more anodyne description of "justice" for her black friend to the rather more accurate one of "revenge" for herself.

. . . When I warned her that prolonged internalized anger, be it well-founded or capricious, could lead to the sort of paranoid disorder—persecutory, delusional, phobic—that she was so determined to dissociate herself from, she said the damage had already been done. "I'm between a rock and a hard place, Dr. Elias. I'm a coward if I give in and a neurotic bitch if I fight back."

. . . In conclusion, I can find no evidence of depression in this patient. She is obsessive and extremely manipulative, but is also well in command of herself. I found her rather frightening. . . .

SIX

In the end I exchanged less than twenty words with Peter Stanhope. He bustled in half an hour late, full of apologies for the delay, only to be sidetracked almost immediately by a telephone call. Pausing only to say it was important, he disappeared into his study and left his wife to murmur courtesies into the receiver until he picked up the extension. It hardly mattered. Wendy was a mine of information, and I was fairly sure they weren't the sort of facts I would ever have had from her husband since most of it was gossip, and some of it was scurrilous.

While waiting for Peter's return we had transferred to the sitting room, where Wendy had tried to relieve me of my small single-shoulder rucksack, not realizing that it was held by a buckle across my chest. She was surprised by how heavy it was and how reluctant I was to let it go. I relented enough to unbuckle the chest strap and lower it to the sofa beside me—but if she wondered why I needed to bring the kitchen sink on my travels she was too polite to say anything. I was clearly an enigma to her, for whatever picture she had in her mind of a crusading zealot it certainly wasn't me.

She made a small moue as she replaced the receiver, and I wondered how often she was left to hold the fort and how accommodating Peter would be if their roles were reversed and she were the vicar and he the helpmeet. My expression must have been more revealing than I realized.

"Has he let you down, my dear?" she said into the silence.

"Not at all," I assured her. "I wanted to talk about Annie's neighbors on Graham Road and I think you probably know more about them anyway."

She fixed me with her all-seeing eyes. "I meant in the past," she said gently. "Did he let you down before?"

"In a way," I said, looking about the room to avoid looking at her. "He told me I was hysterical when I wasn't." Wendy was apparently a collector of porcelain figures because every surface seemed to have them. She had a fine array of white Dresden ladies along her mantelpiece and some tiny hand-painted birds in a small glass cabinet on the wall. Photographs were her other love, with pictures of her family everywhere, and a huge blown-up snapshot of seven laughing children on one wall. "Who are they?" I asked, nodding in their direction.

She accepted the change of tack without demur. "My grandchildren. It was one of those rare moments when they all looked their best." She gave a little chuckle. "Usually one of them can be relied on to scowl."

"Who took it?"

"I did."

"It's brilliant," I said truthfully. "Forget being a vicar, you should have been a professional photographer."

"I was for a time . . . well, semi-professional. I used to do the weddings at St. Mark's, particularly for the couples who didn't have much money to spend." She pulled open a drawer in a desk to one side of the fireplace and produced a bulging photograph album. "I think this might interest you. Most of Annie's neighbors are in here somewhere."

She passed it across to me and I flicked my way through a pictorial history of weddings, christenings, funerals and feast-day services at St. Mark's. The pictures from the '70s made me smile because the fashions were so dated—men in suits with flared trousers, frilly shirts and chunky identity bracelets; women with big hair, wearing empire-line dresses and slingback shoes. There was even a picture of me at Annie's funeral, twenty-four years old and desperately self-conscious in a brand-new black maxi-overcoat which hadn't fitted properly and gave me the look of an orphan in someone else's cast-offs. I recognized very few of the faces because they weren't all from my era, but some I remembered.

"Why did you take so many?" I asked Wendy. "You can't have been paid for all of them."

"I thought it would be interesting for future generations," she said. "I wanted to leave copies with the parish register so that when people came looking for information about their families, there'd be a visual record as well as a written one." She laughed. "It wasn't a very good idea. There was so much time and paperwork involved in cross-referencing pictures with written entries that I got snowed under very quickly. After that I went on doing it for fun."

She does a lot of things for fun, I thought, warming to her. I even began to wonder if I could excuse what I was doing in the same way. Would anyone accept that I was asking questions about Annie's death because I was bored? I touched a finger to a picture of a family group. "The Charleses," I said. "They lived next door to us at number 3."

Wendy moved across to sit next to me on the sofa. "Paul and Julia, plus two children whose names I can't remember. Peter christened one of them and it howled nonstop throughout the service. These were the christening photographs."

"Jennifer," I told her. "She used to cry all night. Sam went 'round once to read the riot act because we couldn't sleep for the row that was going on, but Julia was so exhausted she burst into tears on the doorstep and he couldn't bring himself to do it. After that we took to wearing ear plugs. Jennifer's about twenty-four now and working as a solicitor in Toronto. The whole family emigrated to Canada in 1980."

"Goodness me! You *are* well informed."

"I recognize this man's face," I said, pointing to another picture.

"Derek Slater," she told me. "He was a horrible brute . . . used to beat his wife and children when he was drunk. The poor creature was always taking refuge with us because she was so frightened of him." She turned a page and pointed to a dark-haired woman holding a toddler in her arms. "That's her . . . Maureen Slater. She had four children by him—two boys and two girls—all of whom got thrashed at one time or another. Derek was always being arrested . . . usually for drunk and disorderly . . . although I believe he had theft convictions, too." She placed a finger on the toddler's face. "Derek certainly spent time in prison because this little chap came long after the other three. As far as I know Maureen's still living on Graham Road, but goodness knows where Derek went. There was a terrible fight some time in 1979 or '80 when his elder son finally found the courage to take a baseball bat to him and told him to leave."

"That would be Alan?"

"Yes. Did you know him?"

"I taught him English for a year . . . a tall, heavily built child with hands the size of dinner plates. They lived next to Annie at the end of the terrace. Number 32. Do you have a picture of Alan?"

"I think so . . . but he wasn't in church when I took it. As far as I recall the only time he ever set foot in St. Mark's was to see if there was something worth stealing." She tut-tutted to herself. "He was a frightful thief, stole my mother's brooch from under my nose when I offered Maureen sanctuary one day, and I've never forgiven him for it. Mind you, all her children were thieves . . . only to be expected, I suppose, with a father like Derek. It's very sad the way the sins of the fathers are visited on the next generation."

"Did you report the theft?"

She sighed. "There was no point. He'd just have denied it. And it was my fault, anyway. I should have been more careful. After that I made sure everything was locked away whenever they came to the house."

I wondered what else Alan had got away with. "He tried to steal from me, too," I told her. "I left my bag on my desk while I went to collect some notes from the staff room, and when I came back he was

Maureen and Danny Slater
outside St. Mark's Church,
summer 1978

Derek Slater on a park bench
outside St. Mark's Church,
summer 1978

going through my wallet. I didn't report him either." I tapped a finger against my lip where a tiny tic of hatred pulsed and throbbed beneath the skin. "I'd never have let my own children get away with it."

"No," she said slowly, watching me with her sharp eyes, "but I don't suppose you liked Alan much so you overcompensated."

I didn't answer.

"I'd forgotten you were a teacher," she said to break the silence.

I nodded. "For my sins." I ducked my head down for a closer look at Derek Slater's face. He had long, dark hair and a pleasant smiling face and appeared anything but a wife-beater. "What did Derek go to prison for?"

"I've no idea. Theft? Assault?"

"On his wife?"

"A woman certainly. I don't think he was brave enough to pick fights with men."

"Who's this?" I asked, touching a picture of a heavily made-up blonde, simpering at the camera from beneath a wide-brimmed hat.

"Sharon Percy," said Wendy, turning her mouth down at the corners. "Mutton dressed as lamb. She wasn't far off forty when that was taken but most of her bosom's hanging out and her skirt barely covers her knickers. You must remember her. She lived next to Annie on the other side from the Slaters and was forever complaining about her." She heaved a sigh. "Poor Annie. She was sandwiched between the two worst families in the street—a thieving violent family, the Slaters, on one side and a tart with an out-of-control son on the other."

Sharon Percy—aka Jock's floozy and Libby's "bleached vampire," I thought with amusement. "I don't believe I ever saw her," I said, "or if I did I don't remember. I taught her son, Michael . . . at the same time I was teaching Alan Slater, but I don't think she ever came near the school."

"She was a dreadful woman," said Wendy tartly, "little better than a prostitute . . . entertained a different man in her house every night . . . but she still thought she was superior to a black woman . . . made Annie's life a misery with her endless complaints to the council."

*Sharon Percy at a wedding
at St. Mark's Church,
Spring 1983*

*Alan Slater and Michael Percy in
the alley behind Graham Road,
March 1979*

I studied the young-old face with interest and recalled some of the rednecks we'd met in South Africa. "It's the 'poor white' syndrome," I said slowly. "The lower you are in the pecking order the more important it is to have someone beneath you."

"Mm, well that was certainly true of Sharon."

It seemed a very unchristian attitude and I wondered what the woman had done to make Wendy dislike her. "How do you know so much about her?" I asked curiously. "Was she a regular churchgoer?"

"Oh, yes. Regular as clockwork as long as Peter was willing to give her an hour a week to discuss her problems. Hah!" she snorted suddenly. "*Alleged* problems, I should have said. Called him *Father* Stanhope because she knew it would appeal to his vanity. It was only when she started putting her hand on his thigh that he realized what she was up to and told her he wouldn't see her again unless I sat in on the discussion. After that she never set foot inside the church again."

I hid a smile. For all her declared frustration with her marriage, she could still feel jealousy. "Did she ever marry?"

"Not when we knew her. I couldn't even say who Michael's father was, and I don't suppose Sharon could either. The poor child was always getting into trouble with the police and Peter would be dragged out at midnight to stand in loco parentis because his mother was flat on her back somewhere."

"Turned fourteen in '78," I said, remembering. "Dark-haired, rather adult-looking . . . always wore white T-shirts and blue jeans."

She nodded. "He wasn't a bad lad, just hopelessly out of control. He was very bright and very articulate—the complete opposite to Alan Slater, who could hardly speak without uttering an obscenity. I was rather fond of him, as a matter of fact, but he wasn't the type to give his affection easily." A wistful expression crossed her face. "I read in the newspaper about six years ago that a Michael Percy had been sentenced to eleven years for armed robbery. The age was right but the photograph was very different from the boy I remembered."

I couldn't bring myself to shatter her illusions. "Does Sharon still live at number twenty-eight?"

"Presumably. She was certainly there when we left in '92." She took the album from me and leafed through the pages until she came to a picture of a gray-haired man with a pointed, raddled face like a tortoise. "Geoffrey Spalding," she said. "Married to a woman called Vivienne who died of breast cancer in '82. Poor creature—she fought a long battle against it—nearly five years in all. I took this at her funeral. They lived across the road from Sharon, and it was one of the big scandals that, while his wretched wife was dying, Geoffrey spent more time in Sharon's house than he did in his own. He moved in for good about six months after Vivienne's death." She sighed again. "The whole business upset Geoffrey's children terribly. He had two teenage daughters who refused to acknowledge that Sharon even existed."

"Did they move in with her as well?"

"No. They stayed across the road and took care of themselves. It was all very sad. They had virtually no contact with Geoffrey afterward except to post the gas and electricity bills through his door. I think they blamed him for their mother's death."

"I suppose we all lash out when we're hurt," I said, thinking of Jock and his parents. "It's human nature."

"They were very quiet girls . . . rather too quiet, I always thought. I can't ever remember seeing them laugh. They started caring for their mother when they were much too young, of course. It meant they were never able to make friends with their own age group."

"Do you remember their names?"

"Oh Lord, now you're asking." She pondered for a moment, then shook her head. "No, dear, I'm sorry. They were pretty girls with blonde hair and blue eyes . . . always reminded me of Barbie dolls."

"You said they were teenagers when their mother died. Late teens or early teens?"

"I think the elder was fifteen and the younger thirteen."

I did some mental arithmetic. "So they'd have been eleven and nine when Annie died?"

"More or less."

"They were called Rosie and Bridget," I said. "They used to walk to school every morning, hand-in-hand, wearing beautifully ironed uniforms and looking as if butter wouldn't melt in their mouths."

"That's right," said Wendy. "What a wonderful memory you have."

Not really, I thought. Before Annie's death the two girls and I had been friends. We would greet each other with smiles and hellos, I on my way to one school, they on their way to another. Then, for no reason that I ever understood, everything changed in the months following Annie's death. Their wide smiles vanished and they avoided looking at me. Once upon a time Bridget had had pigtails like her sister until someone cut them off and posted them in long, blond strands through our letter box. At the time I didn't know their surname or which house they lived in. All I knew was that Rosie grew paler and thinner, while nine-year-old Bridget's hair was long one day and short the next. But I had no idea why the ends were sent to me or what their significance was.

"I didn't know their mother was ill," I said sadly. "I used to think what a nice woman she must be because they were so sweetly behaved in contrast to some of the others."

More sighs. "They were very lost after she died. I tried to help them but Geoffrey became appallingly belligerent and told me to stop interfering. There's only so much you can do, unfortunately . . . and Geoffrey made them suspicious of me by saying I was trying to have them put into care. It wasn't true, but they believed him, of course." Her mouth turned down at the memory. "He was a beastly little man . . . I never did like him."

"Are either of the girls still on Graham Road?" I asked.

She looked troubled. "No, and the awful thing is I've no idea where they went or what happened to them. I believe Michael was living with them at one point, but he was in and out of juvenile prison so much it was difficult to keep track. I asked Geoffrey once what had happened to them but he brushed me aside as if I were an irritating gnat. A most pernicious creature. I've always felt he and Sharon deserved each other."

I brought her back to Rosie and Bridget. "Did the girls marry?"

She shook her head. "I couldn't say, my dear. If they did it wasn't in St. Mark's." She paused for reflection. "Mind, the report on the armed robbery—the one about Michael Percy—mentioned a wife called Bridget—and I thought at the time"—she pursed her lips into a tight little rosebud—"well, well! All those children were close. They used to run around in a gang together . . . couldn't prize them apart most of the time."

I wasn't there to score points with superior knowledge so I searched for a photograph of Jock Williams instead. Predictably, I couldn't find one. He vaunted his atheism as loudly as a born-again Christian vaunts Jesus's love, and he wouldn't set foot inside a church if his soul depended on it. There was a picture of Libby talking to Sam and me at Annie's funeral, and I pointed it out to Wendy and asked her if she'd ever met the husband. "His name was Jock Williams. They lived at number 21."

"What did he look like?"

"Late twenties . . . about five years older than Libby . . . dark-haired, quite good-looking, five foot ten." Another shake of her head. "He and Libby divorced eighteen months after Annie died. Libby took herself off to Southampton but Jock moved to a three-story town house in Alveston Road."

Wendy smiled apologetically. "To be honest I wouldn't have known who this woman was if you hadn't told me. Is it important?"

"Probably not."

She watched me for a moment. "Meaning it is," she declared. "But why?"

I concentrated on a small figurine on a side table which was the

Geoffrey Spalding at his wife's funeral, outside St. Mark's Church, Summer 1982

Libby Williams and the Ranelaghs at the funeral of Ann Butts, November 1978

same shade as Sheila Arnold's bracelet. "Most people have to settle for smaller houses when they get divorced," I said mildly, wishing I knew more about jade. "Jock moved into a bigger one."

She was clearly puzzled by my interest. "It was the way we were living then. People took absurd risks on property after Margaret Thatcher came to power. Sometimes it worked and sometimes it didn't. I remember one of our parishioners saddled himself with a mortgage of nearly £200,000 and doubled his investment within five years. Another bought just as the market peaked and within a few months found himself owing more than the house was worth. Your friend was lucky."

I nodded agreement. "What about Maureen Slater's and Sharon Percy's houses?" I asked her. "If they're still living on Graham Road does that mean they remained as council tenants or did they exercise their right to buy?"

"Oh, they bought, of course," she said sourly. "Everything in public ownership was sold off within the first two or three years. It was laughably cheap . . . no one in their right mind would have turned their backs on an offer like that. Sharon paid for hers outright, I believe, and Maureen opted to stagger her payments. Now, of course, they're quids in. Their houses are worth about £200,000 . . . and they paid an absolute pittance for them because the wretched taxpayers subsidized the sales."

I smiled. "You don't approve."

"Why would I?" she countered crossly. "Every time I see a homeless person lying in a doorway I think how criminal it is that there's no housing left for the genuinely deprived."

"Some might say Maureen Slater was genuinely deprived," I murmured. "She took a lot of punishment from her husband."

"Yes, well, Maureen's different," she admitted grudgingly. "Her brain was turned to mush by that brute. Peter used to describe her as 'punch drunk' from all the beatings, but if I'm honest I think real drunkenness probably had more to do with it. She was just as addicted to alcohol as Derek was . . . though with rather more justification." She caught my surprised expression. "Anesthesia," she explained. "It must have been very painful to be used as a sparring partner."

"Still . . ." I said slowly, "if her brain was turned to mush, how could she have afforded to buy her house? Presumably she couldn't work, so what did she use for money . . . even if it was only a pittance that she had to find?"

There was a long silence.

"What aren't you telling me?" demanded Wendy finally.

I took time to consider my answer, but in the end I decided to be straight with her. "I met Sheila Arnold recently . . . Annie's doctor. She told me Annie was robbed. Now I'm wondering who robbed her, how much they made on the deal and what the money was used for."

"Oh, dear, dear," said Wendy with genuine concern. "I really don't think there's any truth in that story. Sheila only came up with it when she was accused of neglecting another patient—and that was three or four years after Annie died. She wasn't remotely interested until her own interests were compromised." She tapped the tips of her fingers together in agitation. "It was all a bit strange. Not a word said for ages . . . then suddenly Sheila expects us to believe that, far from being the vulnerable soul we thought she was, Annie was a wealthy woman, living in comfort, until shortly before she died. It all became very unpleasant very quickly . . . insults being thrown about . . . everyone accusing everyone else of lying."

I didn't say anything, and she seemed to think she'd upset me.

"Are you disappointed?" she asked. "I'm so sorry. Peter told me what a shock Annie's death was to you."

"Please don't apologize." I wondered what else Peter had divulged. "I'm not disappointed." I opened my rucksack to reveal a six-inch-thick file, then took out an envelope of press clippings and flicked through the pile till I came to June 1982. "Is this the story you mean?" I asked her, handing her the "Local doctor denies neglect" report.

"Yes," she said slowly, glancing up from the yellowed paper. "How long have you had it?"

"Sixteen years. It was the fifth time Annie's name was mentioned in the press since the publicity over her death. These"—I removed the remaining clippings from the envelope and flicked my thumb down the guillotined edges—"are all the other references. Her case is generally cited to illustrate the dangers of allowing vulnerable people to fend for themselves." I smiled slightly at Wendy's expression. "Various friends save articles for me. Also, I pay my old university library to monitor the local and national press for any mention of Ann Butts," I explained.

"Good gracious!"

"And for any mention of the two police officers who investigated her death," I went on, removing another envelope. "These are the articles that refer to them. One, PC Quentin, died in a car crash seven years ago. The other, PS Drury, retired from the police in 1990 to take over a pub in the Radley brewery chain. There are also clippings about anyone mentioned in previous articles . . . for example, there's a reference to Dr. Arnold's move to Dorchester . . . and one about you and your husband leaving St. Mark's to take up a parish in the west country."

She looked at the piece on Sheila's alleged negligence. "The previous reference to us being Peter's quote at the end, I suppose?"

I nodded. "He didn't pull any punches either. 'There's no excuse for this kind of neglect. Lessons should have been learnt . . . so that the same mistakes could not happen again.'" My eyes strayed toward the jade figurine. "Did he know what he was talking about? Had he ever been inside Annie's house?"

Wendy shook her head. "She wouldn't give him the time of day because she knew Maureen took refuge at the vicarage."

"Then he had no business to talk about 'this kind of neglect,'" I said lightly. "It suggests an informed comparison, which he couldn't make, and it was hardly surprising that Sheila was upset about it."

"I know," she agreed unhappily. "The only good thing is, he didn't mention her by name."

I shrugged. "He didn't need to. It's perfectly clear who he's talking about. In any case, the newspaper probably edited it out to avoid a libel suit. The whole article's carefully constructed to record Sheila's *denials* of neglect without ever actually accusing her of it."

Wendy gave yet another heartfelt sigh. "It was my fault really. I'm the one who reminded Peter about Annie, and he promptly rushed off in high dudgeon to talk to the press. Sheila never forgave him for it and it made life very difficult afterward."

"I can imagine"—I extracted "Doctor cleared by BMA"—"particularly as Sheila was exonerated. Mr. Potts wasn't even her patient."

"It was too late by then. The damage had been done. Peter did try to apologize but Sheila was having none of it." She paused. "But it wasn't entirely his fault, you know. Sheila was spreading some frightful counteraccusations against him, saying the reason Annie distrusted him so much was because he'd supported the neighbors' attempts to get rid of her from the street. She even suggested he was a racist."

"Is he?"

I thought she might be angry, but she wasn't. "No. He has many faults but racism isn't one of them. Sheila knew it, too. It was an unkind thing to say"

"Not much fun for any of you," I murmured.

"Terrible!"

"But it doesn't mean Sheila was wrong to say Annie was robbed," I pointed out.

"It just seems so unlikely," said Wendy. "No one thought Annie had a house full of treasures while she was alive. Did *you* think she had?"

"No," I admitted, "but Sheila does have evidence to support her story. Letters from the RSPCA inspector, for example, who went in to check on her cats. And if it *is* true that Annie was robbed, then it's also true that the police investigation into her death was flawed because it failed to take into account that someone took a small fortune off her either before or after she died."

"But who, for goodness' sake?"

"That's what I'm trying to find out," I said, putting the press clippings back into their envelopes. "Someone fairly close to home is my guess . . . someone who knew what was in there."

She canted her head to one side to study me closely with her bright, perceptive eyes. "What's your husband's view?"

"He doesn't have one," I said slowly. "The subject hasn't been mentioned in our house for twenty years."

She put a gentle hand on my shoulder. "I'm sorry."

"No need to be," I told her gruffly. "This is my project, not his."

Did she think "project" was an inappropriate word? "It's not your fault Annie died," she said with sincerity. "You've nothing to feel guilty about."

"I don't."

Perhaps she didn't believe me. Perhaps she saw a contradiction between my apparent composure and the evidence of obsession in my lap. "No one escapes justice," she said, dropping her hand to pick up one of mine and rubbing it gently between hers. "It may not be a justice we can see or understand, but the punishment is always appropriate."

"I expect you're right," I agreed, "but I'm not interested in abstract punishment. I want the kind I can *see* . . . the eye for an eye . . . the pound of flesh."

"Then you'll be disappointed," she told me. "There's no joy in causing pain . . . however worthy the motive."

I had no answer to that except to return the pressure of her fingers. It was acknowledgment of a sort and to that extent it mollified her, but worry remained etched around her eyes until I left.

CURRAN HOUSE
Whitehay Road
Torquay
Devon

Wednesday, July 28 1999

Dearest M,

If I can give you any advice at all—and of course there's no reason why you should take it—it's that you talk things through with Sam before your mother and I come for our visit on Saturday. She's still very unhappy about your move to Dorchester and will, I fear, put pressure on the boys to supply answers if she can't get them from you. Sam has told her the farmhouse was the only property you could find at short notice—which is clearly what he believes—and she's now convinced "something's going on" as she says her tame real estate agent faxed you a list of suitable lets in Devon at the beginning of June.

Sorry to be a nuisance but the old adage—"of two evils choose the lesser"—is a good one, I find. You know what your mother's like when she gets the bit between her teeth, and I fear Sam would be very hurt to learn the truth from his children after a quizzing from their grandmother! It won't be easy "coming clean"—secrecy is frighteningly addictive, as I've discovered myself since I realized how much closer you and I have become through our shared crusade, my dear, and how jealously I want to guard that closeness—but I think the time has come for honesty. I know you would never hurt Sam unnecessarily.

Love,

Dad

X X X

seven

The house was full of young people when I arrived back that evening to find an impromptu barbecue taking place on our terrace. "Another end-of-term celebration," explained my younger son en route from the kitchen with a tray of spare ribs. He dropped me a mischievous wink. "Luke and I were voted the people most likely to throw a good party." He had a pretty girl draped off his elbow whose hair was almost as long and blonde as his own. "Georgie," he offered by way of introduction. "Mum."

The girl was too besotted to look at me for long. "It's nice of you to invite me," she said.

I nodded, wondering how Luke and Tom had managed to become the center of attention so quickly. At their age I had hidden behind a fringe, longing to be noticed and invariably overlooked, while Sam had followed in the wake of the Jock Williamses of this world, acquiring girlfriends courtesy of their friends' superior pulling power. The boys would say it was their height, surfers' good looks and neat bums, but I thought it had more to do with taking jobs as checkout cashiers in the local Tesco's, which seemed to be the modern equivalent of the village pump. In the end all paths meet across a supermarket trolley.

With a promise to put in an appearance as soon as I'd changed, I retreated to the bedroom where I found Sam laid out on the bed and glaring at the ceiling. "It's bedlam down there," he said crossly. "Why didn't you tell me the boys were planning to invite half of Dorchester to eat us out of house and home?"

"I forgot," I lied.

"Well, for your information," he growled, "I was sunbathing in the nude when they all came piling round the corner of the house. It was bloody embarrassing."

Smiling, I flopped down beside him. "Is that why you're hiding up here?"

"No," he said, jutting his chin toward some boxes in the corner of the room. "I'm guarding my wine. I found a girl in the kitchen trying to open a bottle of Cloudy Bay because she thought it looked like cheap plonk, so I gave her a lecture on the quality of New Zealand viniculture and she burst into tears."

"I'm not surprised if you had no clothes on. She probably thought you were a rapist."

"Ha-bloody-ha!"

"I suppose you shouted at her?"

He rolled over to face me, propping himself on one elbow. "I told her I'd have her guts for garters if she didn't learn to tell the difference between liebfraumilch and a priceless sauvignon blanc. Matter of fact, I nearly asked for her birth certificate in case we got raided. She didn't look more than twelve."

He had a pleasant face, my husband, with laughter lines raying out around his eyes and mouth, and I thought how well he wore his years and how little he had changed in the quarter of a century I'd known him. He had the kind of temperament that people felt comfortable with because he was slow to anger and quick to pacification, and his face was the mirror of his geniality. Most of the time, anyway.

Now, he eyed me thoughtfully. "How was your day? Did the Reverend Stanhope tell you anything useful?"

I shook my head. "I hardly spoke to him."

"Then why so late back?"

"I talked to his wife," I explained. "She kept a photographic record of their time at St. Mark's and she's lent me pictures of some of the people who were living on Graham Road in '78."

He studied me for a moment. "That was lucky."

Perhaps I should have seized the opportunity to be honest, but as usual I couldn't decide if then was the right time. Instead I just nodded.

"I suppose she knew all their names?"

"Most of them," I agreed.

"And could tell you every last thing about them?"

"Bits and pieces."

He pushed a strand of hair off my forehead with the tips of his fingers. "There can't be many vicar's wives who photograph their husband's parishioners."

I shrugged. "She was semiprofessional, used to cover the weddings of the poorer couples. It grew out of that. She's rather good actually. If she was forty years younger, she'd have made a career out of it."

"Even so"—he let his hand drop to the counterpane—"you could have driven all the way to Exeter to find some dumpy little homebody who'd never done anything more interesting than bake cakes for the Mothers' Union. Instead you come up with David Bailey. That's pretty amazing, don't you think?"

I wondered what was bugging him. "Not really. At the very least I knew she must have some photographs of Annie's funeral. Don't you remember her taking a picture of us with Libby Williams? She's a very striking woman, tall and gaunt . . . like a vulture . . . rather difficult to miss."

He shook his head. "How did you know she was the vicar's wife and not a press photographer?"

"Julia Charles told me. Apparently, Wendy—Mrs. Stanhope—took pictures of Jennifer's christening so Julia knew her quite well." I paused as he shook his head in unhappy denial. "What's the matter?" I asked.

He swung his legs off the bed and stood up, disbelief crackling out of him like small electric charges. "Larry came to see me this afternoon. He says you're stirring up a hornets' nest by asking questions about Annie. He wants you to stop."

"I hope you told him it was none of his business."

"Quite the reverse. I sympathized with him. Apparently Sheila nearly had a breakdown the last time she got involved. She was hauled before the BMA after your precious vicar accused her of neglect. It was all rubbish, of course—she was cleared immediately—but Larry doesn't want a repeat."

He walked to the window where sounds of laughter drifted up from the terrace. I kept my fingers crossed that Tom wouldn't choose that moment to power up his sound system to full volume, which was the one thing guaranteed to drive his father 'round the bend.

"What else did Larry say?" I asked.

"He wanted to know what brought us to Dorchester. Claims he's not much of a believer in coincidences." He frowned at me in hurt recrimination. "I told him he was wrong . . . that it *was* a coincidence . . . that there was no way we could have known in advance where Sheila was working. So he accused me of being naïve. Your *wife* knew, he said. She went into the surgery the day after you moved here to register specifically with Dr. Arnold, then asked for a copy of Sheila's work roster so that she could be sure of getting her."

I frowned back. "Where would he get a story like that?"

"He asked Sheila's receptionist if Mrs. Ranelagh had known in advance which doctor would respond to her request for a home visit."

I sat up and crossed my legs. "I thought that kind of information was confidential," I murmured.

He waited for me to go on and when I didn't he stabbed a finger at me. "Is that it?" he demanded. "You make me look a complete idiot, then talk about confidentiality."

I gave an indifferent shrug. "What do you want me to say? Yes, I knew this house was in Sheila's practice, and that's why we're renting it."

"Why didn't you ask me?"

"Ask you what?"

"If I was happy about it."

"I did. You said Dorchester was as good a place as any."

"You didn't tell me there was a hidden agenda, though, did you?" He was managing to keep his voice under control but I could feel the tremors of a major tantrum building inside him. And that, of course, is the trouble with people with equable temperaments—once they lose it, they lose it big time. "I might have felt differently if you'd told me you were planning to resurrect Annie Butts. *Jesus!* Don't you think we went through enough bloody misery at the time?"

I suppose everyone has a pet subject that triggers their anger—with me it was my mother's wicked talent for stirring, with Sam it was his fear of Mad Annie and everything her death represented: the mask of respectability that overlaid the hatreds and the lies. He always hoped, I think, in a rather free interpretation of the karma principle, that if he refused to look beneath a surface then the surface was the reality. But he could never rid himself of the fear that he was wrong.

I took a moment to reply. "It wouldn't have passed the 'so what' test, Sam. I'd have come anyway."

A look of incomprehension crossed his face. "Without me?"

"Yes."

"Why?"

It was such a little word but its interpretations were endless. Why would I think of deserting him? Why was I being so devious? Why didn't I trust him enough to tell him the truth? If he cared to, of course, he could answer those questions rather better than I could as he'd had a great deal longer to think about them. Admittedly, I'd never challenged him with them directly, but there must have been occasions in the small hours when he prepared his explanations in case I did.

I answered straightforwardly. "I chose Dorchester because I guessed Sheila had more information than anyone else," I explained, "though to be honest, it wouldn't have mattered where we went. The diaspora from Graham Road has been so widespread that we'd have had this conversation whether we'd come here or"—I gave another shrug—

"Timbuktu. Paul and Julia Charles are in Canada . . . Jock and assorted others are still in London . . . Libby remarried and lives happily with her second husband and three children in Leicestershire . . . the Stanhopes are in Devon . . . the coroner retired to Kent . . . John Howlett, the RSPCA inspector, is in Lancashire . . . Michael Percy, the son of Annie's immediate neighbor, is in prison on Portland . . . Bridget Percy, née Spalding—one of the girls who lived opposite Annie—works in Bournemouth . . ." I ran out of names and turned to plucking the dowdy candlewick bedspread which was part of the fixtures and fittings and filled me with loathing every time I looked at it.

I'd shocked him to the core. "How do you know all this?"

"The same way you know that Jock lives in Alveston Road. I kept in touch. I have a file of correspondence from my father, who's been writing letters on my behalf for years, and Julia and Libby drop me a line every six months or so to keep me informed about people's movements."

He looked horrified. "Does Jock know you've been talking to Libby?" He used the sort of tone that suggested I'd been party to a nasty piece of treachery. *Which was pretty rich, all things considered . . .*

"I doubt it," I said. "They haven't spoken since the divorce."

"But he's always believed we were on his side. Dammit, I told him we were."

"You were half-right then," I said, absorbed in teasing the bedspread with my fingernails. "*You've* always been on his side."

"Yes, but . . ." He paused, clearly grappling with some new and unpleasant thoughts. "Does your mother know your father's been writing letters for you?"

"No."

"She'll go apeshit," he said in alarm. "You know bloody well she thought the whole damn mess was dead and buried twenty years ago."

I yanked a particularly large tuft out of the candlewick and poked it back again when I realized I'd made a hole. I wondered if he remembered that my parents were coming to stay with us the following day, or whether like all the other disagreeable things in his life he had pushed it out of his mind. "I wouldn't worry about it," I murmured. "She won't be angry with you . . . only with me."

"What about your father?" he demanded, his voice rising in pitch. "She'll tear strips off him for going behind her back."

"There's no reason why she should ever find out."

"But she will," he said pessimistically. "She always does."

I thought of my father's advice on the lesser of two evils. If nothing else, Sam's inability to hide his feelings would start my mother on a hunt for hidden secrets. "She might be cross for a day or two," I said, "until she persuades herself it's all my fault. She's programmed never to blame men for anything. As far as she's concerned, Eve corrupted Adam"—I held Sam's gaze—"when she ought to know that Adam almost certainly took Eve without permission."

He had the grace to blush. "Is that what this is all about? Getting your own back?"

I didn't answer.

"Couldn't you have told me?"

I sighed. "Told you what? That I was pursuing something that was important to me? As I recall, the last time I used those words to you, you accused me of being a neurotic bitch and said if Annie's name was ever mentioned in your presence again, you'd divorce me."

He waved a despairing hand. "I didn't mean it."

"Yes, you did," I said flatly, "and if I'd been half as confident then as Tom and Luke are now, I'd have told you where to stuff your pathetic little divorce. I only stayed with you because I had nowhere else to go. My mother banned me from going home and none of my friends wanted a loony parked in their spare bedroom."

"You said you wanted to stay."

"I was lying."

Sam lowered himself gingerly on to an unopened box of wine. "I thought this was all over a long time ago. I thought you'd forgotten about it."

"No."

"Jesus," he muttered, dropping his head into his hands and lapsing into a long silence. He roused himself finally. "Have you *ever* loved me?" he asked bitterly.

I wanted to tell him it was a childish question, that if he didn't know the answer after twenty-four years then nothing I could say would make a difference. Did he think anyone could live indefinitely with someone they didn't love? *Could he?* But outside on the terrace Tom's boom box roared into sudden life, causing the walls and floors of the old farmhouse to thump in sympathy, and I was spared the necessity of replying.

I went into the bathroom to change and left my rucksack on the bed for Sam to explore. It was a cowardly way to impart information but I didn't feel badly about it. As the old adage has it—you reap what you sow—and Sam's harvest was well overdue.

M. R.

From: Julia Charles (juliac@cancom.com)

Sent: 11 February 1999 18:50

To: M. Ranelagh

Subject: The Slater children!

You won't believe the trouble we've had just to locate one of the Slater children! Not the one you wanted, I fear—being the youngest (Danny)—but he may be the most amenable to persuading his mother to answer your letters! I won't bore you with full details of the swings and roundabouts—suffice it to say that Jennifer's preschool chum at number 6 (Linda Barry) kept in touch with another preschool chum (Amy Trent) who was at art school with Danny and still keeps in touch with him. We really did bust a gut to find Alan but got nowhere, I'm afraid. Word has it that he married six or seven years ago and is living somewhere in Isleworth, but I don't know how accurate that is. It might be worth trying international directory inquiries to see if there's an A. Slater in that area, but it's a common name and you may come up with several.

Anyway, Danny Slater is living somewhere in Brixton (no address or phone number) and teaching graphic design at a college there. The name and address of the college is: Freetown Community Center, Brixton, London. However, the really good news is that he has an e-mail address—michelangelo@rapmail.com—and collects his messages regularly via an Internet café near Waterloo station. Jennifer's game to make the contact if Luke and Tom don't want to, but it would speed things up, I think, if you approach him direct. NB: Your idea to say it's an IT project using e-mail and Internet only is a good one and worked well with Linda and Amy.

So glad to hear Sam's on the mend. I know what a shock it must have been for you!

Speak soon, love

Julia

Part of the e-mail correspondence between Luke Ranelagh
and Danny Slater during the first six months of 1999

Luke Ranelagh

From: Danny Slater (michelangelo@rapmail.com)
Sent: 20 February 1999 20:50
To: Luke Ranelagh
Subject: IT Project—Database: Graham Road

Listen, mate, anyone who wants to build a database 'round a black hole like Graham Road needs his head examining. Okay, so you're on the other side of the world and you don't know shit about the UK. It's an excuse of sorts—and I guess I can accept it on that basis—but do me a favor and send me some pictures of babes in bikinis. I'm an artist, for Christ's sake! I have an aesthetic appreciation of beautiful women. Word pictures will do if you don't have access to a scanner. The truth is I am DESPERATE to forget I ever lived in Graham f*****g Road. If you'd met my mother you'd understand! Cheers. Danny.

Danny Slater

From: Luke Ranelagh (beachbum@safric.com)
Sent: 22 February 1999 15:12
To: Danny Slater
Subject: Babes in bikinis

How about these? Mine's the blonde babe on the right. Word pictures
of Graham Road will do if you don't have access to a scanner. I'm an
ex-pat, for Christ's sake! I have an aesthetic appreciation of all things
English. Cheers. Luke.

Extracts from an educational psychologist's report on Alan Slater, 32 Graham Road, Richmond. Requested by his head teacher—re: permanent exclusion from school—dated April 1979

. . . Alan shows a pattern of bullying behavior. He employs his strength to intimidate others through unprovoked violence, and uses abusive language toward children of different ethnic groups. He has a history of discipline problems and reacts aggressively toward teachers who attempt to control him—particularly the females . . .

. . . His academic performance across all subjects is poor and this has resulted in feelings of inadequacy and low self-esteem. He regards himself as isolated from his peer group and becomes enraged by seemingly minor slights. He feels rejected by family, peers and teachers, and seeks further rejection through disruptive behavior in order to provide himself with a reason for why no one likes him. There is evidence of violence at home. He speaks about his hatred of his father and refers to his mother as "a vicious bitch." He has a close bond with Michael Percy, a near neighbor and classmate, whom he regards as similarly disaffected. . . .

. . . In conclusion, I have real concerns about Alan's dangerous sense of alienation, which may already have led to criminal behavior. I believe rapid intervention is required to prevent matters from becoming worse. There are problems at home and at school, but permanent exclusion is not a solution. He requires intensive "special needs" teaching to improve his self-esteem, and he should be encouraged to form strong and positive bonds with adults—either inside the school environment or in the broader community. He needs to feel valued: Only then will he have the necessary motivation to correct his aggressive and antisocial attitudes. . . .

eight

I found Luke, my elder son, straddled across a chair in the kitchen. "Your man's outside smoking a spliff," he shouted into my ear over the cacophony of sound from the terrace. "I told him not to make it too obvious in case Dad saw him, so he's lurking behind a hedge at the bottom of the terrace steps." He handed me a can of lager, then stood up to steer me toward the French windows. "He's a bit of a whinger," he warned. "Keeps saying we must be loaded to afford a place like this, then goes on and on about how he's never had any luck in his life."

I nodded.

"So where's Dad?"

"Upstairs," I shouted back.

Luke smiled guiltily. "He's not still angry about his Cloudy Bay, is he?"

"No, but he's going ballistic about the noise."

"Okay." He pushed his way through the crowd and turned the volume down to bearable proportions. When he came back he had a wiry, dark-haired man in tow, about age twenty-five, with a nervous frown on his face. "Danny Slater," he said, introducing us. "He's one of the guys who's been giving me gen on Graham Road . . . teaches art at a community center in Brixton. He's on Portland for the summer learning to carve stone at a workshop in Tout Quarry. I couldn't believe it when we end up in a house just a stone's throw away . . . seemed like a good opportunity to get acquainted."

Luke spoke for Danny's benefit rather than mine. It was hardly tactful, as he'd pointed out several times, to spend months making friends
with a bloke, only for him to guess the first time you meet him that
there was a hidden agenda behind the friendship and that the reason
you're living less than ten miles from his holiday hideaway is because
you want to get close to his parents. "I'd be sodding mad if it happened
to me," he'd told me firmly, "so we take a bit of trouble. Okay? I like
him . . . he's cool . . . and his e-mails are funny."

Did I feel guilty about making an ally of my son? Yes. Did I remember Dr. Elias's words of warning about Sam's sense of betrayal
when he found out? Yes. Would it have stopped me using Luke? *No.* I
had enough faith in my husband to believe he would never blame his
children for something they had done for their mother.

This patient . . . is obsessive . . . manipulative . . . and . . . frightening . . .

Danny wasn't the most attractive young man I'd ever seen, but I put on
my best smile and shook his hand warmly as Luke took his leave and
wandered over to the barbecue. "You won't remember me," I said, "but
my husband and I used to live at number 5 Graham Road. You can't
have been more than three or four at the time, but I knew your elder
brother very well . . . Alan . . . I was his English teacher at King Alfred's."

He shook his head. "It won't have been my brother," he answered.
"Alan's thirty-five. You're thinking of someone else."

"No," I assured him. "It was certainly Alan. I taught him in '78
when he was fourteen. He was a bit of a handful," I finished with a
laugh, "but I expect he's calmed down by now."

Danny examined me closely for a moment, before pulling a packet
of cigarettes from his pocket. "You must have had an easy life then," he
said, more in criticism than compliment. "My mum's not much over
fifty but she looks a damn sight older than you do."

I smiled. "It depends whether you think teaching is easy. *I* don't, but
then I've never taught art. Perhaps that's less stressful than trying to force
Shakespeare down the throats of reluctant adolescent boys."

He rose immediately to the bait and I listened with patience to five minutes of complaint about the intolerable necessity of an artist having to earn a regular income . . . about the wear and tear on the nerves caused by the arrogant egotism of students who hadn't a creative bone in their bodies . . . about how, if he'd been lucky enough to live in a country where culture was valued, he'd have been given a grant to make his own art instead of teaching brain-dead morons how to make theirs . . .

I nodded sympathetically when he drew breath. "And I suppose your family isn't in a position to help you?"

"I'm not married."

"I meant your parents. I remember your father quite well." I thought of the photograph of Derek Slater which Wendy Stanhope had lent me. "Dark-haired, rather good-looking. Very like you, as a matter of fact."

He wasn't easily flattered. "There's only my mother," he said, "and she's on invalidity benefit." He offered me a cigarette and lit one for himself when I shook my head. "Dad abandoned us years ago . . . can't even remember what he looked like anymore."

"I'm sorry."

He shrugged. "It was for the best," he said unemotionally. "He took his belt to all of us at one time or another. Alan worst of all. Dad used to beat him about the head when he tried to protect Mum, and Alan's still got the scars to prove it."

"I did wonder," I said, equally unemotionally. "More often than not he was sporting a black eye at school, but he always told me he'd been in fights with boys from rival gangs. 'You should see the other guys,' he used to say."

For the first time Danny smiled. "He was a good kid. He took a hell of a lot of punishment till he got to fifteen and slammed a baseball bat into Dad's face. That's when Dad took off." Another shrug. "I don't re-member him but everyone says he was a right bastard. He got in touch with one of my sisters a few years ago but nothing much came of it. He was only after money. Sally tried to persuade Alan to help him out, but he refused and we haven't heard from him since."

"Do you know where he is now?"

There was a small hesitation. "Somewhere in London, I think."

Prison? I wondered. "And what of Alan?" I asked in the sort of reassuring tone that said I was more interested in my ex-pupil than I was in his father. "How's he getting on? Is he married?"

Danny nodded. "He's got a couple of kids, a girl and a boy. Never raises his voice to them . . . won't even give them a smack." He sucked moodily on his cigarette. "It fucks my head to visit him. He lives in this great little house in Isleworth and his wife's brilliant. She's called Beth . . . plain as a pikestaff and wide in all the wrong places . . . but every time I go there I think, this is how families are supposed to be, with everybody loving each other and the kids feeling safe. It makes you realize what you missed." His eyes strayed toward Luke and Tom, who were arguing over which CD to put on next. "I'd say your sons are pretty lucky, too."

I realized suddenly how vulnerable he was, and felt ashamed of the way I was using him. Until that evening he had been a name on a computer screen, an unremembered child from twenty years ago who had responded to an e-mail in the innocent belief that he was helping a lad in Cape Town complete a thoroughly trivial IT project. Yet he had no responsibility for Annie's death, and I wondered if he even knew that a black woman had died in Graham Road in '78. Certainly the name Ranelagh meant nothing to him, which suggested that both Annie and I had been long forgotten by the time Danny was old enough to understand that one woman had died on his road and another had accused her neighbors of racially motivated murder.

I followed his gaze. "Luke and Tom might argue that you're the lucky one," I said.

"How do you make that out?"

"Because their upbringing means they will never have your creativity or your commitment to proving yourself. Internalized pain is always a stronger motivator than security and contentment. Contented people take happiness for granted. Anguished people struggle to find it through self-expression. At least you have a chance of greatness."

"Do you honestly believe that?"

"Yes."

"Then why aren't you making your son's lives hell?"

The question was simplistic enough to bring a smile to my face. At the very least, it was predicated on the assumption that parental love can be switched on and off according to circumstance . . . although perhaps for him that was the reality of childhood. "Shouldn't you ask me first if I think greatness is a sensible ambition for a mother to want for her children?"

"Why wouldn't it be?"

"Because the odds are stacked against it. Anguish doesn't guarantee success, it merely offers the possibility. After that it's down to genius. In any case, as far as Luke and Tom are concerned, I'm guided entirely by selfishness. I want them to like me."

He was unimpressed. "Everyone's motivated by selfishness," he said, "including Luke and Tom. They behave the way you expect because they think they'll get something in return. Alan used to kowtow to my father to avoid a thrashing, but I'll bet Luke and Tom only kowtow for money."

I nodded. "More often than not."

"Alan's kids are the same. They're barely out of nappies but they've got him wound 'round their little fingers." He dropped his cigarette butt on to the terrace and ground it out under his heel. "All they have to do is burst into tears and say they want ice cream and he starts emptying his pockets. I told him he's making an ass of himself but he's so fucking paranoid about the way Dad treated us that he won't listen to reason."

I wondered if Danny realized how confused his views on parenting were and what he meant by "reason." Spare the rod and spoil the child, presumably, although why, like so many people, he believed harshness was a better educator than kindness was a perennial mystery to me. "How does your mother feel about it?"

"Christ knows. She's a Prozac junkie," he said bitterly, "so it depends what mood she's in at any given moment. It's a good day if she can drag herself out of bed . . . as for having an opinion on something . . ." He fell silent, staring at the ground.

"I'm sorry," I said again.

"Yeah, it's a mess." He gave a mirthless laugh. "I guess you're pretty disappointed."

"About what?"

"That a type like me responded to Luke's e-mails. You were probably hoping for something better."

"I never make those kinds of judgments," I replied truthfully. "If I did, I'd have to wear a label 'round my own neck, and that's not something I'm prepared to do. In any case, I'm not sure what type you think you are."

He kicked at a flagstone, refusing to meet my eyes. "Fucking useless," he muttered. "The last I heard of my dad he was banged up in the Scrubs for assault, but we've all been there at one time or another. I got six months for twocking—that's taking cars without consent. Alan got four years in juvenile for dealing . . . both my sisters have done time for shoplifting. We're bad news. Poor old Mum used to get the cold shoulder every time she left the house because of the stuff her kids did." He lapsed into a brief, unhappy silence. "I guess that's why she doesn't get out of bed anymore."

The admission clearly wounded him, and I wondered if he hadn't looked for us—or people like us, uninfected by anti-Slater bias—just as assiduously as we had looked for him. *Yet, if that were true, why had he confessed to his family's failings so readily?* The sly glance he gave me when he raised his head persuaded me it was a cynical test of my refusal to label him, and my sympathy waned a little. I guessed he enjoyed holding grudges and sought rejection for the purpose of fueling them . . . and I wondered which of us was the more manipulative.

"I thought you were going to classify yourself as a struggling artist," I said with a small laugh. "I hadn't bargained on 'fucking useless.' Does that mean I'll be wasting my time if I visit you at the sculpture workshop?"

He gave me an unwilling smile. "No. I'm a good sculptor."

"You ought to be," I told him. "Your brother had real talent at fourteen."

He looked surprised. "Alan?"

I nodded. "I've still got a little wooden figure he carved for me. It's in the shape of a snake with feathers 'round its head."

"That's probably right," said Danny. "He's got this thing about an Aztec god who was half snake, half bird. It's a load of crap, but Alan reckons the bastard was an alien who came to earth to create a lost civilization in Mexico."

"Quetzalcoatl?" I suggested.

"That's the one. He's got a mosaic of him on his sitting-room wall."

I learned nothing further about Alan's picture that evening because Danny was more interested in pouring scorn on his brother's belief in extraterrestrials than he was in discussing his taste in art. I clung to my dwindling patience in order to listen to the hoary old arguments on both sides, and was somewhat relieved when a six-foot-tall brunette with legs up to her armpits seduced him away with a cigarette.

I watched them perform the opening moves of a courtship dance—an awkward affair of wriggling shoulders and pretended casualness as they dipped their heads to the cigarette lighter—and was about to go back inside when Sam appeared at my elbow with a peace offering. "It's Cloudy Bay," he said gruffly, shoving a glass of wine into my hand. "I was going to drink the lot to drown my sorrows, then I thought, to hell with it, it's not your fault Larry got me fired up."

It wasn't a white flag exactly but I could always recognize a truce when I saw one. I responded with a chink of glasses and a smile, while wondering if Sam had used the opportunity I'd given him to find out who Danny Slater was and why he was there. If not, I feared the truce would be of short duration. It was one thing for his wife and his father-in-law to keep secrets from him . . . quite another for his sons to do it as well.

He might have read my thoughts. "Who's the dark-haired chap you were talking to?" he asked, nodding in Danny's direction. "I was watching from the window. He seemed to have a lot to say to you."

"His name's Danny Slater," I told him. "He's working up at the sculpture park on Portland."

"Any relation to Derek Slater?"

"His son," I said evenly. "Do you remember Derek?"

"No. I've been going through your rucksack." He hunched his shoulders like a boxer preparing to defend himself. "And don't give me any heartache over it because if you didn't want me looking, you shouldn't have left it on the bed."

"My fault," I agreed, hoping he'd had the sense to go through everything. Ignorance had kept him happy for years; *partial* ignorance would eat away at him like a rotten worm.

"You were right about the Rev's wife. She took some useful photographs. This lad's the spitting image of his father twenty years ago."

"There's a lot of his mother in him," I demurred.

"That would be Maureen Slater?"

I nodded.

"Mm, well, I didn't recognize her. In fact I didn't recognize any of them except Julia Charles and Libby Williams. There's a blonde woman who came into the pub occasionally, I think, but other than that"—he shook his head—"they were all strangers."

I wondered how much of the correspondence he'd read and how much he thought I'd withheld. If he knew the truth, he'd be devastated.

He flicked an abstracted glance across the field of heads in front of the house, looking for Luke and Tom. "That's quite a file the boys have collected on Graham Road. How long have they been doing it?"

"Since your coronary."

He smiled slightly. "On the principle that you'd be coming home whether I lived or died?"

"Something like that."

He paused before his next question, as if considering the wisdom of asking it. He knew as well as I that bridges were best left unburnt, but his need for reassurance was stronger than his caution. "Did you tell them I walked out on you?"

"No. I told them Annie was murdered and that I was trying to get the investigation reopened. Nothing else."

He stared into his wine glass, his mouth working strangely as if trying to formulate unaccustomed words. But in the end, all he said was: "Thank you."

Statement made by Mrs. M. Ranelagh in 1979
re: an alleged assault by Derek Slater of 32 Graham
Road, Richmond.

INCIDENT REPORT

Date: 25.01.79

Time: 10:32

Officer: PS Drury, Richmond Police

Witness: Mrs. M. Ranelagh, 5 Graham Road, Richmond, Surrey

Incident: Alleged assault on Mrs. Ranelagh at 15:00 approx. on 24.01.79

Mrs. Ranelagh states: I went to the shops yesterday afternoon because there was no food in the house and I had had nothing to eat for three days. I thought it would be safe because it was still light. As I turned onto Graham Road, a man came up behind me and pushed me into the alleyway at the back of the even-numbered houses. I was unable to call out because he put a hand over my mouth and clamped my arms to my sides in a bear hug before slamming me face first into a fence and using his weight to hold me there. It all happened very fast and there was nothing I could do to break free. I couldn't see his face because he was behind me, but his breath smelled of drink and his clothes smelled unclean. I was wearing trousers and could feel something being pushed between my thighs. I thought it was the man's penis. He had his face pressed against the side of my head and whispered "slag," "bitch" and "cunt" into my ear. He also said he'd "do for you proper" if I didn't keep my "filthy, nigger-loving mouth shut." He was very strong and I was frightened because I thought he intended to rape me. I believe that is what he wanted me to think. Before releasing me, he forced me to my knees and pushed my head into the mud at the bottom of the fence. He said if I reported what had happened to the police I wouldn't "get away so lightly next time." I raised my head to watch him turn the corner into the main road. He was dressed in a dark jacket, blue jeans and sneakers. It was Derek Slater who lives in the neighboring house to where Ann Butts used to be. I know him by sight, although I have never spoken to him. He had disappeared by the time I found the courage to go back onto Graham Road. I saw no one else and went straight home.

MEMO

To: Police Superintendent Hathaway

From: PS Drury

Date: 29.01.79

Subject: Advice re cautioning Mrs. Ranelagh against wasting police time

Sir,

As you know, Mrs. Ranelagh has made a number of accusations against Derek Slater, including: 1) harassing and murdering Ann Butts; 2) making abusive telephone calls to the Ranelagh household in the middle of the night and; 3) attempting to keep Mrs. Ranelagh a prisoner in her own home by loitering outside her front door. None of these accusations stands up to investigation. 1) The inquest verdict on Ann Butts was unequivocal. 2) The Slaters have no telephone—nor do they have access to the Ranelaghs' new ex-directory number. 3) Mrs. Charles at 3 Graham Road—next-door neighbor and friend of Mrs. Ranelagh—denies ever seeing Derek Slater at their end of the street.

There is no evidence that the above incident took place other than Mrs. Ranelagh's word. The clothes she claims to have been wearing are unmarked and unstained—i.e., there are no muddy marks on the knees of her trousers and no semen staining between the thighs. Despite the aggressive way in which she says she was held "in a bear hug" and slammed against a fence, her face and arms are unmarked. (N.B.: She waited nineteen hours to report the incident and claimed to have cleaned herself up.)

Mrs. Ranelagh admitted to me that her husband has left her. She is clearly disturbed by Mr. Ranelagh's desertion. She says she phoned him to tell him about the alleged assault and was upset when he accused her of lying. "He said I'd invented it to make him jealous. I sometimes think the only thing he thinks about is sex." (N.B.: Mrs. Ranelagh has lost a lot of weight and appears to be anorexic. Also, her behavior is irrational—she breaks off in the middle of a conversation to listen for rats.)

I spoke to Mr. Ranelagh by telephone. He claims his wife is "bored with being a teacher and is reveling in her fifteen minutes of fame." According to him, nothing she says can be believed at the moment.

I have questioned Derek Slater and he denies being anywhere near Graham Road at 15:00 hours on 24.01.79. He says he was at Kempton Park Races until the early evening and has a ticket stub to support this. He has supplied names and telephone numbers of three friends who were with him—one supports the alibi; two yet to be checked.

Please advise. My personal view is that Mrs. Ranelagh is pursuing a vendetta against Derek Slater because she believes him to be responsible for the death of Ann Butts. I consider this vendetta to be: a) an invention; b) paranoid; and c) strongly linked to shock and/or the failure of her marriage. I strongly recommend an official caution against wasting police time.

F Drury

nine

We survived the party wreckage on the terrace the following morning with sore heads and mixed feelings. The boys were savoring last night's success, while Sam and I peered into a black hole as I reminded them all that my parents were due at noon. Luke and Tom, who were both on the afternoon shift at Tesco's, took the news in stride. Forget lunch, they said cheerfully, but as long as dinner was late they'd make an effort to get back for it. Sam, by contrast, crumpled dramatically as if he'd been axed by a pole.

"It's been on the calendar for ages," I said unsympathetically, handling him a cup of black coffee as he slumped into a chair, "so don't blame me if you never bother to read it."

"I don't feel well."

The boys were immediately solicitous, worried that "not feeling well" had more to do with Sam's coronary than too much to drink the night before. They fussed about him, staring anxiously into his face and patting him encouragingly on the shoulder as if that would somehow prevent another attack. Sam eyed me with sudden mischief, as if seeing a way out of a nightmare weekend, so I gave him the Ranelagh glare.

"Don't even think about it," I warned, massaging my hangover. "You know my mother. Nothing prevents her turning up. And do not *dream* of disappearing off to bed. It's your job to charm her until the boys get back."

"Oh God!" he groaned theatrically, sinking his head into his hands.

"She'll *kill* me. I've told her at least ten times that it was chance that brought us to Dorchester."

Luke and Tom eyed him curiously, wondering at this sudden reversal in their father's usually sanguine, if never very thrilled, acceptance of his mother-in-law.

"What's up?" asked Luke.

"Nothing," I said. "Dad's looking for trouble where it doesn't exist."

"We could call in sick," said Tom helpfully. "I quite like Gran."

"Only because you've never seen her breathing fire," muttered Sam. "She's even more scary than your mother when she's angry"—another mischievous glance in my direction—"probably because there's so much more of her."

I handed Tom a black plastic bag to start clearing the mess on the terrace. "Your father's being ridiculous. Granny adores him. He only has to smile and she's putty in his hands."

It didn't work out like that, of course. Nothing ever does. My father had taken his own advice—*of two evils choose the lesser*—and had tucked a magazine article on racially motivated murder into his overnight bag, which my mother unearthed and read when she decided unilaterally to repack their clothes into one large case. Dad swore it was an accident, but I didn't believe him any more than he would have believed that Sam had read my files "by accident." I remarked to him afterward that it was a damn good thing I hadn't ignored his letter of warning, otherwise we'd have had a repetition of the mother/son-in-law alliance of twenty years ago, but Dad just laughed and said Sam wasn't the kind of man to make the same mistake twice.

The article in question had been written in the wake of the official inquiry into the murder in London in 1993 of a young middle-class black man called Stephen Lawrence. The inquiry—not held until 1999— had condemned the police for "institutionalized racism" following the shoddy and lackluster investigation into Stephen's murder by a gang of youthful white supremacists, all known to the police, who escaped

conviction because of the culture of legal carelessness that existed in regard to the deaths of black people. My mother might have thought it
was a general interest story if my father hadn't taken the trouble to
highlight a paragraph and make this note to me in the margin: *M. Some
good points here. Suggest you contact the journalist re police apathy and violent
treatment of offenders. N.B.: River of Blood speech, 1968—Annie Butts's murder, 1978.*

The paragraph read:

> *By definition, to describe anything as "institutionalized" means the tra-
> dition is a deep-seated one, and this suggests that Stephen Lawrence's
> murder isn't the only investigation to be bungled by a predominantly
> white police force, long riddled with apathy and indifference toward black
> victims. In the thirty-one years since Enoch Powell M.P. predicted war be-
> tween the races in his notorious "River of Blood" speech, little has been
> done by police and government to address the issue of racially motivated
> attacks on Afro-Caribbeans and Asians. Indeed, many in these commu-
> nities point to the number of black people who have died while in police
> custody or while resisting arrest, and argue that some of the worst treat-
> ment they receive is at the hands of the very people whose duty it is to
> protect them.*

My mother sniffed a conspiracy immediately, and set out to prove it
by berating my father nonstop all the way from Devon. By the time
they reached our house she had worked herself into a fine fury, made
worse by my father's stubborn refusal to comment. He hoped, I think,
that good manners would prevail once they reached the farmhouse, but
he had forgotten how much she enjoyed confrontation, particularly
where her daughter was concerned. She assumed—with some justification—that Sam was as much in the dark as she was and, all too predictably, the full weight of her moral outrage descended on me.

She cornered me in the kitchen. "It's the deceit I can't stand," she
said. "All your life you've been saying one thing and doing another. I

wouldn't mind so much if you didn't involve other people in your lies. I remember the time you and that beastly little friend of yours . . . Hazel Wright . . . swore you'd spent the night at her house when the reality was you were both passed out, drunk, on the floor of some boy's bedroom." She clenched her fists at her sides. "You *promised* us," she declared aggressively. "'A new start,' you said. No more recriminations. No more dragging the family down with your dreadful fantasies. And what do you do? Break your word at the first opportunity, then manipulate your father into helping you."

I put some glasses on a tray. "Is Dad still on the pink gins?" I asked her, searching the larder for Angostura bitters.

"Are you listening to me?"

"No." I raised my voice to reach the open French windows which led directly from the quarry-tiled kitchen on to the Portland flags of the terrace. "Sam! Find out if Dad wants his gin pink, will you?"

"He does," came the shout back. "Do you need a hand?"

"Not at the moment," I called, taking a lemon from the fruit bowl and cutting it in half.

"I'll talk to Sam if you insist on ignoring me," my mother warned. "I've already given your father a piece of my mind. God knows what he thought he was doing, encouraging you like this."

I watched her for a moment, wishing I hadn't inherited so many of her features. She was a good-looking woman, although she rarely smiled because of worries about wrinkles, but I'd done my damnedest in twenty years to wipe out the similarities between us—slimmed down, changed my hair color, forced a permanently cheerful expression to my face—but it was all just window dressing. Every time I saw her, I was seeing myself thirty years on, and my smile would become a little more fixed and my resolve not to leap to critical judgments a little more determined. It made me wonder who I really was, and whether I had any substance beyond a childish desire to prove I was a better person than she was. I recalled my father telling me once—as if it were something that needed saying—that my mother *did* love me, and I answered, "Of course she does, as long as I agree with her. Not otherwise."

"You're her proudest achievement," he had said simply. "If you reject her views, you reject her."

I turned one of the lemon halves on its side and sliced into the oozing flesh. "You look as if you've been sucking one of these," I murmured, "and if the wind changes you'll be stuck with that sour expression forever."

Her mouth turned down even further. "That's not funny."

"You found it funny when you said it to me."

There was a short silence.

"You have a cruel streak in you," she said. "You don't mind who you hurt, just as long as you can have your petty little revenges. I've often wondered where you get it from. There's no forgiveness in your nature. You brood over people's mistakes in a way that neither I nor your father has ever done."

I gave a laugh of genuine amusement. "My God! And this from elephant-brain who's just been quoting Hazel Wright at me. I was thirteen years old, Ma, and Hazel and I drank two shandies each before falling asleep on Bobby Simpkin's bed." I shook my head. "You wouldn't let it rest. I don't know what you thought we'd been doing but from that moment on, I had nothing but lectures on how no decent man would take on shop-soiled goods."

"There you go again," she snapped. "Always blaming others, never yourself."

I shrugged. "I was merely pointing out that my cruel streak, assuming it exists, comes from you."

"Have I ever broken my word? Do I lie?"

Maybe not, I thought, *but I might prefer a few white lies and broken promises to the painful recognition that she would rather I had been a son.* "The only promise I made," I reminded her, "was never to mention Annie Butts in front of you or Sam again, and the fact that you're now interpreting my keeping of that promise as deceit is hardly my fault."

"Then how did your father get caught up in it?"

"In what?"

"Whatever it is you're doing . . . the reason you chose to come here despite the trouble I went to to find you a house in Devon."

"I didn't make the promise to Dad," I said, "and he wouldn't have accepted it if I had. He offered to help me before Sam and I left England, and he's been a tower of strength ever since. As a matter of fact, he's the one who spotted the ad for this place in the *Sunday Times* and phoned me in Cape Town to suggest we rent it for the summer."

Another silence, rather longer this time. She wanted to ask me why—much as Sam had done last night—but she was embarrassed to admit just how far she'd been excluded from our lives and decisions. Instead she adopted an injured air. "I hope you haven't turned Sam's sons against him as well," she said. "That really would be unforgivable."

"I haven't turned anyone against him," I answered, searching the cupboards for a jug.

"Oh, for goodness' sake!" she said sharply. "Don't be so naïve. When you persuaded your father to take your side against your husband's, you effectively set them at each other's throats."

"It was never a question of taking sides," I said, finding a glass carafe, "only a question of research. In any case you took Sam's side against mine, so Dad thought it reasonable for at least one of my parents to redress the balance."

"I did it for your own good. You were behaving like a spoiled child."

"How odd," I said with a laugh. "That's exactly what Dad said about Sam."

"That's nonsense. Your father and Sam used to get on like a house on fire until you insisted on jeopardizing your marriage over that wretched negro." She paused. "Dad's worked hard to restore their relationship, which is why it's so unkind of you to persuade him to go behind Sam's back like this."

I cocked an ear to the rumble of relaxed conversation outside. "They're certainly not at each other's throats yet, so let's hope you're worrying unnecessarily."

"For how much longer? You can't have forgotten how upset Sam was in the wake of that woman's death. What on earth induced you to raise the whole sorry business so soon after his coronary? Do you want to cause another one?"

I filled the carafe with water and put it on the tray. "It doesn't seem to have worried him so far," I said mildly, "but feel free to ask him yourself if you don't believe me." I lifted the tray. "That's everything, I think. Could you bring the lemon?"

We talked about everything under the sun except Annie Butts, yet her presence was powerfully felt—in my father's refusal to meet my mother's eyes, in Sam's obvious discomfort every time the subject of Dorchester was raised, in my mother's dreadful attempts at flirtatiousness to reestablish a hold on her menfolk. When it became obvious that I was *de trop* as far as she was concerned, I took the hint and vanished inside to make lunch. Ten minutes later a monumental row erupted on the terrace. I caught it only in snatches but so much heat was generated, particularly between my parents, that their rapidly rising voices carried through to the kitchen.

It does me no credit to say I enjoyed every minute of it. But I did. It was the first of my petty little revenges and I raised a silent cheer when my father told my mother it was a pity her life was so bereft of interest that her only joy came from stirring up trouble within her family.

The silence that followed my reappearance on the terrace with trays of salad was interminable. I remember thinking there was a multitude of wasps that summer. I watched them drone in their black and yellow stripes around the spirit-sugared glasses, and wondered if there was a nest nearby that needed destroying. I also remember thinking that wasps were less harmful than people, and that a sting was a bagatelle compared with the poison of a long-suppressed grievance.

"Why does your father stay with her?" Sam asked me in bed that night.

"Once he signs up to something he always sees it through."

"Is that the only reason they're still together? Because your father has a sense of duty?"

I shook my head.

"What else is there?"

"Love," I said. "He's a very affectionate man and he never gives up on anyone."

"Like father like daughter then?"

I turned to look at him. "Is that how you see me?"

"Of course. How else would I see you?"

QUEEN VICTORIA HOSPITAL

Hong Kong

Dept. of Psychiatry

Mrs. M. Ranelagh

12 Greenhough Lane

Pokfulam

February 14, 1980

Dear Mrs. Ranelagh,

   Thank you for your letter of July 3. I'm sorry you feel that a follow-up visit would be of no benefit, particularly as your reference to "a new calm" suggested that our previous conversation had been valuable. However, as you so rightly point out, there is no compulsion on you to attend further sessions.

   I have pondered deeply on the question you posed toward the end of our session. Why should your husband escape punishment for raping you? And I pass on some wisdom I received as a child in Auschwitz concentration camp when I asked a rabbi if the Germans would ever be forgiven for what they were doing to the Jews. "They will never forgive themselves," he said. That is their future and also their punishment.

   Should you not have asked, however, whether it was right for Sam to escape your punishment? And

are you so free of guilt yourself, Mrs. Ranelagh,
that you feel comfortable standing in judgment on
your husband?
With best wishes,
Yours sincerely,

J. Elias

Dr. J. Elias

THE CHESHIRE CAT HOSPITAL
Cheadle Hulme, Cheshire, UK

Mrs. M. Ranelagh

Jacaranda

Hightor Road

Cape Town

South Africa

December 3, 1998

Dear Mrs. Ranelagh,

In response to your detailed inquiry about the ill treatment of cats in the UK, I enclose a copy of a leaflet we produced last year to boost interest in a fund-raising drive. As you will see, it makes grim reading, but I make no apology for the contents. The work we do is costly and time-consuming and would be entirely unnecessary were it not for the terrible cruelty that is regularly inflicted on defenseless animals.

I have no difficulty in believing that someone would put superglue in a cat's mouth and tape its muzzle with Elastoplast or parcel tape to stop it from eating or crying. In the past, we have seen cats with their paws dipped in quick-drying cement to prevent them walking; cats with their back legs paralyzed by broken spines; cats with their claws and teeth pulled out by pliers; cats blinded with red-hot pokers; and cats with rubber bands wound so tightly round their muzzles that the flesh of their mouths had closed over the band. And all, apparently, to the same purpose: to stop them from catching birds and mice.

I would like to be able to tell you that a person who pursues this sort of vendetta against cats is easily identifiable, but I'm afraid I can't. There is considerable evidence—largely through behavioral-science studies in the U.S. and the UK—to indicate that cruelty to animals in childhood leads to sociopathic behavior in adulthood. However, cruelty is far more common in adults than it is in children, and such cruelty is usually the result of an obsessional dislike of certain animals or an uncontrollable temper—often drink-related—which lashes out at anything it finds irritating.

Sadly, I cannot say with any certainty that because Miss Butts treated her own cats with kindness she would not have inflicted cruelty on strays intruding into her house. I can only draw parallels with people, and people are notoriously unwilling to show the same charity to foreigners as they show to their family and friends.

Yours sincerely,

Betty Hepinstall

Betty Hepinstall

t e n

The following day I drove my mother to Kim-
meridge Bay on the Isle of Purbeck. It was a beautiful summer morning with puffs of white cloud dotted across the sky, and we climbed the
cliff path to the Clay Tower on the eastern arm of the bight. Larks sang
in the air above us, and the occasional walker passed us by, nodding
good day or pausing to look at the bizarre folly behind us that some
long-dead person had built as a permanent sentinel to guard the ocean
approaches. Mother and I conversed with the strangers but not with
each other and, in the silences between, we stared as resolutely across
the channel at the tower, unwilling to speak in case we started another
argument, locked in mutual ignorance despite the genes and experiences we shared.

In the end I mentioned a vicar's wife I knew who drove to clifftops
whenever the pressures of life became too much and screamed her frustrations to the heavens. I suggested my mother had a go. She refused. It
wasn't her sort of thing, she told me. Nor could she understand why a
vicar's wife would want to do something so common. What sort of
woman was she?

"Eccentric," I murmured, as I watched the seagulls float effortlessly
over the sea like fragments of tissue paper. "Very thin and gaunt . . .
hates being married to a vicar . . . likes her booze . . . fancies being a
lap dancer . . . looks like a vulture."

"That explains it then," said my mother.

"What?"

"The screaming. Thin people are always more high-strung than fat ones."

It sounded reasonable, but then much of what my mother said sounded reasonable. Whether it was true or not was another matter. I decided she was being snide because *she* was plump and *I* was thin but, for once, I chose to ignore the bait. "I've been wondering if it works," I said idly. "My screams are always silent ones that circle 'round my head for days until they run out of steam and die naturally."

"It's pure affectation to scream at all. You should learn to deal with your problems quietly instead of making a song and dance about them." I gave a weary sigh as I thought to myself that that was precisely what I had done, and she cast me a suspicious glance. "I suppose that's why you brought me here? So you can scream at me?"

"Not at *you*," I corrected her. "At the wind."

"You'll only embarrass yourself," she said. "Someone's bound to appear up the path at the wrong moment."

"Perhaps that's the point," I murmured reflectively. "A double whammy. Physical and mental adrenaline all in one shot." I watched a dinghy, full of divers in wetsuits, motor out of the bay and head toward the southwest. "Would it embarrass you?"

"Not in the least." She perched her behind on the edge of a rock. "If I wasn't embarrassed twenty years ago when you were behaving like a madwoman then I'm hardly likely to start now."

She has a short memory, I thought, as I lowered myself to the ground to sit cross-legged in front of her. Her embarrassment had been colossal. I concentrated my attention on a clump of pink thrift that had rooted itself tenaciously in a crevice. "I wasn't mad, Ma, I was exhausted. We were kept awake night after night by the phone ringing nonstop, and even when we changed our number the calls just kept on coming. If we took the damn thing off the hook, we had mud thrown against our windows or constant hammering on the front door. We were *both* suffering from sleep deprivation, *both* behaving like zombies, yet for some reason you decided that everything Sam told you was true while everything I said was a lie."

She examined the distant horizon where the blue of the sea met the blue of the sky, and I remembered her telling me once that the difference between a woman and a lady was that a woman spoke without thinking while a lady always considered what she was about to say. "You screamed and yelled about rats in your downstairs lavatory," she said at last. "Are you saying *that* wasn't true? You poured gallons of bleach down the loo in order to kill them, then became hysterical because you said they'd moved into the sitting room."

"I'm not denying I said some strange things, but they weren't lies. I kept hearing scratching sounds and I could only think of rats."

"Sam didn't hear them."

"He most certainly did," I contradicted her. "If he told you he didn't, he was lying."

"Why would he want to?"

I thought back. "For a lot of very complicated reasons . . . mostly, I imagine, because he didn't like me much at the time and thought that everything was my fault. He said I was making the noises myself to get attention and was damned if he was going to pander to any more of my childishness."

She frowned. "I remember him saying he called in the rat catcher to try to persuade you it was all in your imagination."

I shook my head. "It was me who called in the rat catcher, and for exactly the opposite reason. I wanted proof that there *were* rats."

"And were there?"

"No. The man said there was no evidence of rodent infestation, no nests, no indication that any food had been eaten, and no droppings. He also said that if we had rats then our neighbors would be complaining as well." I ran my finger lightly over the thrift and watched the pink heads shiver. "The next day Sam phoned you to tell you I was going 'round the bend and he wanted a divorce."

She didn't say anything for several moments, and I raised my head to look at her. There was a perplexed expression on her face. "Well, I'm completely lost. If you and Sam both heard it but it wasn't rats and it wasn't you, then what was it?"

"I think it might have been cats," I said.

"Oh, for goodness' sake!" she declared crossly. "How could there be cats in your house without your noticing?"

"Not *in*," I said, "*under*. It took me a long time to work it out because I didn't know the first thing about building houses. I couldn't even change a plug when I married, let alone get to grips with the importance of underfloor ventilation."

Her mouth thinned immediately. "I suppose that's a sly dig at me and your father."

"No," I said with an inward sigh, "just a fact."

"What does it have to do with cats?"

"Houses have holes in their walls below ground level to allow a free flow of air under the floorboards. It prevents the wood from becoming rotten. They're usually constructed out of airbricks, but the houses in Graham Road were built in the 1880s and in those days they used wrought-iron grills to make a design feature out of them. Before he left, the rat catcher mentioned that one of ours was missing from the back of the house. It happened all the time, he said, because there was quite a market for them in architectural salvage. It wasn't a problem because someone had wedged a metal bootscraper over the hole, but he suggested we get it replaced at some stage if we didn't want trouble in the future. He kept calling it a ventilation grill, and I assumed he was talking about something that was attached to the extractor fan in the upstairs bathroom because that was the only ventilation I knew about."

I fell silent and she made an impatient gesture with her hand, as if to say, "Get on with it."

"I wasn't very with it at the time—all I wanted was confirmation that rats existed—so it went in one ear and out the other because whatever was missing didn't seem to stop the extractor fan working. Then, one day in Sydney, I watched our neighbor's Jack Russell dig a hole in

the flower bed beside our house and vanish through a hole into the
crawl space beneath the house, and I realized the rat catcher had probably been talking about underfloor ventilation. He was telling me we
had a hole in our back wall at ground level, and probably quite a size-
able one if a wrought-iron grill had been hacked out."

"And because of that you think cats got in?"

"Yes."

"Didn't you say the rat catcher said it wasn't a problem because a
boot scraper was wedged over the hole?"

"Yes."

"Then how did they get in?"

"I think someone carried them down the alleyway at the back of
our house, pushed them in and covered the hole afterward."

She gave a snort of incredulity. "That's too absurd. The rat catcher
would have heard them. They'd have been yowling their heads off. And
why cats? Why not dogs? You said it was a Jack Russell that went into
your crawl space in Sydney."

"Because Annie's house was full of cats."

"Now you really *are* being ridiculous! The woman had been dead
for weeks by that time. They can't possibly have been hers."

"I'm not suggesting they were," I said, "just that cats are more likely
than dogs in the circumstances. My guess is they were pushed in under
our floorboards to die because there was no convenient cat flap in our
back door. If there had been, I think I'd have found them dying in my
kitchen. I called out the gas board twice because I thought I could smell
gas, but each time they said there was nothing wrong. One of the men
said it smelled like a dead mouse, but I said it couldn't be because we
didn't have any."

I could feel the weight of her disbelief bearing down on my bent
head. "You'd have known if something had died. The smell of death is
terrible."

"Only when it's warm. This happened in winter—a particularly
cold winter—and we had fitted carpets over all the floors."

"But—" She broke off to marshal her thoughts. "Why didn't you hear them? Tomcats make a terrible noise when they yowl."

"It depends what was done to them first." I shook my head. "In any case, I think they must have died of hypothermia very quickly."

Another pause. "What on earth could be done to a cat to stop it crying?"

I hunched my shoulders as I thought of the chilling research I'd done on the subject. "At a guess, they had superglue pumped into their mouths and eyes and Elastoplast wrapped tightly 'round their faces so they couldn't see, eat, drink or cry. Then they were pushed under our house to try to scratch their way out with the only things left to them . . . their claws."

My mother drew a disgusted breath, although whether her disgust was leveled at me for making the suggestion or at the suggestion itself, I couldn't tell. "What sort of people would do a thing like that?"

I reached into my pocket for a copy of the police report describing the entry into Annie's house the day after her death and passed it across to her. "The same people who tortured cats for Annie's benefit," I said. "The only difference is, they pushed the wretched creatures through her cat flap so she could see what was happening to them."

She glanced at the report but didn't read it. "Why? What was the point?"

"Any reason you like. Sometimes I think it was done to cause fear, other times I think it was done for pleasure." I turned my face to the wind. "In a perverted sort of way, I ought to feel flattered. I think the assumption was I was cleverer than Annie and could work out for myself that animals were dying in dreadful agony under my house. And the fact that I wasn't . . . and didn't . . . must have been a disappointment."

If my mother asked me why once, she asked it a hundred times on our journey home. Why hadn't Annie gone to the police? Why hadn't Annie phoned the RSPCA? Why would anyone feel confident about tormenting me in the same way they'd tormented Annie? Why weren't they afraid I'd go to the police? Why *hadn't* I gone to the police? Why would anyone want to reinforce my suspicions about Annie's death? Why risk getting Sam involved? Why risk getting the rat catcher involved? Why hadn't I questioned the RSPCA findings at the inquest? Why . . . ? Why . . . ? Why . . . ?

Was she finally beginning to understand how betrayed I'd felt when she hadn't believed me at the time? Or was I being cynical in my absolute conviction that it was only her recognition of my father's tireless support of me that had shamed her into asking any questions at all?

In any case, I had few answers for her, other than to say no one believes a mad woman. "But why assume there was a logical thought process at work," I asked her finally, "when whoever tortured the cats was clearly unbalanced?" It was done for the pleasure of inflicting pain, not because it was possible to predict how Mad Annie or I would react to having mutilated animals left on our doorsteps.

CURRAN HOUSE
Whitehay Road
Torquay
Devon

Monday

Darling,

Just a quick note to thank you and Sam for the weekend. It was good to see the boys again, although I do think you should persuade them to have their hair cut. Your father and I both liked the house, despite its dilapidation, and feel it would be sensible to make an offer for it. Sam is clearly at a loose end at the moment (country life doesn't really suit him, does it?) and a renovation project would keep him occupied. You can always sell it afterward if and when he manages to find a job.

With regard to what we talked about yesterday: I have since had a word with our local RSPCA inspector. He tells me stories like yours are not unusual and that cruelty to cats is more common than anyone realizes. He gave me some horrific examples—cats tied in sacks to be used as footballs; claws pulled out with pliers; and fur doused in gasoline and set alight. Apparently the favorite sport is to use them as target practice for airguns and crossbows.

He's given me the name of a solicitor down here whose wife runs a rescue home for abused animals, and suggests we consult him with a view to a prosecution. I said I was sure you had some idea of who was responsible and, while he is not optimistic of a successful prosecution twenty years after the event, he believes it may be worth a try, particularly as the RSPCA inspector involved at the time is still alive and able to give evidence.

Let me know what you'd like me to do.

All my love,

Ma

PS I know she's barking up the wrong tree but do give her credit for trying. She's very "down" at the moment because she feels we ganged up on her and can't understand why. I said she should have expected it—i.e., what goes around comes around—but she doesn't want to be reminded of how she ganged up on you all those years ago. It would be tactful, my dear, to avoid saying "I told you so," however strong the temptation. I would think less of you if you did!

Dad

X X X

eleven

Portland Peninsula was under assault from a blustery southwest wind the following Wednesday when Sam and I drove up from Chesil Beach in search of the sculpture park. Given the choice, I'd rather have gone on my own. There was too much that still needed explaining—my more-than-passing interest in Danny, for example—but I balked at telling Sam his presence would only exacerbate the problem when, like my mother, his way of making up for past indifference was a belated wish to be involved.

I had made a halfhearted attempt the previous day to talk about the three weeks at the end of January and beginning of February '79 that I spent alone on Graham Road, but my habit of silence was so ingrained that I gave it up after a few minutes. I found I couldn't talk about fear without becoming cruel, and I couldn't become cruel without turning on Sam because he had abandoned me when I needed him most. In the end, as so often in my life, I took the fatalistic view that whatever would be would be. Sam was a grown man. If he couldn't learn to live with the truth, irrespective of how it was revealed to him, then nothing I did or said would make a difference.

The Isle of Portland, a tilted slab of limestone four miles long and one mile wide, forms a natural breakwater between Lyme Bay to the west and the sweep of sheltered water between Weymouth and the Isle of Purbeck to the east. Its precipitous cliffs rise out of the sea to a high point of nearly five hundred feet, with only the hardiest of vegetation surviving the mercurial English weather. As Sam and I wound our way up its spine, I thought how bleak it was, and how unsurprising that successive governments had claimed it both as a fortress against foreign invasion and as a colony for prisoners.

In 1847 the Admiralty had employed convict labor awaiting transportation to Australia to construct a mighty harbor on Portland's eastern shores, which remained the preserve of the Ministry of Defense until the government abandoned it in the early 1990s. It seemed fitting somehow, in view of the convicted men who had toiled to create the anchorage, that the most prominent feature in Portland harbor that Wednesday was a gray prison ship that had been imported from America some four years previously to deal with the chronic overcrowding in Her Majesty's inland gaols.

"Is Michael Percy being held there?" Sam asked me.

"No. He's in the adult prison here on the island. It's called the Verne. It's off to our left somewhere." I pointed to a sprawling Victorian building ahead of us which dominated the skyline. "That's the young offenders' institution. It was built to house the convicts who worked on the harbor."

"Good God! How many prisons are there?"

"Three, including the ship." I laughed at his expression. "I don't think it means Dorset's a hive of criminal activity," I said, "just that desolate lumps of rock make good holding pens for society's rejects. Think of Alcatraz."

"So what did Michael do?"

I thought back to the press cuttings of his trial which had arrived toward the end of 1993. "Went into a village post office in leathers and a crash helmet, and pistol-whipped an elderly customer until the postmaster agreed to open his security door and hand over what was in his till."

Sam whistled. "A bit of a bastard then?"

"It depends on your viewpoint. Wendy Stanhope would say it was his mother's fault for letting him run out of control. Her name was Sharon Percy. She's the blonde you saw in the pub occasionally."

He made a wry face. "The prostitute? She used to haunt the flaming place looking for customers. She tried to hit on me and Jock once so I gave her a piece of my mind. Jock was furious with me afterward. He said Libby was giving him a hard time, and he'd have been up for it like a shot if I hadn't queered his pitch."

"Mm. Well, at a guess he was double-bluffing you in case you got suspicious about her approach. According to Libby, he was paying out thirty quid a week to Sharon for most of '78. They didn't bother to keep it much of a secret either, except from the people who mattered . . . like you and me and his long-suffering wife." I watched him out of the corner of my eye. "Paul and Julia Charles worked out what was going on because Paul saw Jock coming out of Sharon's house one evening and put two and two together."

He threw me a startled glance. "You're joking!"

"No. She charged twenty for straight sex, thirty for a blow job, and Jock visited her every Tuesday for months." I was amused. "You can work out for yourself which service he was getting."

"Shit!" He sounded so shocked that I wondered if "Tuesday" had registered as the day Annie died, and if he was now trying to remember the details of the alibi he'd given Jock. "Who told you?"

"Libby."

"When?"

"A year or so after we left. It all came out in court when Jock decided to contest the divorce settlement. Libby hired a hotshot solicitor who demanded an explanation for the £30 withdrawals from the joint bank account every Tuesday, along with an explanation for the numerous other bank accounts he'd set up without Libby's knowledge. He wasn't very good at hiding his peccadillos and the judge took him to the cleaners for it." I pointed to a sign for Tout Quarry. "I think this is where we need to turn off."

He flicked his indicator. "Where did they do it?"

"In her house. Sharon used to smuggle her clients down the alley-way at the back as a way of protecting her reputation . . . such as it was."

"What about her kid?"

"Michael? I'm not sure he was there very much. Wendy said he was always in trouble with the police so I imagine he was made to roam the streets."

"Jesus!" said Sam in disgust, as he drove onto a rough unmade track that led down to the sculpture park. "No wonder he went to the bad." He drew the car to a halt and switched off the engine. "How was he caught for the post-office job?"

"He confessed to his wife three months later and she promptly turned him in. She gave the police a black leather jacket which she said Michael was wearing on the day of the robbery. It still had blood spots round the cuffs which matched the customer's in the post office." I thought back. "Michael pleaded guilty but it didn't do him much good. The judge commended Bridget for the brave assistance she'd given the police, and said he was sending her husband down for eleven years as a result of her efforts."

"And this is the Bridget who lived on Graham Road?"

"Mm. She was at number 27 . . . opposite Annie's house. Her father, Geoffrey Spalding, shacked up with Michael's mother when Bridget was thirteen, leaving her and her older sister, Rosie, to fend for them-selves. I don't know what happened to Rosie, but Bridget and Michael married sometime in 1992, just after Michael finished a long sentence for aggravated burglary and ten counts of breaking and entering. He stayed out of trouble for about six months then robbed the post office. All in all, he and Bridget have spent less than a year living together as a married couple."

"And now they're divorced?"

"No. The last I heard she was working in Bournemouth and mak-ing a monthly trip to Portland to visit Michael. That's why he was moved down here . . . because no one visits him except his wife. She said at the trial that she still loved him—said she can't rely on anyone the way she relies on Michael because they've known each other since they were children—and the only reason she turned him in was because she was afraid he was going to kill somebody. I thought how brave she was," I said dryly. "His mother's a coward by contrast—that's Sharon—won't go near him . . . hasn't done for years because of the shame he's brought on her. She's been respectable ever since Bridget's dad moved in with her and she was able to give up the game."

"She sounds a right bitch," he said grimly.

"She's not much of a mother, that's for sure."

Sam leaned his arms on the steering wheel and stared thoughtfully out of the window. "Were all the kids as bad?" he asked. "What about the Charles children next door?"

"The oldest was only five," I said, "and Julia never let them out of her sight. It was really only Michael and the Slaters who ran wild . . . in both cases because their mothers had given up on them. Sharon didn't care . . . and Maureen was so brutalized by Derek that she spent most of her time getting stoned in her bedroom."

"Did you know all this in '78?"

"No. Most of it came from Libby after we moved. I knew Alan Slater was getting into fights because he had so many bruises, but I didn't realize it was his father who was hitting him. I talked it over with the head on one occasion, but he just said it would do Alan good to be thrashed by his own peer group because he was a bully himself. As for Michael"—I gave a small laugh—"I always thought how mature he was for his age. He wrote me a couple of love poems and left them on my desk, signed: The Prisoner of Zenda."

"How did you know they were from him?"

"I recognized his handwriting. He was an incredibly bright child. If he'd come from a different background, he'd have an M.A. from Oxford by now instead of a ten-page criminal record. The trouble was he was a persistent truant so he only ever attended one class in three." I sighed. "If I'd been a little more experienced—or less intimidated by the bloody headmaster—I could have helped him. As it was, I let him down." I paused. "Alan, too," I added as an afterthought.

"Did Jock know Michael was truanting?"

I reached for my door handle. "I shouldn't think so," I said bluntly. "He was paying to have his dick sucked, not listen to stories about Sharon's only child."

It was years before I understood that Michael's poems were more about loneliness than love. At the time I swung between suspicion that he had plagiarized them, possibly from song lyrics, and admiration that a fourteen-year-old could write so poignantly. Either way, I decided he had an unhealthy crush on me and made a point of keeping him at arm's length to prevent him becoming a nuisance.

If I was older. If I was wise.
You'd look at me with different eyes
and love me.
If I was handsome. If I was strong.
No one would say that you were wrong
to love me.
It always makes me sad to see
a weed grow where a flower should be.
So I think of flowers when I think of you.
It always makes me sad to hear
the deathly silence in the air.
So I think of music when I think of you.

Letter from Libby Garth—ex-wife of Jock Williams,
formerly of 21 Graham Road, Richmond—
now resident in Leicestershire

Windrush
Henchard Lane
Melton Mowbray
Leicestershire

December 4, 1989

M'dear,

Happy Christmas! I'd send a card if I didn't think Sam
would go ballistic at the idea. It still hurts, you know, that
he took Jock's side without ever bothering to hear mine. I
know you say it's not in his nature to think ill of anyone—
let alone a close friend—but he must think ill of me if you
can't even tell him we're still in touch. It's one of the
horrible truisms that divorce doesn't just divide property,
but friends as well. That being said, it's probably better this
way if he's still shying away from the whole subject of
Annie's death.

Have you ever worked out why that is? I know you say
he has a habit of forgetting anything he doesn't want to
remember—like your frigid spell, your near-divorce, your
"fits of the vapors," your police caution, etc.—but surely
Annie doesn't hold any fears for him now? He can't possibly
have killed her because he's not the type to push people
under trucks! Surely, that had to be Derek Slater? He was
the only man on Graham Road who was vicious enough.

Jim and the girls are fine. At the moment I'm resisting

Jim's blandishments for one more try to see if we can make a boy. I keep telling him a three-year-old, a nine-month-old and a teaching job are more than enough to occupy anyone, but he seems to think I'm Superwoman. I don't know how you managed without a nanny. The only thing that keeps me sane is to get into my car every morning and spend the day with my alternative "family" at school, though I'm still trying to work out how to persuade fourteen-year-old gorillas with twice as much testosterone as brain that learning is a "good thing." I leave every class feeling as if I've been raped and ravaged by their revolting imaginations. Did that contribute to your agoraphobia after Annie died? I've often wondered. I remember you telling me that you couldn't stand the way Alan Slater and Michael Percy looked at you.

Apropos, I enclose two cuttings. One about Michael, who goes from bad to worse, which is only to be expected of the tart's son. Yes, I'm being beastly, but I'd have to be a saint to view the "bleached vampire" and her progeny with anything other than hatred since they received a rather more regular income from Jock than I ever did! The second is about the policeman, Sergeant Drury—the one you had a yen for at the beginning. (Looked like a shorter-haired version of Patrick Swayze in <u>Dirty Dancing</u>—have you seen the movie? It's to die for!) I might have fancied him myself if he hadn't turned out to be such a shit. It was unforgivable of him to "kiss and tell" to Sam. Have you considered that that might be Sam's problem with the Annie saga? It was certainly his problem the night before he took himself off for three weeks. Have you forgiven him for forcing you yet?

It was a shabby and beastly way to treat you when you were struggling with agoraphobia and depression. But that's men for you—act first, think later! I bet he regrets it now, especially if you managed to persuade him that Drury was lying.

Anyway, Drury's taken early retirement, though by the way the piece is worded the implication is he was given the boot for whacking a seventeen-year-old Asian boy.

Keep smiling,

All my love,

Libby

Local Man Convicted

Michael Percy, 25, of Graham Road, Richmond, pleaded guilty yesterday to aggravated burglary at a house in Sheen Common Drive. He admitted carrying a chisel and using it to threaten the homeowner when he was surprised to find the house occupied. He asked for 10 other charges of burglary to be taken into account. The judged described Percy as a "persistent criminal" and a "dangerous man" before passing a sentence of four years.

Richmond & Twickenham Times—
September 14, 1989

Police Sergeant Retires

Sergeant James Drury, 41, is retiring early after 15 years with the Metropolitan Police in Richmond. He has been absent on sick leave since a fight broke out between him and a group of youths behind the William of Orange pub two months ago. One of the youths, Javinda Patel, 17, sustained a broken cheekbone and was taken to hospital. The rest of the gang fled before P.S. Drury's colleagues reached the scene. A police spokesman said today, "Mr. Drury was very shaken by the incident and this was a contributory factor in his decision to take early retirement. We're always sorry to lose good officers." He denied that Mr. Drury started the fight.

Richmond & Twickenham Times—
November 24, 1989

twelve

Tout Quarry, home to the sculpture park and once a source of hand-quarried Portland stone, had been long worked out and abandoned. It was a wild and wonderful place. A man-made labyrinth of tangled gorges and wide-open spaces like amphitheaters where stunted shrubs and trees grew among blocks of half-excavated sedimentary rock. It looked as if a giant hand had rummaged in the belly of the earth and stirred the stone into a chaotic, tumbling dance.

Sam was fascinated by the intermittent sculptures which had been carved in situ and introduced subtle shape to the craggy landscape. Antony Gormley's *Still Falling*—a cameo figure plunging down a rocky cliffside. Robert Harding's *Philosopher's Stone*—an intricate layer of cut stones perched between V-shaped rocks. A crouching man with his chin resting on his knees. Footsteps. A tulip, prized from the rock to lie in reflection on the ground. "Is anyone allowed to have a go?" he asked, examining a fossil in a slab and trying to work out if it was a real ammonite or a simulated one.

"I think you have to be invited."

"Pity," he said wistfully. "I quite fancy leaving my mark for posterity."

I laughed. "Which is probably why people like you aren't allowed to do it. You'd get bored after a while and carve out 'Sam woz 'ere, 1999,' then the whole place would be desecrated with graffiti."

We heard the sculpture workshop before we saw it. A constant rat-a–tat of hammers on chisels, overlaid by the whistle of wind through a polythene canopy that had been rigged above the sculptors' heads. It was a scene of intense industry because everyone was there for a purpose, to learn how to work in three dimensions. White stone chippings littered the ground, and a fine dust clung to arms, hair and clothing like baker's flour. It might have been a Renaissance atelier in Italy but for the polythene canopy, the uniform prevalence of T-shirts and jeans, and the fact that half the sculptors were women.

It was situated in a sheltered gulley, and Danny stood out from the rest of the group, not just because he'd positioned himself near the entrance but because his block of stone was three times the size of anybody else's. It was also a great deal more advanced. Where most of the others were still working to establish basic form, Danny had already released a bespectacled head and upper torso from the limestone's grip and was using a claw chisel to give grained texture to the skin of the face.

He looked up as we approached. "What do you think?" he asked, stepping back and letting his hands fall to his sides, unsurprised that we'd come to admire his work. His physique interested me. I was amazed by how well developed his shoulders and arms were without a jacket to hide them.

"Excellent," observed Sam with the overdone bonhomie that he reserved for men he didn't know very well. "Who is it? Anyone we know?"

A scowl of irritation narrowed Danny's eyes.

"Mahatma Gandhi," I said, casting a quick verifying glance at the drawings and photographs on the ground beside him. I didn't need to. The likeness was there, even if more reliant on intuition than reality. "It's an ambitious subject."

That didn't please him either. "I can tell you're a teacher," he said witheringly, glancing toward the canopy where instructors were passing on advice and help to the other students. "That's what they keep telling me."

I eyed him curiously. "Why don't you take it as a compliment?"

He shrugged. "Because I know a put-down when I hear it."

"You're too sensitive," I said. "In my case it's a spur to keep you going. You're obviously the star here—head and shoulders above the others—and unless you're blind and stupid you must recognize the fact."

"I do."

"Then stop bellyaching and prove you can cope with an ambitious subject." I ran a finger along the larger-than-life spectacles which grew at a forty-five-degree angle from the wrinkled stone cheeks. "How did you do these?"

"Carefully," he said, more serious than ironic.

I smiled. "Weren't you afraid of knocking them off?"

"I still am."

"There's a bronze statue of Gandhi in Ladysmith in South Africa. It commemorates the ambulance corps that he set up there during the Boer war. It's the only other one I've ever seen of him."

"How does it compare?"

"With this one?"

He nodded. I might have mistaken his question for arrogance if the muscles in his shoulders had been less rigid or his scowl less ferocious. *He is preparing to defend himself again,* I thought.

"It's a thoroughly professional life-size representation in bronze of a tiny little man who did his duty by the Empire after accepting British citizenship," I said. "But that's all it is. It gave me no sense of his greatness, no sense of the extraordinary effect his humility had on the world, no sense of inner strength." I moved my fingers to touch the rough limestone face. "Gandhi was a giant with no pretensions. For myself, I'd rather have him larger-than-life and rough-hewn in stone than realistically small and neatly polished in bronze."

His scowl relaxed. "Will you buy it?"

I shook my head regretfully.

"Why not? You just said you liked it."

"Where would I put it?"

"In your garden."

"We don't have a garden. We're only renting the farmhouse for the summer. After that"—I shrugged—"who knows? If we're lucky we may be able to afford a brick box with a tablecloth for a garden and a few roses 'round the border . . . and, frankly, a bust of Mahatma Gandhi in the middle of it would look very out of place."

He was disappointed. "I thought you were loaded."

"Sadly not."

He pulled out his cigarettes. "Just keeping up appearances, eh?"

"Something like that."

"Ah, well," he said with resignation, bending his head to shield his lighter from the wind. "Maybe I'll give him to you for free." He blew smoke through his nose. "It'll cost me an arm and a leg to get him back to London, and the chances are the specs'll get knocked off in the process. You can start a collection . . . put him next to Alan's Quetzalcoatl . . . make the Slaters famous for something other than drugs, burglary and wife-beating . . ."

I suggested we treat Danny to lunch at the Sailor's Rest in Weymouth but Sam wasn't keen. "The food's good," he admitted, "but the landlord's an asshole."

"I think you already know him," I told Danny as we made our way back to the car. "He's the policeman who got Alan sent down. I thought it might amuse you to see him in different surroundings." I interrupted the silence that followed this remark to point at the wreck of a Viking long ship that was creatively cast upon some rocks to our left. "That's a clever use of materials," I murmured.

"What's his name?" asked Danny.

"James Drury. He was a uniformed sergeant in Richmond until he was forced to take early retirement and took himself off to train as a pub manager for Radley's Brewery. They started him off in Guildford, then moved him to the Sailor's Rest in '95."

Danny eyed me with understandable suspicion. "How do you know he's the one who nicked Alan?"

"A neighbor of ours in Graham Road told me," I explained. "Libby Williams?" He shook his head. "She knew I was interested in anything Mr. Drury did, particularly if it concerned an ex-pupil." I tucked my hand companionably into the crook of Sam's elbow to soften the blows of revelation. "I had several encounters with him before we moved abroad. He's probably the most corrupt person I've ever met . . . a thief, a liar, a bully . . . and a racist. Quite the wrong sort of man to be given a police uniform."

A mirthless laugh escaped Danny's mouth. "He sure as hell stitched Alan up. Okay, I'm not saying my brother was an angel, but he was no drug pusher. A user, maybe—never a pusher."

"What happened?"

"I don't know the exact details . . . I was just a kid at the time . . . but Ma said Drury nicked him in a pub one night, and dropped four ounces of hash into his pocket while he was slapping on the handcuffs. He was a right bastard. If he couldn't get you for one thing, he'd get you for another."

"What had Alan really done?"

Danny made fists of his hands and punched the knuckles against each other. "Couldn't stay out of a fight, particularly when he was drunk. Took the whole damn police force on one evening and laid about him like a good 'un, never mind he was only fifteen." A reminiscent smile curled his mouth. "He got five thousand quid compensation for it."

"That's some trick," said Sam.

"Not really. Al's injuries were much worse than the coppers'. Three broken ribs . . . boot marks all over him from the kicking they gave him . . . internal bleeding. You name it, he had it. The only problem is"—Danny sent a stone flying with a well-aimed toecap—"Drury had it in for the Slater kids from that moment on. He arrested us all at one time or another. He rubbed his arm in tender recollection. "*And* gave us a damn good thrashing whenever he got the chance."

"So what was Alan actually convicted of?" I asked curiously. "Possession or assault on the police?"

Danny frowned. "Dealing, I think," he said vaguely. "But it was a stitch-up whichever way you look at it. They reckoned he was a bad influence on the rest of us, so Drury had him put away till he calmed down. He's been straight ever since . . . so I guess it worked."

I wondered if any of it was true, or if it was a story the family had invented for public consumption.

Sam turned to me with a puzzled look. "And this Drury is the man who was staring at you?"

I nodded. "I think he was trying to work out who I was."

"Well, he'll know by now. I paid by credit card."

"Yes," I agreed. "That's why we went there."

He looked away, racing to put the pieces of his own personal jigsaw puzzle together. "So what's the plan?" he asked as we approached the car. "Do we walk up to this thug and confront him? Or do we behave with civilized disdain?"

"We behaved with civilized disdain last time," I reminded him.

"*You* may have done," he snapped irritably, inserting his key into the car door. "*I* didn't know him from Adam. All I saw was a middle-aged prick ogling my wife." He frowned at us across the roof. "If you're intending to talk to him about the robbery you won't get anywhere. Larry said he wasn't remotely interested when Sheila tried to raise it with him. He just became extremely offensive and reduced Sheila to a nervous wreck."

I exchanged a quick glance with Danny and saw only curiosity in his eyes. "I want to unsettle him a little," I said. "Make him wonder what three ex-residents of Graham Road are doing in his pub."

Sam shook his head, clearly unimpressed. "Yes, but *why*? What are you expecting to achieve? There's no reason to think you'll be any more successful than Sheila, and I'm not keen to end up in the middle of a screaming match in public."

Danny spoke before I could answer, after shoving his hands into his pockets to protect whatever was there. *Cannabis?* I wondered. "I've done my best to put distance between me and Mr. Drury these last ten years," he grumbled, "and I'd be well pleased if he thought I was dead."

I gave a noncommittal shrug. "Okay, we'll go somewhere else. I always planned to confront him on my own anyway. He doesn't scare *me* . . . or not as much as he'd like to think."

I was lying of course.

Sam took up the gauntlet as I hoped he would, albeit reluctantly since he obviously thought I was planning a scene, while Danny muttered that the issue had nothing to do with being scared and everything to do with common sense. He asked me if we intended to drive him back to the sculpture park afterward, and when I said we would, he brightened visibly and tucked something down between the cushions of the back seat before we left the car.

When we reached the Sailor's Rest, Sam chose a table near the harbor wall and eyed the other customers warily to see if he recognized anyone. "Just try to keep your voice under control," he muttered irritably. "You get very strident when you talk about Annie."

"Not anymore," I said, switching my attention to Danny and asking him to come inside with me. "Sam can guard the table," I told him, "while you and I sort out the drinks."

"What you mean is, you want the ferret to see the rabbit," Danny muttered despondently as I led the way across the cobbles to the front door of the pub.

I smiled, liking him a great deal. "Rabbits plural," I said. "We're both in the same boat. But there's strength in numbers . . . any rabbit will tell you that."

"So who's this Annie you get strident about?" he asked as we paused on the threshold to let our eyes adjust from brilliant sunshine to the Stygian gloom inside.

"Annie Butts," I told him. "She was living next door to you in Graham Road while Sam and I were there. Your mother would probably remember her. She was a black lady who was killed by a truck shortly before we left. Her death was one of the reasons Mr. Drury and I came to blows."

He shook his head. "Never heard of her."

I believed him. He seemed to have no memories of his early childhood—perhaps because it was too painful and he had chosen to blank it, just as I had done with some of my more disturbing memories—and I was grateful for his ignorance. If nothing else, it meant my conscience could ride a little lighter. "There's no reason why you should," I said. "People die every day, but they're usually only remembered by their families."

He looked toward the bar where Drury was standing. "So why did you and him come to blows over her?"

It was a good question. "I don't know," I answered honestly. "It's something I've never understood. But I'll get an explanation one day . . . assuming there is one."

"Is that why we're here?" he asked in an unconscious echo of my mother three days before. In a way it was flattering. They both assumed I knew what I was doing.

*Correspondence from Michael Percy, son of Sharon—
convicted of armed robbery and serving out his sentence at
the Verne Prison, Portland—formerly of 28 Graham
Road—dated 1999*

In replying to this letter, please write on the envelope:

Number: V50934   **Name:** *Michael Percy*

Wing: B2

B2 WING
HMP THE VERNE
PORTLAND
DORSET
DT5 1EQ

To: Mrs. M. Ranelagh
Jacaranda
Hightor Road
Cape Town
South Africa

February 1, 1999

Dear Mrs. Ranelagh,

*First, don't worry about getting your dad to send me stamps.
There's a lot of foreign guys at the Verne—drug smugglers and
suchlike who get picked up at the airports as they come in—so
the prison lets us swap inland stamps for airmail letters. That's
okay, as I've no one to write to except Bridget.*

*As you can imagine, life's pretty grim inside, but I've only
myself to blame. Every prisoner's a volunteer, if you think about it.
You say you read what I did in the newspapers and your dad used
a mate of his in the prison service to locate me. Well, I'm glad
about that. You were always my favorite teacher though you may*

not want to keep writing when I tell you everything they said about me was true. I'm ashamed of it now, but it's pretty two-faced to say sorry afterward, don't you reckon? The judge said I was dangerous because I had no conscience, but I'd say it's lack of wisdom that's the problem. I've never been able to recognize in advance the things I was going to regret—simple as that.

You ask me what I remember about the black lady who lived next door to us on Graham Road. Quite a lot, as it happens. She used to drive my mother nuts with her bad-mouthing about "whores" and "cunts" and "trash" and suchlike. One time Mum emptied a bucket of water over her head from our upstairs window when she spotted her peering over our fence, and old Annie howled like a banshee because she thought it was piss. It's probably cruel to say it now—seeing as how she's dead—but it was pretty funny at the time.

It'd be easier if you listed the things you want to know. I never liked her much, that's for sure. She damn near chopped Alan Slater's hand off when she caught him inside her house—went for him with a meat cleaver and only missed by inches. He was shaking like a leaf for days afterward. Okay, he shouldn't have been nicking off of her but it's a bit heavy to go for a kid with a hatchet when all he did was take a useless wooden statue from her sitting room.

Still, like I say, you need to tell me what you want. It wasn't just my mum and Alan's mum she drove mad. She got most of the street riled up. I remember this woman she used to follow home every time she went shopping and shout "dirty tart" after her, and it didn't half make her mad. I watched her take a swipe at Mad Annie once with her shopping bag, then end up ass over tit in the gutter. That was pretty funny, too. The silly cow fancied herself something rotten.

I guess what you really want to know is who killed old Annie, but that's not something I can tell you. I remember my mum being gobsmacked to hear she was dead so I guess the one thing I can say is that she and me didn't do it. In the end, I'd go with it being a truck, like the police said, and I'm sorry if that's disappointing.

Your friend,
Michael Percy

B2 WING
HMP THE VERNE
PORTLAND
DORSET
DT5 1EQ

To: *Mrs. M. Ranelagh*
   Jacaranda
   Hightor Road
   Cape Town
   South Africa

February 23, 1999

Dear Mrs. Ranelagh,

You're the one who should take credit for my handwriting. I remember you teaching us italics in class and telling us that if we wrote well we'd always get a job. It didn't work out like that for me, but only because I couldn't see the point of slaving for peanuts when a hit on a shop or a post office could give a better return for a few minutes' sweat. But I've always liked nice writing, so you scored on that at least. Also—sure!—I've still got the gift of the gab! You should take credit for that, too. It was you who said a good vocabulary means you'll always make a good impression.

One day I'll tell you about me and Bridget—she's the reason I'm in here. Trust me to marry the only girl in the world who'd rather shop her husband and visit him in prison than wait till he murdered someone! You might remember her. She lived across the street from us in Graham Road and had blond hair down to her ass till she cut it off and posted it through your letterbox as a sacrifice. She's still as pretty as a picture and refuses to give me up even though I keep telling her she's young enough to find someone else and have kids. The good news is, I could be out next year if I keep behaving myself.

Okay, to business. The answers to your questions are as follows:

1. I don't know the name of the woman Annie called a "dirty tart" but I think her man was one of Mum's clients, though I never hung around long enough to get much of a look at him. They were all shits as far as I was concerned.

2. Everyone stole from Annie. I'd say Alan and his sisters were the worst, but the rest of us did, too. It was the girls who kept egging us on. There were stacks of little trinkets in drawers and cupboards, which they really liked. She used to leave her back door open for her cats, and it was a doddle for one of us to keep her occupied at the front while the other nipped in through the back. It wasn't so easy after she had the cat flap put in and started bolting her door, but the catch on her toilet window was broken and little Danny Slater was skinny enough to slither through the gap. He was a bright little kid, no more than four years old, but he'd creep through to the kitchen and climb on a chair to pull back the bolts. Alan even taught him to shove 'em home again afterward, then use the bog seat to climb out the window. I've never been too sure if Annie noticed her stuff was going—we always rearranged things so it didn't look too obvious—but Alan said she got some bloke in to make a list of everything in her house so I guess she must have done. We gave the whole caper up after she went for Alan with the cleaver. It didn't seem sensible once she'd sussed us. If I remember right, that was a month or two before she died.

3. Why did we do it? For kicks, I guess. To be honest, I'm not sure any of us ever asked ourselves that kind of question. All I know is it was a hell of an adrenaline buzz to creep around a crazy woman's house, especially one that had so much in it. We didn't do it for money because we reckoned most of what she had was rubbish—like the wooden statue—though I remember Alan's mum taking a ring off Bridget one time because she thought it looked valuable. She got rid of it to buy vodka, so I guess it might have been.

4. All I remember about the night of the accident is coming home around midnight and Mum telling me I'd missed all the fun. The mad cow next door got run over by a truck, she said. I haven't a clue what I was doing. The same as usual, I expect. Playing the machines in the arcade.

5. All I remember about the next day is Mum and me being staggered by the number of cats that came out because we didn't know Annie had that many.

None of this sounds good when you read it back and I hope you aren't too shocked. The trouble is the truth is always worse when you tell it bald. It kind of ignores the fact that there are two sides to everything. I mean, we were dead scared of her because she was mad, and Alan's mum kept saying she practiced voodoo with chickens. I know that sounds pretty off the wall now, but at the time—hell, we thought we were heroes just going in there. Alan reckoned she could turn us into frogs or something just by looking at us!

Hoping this helps,
Your friend,
Michael

thirteen

I don't know if it's enough to say I wanted revenge on Drury because I hated him. One should have reasons for hatred, not just a visceral antipathy that causes a red mist before the eyes at the mere mention of a name. Dr. Elias had asked me several times why I bothered to invest so much emotion in a man I had known for only a matter of weeks, but I could never bring myself to answer for fear of sounding paranoid.

He had changed very little in twenty years except that his hair was grayer and his eyes darker and more impenetrable. He was the same age as Sam, but he'd always been tougher, stronger and more attractive. He was a type that women invariably fell for and invariably wished they hadn't when the hard-man image—a thin disguise for misogyny—proved to be an immutable reality.

He studied us with amusement as we approached. "Mrs. Ranelagh." He gave an ironic nod in Danny's direction. "You're scraping the bottom of the barrel with this one, aren't you? What is he? Toy boy or minder?"

I had to run my tongue around my mouth to stimulate some saliva. "Moral support," I replied.

His smile broadened. "Why would you need it?"

"Because you won't like these," I said, taking some photographs from my pocket and laying them on the bar.

He reached out a hand to pick them up but Danny was there before him. "Is this the black lady you were talking about?" he asked.

166

"Yes."

"She looks as if she's been hit with a baseball bat," he said, laying them back on the counter.

"She does, doesn't she?" I put my finger on the top picture and pushed it aside to fan out the five others underneath. None of them was pleasant. Each showed Annie in death, bruised and battered about the face, and with a discolored right arm where blood had seeped under the skin to form an extended hematoma from shoulder to wrist. "Mr. Drury decided all these injuries came from a single glancing blow from a truck, which resulted in death within thirty minutes . . . but I can't find anyone who agrees with him. These pictures were taken during her autopsy in 1978. I've had them examined by two independent pathologists and they both say the bruising to the arm points to severe physical trauma some hours before she died."

"What's that in English?"

"Annie was murdered."

The irritation from across the counter heightened abruptly, and I wondered why Drury thought I was there. A desire to renew an old friendship? Lust?

"Jesus wept!" he growled. "Don't you ever give up? It's like listening to a skipping record. Haven't you anything better to do with your life than make a martyr out of a miserable black who couldn't hold her drink?" He lifted the top picture and turned it over to inspect the back for an official stamp. "Where the hell did you get these?"

"PC Quentin sent them to me."

"Andrew?"

I nodded.

"He's been dead seven years," he said dismissively. "Died in a car crash after chasing a joyrider at high speed for three miles."

"I know. He sent them to me shortly after we left England. I wrote and asked him for copies because I knew he was unhappy with the inquest verdict."

Drury gave a grunt of irritation. "What would he know? The guy was still wet behind the ears. He had a half-assed degree in sociology, and he reckoned it gave him an edge over a home office pathologist and a beat copper with ten years' graft on the streets."

"He was right, though," I said. "This kind of bruising"—I touched one of the photographs—"takes time to develop. It also suggests more than one contact. If her arm was hit in several places, the individual hematomas would have spread out, darkening the skin from shoulder to wrist."

"A photograph proves nothing. She was black. You can't say what's a bruise and what's not."

"These are color photos," I pointed out mildly, "so unless you're blind you can certainly see the bruising."

He shook his head angrily. "What difference does it make? The accepted version was given by the man who performed the postmortem and he said her injuries were caused by a glancing blow from a truck."

"But not fifteen to thirty minutes before I found her. Two or three hours *perhaps*. And that means the people who say they saw her staggering about the road were probably looking at someone with severe head injuries."

His eyes flickered unwillingly toward the pictures again, as if he were both repelled and fascinated by them. "Even if that's true, you can't blame them for assuming she was drunk."

"I don't."

"Then what the hell is this in aid of?"

I licked the inside of my treacherous mouth again. "I'm going to have the case reopened," I said. "I want the way you handled it investigated. I want questions asked about why a rookie cop with a half-assed degree in sociology could see that something was wrong . . . but *you* couldn't. I want to know why, when he tried to raise it with you, you had him thrown off the case."

He tore the photographs in half and tossed the pieces across the bar to flutter at my feet. "Problem sorted. And if that's all you've got to show for the last twenty years then you've been wasting your time."

Danny stooped to retrieve the bits. "You don't want to let him get to you," he said as he handed them back to me. "He's a bully. It's the only way he knows how to control people. He's busting a gut to change the subject rather than explain why he did fuck all about this poor black lady having her face smashed in."

Drury stared him down. "What would you know about it, shithead? You were still in nappies." He jerked his chin at me. "And you're backing the wrong horse if you back her. It was your dad she wanted locked up . . . your dad she accused of murder. No one else."

There was a long silence.

Danny cast me an uncertain glance. "Is that true?"

"No," I said honestly. "Mr. Drury asked me if I knew of anyone who had a grudge against Annie, so I named your father, mother and Sharon Percy. I never at any point suggested they'd murdered her. That was Mr. Drury's interpretation."

Drury laughed. "You were always good at twisting the facts."

"Really? I thought that was your speciality."

He held my gaze for a moment, searching for chinks in my armor, then crossed his arms and turned to Danny. "Ask yourself why she brought you here and why she wanted you to see those photographs. She's planning to use you to get at your family, preferably by turning you against them first. It's what she's good at—manipulating people."

Danny hunched his shoulders unhappily as if all his worst fears had been confirmed, and my son's voice echoed uncomfortably in my ear. *I'd be sodding mad if it happened to me. . . .*

"Your father had an alibi from five o'clock until midnight," I told him, "and it was Mr. Drury who established it. He knows as well as I that Derek couldn't have killed Annie."

"Then why am I here?"

"Because Mr. Drury lied about me to your family. He told your parents I was saying things that I wasn't . . . and I need you to pass on to your mother and brother that all I ever accused them of was racism.

And that was true, Danny. They *were* racists—probably still are—and they weren't ashamed of it."

I touched a hand to his shoulder by way of apology because it was cruel to associate him with his family's hate when he'd stated so often in his e-mails to Luke that he didn't approve of white people living in South Africa. "But my argument isn't with the Slaters," I told Drury, "it's with *you*." I stirred the torn photographs with the point of my finger. "Because when I accused you and your colleagues of the same thing, it frightened you so badly that you manipulated every piece of evidence to support the theory that Annie had died in an accident. And I'd like to know why you did that."

Did I imagine the flicker of fear in his cold, reptilian eyes or was it real? "We didn't have to manipulate anything," he said sharply. "We accepted the inquest verdict . . . accidental death after stumbling under a truck some fifteen to thirty minutes before you found her."

"But you didn't know what the verdict was going to be when you began the investigation into Annie's death."

"So?"

"So you can't claim it as justification for your refusal to make proper inquiries. The only evidence you put forward was a description of Annie's house after she was dead, but it didn't stop you weighing in with a conclusion that she was a chronic drunk, an abuser of animals and a mental incompetent who neglected herself. I even remember your words. You said that in view of 'Mad Annie's' numerous problems your only surprise was that she'd lived as long as she had."

"Which was a view endorsed by everyone except you."

"Her doctor didn't endorse it."

He looked beyond me toward the door. "Your husband did," he murmured. "He and Mr. Williams described Annie as paralytic outside your house when they came home an hour and a half before you did. They also implied it wasn't unusual."

I followed his gaze to where Sam was hovering uncertainly in the doorway. We'd tarried too long, I thought. In the end everyone's patience ran out, even the guilty's. "They were lying," I said flatly.

"So you kept saying in '78."

"It's the truth."

"Why would they want to? If anyone was going to back you it ought to have been the man you married."

Once upon a time that had been my view, too, but only because I'd believed that truth was simple. "He was trying to protect his friend," I said carefully. "The two people I saw under the street lamp that night were Jock Williams and Sharon Percy. I suppose Jock was afraid I'd seen him . . . and didn't want his wife finding out he'd been with a prostitute. So he and Sam concocted their story about going back to our house for a beer."

Drury glanced toward the door again, but Sam had disappeared. "Why didn't you tell me this twenty years ago?"

"I did. I gave you Jock's name as the man I thought I saw."

"But that's the point," he said sarcastically. "You only *thought* you saw him . . . and you didn't say he was with Sharon Percy."

"At the time I didn't know who she was."

He gave a dismissive shake of his head. "Sharon had an alibi and Mr. Williams was ruled out when your husband vouched for him."

"But you never even questioned him," I said, "just accepted Sam's word against mine. But why? Wasn't a woman's word as good as a man's?"

He leaned his hands on the counter and shoved his face close to mine. "You were 'round the bend, Mrs. Ranelagh. Nothing you said was believable. Everyone agreed with that . . . even your husband and mother. And they should know because they had to live with you."

If I'd had a gun at that moment, I'd have killed him. *Bang! Straight between the eyes.* How dare he quote my family at me when he had been the cause of their distrust? But hatred is a futile emotion which damages the hater more than the hated. Yes, he'd have been dead . . . but so would I . . . to everything that mattered to me. Perhaps my expression said more than I realized because he straightened abruptly.

"Sam and Jock invented their story to conform with what you told Jock's wife the next morning," I said evenly. "You told Libby Williams, and anyone else who was interested, that Annie had been seen staggering about the road an hour before she died, you also mentioned the outside time she could have stumbled in front of the lorry. All Sam and Jock did was recycle that information to give you what you wanted—a stupid, drunk nigger lurching around from 7:45—and the fact that none of it was true didn't bother you one little bit."

"Why would your husband and Mr. Williams do that?"

I shrugged. "It was easier for everyone if she died in an accident. For the police, too. It meant no one had to address the issue of racism."

He stared at me for a moment, his brows furrowed in what looked like genuine perplexity. "When did your husband tell you this?"

"Six months after we left England."

It was in the wake of the Hong Kong policeman debacle. Sam had drowned himself in whisky while stomping about the room, lecturing me on my behavior. Most of it—the issue of how my "madness" was affecting his career and social life—washed over me. Some of it did not, particularly when he started to feel sorry for himself at three o'clock in the morning. He was missing England . . . and it was my fault. What the hell had induced me to go spouting off to the police about murder . . . ? He could hardly switch horses midstream . . . not when poor old Jock was caught between a rock and a hard place. Half the bloody road had seen the stupid woman roaring around like a bear with a sore head. All he did was agree with them . . .

I fancied I could hear Drury's brain whirring.

"You told me your husband was lying as soon as I read his statement to you. How could you know that if he didn't admit it until six months later?"

"There were no beer cans in the rubbish bin," I said.

Danny took a swig of Radley's draught lager and eyed Sam suspiciously across the table as he wiped the froth from his lips. "How come you didn't recognize Mr. Drury when your missus brought you here the other day?" he demanded. "I haven't seen him in years but he hasn't changed that much."

Sam went on the defensive immediately. "I only met him a couple of times. As far as I remember, I was more interested in what he was saying than what he looked like."

"Sam's not very good with faces," I offered by way of mitigation.

Danny ignored me. "How about when you made your statement? He must have interviewed you first. Didn't you look at him then?"

"It wasn't Drury who took it. It was a constable. And, no, I was never interviewed . . . just asked to write out where I was and what I was doing." He raised his eyes briefly to mine. "The statement ended my involvement. I wasn't even required to appear at the inquest."

Danny was unimpressed. "Yeah, but you don't walk away when your family's in trouble," he said. "You should have insisted on being there whenever your missus was questioned. Christ! I wouldn't let my lady go through Drury's wringer on her own."

Sam cupped his own glass in his hands but made no move to drink from it. "You're describing a different scenario. My wife wasn't facing charges, she was the one who was asking for charges to be brought."

"I don't blame her. That poor black lady looks as though she had the shit beaten out of her. It doesn't make any difference anyway. Your wife is family. You should have been there for her. That's the way it works."

Sam buried his face in his hands, and I had to harden my heart to his pain because there was no avoiding the issue that my husband was part of the problem . . . not part of the solution . . .

"It wasn't that simple," he muttered wretchedly.

"Sure it was," said Danny scathingly. "Trust me. I know this stuff backward. Families pull together . . . rats jump ship."

Letter from Danny's mother, Maureen Slater, dated 1999

32 Graham Road
Richmond
2 August

Dear Mrs. Ranelagh,

The reason I'm agreeing to see you is because Danny likes you and you did a kind thing for Alan all those years ago when you caught him thieving off of you. He's a fine man now—married with kiddies—and I think you'll be glad you gave him a second chance. Also I appreciated you visiting me in hospital that time. I know I told you I'd fallen down the stairs, but I think you guessed it was Derek who gave me the injuries.

You say a lot's changed since 1978 and that's true. There's hardly anybody left who remembers Annie. I still don't think she was murdered, but like you say there's probably no harm talking about it now. Derek walked out on me twenty years ago and I haven't seen him since.

Around midday next Monday will be fine.

Yours,
Maureen Slater

Letter to Sergeant James Drury—dated 1999

Leavenham Farm

Leavenham

Nr Dorchester

Dorset DT2 XXY

Thursday, August 5, 1999

Dear Mr. Drury,

Following our conversation yesterday, I enclose a copy of a letter I received in 1985 from a colleague of Dr. Benjamin Hanley, the pathologist who performed the postmortem on Ann Butts. In view of your confidence in Dr. Hanley's findings, you may find it interesting reading. The colleague's name was Dr. Anthony Deverill and he worked with Benjamin Hanley from 1979 until Hanley's compulsory retirement on medical grounds in 1982.

Yours sincerely,

M. Ranelagh

PS: Following the investigations referred to in (3) of Anthony Deverill's letter, both cases (believed at the time to be murders) were referred back to the Court of Appeal and the convictions against two innocent men were overturned. The evidence provided by Dr. Hanley was deemed "unsafe" and the deaths of the alleged "victims" were subsequently ruled to have occurred from "natural causes."

PPS: I have several sets of the postmortem photographs.

Dr. Anthony Deverill, MRCPath

25 Avenue Road

Chiswick

London W4

Mrs. M. Ranelagh

P.O. Box 103

Langley

Sydney

Australia

February 6, 1985

Dear Mrs. Ranelagh,

Thank you for your letter of January 10, together with the enclosed postmortem photographs of Miss Ann Butts and the written report from Professor James Webber. As you so rightly say, I have met Professor Webber on several occasions and have a high regard for his judgment. Indeed, after studying the photographs myself, I have no reason to disagree with his detailed assessment that Miss Butts received the injuries to her face and arm some hours before her death.

Your specific request was for information on my predecessor Dr. Benjamin Hanley, who conducted the postmortem in November '78. You say that both you and your father made unsuccessful attempts to contact him over the years, and that the only response either of you had was when his secretary admitted to your father over the telephone in 1982 that the file relating to Miss Butts's postmortem was "missing." Unfortunately, a search of the archive files appears to confirm this last statement, as the only evidence that Dr. Hanley conducted a postmortem on Miss Butts is an entry beside his name on the work schedule for 15.11.78—"10:30 A.M. Butts. RTA. Report requested by PS Drury, Richmond."

You may be interested to learn that Miss Butts's file is not the only one we have been unable to locate. Of the 103 entries against Dr. Hanley's name on the '78, '79 and '81 rosters, nine are currently "missing."

Re your specific inquiries:

1. As you already know, Dr. Hanley was compulsorily retired on medical grounds in 1982 and died of liver failure eighteen months later. However, the compulsory element to his retirement related to a deterioration in his work and performance over a twelve-month period and not to a diagnosed medical condition since he refused to consult a doctor. This is not unusual among pathologists who deal with death every day and can forecast their own prognoses. In simple terms, Dr. Hanley was a chronic alcoholic who became increasingly incapable of doing the job assigned to him. The "medical" tag was attached to the retirement order to allow him to keep his pension, but the cirrhosis that killed him was not discovered until shortly before his death when he was admitted to hospital. These facts are a matter of public record, and I betray no confidences by passing them on to you.

2. I worked alongside Dr. Hanley for two and half years— from September '79, to March '82, when he retired—and I am sorry to say that I had serious reservations about his competence from the beginning. It is, of course, impossible

for me to comment on a postmortem that a) took place before I joined the team and b) has no supporting documentation on file; however, it is my considered opinion that Dr. Hanley's alcoholism would certainly have affected his judgment in November '78.

3. I have no precise knowledge of Dr. Hanley's relationship with PS Drury of Richmond Police, nor can I validate your contention that: "Dr. Hanley may have taken direction from PS Drury and produced a report that suited Richmond Police." However, I expressed concern on several occasions that Dr. Hanley was compromising the independence of his department by writing postmortem reports that appeared to mimic the police version of affairs. Two of these incidents are now under official investigation. In defense of Dr. Hanley, I do not believe there was any malicious intent behind his actions, simply a recognition that he could no longer cope with the demands of his job and a compensatory willingness to place too much confidence in the "hunches" of certain police officers. I should say that in most cases this would not be a cause for concern—most of the deaths we see are "natural"—but clearly it could create problems where facts are disputed.

4. I can say with absolute certainty that Dr. Hanley would have had no racist motive for ignoring evidence of murder in the case of Miss Butts. I am black myself and never experienced any sort of prejudice at his hands. He was a kindly man who had no interest in politics and clearly found his job distressing, particularly when he was obliged to open the chest cavities of women and children, which he began to see as an "unnecessary mutilation."

5. In the absence of a file, I am afraid there is very little assistance I can give you other than to support Professor Webber's interpretation of the photographs. As mentioned above, nine sets of case notes seem to be missing and there is some evidence that Dr. Hanley destroyed them himself prior to leaving the department. In view of his long service record, a decision was taken to allow him to "work out" a three-month notice and we believe he used that time to remove any files that he believed to contain questionable findings. Sadly, he appeared to become deeply confused about the "examiner's" role in society and consistently questioned the value of "righteous judges." However, there is no proof of this and any such speculation could never be used in court.

In conclusion, I am happy to give my permission for this letter to be used as supporting evidence for the deterioration in Dr. Hanley's performance and standard of work during the years I worked with him, all of which is already in the public domain. Beyond that, I can only advise you to gather as much supporting evidence as you can, from whichever source, in order to present a tight and compelling argument for a reopening of the investigation into Miss Butts's death. Trusting this is of help,
With all best wishes,

A. Deverill

Dr. Anthony Deverill

fourteen

I took the train to London on my own the following Monday. It caused a row because I refused to tell Sam where I was going or what I was planning to do, and he drove off in a huff after dropping me at Dorchester South station at eight o'clock in the morning. His mood had been depressed since Danny's throwaway line about rats jumping ship—*It wasn't like that. . . . I needed time to get my head together. . . . Jock was on my back all the time trying to persuade me to make you take those flaming tranquillizers. . . . He said you needed help . . . he said you'd flipped . . . he said . . . he said*—and his temper was not improved by my sour comment that if Jock was such a guru he should be talking to him and not to me.

I didn't keep tabs on him, so when I set out on Monday morning I had no idea if he'd taken my advice or not. I thought it unlikely. Sam wasn't the type to poke a sleeping dog unnecessarily, particularly when he was the most afraid of being bitten.

I found Graham Road changed beyond recognition that August morning. It had become a one-way street with speed bumps down the center. Parking was restricted to permit holders only, and trucks were banned. The houses were smarter than I remembered, the pavements wider, the sunlight brighter and more diffuse. It had lived for so long in my memory as a dark, foreboding place that I found myself wondering what else my mind had poisoned over the years. Or perhaps it wasn't my memory that was at fault? Perhaps Annie's death had actually achieved something?

I glanced at number 5 as I passed and was put to shame by its natty appearance. Someone had lavished the love and care on it that we should have done. Window boxes splashed the front with brilliant color, a new stained wood door had taken the place of our elderly blue one and the tiny front garden, barely three feet deep, boasted a neat brick wall, tubs of scarlet petunias and a semicircle of clipped green grass beside the path to the door. Nor was it alone. Here and there, untidy front gardens and peeling paintwork spoke of residents who were unable or unwilling to conform, but for the most part the road had moved decisively upmarket and made sense of Jock's statement that property prices had skyrocketed.

I guessed that some of that was due to the sale of the council-owned properties, which had stood out like sore thumbs twenty years before because of their uniform yellow doors. Now it was impossible to distinguish them from those that had always been in the private sector, and I wondered how many of them were still owned by the council tenants who had bought at rock-bottom prices. If Wendy Stanhope was to be believed, most of them had sold up within a year to achieve a 100 percent return on their investment, but the wiser ones had stayed and watched their investments grow.

I crossed the road and paused beside Sharon Percy's gate. Her house was almost as natty as ours, with Austrian blinds in the windows and a clump of Pampas grass in the front garden, but I couldn't believe she hadn't cut and run the minute she saw a profit. I knew she'd bought the house because Libby's letters had ranted on for months about how Jock's thirty quid a week had paid for Sharon's bedroom, but I found it difficult to equate the new subdued classiness of number 28 with the simpering peroxide blonde in Wendy's photograph.

I looked into her downstairs window—more curious than expectant—and was taken aback when her flour-white face, slashed red lips and heavily outlined eyes appeared briefly behind the pane. I recalled

Libby's nickname for her, "the bleached vampire," but she looked more pathetic than predatory that morning. An aging woman trying to paint away the ravages of time. Was Geoffrey Spalding still with her? Or had his infatuation died along with her sex appeal? I felt an absurd desire to raise my hand in greeting before I remembered that we'd never spoken and that, if she'd known me at all twenty years ago, she certainly wouldn't recognize me now.

I barely glanced at Annie's house as I moved on to number 32. Even when I'd stood in front of her boarded-up house in the months following her death, her ghost had never troubled me, and I certainly didn't expect to be bothered by it now.

In the end, the only ghosts that lingered here were lonely mothers. . . .

Maureen Slater opened her door before I could knock, and thrust out a miniature hand to pull me inside. "I don't want anyone to see you," she said.

"They won't know who I am."

"They'll guess. Everyone talks."

I wondered why that mattered when there was no one left who remembered Annie, and decided that by "everyone" she meant Sharon. I thought it would be counterproductive to say I'd already been seen, and followed her down the corridor to the kitchen, catching glimpses of the two ground-floor rooms as I passed their open doors.

The sitting room looked as though it was rarely used, but the dining room had been converted into a comfortable den with brightly colored bean bags littering the floor, a cushioned sofa along one wall and a wide-screen television in the corner. It was already switched on, showing a daytime magazine program, and the rumpled duvet on the sofa and the fug of smoke in the room suggested Maureen had either been watching it all night or had started early. She closed the door as we passed to deaden the volume.

Even though Maureen's was an end-of-terrace house, the layout inside was identical to ours, as indeed was every alternate house in the row: sitting room and dining room on the right with the corridor running past the stairs on the left-hand side toward the kitchen at the back. The in-between houses were built in mirror image so that corridors adjoined corridors on one side, and living space adjoined living space on the other. Upstairs, in precisely the same way, it was either the bedrooms or stairwells that adjoined. In order to allow for a window in the dining rooms, the kitchens were offset against the ends of the houses and shared a party wall with the people on the corridor side. As none of the structures was built to modern soundproof standards, the inevitable result was that we all came to know our neighbors rather better than we would have liked.

Indeed, it had been Sam's permanent complaint that we should have done some "noise" research before we bought number 5. On the corridor side, number 7—the side that acted as a sound buffer—lived an elderly couple, who rarely spoke above whispers even when they were in their kitchen. On the living-space side, number 3—the side that acted like a huge echo chamber divided by a thin vibrating wall—were the Charles children, whose nighttime screaming had kept us awake. One day, in a spirit of optimism, Sam invited both couples in for drinks and suggested they swap houses so that peace could break out all 'round, but Paul Charles took exception to some of the things Sam claimed to have heard through the wall and treated him with hostility from that moment on.

I had often wondered if a similar situation had existed with Annie, although, of the many complaints made against her, the question of noise had never been mentioned. In fact it was more likely she had been a victim of it and had suffered in silence while her life was made a misery. Certainly Michael Percy and Alan Slater had taken great pleasure from teasing her in public, and I couldn't believe they hadn't continued the sport in private by shouting insults at her through the party walls.

"Danny phoned last night," said Maureen, pulling out a chair in the kitchen and pressing me on to it. "You seem to be making quite a hit with him." She had a trace of the Midlands in her voice, which showed itself in the hard "g" she added to "ing," but whether she had been born there or whether she had learned it from her parents I didn't know.

Like everything else about her it set my teeth on edge, and I had to glue a smile to my face to mask my dislike. Whatever Wendy Stanhope may have said about her brutal treatment at the hands of her husband, I'd always thought there was something evil about Maureen Slater, perhaps because I held her responsible for the hate campaign against Annie. I'm sure she knew what my real feelings were, but for the moment she was prepared to go along with the pretense of friendship.

"The feeling's mutual," I assured her. "Danny's a nice fellow."

She busied herself with cups and saucers. I had written to her many times over the years, seeking answers, but the only response I had ever received was the one a week ago, agreeing to this meeting. I assumed it was my contact with Danny that had persuaded her to change her mind, and I wondered how far she suspected that I had sought him out deliberately and how far she was worried about what he had been telling me. There was, after all, so much that she wouldn't want me to know.

"You're the only person who thinks so," she said, filling a kettle at the sink. "Danny's been in and out of trouble since he was ten . . . fighting . . . stealing cars . . . he started shooting heroin when he was twelve." She paused, waiting for an answer. When I didn't give one, she went on a little tartly, "Not the type most mothers want hanging around teenage boys. He says he's been out drinking with your lads."

"He has. They've met up with him on Portland a couple of times."

"You know he smokes cannabis."

"Yes."

"He's probably offering it to your kids," she said with a touch of malice, as if the idea pleased her.

"Then he isn't the first, and he won't be the last."

She eyed me suspiciously. "You're pretty laid back about it. You must have a lot of faith in your boys."

I gave a noncommittal smile. "I'd be more worried if Danny was still on heroin."

"No chance of that." She plugged in the kettle. "It's the one good thing Mr. Drury did for me . . . caught the stupid little bastard at it one day and put the fear of God into him so he'd never go near a needle again."

"How did he do that?"

"He gave him a choice: punishment now, or a care order imposed by the juvenile court. Danny chose punishment now." She laughed. "I think he thought Drury was going to slap him about a bit . . . didn't reckon on honest-to-God sadism." The idea seemed to amuse her.

"What did he do?"

"He broke off the needle and pressed it into Danny's arm with the edge of his handcuffs, then told him if he went to a doctor to get it removed there'd be that many questions asked he'd find himself in care so quick his legs wouldn't touch the ground. It was two days before Danny could find the courage to cut down deep enough to pull the needle out with a pair of tweezers. He's never been able to look at a syringe again without turning green."

"That sounds like Mr. Drury's style," I murmured. "Brutal but effective. Did you report him for it?"

"Did I hell!" She spooned coffee into the mugs. "In any case I was grateful. The last thing I wanted was one of my children dead of an overdose."

A silence fell while we waited for the kettle to boil. I had no idea what kind of background she came from, but Drury's parting shot to Danny—"How's that downtrodden slut of a mother of yours? Still on the booze?"—was uncomfortably close to the mark. My mother would say it was breeding (or lack of it)—a scientist would say it was genes— I would say it was poor education and low self-esteem. If she cared about anything at all, I thought, it was probably her benefit checks and whether they would buy enough smokes and alcohol to last her through the week.

Her windowsill was lined with empties, testimony to the drinking habit she hadn't been able to kick. An unopened bottle of vodka stood beside the salt and pepper on the table like an unearned reward. But if she was drunk or stoned on Prozac that day it wasn't noticeable. Indeed in some ways the sharp, assessing glances she kept flicking in my direction reminded me of Wendy Stanhope, although there was no kindness in them, only suspicion.

"Thank you," I said when she put a mug of coffee in front of me. Out of habit, she had added milk and sugar, neither of which I could stand, but I sipped enthusiastically as she sat herself in the chair opposite and lit a cigarette.

"Do you want one?" she asked.

I shook my head. "I never got hooked, thank God. If I had, I'd be a sixty-a-day woman by now."

"How do you know?"

"I have an addictive personality. Once started, I can't stop."

"Like this thing with Annie?"

"Yes."

Maureen gave a baffled shake of her head. "You wouldn't have liked her, you know. That's what makes this all so . . . *stupid*. If anyone else had found her, there'd have been no fuss, she'd have been quietly buried and we could all have got on with our lives." She paused to draw pensively on her cigarette. "You, too," she added, watching me through the smoke.

"I haven't done badly so far."

She dropped ash into her saucer. "Except you can't let her go, and that's not healthy."

I might have answered that Annie was the least of my obsessions but I didn't want to put her on her guard. Instead I asked, "Why wouldn't I have liked her?"

"Because she wouldn't have liked *you*. She didn't like any white people. We were all 'white trash' to her. She used to chant it through the kitchen wall whenever Derek raised his voice. 'White trash . . . white trash . . .' On and on for minutes on end. It used to drive him mad."

"Is that why he hated her?"

She nodded.

"Perhaps he didn't like hearing the truth?" I remarked dryly.

A wary expression crept into her eyes. "We never claimed to be anything we weren't."

The pretense at friendship began to unravel at speed. "You were known as 'the family from hell,' Maureen. When you and Derek weren't screaming at each other, your children were running riot in the street. I've never known a group of people make their presence felt so rapidly in so short a time. Alan's favorite occupation was to practice his jump kicks against other people's front fences. He flattened Annie's within a month of you being rehoused here . . . and ours within three months."

She bridled immediately. "He wasn't the only one. Michael Percy was just as bad."

"I agree."

"But it was always my Alan who got the blame."

I shook my head in disagreement. "Michael faced up to what he'd done. Your son never did. Alan used to run away the minute trouble appeared and leave Michael to take the flak."

"Only because he knew his father would give him a larruping if he got caught."

"But it was all right for Michael to be given a larruping?"

Her mouth thinned immediately. "It never happened. Who was going to give it to him? Sharon? He'd have thumped her first. He was a nasty piece of work that Michael . . . a bad influence on all the kids 'round here. He was the one got my lad into trouble, never the other way 'round."

I wondered if Sharon saw it that way, or if she cared. "I watched a man hurl him head first into a brick wall once," I said idly. "It all happened very quickly and I was too far away to stop it. The wretched child was only fourteen—and he wasn't very big for his age—so he went down like a sack of potatoes."

"Serves him right," said Maureen balefully. "He almost killed somebody not so long ago . . . got eleven years for his troubles. That should tell you the sort of boy he was. It makes me sick the way we got dumped on all the time, when it was him and his tart of a mother caused all the problems in the street." A sly expression crept into her eyes. "Annie had their measure all right. She called Sharon a 'whore' and Michael a 'son of a bitch.'"

"Did she call her 'white trash'?"

"Nn-nn. 'Whore' . . . 'ho' . . . 'cunt.' Annie'd get going at the top of her voice every time she was with a client. It was pretty funny."

There was a time, I remembered, when she and Sharon had been thick as thieves, and I wondered what had happened to make them fall out. Something to do with money, I guessed, as it was the single passion they both shared. "So it was just the Slaters who were 'white trash'?" I murmured.

Maureen studied the end of her cigarette. "Think what you like," she said.

"Do you know who the man was who knocked Michael down?" I asked her.

She gave an indifferent shrug.

"It was your husband," I told her. "He was fighting drunk and caught Alan and Michael trying car doors to see if any of them were unlocked. Alan took to his heels but Michael stood his ground and ended up with a bloody face. I wanted to report Derek, but Michael said he'd take his anger out on you if we grassed him up. 'Mr. Slater's a right bastard,' he told me. 'He beats up on his missus every time his kids get the better of him.'" I watched her for a reaction, but there was none. "So I let Derek get away with it, and took Michael to my house instead of a police station. It was three hours before his nose stopped bleeding."

She stubbed out her cigarette, refusing to meet my eyes. "You can't blame me for that. Most of the time I didn't even know where Derek was, let alone what he was doing."

It sounded like the beginnings of a defense. "I'm not blaming you."

"Sure you are. You're like everyone else. It's Maureen's fault her kids were out of control. Maureen's fault she married a lousy husband. Well, maybe it was and maybe it wasn't. But who the fuck ever cared about me? Tell me that."

"The vicar and his wife?"

Anger sparked briefly in her eyes. "They were more interested in the nigger than they were in me."

I looked away to hide my anger, recalling what Wendy Stanhope had said. *The poor woman was always taking refuge with us. . . .* "I understood they took you in whenever Derek became violent."

"Only out of charity, never out of liking."

It was something she resented, I thought.

"The vicar knocked next door once a week. He never did that for me. I had to go looking for help."

"Perhaps he felt Annie had more to put up with."

"No more than we did. You should have heard her cursing and swearing at us through the wall."

"You said she only did it when you made a noise."

"Not always. Sometimes it was hard to say which came first . . . her or us. She had a mouth like a sewer. When it wasn't 'white trash,' it was 'honkies' or 'scum.' It used to rile us up something rotten."

"She couldn't help herself," I said. "She suffered from a neuropsychiatric disorder called Tourette's syndrome. Sometimes it manifests itself as *coprolalia,* which is a compulsion to utter obscenities. Her mother was far more prone to it than Annie, but maybe Annie resorted to it when she was stressed."

"Then she should have been in a loony bin."

Does she believe that? I wondered. Or was it something she repeated like a mantra to excuse what she did? "A more sensible solution would have been for the council to rehouse you and your family somewhere else," I suggested. "To be honest, I never understood why they didn't. You lived entirely on benefit, had more social workers allocated to you than anyone else in the street, yet for some reason the pressure was always on Annie to move and never on you. That always seemed grossly unfair to me when she was a householder, paying rates, and you were paying nothing."

"That wasn't our fault. Derek was out of work. Would you have liked it better if we'd starved?"

I refused to be sidetracked. "Why did the council take your side against Annie's, Maureen? It must have been clear to them that she wasn't getting on with her neighbors."

"Why would it? She never complained."

"She called you 'white trash.' What's that if it's not a complaint?"

She lit another cigarette and shook her head at my stupidity. "I meant she didn't complain to the council."

I had to make a conscious effort to stop my mouth dropping open. I had imagined any number of conspiracy theories to account for why the Slaters and the Percys had been allowed to wage a terror campaign against Annie, but it had never entered my head that the explanation was so simple. "Are you saying that, despite all the complaints you and Sharon made against her, she never once retaliated?"

Maureen nodded.

"Why not?"

She didn't answer and another silence developed between us. She wore her hair in a tight ponytail and kept running the flat of her hand across her crown as if to check that the elastic was still in place. She seemed to be debating with herself whether after twenty years there was anything to be gained by telling the truth, although I guessed that her real concern—indeed the only reason we were having this conversation—was to find out how much I knew and what I was planning to do about it.

"She was too afraid of Derek," she admitted suddenly.

"To make an official complaint?"

"Yes."

"What did he do to stop her?"

Another silence, longer this time, before she gave an embarrassed shrug. "Killed one of her cats and said he'd kill the others if she ever spoke out against us. The thing is"—she wriggled her shoulders uncomfortably, knowing that nothing could excuse her husband's behavior or her complicity in it—"we'd been moved three times in three years, and we didn't want to move again. We sure as hell didn't want to go back to a high rise."

"No," I said slowly. "I don't suppose you did."

"It was only a cat."

"Mm." I paused to glance along the corridor. "It was quite a bargain when you think about it . . . a cat for a house."

"There you are, then."

"Oh, no." I gave a small laugh. "Don't you dare bracket me with a sadist. If Derek had been married to me, he'd never have got near a cat. I'd have beaten his brains out with a sledgehammer the minute he lifted a finger against one of my children. Why were you such a coward? Why didn't you fight back?"

Her malice intensified. "You don't know what it was like. You didn't go in fear of your life every day. What do you think he'd have done to me and the kids if I'd tried to stop him?"

"Why didn't you go to the police?"

She shook her head scornfully as if the question weren't worth answering, and in fairness, it probably wasn't. Domestic violence was a low priority in 1978. As was harassment of black people.

"How did he kill the cat?" I asked, reverting to what interested me.

"Strangled it," she said irritably. "They kept coming into our garden, and he'd already warned her he wasn't going to stand for it. He chucked the body back over the fence with a note tied to its collar so she'd get the message."

"What did the note say?"

"I don't know, for sure. Something like he'd nail the next one to the fence. He didn't tell me about it till afterward." She watched me slyly through her lashes while she cooked up another defense. "I like cats. I'd have stopped him if I could. The children were all over them when we first came here . . . they kept asking where the marmalade one was."

"When did it happen?"

"About two months before she died."

"September '78?"

"Probably."

I recalled John Howlett's letter to Sheila Arnold. *I made two recommendations on my first visit in March 1978: 1) that she install a cat flap in the kitchen door to allow the animals free access to and from the garden. . . .* "After you'd set the RSPCA inspector on to her then?"

Maureen tapped the glowing end of her cigarette against her saucer and watched a curl of ash deposit itself against the side. "I can't remember."

"His first visit was in March. He ordered her to put a cat flap in her door because you and Sharon kept complaining about the smell coming from her house."

She lifted a shoulder in a careless shrug.

"Weren't you worried she'd show Derek's note to him the next time he came?"

"She wouldn't have dared. She was almost as frightened of the RSPCA as she was of Derek."

"How did she let the cats out before she had the flap installed?"

"She never did. That's why the house stank."

"That's not true," I said bluntly. "You just told me how your children were all over the cats when you first came here. How could they have had any contact if there was no way for the animals to get out until the flap was installed?"

A stubborn note crept into Maureen's voice. "Maybe she didn't bother to close her back door."

"Well, did she or didn't she? You must have known. Your kitchens were next door to each other."

"Most of the time it was open." Her eyes caught mine, then slid away to hide their cunning. "That's what made us think she had chickens in there. The smell that came out of it was disgusting."

"Oh, for Christ's sake!" I said wearily. "The only stink 'round here was your family's body odor. God knows if you ever gave Alan a bath or washed his clothes, but no one wanted to sit next to him at school. Poor kid. He was always the first to be checked for head lice . . . and *always* had them. Always the first to have his locker searched for missing games kit . . . and *always* had it. The PE teacher asked him once what his problem was, and he said he liked things that smelled clean."

"It wasn't my fault," she said again, her voice rising to an irritating whine. "We didn't have a washing machine."

"Neither did we. I used the laundrette on the main road."

"You didn't have kids."

"Two machines take the same time as one."

"The bags were too heavy. . . . I couldn't abandon Danny. . . . In any case, I never had any money. Derek spent it all on drink."

I looked at the vodka bottle on the table. "He wasn't the only one." I rode roughshod over her attempt at a retort. "Why didn't you do the washing by hand in the bath? You weren't working. You had all day to devote to your children. The one thing you could have done was keep them clean."

"I did my best."

I'd waited so long to get this off my chest that caution gave way to honesty. "Then you should be ashamed of yourself," I said flatly. "I've seen women in Africa do better than that when all they had was a tub of cold water. You did nothing for your children, and the only reason Danny's a nice kid now is because somewhere along the line someone took an interest in him. I suspect it was Alan's wife"—I could see from her expression that I was right—"because it certainly wasn't you. You were in a drunken stupor most of the time . . . like your husband."

She was surprisingly indifferent, as if she'd heard the same accusations many times before. "You do what you can to get by," she said, "and it wasn't always like that. Some days were better than others. In any case, you don't feel the pain so much when you're drunk. You should try having your face smashed into a brick wall once in a while and see how you like it."

Letter from Ann Butts to Councillor J. M. Davies,
Richmond—dated 1978

30 Graham Road
Richmond
Surrey
June 12, 1978

Dear Mr. Davies,

I got your name and address from a leaflet that was pushed through my door. You said to write if I had a problem. I think something should be done for Morin. She cries because her husband hits her. I have tried to make him stop but he is a nasty man who likes hurting children and animals.

Yours very worried,

Ann Butts (Miss)

Pendlebury
Duke's Avenue
Richmond
Surrey
01-940-0000

June 20, 1978

Dear Miss Butts,

Thank you for your letter of June 12, 1978. I am deeply disturbed by what you say, however, there is little I can do without more information. You did not give me Morin's surname, nor the name of her husband, nor indeed did you say where she lives. As I'm sure you appreciate, it will be difficult for me to raise the matter with the appropriate authorities without these details.

If you wish me to pursue the matter, please write again or telephone me on the above number. Alternatively, you may prefer to attend one of my "surgeries" at the above address, which would give you a chance to discuss your concerns in person. They take place between 9 A.M. and midday on the first Saturday of every month and do not require an appointment.

Yours sincerely,

(Update: No response received therefore no action taken. Possibility that a strange phone call at 11 P.M. on July 3 with much reference to "white trash" may have been Miss Butts, but caller was very incoherent. Suspect original letter was malicious. J.M.D.)

fifteen

I stared into my coffee. "How did she stop her cats coming into your garden after Derek killed the marmalade one? It was long after the cat flap had been installed."

"She propped a board in front of it so they couldn't use it, then let them out one at a time to do their business. It was quite funny watching her. She used to run up and down flapping her arms to stop them coming anywhere near our fence. We reckoned she'd have lost a couple of stone with all the exercise if she hadn't had her face in the trough all the time. You should have heard her . . . right noisy she was. Gobble, gobble, gobble. It made us sick just to listen."

My expression must have given away more than I intended because she dropped her eyes immediately. I thought what a vile little woman she was and how injurious her poison must have been to her family.

"You asked. . . . I told you," she muttered. "Don't blame me if you don't like the answers."

I caught at the edges of my anger and drew it back inside. "How do you know she used a board?"

"The kids used to climb over the fence at night and push the flap open to make the board fall on the floor."

"That must have frightened her."

"It did. She used to wail her head off."

"Why didn't she fix the board to the door?"

"Because she didn't want the RSPCA to know she was blocking the flap. She'd keep the inspector waiting at the door while she scurried around trying to find somewhere to hide the stupid thing."

"Is that why you and Sharon kept pestering the RSPCA? So they'd catch her out?"

She blew a smoke ring in my direction, then stabbed it through the heart with the point of her cigarette. "Maybe."

I gave my coffee cup a violent shove and watched it slop across the table. "You had her in a vise. On the one hand Derek was threatening to kill her cats if they *did* run free; on the other, the RSPCA was telling her she could face prosecution if they *didn't* run free."

She took to smoothing her hair again.

"What was she supposed to do?"

"Leave," she said matter-of-factly, "and take her cats with her."

"Just because she was black?"

"Why not? We didn't want a coon for a neighbor." She retreated rapidly as she saw my expression. "Look, it wasn't my idea. . . . I'd have done it differently if I could. But Derek wanted rid of her . . . he had this thing about nig—" She corrected herself—"blacks . . . really hated them. In any case, she had her chance. The social workers told her she only had to say the word and they'd rehouse us. But she said no, she was happy the way things were."

"She had no choice. Derek knew where she lived. Her cats were never going to be safe from him."

"Right, and she got so scared of him in the end, we reckoned she'd leave before Christmas." She paused. "Then the silly cow falls under a flaming truck," she finished lamely, "and the cops find she's been killing the cats herself."

I rested my chin in my hands and studied her with grim curiosity. "They were already half-dead when they were pushed through her flap," I told her. "Someone thought it was funny to catch strays and bind their mouths with superglue and parcel tape so they'd either starve to death or have most of the fur ripped out of their heads if Annie tried to save them. I think she killed the weakest ones when the others started attacking them, but it was done out of kindness, not out of cruelty." I favored her with a crooked smile. "So whose bright idea was that? Yours? Or your husband's?"

She squashed her cigarette into the ashtray, mashing it to shreds with nicotine-stained fingers. "It weren't nothing to do with us," she said flatly, while apparently agreeing with the facts. "We weren't like that."

"Oh, come on!" I said sarcastically. "You've just told me Derek strangled one cat and threatened to nail another to a fence. And all for what? Because he was thick as pig shit and had to terrorize women to give himself a sense of authority."

She didn't like the way the conversation was going, and licked her lips nervously. "I don't know anything about that."

"What? The way he liked to terrorize women?"

She recovered quickly. "All I know is what he did to me and the kids. But he was more talk than action. Most of the time he never followed through."

"Maybe not when Annie was alive," I agreed, "but he certainly made up for it after she was dead. He was far more violent when he knew there were no witnesses."

I recalled my visit to her in hospital. It was a wet afternoon at the end of November, and I'd dripped water all over the vinyl floor beside her bed while I tried not to show my shock at Derek's handiwork. I couldn't believe how small she was, how damaged she was, and how panic-stricken her eyes were. It was a wasted journey in terms of gathering information because she was too suspicious of me to answer questions. I listened to her dreary insistence that, far from Derek using her as a punchbag, she'd been alone in the house and had missed her footing at the top of the stairs, while saying in her next breath that she'd be dead if Alan hadn't been there to call an ambulance for her. It was a ridiculous story because her broken cheekbone and blackened eyes looked too much like Annie's death mask for anyone to believe that either of them had suffered an accident; but all too belatedly I was given a glimpse of the walls of terrified silence that protect violent men.

"What are you talking about?"

"Derek putting you in hospital two weeks after Annie's death. Didn't you ask yourself why that happened? He'd never hit you so hard before that you went into a coma and had to rely on your children calling an ambulance for you." I jerked my head toward the party wall. "Your protector was dead. Her house was empty. Derek was free to break every bone in your body if he wanted to, then dump you in the road somewhere and claim you were run over by a truck . . ."

Maureen rejected my suggestion that Annie had been her "protector." It was rubbish, she protested—Annie hated her. I repeated what she'd said herself, that Annie had wailed every time Derek raised his voice. "You asked me earlier who had ever cared about you," I reminded her. "Well, Annie did. I know it isn't what you want to hear, but it *is* the truth." I took two letters from my rucksack and pushed them across the table. "The top one's a copy of a note she wrote to your then councillor, J. M. Davies, in June '78. The one underneath is his reply. She obviously didn't know how to spell your name and, because she was incoherent when she tried to raise the matter over the telephone, he put the whole thing down to maliciousness."

Maureen looked uncomfortable reading Annie's bold handwriting as if, even in reproduction, it had the power to summon her into the room with us. "Perhaps it *was* malicious," she said, laying the letters aside. "Perhaps she was just trying to cause trouble for me and Derek."

"Oh, for God's sake!" I sighed impatiently. "If that was her intention, she'd have made a better job of it. She'd have written a barrage of letters, almost certainly unsigned, and she'd have accused Derek of killing animals instead of hurting them. Can't you see her concern was for *you*? She says, 'something should be done for Maureen,' not, 'something should be done about the white trash next door because they keep stealing from me.'"

She fumbled nervously at her cigarette packet. "She'd have been lying if she had."

I shook my head in contradiction. "Alan gave me a tiny wooden statuette which he told me he'd carved himself from an old table leg as an end-of-year present. I believed him because it's very primitive, and looks like something a child might do, but I'm certain he stole it from Annie."

"You can't prove that."

"No," I agreed, "but I can certainly prove he never carved it. It's been analyzed by an expert. It's a representation of an Aztec god, called Quetzalcoatl, and was cut from pine, probably around the turn of the century, in a style common to natives of Central America. Annie's father made a collection of Central American artifacts during the '30s and '40s, so the circumstantial evidence suggests that the Quetzalcoatl in my possession once belonged to her. The only question is, did she give it to Alan, or did he steal it?"

Maureen leaped at the bait. "She gave it to him."

"How do you know?"

She thought for a moment. "He ran an errand for her . . . it was her way of saying thank you. Matter of fact, I was the one who made him pass it on to you. He kept on about what a nice lady you were, and how you'd kept quiet about the time you caught him thieving from your wallet. 'One kindness deserves another,' I said, 'and Mrs. Ranelagh's more likely to appreciate a wooden statue than you are.'"

"Why did he tell me he'd carved it?"

She caught my eye briefly. "I expect he wanted to impress you."

I laughed. "I'd have been more impressed if he'd told me he earned it running errands for Mad Annie. He used to shout 'daft nigger' after her in the street. She turned on him once with a growl and grabbed at the sleeve of his jacket. He was so terrified he took to his heels and left the jacket in her hand." I paused. "She'd never have asked him to run an errand for her. And, even if she had, she'd have cut off her right hand before she rewarded him with one of her treasures. She disliked him even more than she disliked Derek. The little brute never left her alone. . . . He was always on the lookout for her. . . ." I fell silent before anger made me strident.

"That's lies. You're inventing things to suit yourself. All you're saying is that Alan played in the street a lot. It doesn't mean he was on the lookout for Annie."

"He was an abused and neglected child, Maureen, who was too frightened to take on his father and saw Annie as easy meat. He learned that bullying worked and put it into practice on the most vulnerable person he could find." I gave a humorless laugh. "I wish I'd known how you and Derek were treating him. I wish I'd had him prosecuted when I had the chance. Most of all, I wish he'd been taken away from you and taught some decent values when it mattered."

"You were just as responsible as us," she muttered. "You were his teacher. Why didn't you say something to him when he called her a 'daft nigger'?"

It was a good question. Why hadn't I? And what sort of excuse was it to say I was frightened of a fourteen-year-old? But I was. Alan was a huge child for his age, tall and heavily built, with a low IQ and little understanding of anything except aggression, which both emboldened and scared him. Had there been no Michael Percy to take the flak, then I think Alan's problems would have been more obvious and he might have attracted sympathy instead of dislike and disgust. As it was, most people avoided him and, in the process, turned a blind eye to the way he and his gang terrorized Mad Annie. It seemed an even contest, after all. She was bigger than they were, crazier than they were, older, bulkier and perceptibly more aggressive—particularly when she'd been drinking—and she had no compunction about lashing out when their teasing became intolerable.

"I've spent twenty years regretting my silence," I told Maureen. "If I'd been a little braver, or a little more experienced"—I gave an uneasy laugh—"maybe I wouldn't feel so guilty now."

She shrugged. "I wouldn't fret about it. Alan wouldn't have listened to you even if you had taken him to task. The only person he paid any mind to was his father."

"Until he turned on him with a baseball bat."

"It was bound to happen one day," she said indifferently. "Kids grow up. It was Derek's fault anyway. He didn't realize Alan wasn't up for a thrashing anymore."

I looked again at the cluster of empty bottles on her windowsill. "Do *you* ever feel guilty, Maureen?"

"Why should I?"

I gave her a copy of Michael Percy's letter, detailing how her children had stolen trinkets from Annie. She was more amused than fazed by it for, as she said herself, I'd have a job proving it. "No one's going to believe Michael," she pointed out, "and he wouldn't talk to the police anyway, not while he's in prison. It's more than his life's worth to be known as a grass."

"They might believe Alan," I suggested.

"He'll just deny it. He's got a family now . . . doesn't want something he did as a kid coming back to haunt him this long afterward. And Danny doesn't even remember his dad, let alone who lived next to us twenty years ago. He asked me down the phone what Annie was like and why I've never mentioned her."

"What did you say?"

"That she was a fat bitch who made our lives hell, and he didn't ought to believe anything you said because you had about as many screws loose as she did."

I smiled at her as I pulled a manila envelope from the bottom of my rucksack and put it on the table in front of her. "He'll probably believe this, though. I made this copy for you. When you've read it, give me a call. My number's on the front."

"What is it?"

"An affidavit from a jeweler in Chiswick who bought several items off a woman called Ann Butts. It took me and my father about two hundred letters to find him after Michael suggested you'd sold the ring you took off Bridget. We started with jewelers and pawnbrokers in

Richmond and radiated out until we hit pay dirt in Chiswick. He's still in business and keeps a record of every item that passes through his hands . . . together with the name of the seller and purchaser."

She dropped the envelope on to the table as if it were a red-hot coal.

"He's an honest trader and pays an honest price, so he requests proof of identity and ownership in order to be sure that the goods aren't stolen. He also records the type of proof that's offered. In the case of Ann Butts, it was a bank card and supporting statement, and a Sotheby's valuation of a list of items, including the jewelery, which were viewed on site at 30 Graham Road, Richmond. I presume you don't still have it?" I said with a lift of my eyebrows. "You wouldn't have been that stupid, would you?"

She reached for another cigarette but I took the packet away from her and flattened it under my heel as I stood up.

"The really interesting fact," I finished, leaning my hands on the table, "is that the first item wasn't sold until June '79, and my jeweler friend is positive that the Ann Butts he dealt with was a small white woman with a Brummy accent."

She had a quick mind for a Prozac junkie and a drinker. "Just like half a million others then," she said.

"My phone number's on the envelope," I reminded her. "Call me if you want to trade. If you don't, I'll give the affidavit to the police."

"Trade what?"

"Information. I want to know who murdered Annie, Maureen . . . not who stole from her."

Sharon Percy refused to open her door beyond the burglar chain. "I'm not going to talk to you," she said. "You thought I wouldn't recognize you, but I watched you go into Maureen's so it didn't take much guessing."

A tortoise head loomed behind her in the hallway. "First you pester us with bloody letters," Geoffrey spat at me, "now you turn up in the flesh. Why don't you just bugger off and leave us alone?"

"I would have done if you'd written back," I said.

"What's to say?" he growled. "We don't know anything. Never did."

"Then why did you lie in your statements to the police?"

There was a look of panic on both their faces before the door was slammed against me. As I hadn't expected anything else, I set off on the two-mile walk to Jock Williams's house.

*Letter from Libby Garth—ex-wife of Jock Williams,
formerly of 21 Graham Road, Richmond—now resident in
Leicestershire—dated 1997*

Windrush

Henchard Lane

Melton Mowbray

Leicestershire

June 19, 1997

M'dear,

Written in haste before I start cooking supper for the
hungry horde. Would you believe Jock's moved yet another
bimbo into that mansion of his! He seems to replace them
every few months, yet he's hardly sex on wheels, for God's
sake! How on earth does he attract them? I know he makes
money from time to time but it's not as if he holds on to it for
very long.

His new project, "Systel"—something to do with mobile
phones—looks optimistic, but if it goes the way of the others
he'll be looking for a huge injection of cash within a year or
so. Word has it (the new bimbo) he has such a lousy
reputation with venture capitalists he's now looking at loans
secured against the house. He needs his head examined if he
does because he'll end up without a roof over his head if he
overreaches himself. Heh! Heh!

God, I'm a bitch! And why am I still doing this? Perhaps
I'm a *voyeur manqué?* If so, I blame you for it. You should
never have encouraged me to keep tabs on him, because it is
so addictive chatting up his "crumpet." It must be a "comfort

thing." I feel better knowing I wasn't the only one who couldn't make a relationship work with him.

All love,

Libby

XXX

PS: Jim keeps complaining about the amount of time I spend at teachers' conferences. Did I tell you I'm now a union rep? Next stop Parliament! And this from a man who expects me to entertain his major account-holders every weekend with cordon bleu cookery! Men, eh? Who needs 'em?

sixteen

Jock kept me standing on the step for several minutes before he opened the door, and I took the time to catch my breath after my hike from Graham Road to the rather grander street between Queen's Road and Richmond Hill where he was now living. The area had been developed in the wake of rail travel when the middle classes first began to exploit the benefits of living at a distance from their workplaces in noisy city centers; and the houses, though still in terraces, were more substantial than their humbler counterparts in Mortlake, with a third story to accommodate servants. A hundred years ago, each house would have had a walled front garden with trees and shrubs for privacy, but since the advent of the two-car family the gardens had been opened and paved to provide off-street parking.

To one side of Jock's frontage was an elderly black Mercedes with worn leather seats, and I was peering through the windscreen wondering if it was his when the door to the house snapped open and he appeared at my side. "You're half an hour early," he said irritably. "I thought we agreed two o'clock."

I had expected age, divorce and thwarted ambition to have mellowed him a little, but attack, I saw, was still his favored form of defense. I was surprised by the sense of pleasurable recognition I felt, as of an old friend, and offered my cheek for a kiss. "Hello, Jock," I said. "How are you?"

He gave me a quick peck. "Where's Sam?"

"Didn't he phone you?"

"No."

"He got tied up at the last minute and couldn't make it," I lied with convincing regret, "so I'm on my own." There was a beat of time while I pretended not to see the swift look of relief that crossed Jock's face. "I didn't know you were into classic cars," I said mischievously, patting the Mercedes's hood. "You always hankered after the newest model in the old days. I remember how rude you were when Sam and I bought that secondhand Allegro estate."

He made a dismissive gesture. "I keep the Merc as a runabout. The Jag's in a lockup garage down the road."

"A Jag!" I exclaimed. "My God! Sam will be green with envy. He's been wanting an XK8 since they came out." I looked past him into the shadows of the hall where a coin-operated telephone hung off the wall. "Don't let me stop you if I've interrupted something," I said. "I'm in no hurry."

He pulled the door to. "I've some e-mails to answer."

"I can wait." I hitched a buttock onto the bonnet of the Mercedes and lifted my head to look at the house. It was an attractive building with sandstone bays containing the high, wide windows of which Victorian architects were so fond. According to Libby the house had cost him £70,000 in 1979 and, according to a local real estate agent, it was now worth upward of three-quarters of a million. "Nice place," I murmured when he made no move to return inside.

He nodded. "I like it."

"So what was wrong with it when you bought it? Sitting tenants? Subsidence? Dry rot?"

He looked surprised. "Nothing."

"You're joking! How on earth did you afford it? I thought you got a pittance out of the divorce settlement."

He recoiled slightly as if I'd just revealed teeth. "Who told you that?"

"Libby."

"I didn't know you were still in touch."

"On and off."

"Well, she's wrong," he said warily. "She thought she could clobber me by hiring an expensive solicitor but he never came close to finding the investments that mattered."

It is odd, I thought, *how the memory plays tricks.* In my mind, I had likened him for so long to a weasel that his rather charming face surprised me. "It must have been a first then," I said with a small laugh. "You never managed to hide anything else from your wife."

"What else has she told you?"

"That you moved a blonde in here before the ink was dry on the divorce. 'Young enough to be his daughter,' she said, 'but old enough to recognize a sucker when she sees one.'"

Another flash of relief. "That's her jealousy talking," he scoffed.

I laughed again, amused by his cocky expression. "You always were a hopeless liar, Jock. It used to irritate me . . . now it amuses me . . . probably because I know so much more about your business affairs than Sam does."

His expression soured. "Like what?"

"Like you have an outstanding loan on this place of £500,000 which you took out to keep Systel afloat and now can't repay."

There was a short silence while he considered his response. "Is this something else Libby told you?"

I nodded.

"Well, it's a lie," he said curtly. "She doesn't know a damn thing about my finances. Hell, she didn't even know what they were twenty years ago, so she certainly wouldn't know now. I haven't spoken to her since the divorce." He waited for me to say something and, when I didn't, he ratcheted up his aggression. "I could sue you both for slander if you repeat it to anyone else. You can't go 'round destroying people's reputations just because you hold a grudge against them."

I was tempted to say such considerations hadn't stopped him twenty years ago from helping Sam to destroy *my* reputation. Instead I said mildly: "I'm always happy to be put straight, Jock. So which is the lie?

That you don't have an outstanding loan, that you didn't plow it into Systel and lose it or that you can't repay it?"

He didn't answer.

"Perhaps you should have been a little more selective in your girl–friends," I suggested. "According to Libby, the blonde bimbette was the first of many, and none of them knew how to keep her mouth shut."

"What's that supposed to mean?"

"Libby's been prying information out of them for years while you were out at work, and even she couldn't believe how indiscreet some of them were. All she had to say was that she was conducting research for a hosiery manufacturer, then offer them a dozen free packs of luxury tights in return for twenty minutes of their time answering lifestyle questions, and the floodgates would open."

He frowned. "Why the hell would she do a thing like that?"

It was a good question, but not one I was ready to answer. I needed him off balance if I was ever to get at the truth. "She wanted to know how much you ripped her off in the divorce settlement."

"None of my exes could have told her that," he said confidently.

"No," I agreed, "but she never asked anything so direct. She was far more subtle" I smiled—"and *very* patient. She built on what she al–ready knew about you." I thought of the regular lists Libby had sent me with updated information on Jock. "Do you or your partner own the house? Was the value of the house more or less than £50,000 at the time of purchase? Is the present value of the house more or less than £100,000 . . . £200,000, et cetera? Is your partner self-employed? Does he earn more or less than £50,000 . . . £100,000, et cetera? Does he have a mortgage? Is it more or less than £50,000, et cetera, et cetera?" I laughed unkindly. "She never got a straightforward yes or no. One of your girlfriends even fished out your bank statements so that the figures would be accurate."

"That's illegal."

"Undoubtedly."

"You're lying," he said with more certainty than his expression suggested he felt. "Why would she keep on with something like that? It doesn't make sense."

I smiled ruefully as if I agreed with him.

"What answers did she get?"

"That your mortgage went from £20,000 to £500,000 in fifteen years, and you worked your way through seven girlfriends in the process. Two of your start-up businesses failed and the half million you made on the one you sold last year went straight into staving off bankruptcy. The only reason you're still here"—I nodded toward his front door—"is because the capital value of the house exceeds the loan and the bank's allowing you to make interest-only repayments while you look for a job with a six-figure salary. You're not having much success because you're almost fifty and your track record is far from impressive. You're fighting the bank's pressure to sell the house because you're afraid you'll only walk away with £200,000 once the bills have been paid, and that's barely enough to buy back your old place in Graham Road."

He looked devastated, as if I'd just torn his life apart and tossed the pieces to the winds. I felt no remorse. In a small way he was beginning to understand what he had once done to me.

"If it's any consolation," I went on amiably, "Sam's been just as economical with the truth. We didn't make a killing in Hong Kong, there's no eight-bedroom mansion on the horizon, and the farmhouse we're renting is falling down. In fact we're not much better off than you are, so it seems rather pointless to spend the next half-hour trying to impress each other with our nonexistent fortunes."

He sighed—more in resignation than anger, I thought—and gestured toward the door. "You'd better come in, though I warn you I'm pretty much confined to my study these days. The rest of the house is let out to foreign students as the only way to cover the bills. Matter of fact, I was planning to take you to the pub so you wouldn't find out, but it's a hell of a sight easier this way." He led me across the hall toward a room at the back. "Have you told Sam any of this?" he asked, opening the door and ushering me in.

"No. He still believes everything you tell him." I took stock of the room, which had barely enough space to maneuver. It was packed to the scuppers with sealed boxes, piles of books and pictures hung in tiers on every wall, and if anything of Annie's was in here, it was stubbornly invisible. "My God!" I said, unbuckling my rucksack and dropping it to the floor. "Where the hell did all this come from? You haven't taken to burglary, have you?"

"Don't be an idiot," he said tetchily. "It's the stuff I'm keeping from the lodgers. If they don't steal it they'll break it. You know what they're like."

"No," I assured him. "I haven't met them."

"I meant foreigners in general."

"Ah!" I gave a snort of laughter, enjoying the irony of Jock sharing his house with strangers. "Are we talking *black* foreigners, Jock?"

"Arabs," he said crossly. "They're the only ones with any money these days."

"Is that why you're sleeping in here?" I asked, looking at the bed in the corner. "To guard your possessions from dusky predators?"

"Ha-bloody-ha!" He took the swivel seat in front of his desk, leaving the armchair for me. "Only when the other rooms are full. It's a bit hand-to-mouth but it's tiding me over."

He had grown a beard since the last time I saw him and his dark hair was going gray, but it suited him and I decided he must thrive on adversity because he had none of the worry lines that characterized Sam's face. "You look good," I said, settling myself in the chair. "Sam's lost most of his hair and is very sensitive about it. He'll be upset to hear you've kept all yours."

"Poor bugger," he said with surprising sympathy. "He was always paranoid about going bald . . . used to count the hairs in his comb every day."

"He still does." I transferred my attention to a tortoiseshell cat that was curled up on a padded footstool in the corner of the room. "I didn't know you liked cats."

He followed my gaze. "This fellow's grown on me. One of the exes stormed out when I refused to pay her credit-card bill and poor old Boozey got abandoned in the rush. . . . Either that, or he went to ground the minute the estrogen started to fly. He's more interested in me than my wallet so we rub along pretty well together."

"Do you have a girlfriend now?"

"You mean Libby hasn't told you?" he asked sarcastically. "I thought she knew everything."

"She gave up calling when foreigners started answering the phone."

"Why wasn't she worried about me picking it up?"

"You did," I told him, "several times. She always pretended to be an old lady phoning the doctor's surgery. You were very patient with her. Kept telling her to correct the number in her book so she wouldn't get it wrong again."

"Godammit! Was that Libby? It didn't sound like her." He looked impressed, as if I'd just said something laudable about a nonexistent daughter instead of the wife who'd cast him aside nearly a quarter of a century before.

"She's good at putting a tremble in her voice." I paused. "Do you miss her?"

It was a question he hadn't expected and he stroked his beard pensively while he considered his answer. "Sometimes," he admitted. "Where is she now? I know she remarried because one of her friends told me, but I've no idea where she went."

"Melton Mowbray in Leicestershire. She did a postgraduate course in Southampton after you and she split up and now she's head of the history department at a comprehensive in Leicester. Her husband's a bank manager called Jim Garth. They have three daughters. The eldest is thirteen and the youngest seven."

His lips twisted in a regretful smile. "She always said she could do better without me."

"She wanted an identity of her own, Jock"—I leaned forward, clamping my hands between my knees—"and if you'd encouraged her to train as a teacher while you were still married . . . who knows? Maybe you'd still be together."

He didn't believe that any more than I did. "Hardly. We weren't even on speaking terms by the end." His eyes narrowed as he looked at me, and I guessed he had as much pent-up distrust of me as I had of him. "I've always blamed you for the divorce, you know. Libby didn't have a problem till you came along, all she wanted was babies . . . then *you* move into the street and, suddenly, babies aren't good enough. She *has* to have a career, and it *has* to be teaching."

"I didn't know she was so easily influenced."

"Oh come on! Every idea she had was recycled from the last person she spoke to. That's probably why she became a history teacher," he said sarcastically. "You don't have to think so much when your subject's been chewed over for centuries by other people."

"That's rubbish, Jock. Libby knew exactly what she wanted out of life . . . also what she *didn't* want."

"Yes, well, I could always tell when she'd been with you. She was a hell of a sight more belligerent about her rights when she'd had a dose of Ranelagh left-wing feminism."

"Maybe it's a good thing you never introduced her to Sharon then," I said dryly. "Or you'd have had a prostitute for a wife."

He wouldn't look at me—afraid, I think, of what I might read in his eyes—but his neck flushed an angry red. "That's a stupid thing to say."

"No more stupid than you trying to blame me for your divorce," I said evenly. "Nothing I said or didn't say could alter the fact that Libby was sick to death of your gambling. She wanted some stability in her life, not a roller-coaster ride of wins one day and losses the next. It was bad enough when it was just the stock market, but when you admitted to losing three thousand quid on a poker game. . . ." I shook my head. "What did you expect her to do? Pat you on the back?"

"It was *my* money," he said sulkily.

"It was also your money when you won," I pointed out, "but you never shared your winnings with her, only your losses. You put Libby through hell every time you lost and used your winnings to buy blow jobs off Sharon."

It began to dawn on him just how much Libby had told me and he retreated into an offended silence, punctuated only by the regular ticking of a pendulum clock on the mantelpiece. I made no effort to break it. Instead I glanced about the study, trying to imprint what I could see on my memory. It was an impossible task, so I looked for what wasn't there: silhouette pictures of Annie's grandparents, mosaics of Quetzalcoatl, items of jade, artillery shells and peacock feathers . . .

There was a fine seascape in a gilded frame on the wall opposite showing a ship under full sail battling with a storm-tossed sea, and I could just make out the words on the small plaque screwed to the bottom of the frame. *Spanish Privateer in Great Storm off Kingston, Jamaica, 1823.* I was so absorbed in trying to decide whether the date represented the year the storm happened or the year the picture was painted, that it was a while before I realized Jock was watching me.

"What the hell's going on?" he asked suspiciously, following my gaze. "Has Libby got some crazy idea that she can get more money out of me?"

I shook my head. "I came to ask you about the night Annie Butts died."

He gave an exasperated sigh. "So why drag Libby into it? Why not be upfront at the beginning?"

It was an obtuse remark from a man who always attacked first and asked questions later. "Sorry," I said apologetically.

"You could have talked to me on the phone," he said, warming to his grievance. "I've always answered your questions in the past. I even drove round to St. Mark's Church the other day to find out the vicar's name for you."

"That was kind," I agreed.

"Then what's the big deal?"

I pulled a wry expression. "Nothing really. I'm just not very good at this. I was afraid you'd clam up if I dived straight in with questions about where you were and who you were with that night."

He looked surprised. "You already know all that. It was in my statement. I was with Sam at your place. We had a couple of beers and then I went home."

"Except it was a Tuesday," I reminded him, "and Libby told me Tuesday was your fellatio day."

"God almighty," he growled angrily, hating the whole subject, "I went to Sharon first. Okay? I came out at about half-seven, bumped into Sam and went back to his place for a beer."

"Sam said you bumped into each other at the tube station."

He shifted uncomfortably. "It was twenty years ago. You can't expect me to remember every wretched detail."

"Why would you be at the tube if you'd just left Sharon? I thought you had sex in her house."

"What the hell difference does it make? Annie was alive and well when we passed her in the street."

I shrugged. "The reason Sam knows he met you at the station is because you were on your way home from a poker game."

He was taken by surprise. "A poker game?" he echoed. "Where on earth did that spring from?

"It's what Sam said."

"Not in his statement, he didn't."

"No, it was the explanation he gave me afterward," I lied. "He said he took you home for a drink because you were in a blue funk about how to tell Libby you'd lost another fortune."

Surprise was abruptly replaced by irritation. "You didn't pass that on to Libby, did you?"

"No. I didn't hear about it until after we'd left England."

He pondered for a moment. "Maybe Sam didn't want to say I'd been with Sharon."

"Did he know about her?"

He gave a half-hearted nod.

"But who could have told him, Jock? *You?*" I said in amazement when he didn't answer. "God! I'd have put money on you keeping that a secret. It wasn't something to be proud of, was it?"

His mouth thinned. "Give it a rest, all right? None of this has anything to do with Annie's death."

I shook my head. "It has everything to do with it, Jock. She died because she was beaten half to death some hours before she managed to drag herself down to our end of the street for me to find, yet you just said she was alive and well when you came out of Sharon's house at a quarter to eight." I lifted copies of the autopsy photographs from the front pocket of the rucksack and spread them on my lap. "Look at the bruising. It's too extensive to have come from injuries inflicted fifteen to thirty minutes before she died." I isolated a close-up of Annie's right arm. "This is a classic picture of a multitude of defense wounds sustained hours before death. The probability is that she curled herself in a ball to try to protect her head and, instead of a few individual bruises, which is what you would expect to see if a truck had flung her against a lamp-post minutes before she died, all the bruises have merged over a period of hours to produce one massive hematoma from shoulder to wrist."

He stared at the photographs with shocked fascination but instead of expressing revulsion over Annie's bludgeoned face, he offered a poignant non sequitur. "I'd forgotten how young she was."

"Younger than you are now," I agreed, "and very strong, which is why she took so much punishment before she passed out. This bruising at the top of her thighs"—I turned a picture of Annie's torso toward him—"suggests massive internal injuries from being kicked or beaten around her abdomen, causing blood to seep into the tissue of her legs. It's what's usually described as a 'frenzied attack' and it almost certainly happened in her own house because anywhere else would have been too public."

He took time to assimilate what I was saying. "I thought she was wearing her coat. Why would she wear a coat in the house?"

It was a question I'd asked myself many times because she certainly wouldn't have been in any condition to put it on after she'd been attacked. "I can only guess that someone pushed in behind her when she came home from the pub and attacked her before she had time to remove it."

He began to look worried. "The police would have found some evidence," he protested. "There'd have been blood on the walls."

"Not if most of her injuries were internal. In any case, there *was* evidence. The police recorded it themselves. Broken furniture which suggested a fight . . . absent floor coverings which suggested she *did* bleed and the rugs were removed . . . human waste in the hall, which is a classic fear response from intruders. She stank of urine when I found her, Jock, which suggests they pissed on her as well."

He turned away to fiddle with the pens on his desk. "That's disgusting."

"Yes." I gave a tired shrug. "And if you and Sam hadn't lied about seeing her at a quarter to eight, then maybe the police would have interpreted the evidence properly instead of condemning her as a tramp."

He licked his lips nervously. "Does Sam say we lied?"

I nodded, carefully squaring the photographs in my lap. "He was feeling homesick one night in Hong Kong and started blaming me for the fact that we'd had to leave England. It all came out at about three o'clock in the morning . . . how you'd phoned him and begged him to give you an alibi . . . how I'd made his life impossible by telling the police it was murder . . . how the choice between supporting me or his closest friend had been one of the hardest he'd ever had to make." I shrugged. "I've not had much sympathy for you since. You put me through hell and I've never forgiven you for it."

"I'm sorry," he said awkwardly.

I couldn't help admiring his loyalty. It was more than Sam deserved but it said much for their friendship, which had stayed healthy through their regular exchange of phone calls, faxes and e-mails. "It's only a matter of time before the police reopen the case," I told him, "and the first thing they're going to look at is where people were in the hours before Annie's death. She died shortly after 9:30," I reminded him. "So if you spent thirty to forty minutes in Sharon's house and left at half-seven, then you were there within the timespan that bruises like this"—I tapped the photographs—"need to develop."

His eyes flicked toward my lap.

"And that means you must have heard what was going on next door," I went on matter-of-factly, "or you joined Sharon shortly after she heard it. Either way you'd have noticed something. You don't get good sex off a woman who's just listened to her neighbor being clubbed into unconsciousness." I eyed him curiously. "But Sharon's bound to claim your story's bullshit anyway because, according to her inquest testimony, she was in the pub from 6 till 9:15."

"This is crazy," he said, his eyes straying toward the telephone on his desk. "What does Sam say?"

"Nothing much . . . except that he's adamant he didn't know about Sharon and refuses to take the blame if you lied to him about why you needed an alibi."

It was the accusation of lying to Sam that seemed to goad him toward honesty. Either that or his resentment at being made everybody's scapegoat finally boiled over. "Sam knew better than anyone that I didn't have the bottle to go near another card game," he said bitterly. "I may be a risk taker but I'm not a bloody fool. I was taken to the cleaners by some pros the first time and I wasn't going to give them a second chance." He squeezed the bridge of his nose between finger and thumb. "And there's no way Sharon was an issue. I could have paraded half the whores in London in front of Libby without her turning a hair. The marriage had been dead for months . . . it was just a question of which one of us was going to pack our bags first."

"Then why did you lie in your statement?"

He saw in my eyes that I knew the answer. "Do you really want it spelled out? It was dead and buried before you even left England."

"For Sam maybe," I said. "Not for me. That's why I'm here. I've waited a long time to find out who he was with that night . . . and what they were doing . . ."

E-mail from Libby Garth—ex-wife of Jock Williams,
formerly of 21 Graham Road, Richmond—now resident in
Leicestershire—dated 1999

M. R.

From: Libby Garth (liga@netcomuk.co)
Sent: 05 May 1999 14:37
To: M.R.
Subject: Re coming home at last!

M'dear, this is such marvellous news! I truly believed you were gone for good! I suppose Sam's coronary accounts for it—so every cloud does have a silver lining then? Anyway, I can't wait to see you again. Perhaps you can persuade Sam to visit Jock one weekend while you and the boys come up to visit us in Leicestershire? I can't imagine Sam will want to buddy up to Jim for fear of betraying his old friend—and Jim would be v. nervous to have a suspicious mate of Jock's about the place.

Talking about suspicious mates (ha! ha!) are you planning to confront Jock after you get back? As you know, I've never managed to find out how he bought that house in Alveston Road, although I met a university friend of his at a party a while back who made an oblique reference to the effect that Jock's parents had helped him—viz.: "Jock's never been known to miss a trick. He told me once he'd screwed a small fortune out of the pair of them because each one thinks he doesn't talk to the other, and they can't check because they haven't exchanged a word since the brother died." Could that be where the money came from? It sounds like Jock's modus operandi, whatever he may say about being a "self-made man."

Have I ever told you how impressed I am by all your efforts? Who'd have thought the little teacher from Graham Road would have turned into such a tigress! Poor old Sam must wonder what's hit him. You say he still won't talk about the night Annie died, but perhaps that's only to be expected. The longer you remain married the harder it must be for him to admit that he was prepared to put a friend before his wife.

You're too wise not to put something that happened twenty-plus years ago into perspective. Let's face it, we all make mistakes, and in fairness to Sam you did go a little crazy afterward—classic post-traumatic stress reaction for which you should have had counseling—and neither he, Jock, nor anyone else had reason to doubt the police view that Annie died in a tragic accident. I know you'll say it doesn't pass the "so what" test, but I can't help feeling it would put your marriage under unnecessary strain to keep reminding Sam of his "failure" when all the police will require is a straightforward admission that they didn't see Annie that night.

Re the Slaters, Percys and Spaldings. Do be careful how you approach them as there is no doubt in my mind that they'll be extremely hostile to answering questions. Hate groups are notoriously violent—they're too low on the pecking order to be anything else—and I really don't want to read in my newspaper that your body's been fished out of the Thames! The burning fiery cross is a frightening reality, my darling, not a figment of KKK imagination. They believe in terror because terror gives them status. (It probably gives them orgasms as well because they're all sadists, but they would never admit to that!) Anyway, I do wonder if you shouldn't leave the Slaters to the police, particularly as you've amassed so much evidence already of their petty thieving.

Speak soon,

All my love,

L

seventeen

It was an involved tale about a pretty little secretary in Sam's office who had ensnared him during the August of '78 while I was in Hampshire dog-sitting for my parents, who were on holiday. It was a brief madness, Jock assured me, a fatal attraction that went sour almost as soon as it started. Sam wanted to dump her the minute I came home, but the girl was having none of it. If she'd worked anywhere else it wouldn't have been a problem, but Sam was worried about how it would affect his career if she turned on him out of spite. It was the early days of sexual harassment cases, and this was a girl who knew what she was doing.

Sam strung her along for a couple of months, then made an attempt to end it on the night I was due to stay late at school for a parents' evening. By malign chance, it was also the night Mad Annie died. "Sam was way out of his depth," said Jock. "He had this crazy idea that if he wined and dined his mistress first, then told her he planned to do the decent and honorable thing and stay with his wife, the girl would accept it. Instead she went ballistic . . . screamed and yelled at him in the restaurant . . . poured wine down his suit . . . and, what with one thing and another, he was in a pretty dire state by the time he reached home.

"He passed Annie in the gutter," said Jock. "She was under the lamppost so he could hardly miss her, but she reeked of drink so he left her. He knew you'd be back any minute and his first priority was to get out of the suit, clean himself up and pretend he'd been in all evening."

A glint of humor flashed in his eyes. "Then you come running in fifteen minutes later to ring for an ambulance and the silly sod promptly
shoots himself in the foot."

I frowned. "He was watching television. I never even questioned
where he'd been."

"You told him Annie Butts was dying in the road outside and he
said, 'No, she's not, she's paralytic.'"

"So?"

"Why would he say that if he hadn't seen her?"

I bit back a laugh. "Are you telling me you lied to the police because
of some half-assed remark he made while I was screaming down the
telephone for an ambulance? He could have told me she was standing
on her head and waggling her legs in the air for all the notice I paid
him. I wouldn't have remembered afterward."

Jock shrugged. "That's exactly what I said, but he didn't believe me.
He reckoned you had a memory like an elephant. He said it would be
easier all round if we supported the police version that Annie was staggering drunk at a quarter to eight. I mean it wasn't as if we were the
only ones to say it . . . *everyone* was saying it. We thought it was the
truth."

"There were only five other people who claimed to have seen her,"
I reminded him. "One was Geoffrey Spalding who lived opposite Annie at number 27. He's the man who said at the inquest that he tried to
persuade Annie to go home but gave up when she started cursing him.
His estimate of the time was between 8 and 8:30. Two were an elderly
couple at number 8, Mr. and Mrs. Pardoe, who went up to bed at approximately nine o'clock because they were cold and saw her from
their upstairs window, but decided against doing anything because she
was clearly drunk and the last time they'd tried to help her she spat at
them. And the remaining two were a man and a woman in a car who
were using Graham Road as a shortcut and said they had to slam on the
brakes when a bulky figure in a dark coat suddenly lurched in front of
them, screaming abuse. They decided she was 'an aggressive drunk' and

drove on to avoid a confrontation. They couldn't be accurate about the time, but thought it was shortly after nine o'clock."

He looked at the photographs that were still in my lap. "You've just destroyed your own argument," he said. "Why would any of those people lie about seeing her?"

"I don't think they did," I answered slowly, "except possibly Geoffrey Spalding, and he may only have been lying about the time. You see, timing's important. One of the reasons the police estimated that she received her injuries fifteen to thirty minutes before I found her was because the Pardoes and the couple in the car both said she was on her feet at or around nine o'clock. If she was dead by 9:30, then ipso facto something must have hit her during those thirty minutes."

"Then how can you expect anyone to believe she was beaten to death hours earlier?"

"I said she was beaten unconscious, Jock, I didn't say she was dead. There *is* a difference . . . particularly when you're talking about someone as well-built and powerful as Annie." I ran an exploratory finger across her celluloid face as if it could tell me something. "I think she came 'round inside her house and managed to get herself out in search of help. The miracle is she had enough strength left to try to stop a passing car. A doctor would probably say it was impossible because her skull was so badly fractured, but it's the only explanation for why she was in the road and why she appeared drunk."

"Or the police were right all the time," suggested Jock. "I remember reading the inquest report. It said there was a high level of alcohol in her blood."

I shook my head. "It was ninety-five milligrams per hundred millilitres of blood—or fifteen milligrams above the legal driving limit. That's the equivalent of four or five shots of rum . . . a drop in the ocean for someone who drank as much as Annie. Sam and I can manage that with no trouble at weekends . . . you, too, I expect . . . but it doesn't make us stagger about like zombies." I gave a weary shake of my head. "She was labeled a road-traffic accident, so the pathologist routinely recorded her as 'unfit to drive,' which the police and the coroner then interpreted as a 'high concentration of alcohol.' In fairness they had witness statements that described her as 'paralytic' and the police found cases of empty vodka bottles in her house, but if the pathologist had done his job properly he would have questioned whether ninety-five milligrams was enough to cause staggering in a fourteen-stone woman with a known alcohol habit."

"You really have done your homework, haven't you?"

"Yes."

"What do the police say?"

"Nothing yet. I want my evidence so watertight that they'll be forced to reopen the case whether they like it or not." I paused. "I'll need you and Sharon to admit you were the couple I followed into Graham Road that night," I told him.

He shrugged. "That won't worry me. It might worry her, though."

"Why?"

"She lied at the inquest. She didn't get to the William of Orange till 9:15. We usually met up about half-eight, had a quick drink, then cut down the alleyway at the back of her house, but she was dropped off by a taxi that night, high as a kite, and totally uninterested in making any more money. So I walked her along the A316 and split away from her when we turned into Graham Road." He went on before I could ask the obvious question. "She said she'd been at a hotel with another client. I assume it was true because she was dressed up like a dog's dinner and stank of fags." He gave a small shake of his head as he recalled the memory. "She certainly didn't give the impression that she'd come from her house. Rather the reverse, in fact. Kept saying she wanted to get back to it because she was sick as a dog from all the champagne she'd drunk."

"But if Tuesday was *your* day, why would she go with somebody else?"

"She was a pro," he said sarcastically. "Someone else offered her more money."

"Did she say who it was?"

"She didn't give me a name . . . just said it was another regular whom she couldn't afford to disappoint."

"Geoffrey Spalding was one of her clients," I said slowly. "His wife was dying of breast cancer and he didn't want her or his daughters to know he was paying for sex. He took Sharon to a hotel once a month." I laughed at his expression. "No, it wasn't Libby who told me. It was Sharon's son, Michael. I've been writing to him in prison."

"Jesus! Rather you than me then," he said dryly. "He was a right little sadist when I knew him . . . used to pluck the whiskers out of Annie's cats just for the fun of it. Do you know why he's in prison?" I nodded. "Then you ought to be careful. His mother was shit-scared of him. And with reason. He had a real temper when he was roused."

I watched the cat lick itself drowsily in the afternoon sun. "You know the one thing that's always puzzled me, Jock . . . why neither you nor Sharon stopped to find out if Annie was alive. You must have seen her. Sharon virtually had to step over her to cross the road."

"We truly didn't," he said. "I asked Sharon about it afterward and she went white as a sheet . . . kept begging me to keep my mouth shut in case we got accused of being involved in some way."

There seemed little else to say, but I couldn't find the energy to rise from the chair. The journey home held few attractions and, like the cat, I wanted nothing better than to curl into a ball and forget that life was complicated. Perhaps Jock felt the same because the shadows lengthened noticeably before he spoke again.

"You've changed," he said finally.

"Yes," I agreed.

He smiled. "Aren't you going to ask me how?"

"There's no point." I leaned my head against the back of the chair and stared at the ceiling. "I know what you're going to say."

"What?"

"I'm more relaxed than I used to be."

"How did you know?"

"It's what Sam always says."

"You used to get pretty hyped-up in the old days," he said. "I remember going into your house one day and having to duck a flying saucepan."

I turned my head to look at him, laughing at the memory. "Only because you and Sam came home plastered at some god-awful hour in the morning and got me out of bed with the row you were making downstairs. The minute you saw me you started demanding food, so I tossed the saucepan in your direction and told you to cook it yourselves. You were supposed to catch it, not duck it."

"Is that right?" he asked dryly. "Then how come most of the crockery ended up on the floor as well?"

I thought back. "I was hopping mad, particularly as we had a school inspection the next day. In any case, I never liked those plates. Sam's mother gave them to us."

He grinned at me. "We were so damn legless we probably thought you'd be thrilled to see us. And at least we never did it again. As Sam said, you'd probably start hurling knives the next time."

We exchanged smiles. "I never did find out where you'd been," I murmured lazily. "You swore it was the pub, but it can't have been because pubs closed at 11."

There was the smallest of hesitations before he answered. "A strip club in Soho," he said. "Sam didn't think you'd approve."

I gave a noncommittal shrug. "Was the pretty little secretary with you?" I asked. "It was October-time, so she must have been around."

He shook his head. "Sam wouldn't take a woman to a strip club."

I leaned forward to tuck the photographs of Annie into my rucksack. "Did you ever meet her, Jock?"

"No," he admitted.

"So you've only Sam's word that she existed?"

There was real surprise in his voice when he answered. "Of course she existed! You can't hate someone who isn't real. He told me that night that strangling was too good for her, and trust me . . . I was *there. . . . I heard* him. He meant every word. That's why I took him to the club in the first place . . . to try to get his mind on to something else. He was terrified she was going to come to you with the sordid details . . . either that or blackmail him. I'd just about persuaded him to come clean and tell you about it"—he gave a dispirited sigh—"then we walk through the door and you start throwing bloody saucepans at us."

I smiled at his innocence, thinking it was no wonder Sam loved him as a guru. Pupils always preferred a teacher they could manipulate. "Sorry," I said without contrition, "but if it's any consolation there's no way he was going to own up to it. I'm not questioning the affair, Jock, only the conveniently streetwise secretary. He invented her for your sake. He's always been useless at keeping secrets and you were bound to get suspicious if he started saying he was too busy to have a drink with you. I think you'll find he was performing closer to home."

He rubbed his head ferociously. "I don't understand."

"Oh, come on, it's not that hard to work out." I started gathering my bits and pieces together. "What do you think Libby was doing the night Annie died? Darning your socks?"

He wouldn't accept it. "She can't have been with Sam," he said. "Hell, I'd have known if she'd been out. She had my supper waiting, and all the laundry done, for Christ's sake."

"There was a perfectly good bed in your house," I murmured. "What makes you think they didn't use that?"

He stared at me with a look of bewildered hurt on his face, and I was reminded of my own devastation as I listened to Sam's drunken ramblings that night in Hong Kong. *It's your fault we're here. . . . If you hadn't left me in the lurch none of this would have happened. . . . Women are crooked. . . . They do one thing and say another. . . . Why the hell did you have to ask people what they were doing that night? Did you expect them to be honest?*

"I could have walked in at any moment," protested Jock, clutching at straws.

"It was a Tuesday," I said, "and you never got home before 10 on a Tuesday."

"But . . ." His bewilderment increased. "Was anything Sam told me true?"

"I think it was true that it started during the two weeks I was away. I remember him telling me over the phone that Libby had offered to do his washing for him, but when I asked him later if he'd taken her up on it he became incredibly tetchy and said he hadn't seen her. At the time I thought he was cross because she'd let him down, but now I think he was just frightened of giving too much away . . ."

I watched resentment steal into Jock's face like a thief, and was surprised at how hollow my little victory felt.

"I think it's also true that he wanted to end it," I went on, "and was terrified of making an enemy of her. Personally, I doubt Libby would ever have confessed to it herself—she didn't want to give you ammunition for a divorce—but Sam certainly believed she would." I smiled slightly. "The irony is, I suspect he was far more worried about you finding out than he was about me. He says your friendship is important to him."

"He's a bloody hypocrite."

I didn't disagree. "Why do you care?" I asked. "As you said yourself it was dead and buried years ago."

But Jock didn't want to be reminded of his own mealymouthed platitudes. "He got me to lie for him."

"You were happy to do it," I pointed out.

"I might have felt differently if I'd known he was with Libby."

I lifted a shoulder in a half-shrug. "Who's the hypocrite now?"

He turned away, pulling a handkerchief from his pocket.

"In any case," I went on, "I'm betting it was Libby who pushed him into it. The police were asking everyone in the street if they'd seen or heard anything at the time of the accident, and I think she was afraid someone would say they'd spotted Sam leaving your house around nine o'clock. It was safer all 'round if he could deny it and say he was with you at our place."

The steps from bewilderment to hate were short and ugly and could be measured in their passage across his face. I had taken those steps myself and recognized the signs. Yet the object of his hatred was not the man who'd betrayed him, but the woman. "She loved making a fool of me, you know. She's probably been wetting herself for years knowing I was the one who covered their tracks."

I shook my head. "You shouldn't dwell on it. If Sam had been anything more to Libby than a stopgap lover, you'd have been out on your ear and he and I wouldn't still be married."

"I was out anyway," he said angrily. "I never had a chance."

"You had the same chances I did," I said coolly. "If either of us had known what was going on, then both our marriages would have ended in divorce. Because we didn't, yours held together a little longer and mine survived. But yours was on the rocks already, Jock, and you can't blame Sam for that. He was a symptom, not a cause."

He began a rambling defense of his own part in that long-dead relationship. Did I have any idea what it was like to be rejected by someone I loved? Why would he have taken up with Sharon if Libby had shown the slightest bit of interest in him? What did I think it did to a man's self-esteem to have to pay for sex? Of course he hadn't told Sam about her. No man in his right mind would want his friends laughing at him behind his back. . . .

Listening to him expose his heartache in that room stuffed with hidden secrets, I was more amused than sympathetic. Was he so blind to his own duplicity that double standards held no embarrassment for him? And why did he think he could trust me with his pain, when mine was older, more monstrous and a great deal crueller? Like Sam, he saw himself more sinned against than sinning, and, like Sam, his belligerence grew as his own guilt paled before the guilt of others.

When he finally ran out of steam, I stood up and pulled on my rucksack. "I wouldn't waste any more time on it if I were you," I said kindly. "It won't change anything, just make you angry."

"If that's what you wanted you should have left me in ignorance." He watched morosely as I checked to see I'd left nothing behind. "Why didn't you?"

"I didn't think it was fair."

He gave a mirthless laugh. "Well, maybe I don't put such a high price on fairness as you do. Did you think about that? Sam and I go back a long way. Maybe I'd have been happier not knowing."

I was sure he was right. It was truly said that what you don't know can't hurt you, and Sam and he could have gone on forever, the one lying about his stalwart support of his friend, the other lying about his success. It was also truly said that misery loves company and I laid a quiet bet with myself that Jock—a man not given to suffering in silence—would pick up the telephone after I left and offload some of his misery onto my husband.

It seemed eminently fair to me—justice demands a penalty—but whether they would ever speak again was questionable. I wasn't troubled by it. I had waited a very long time for my pound of flesh.

CURRAN HOUSE
Whitehay Road
Torquay
Devon

Friday

Dearest M,

I can't help feeling Libby is right, and you should rethink these visits on Monday, particularly the one to Alan's house. I know Danny's told you Alan won't be there—but do at least consider how he's likely to react when his wife tells him you've taken photographs of what's there. Are you sure it wouldn't be more sensible to involve the police? I know I don't need to remind you of what Alan and his father did to you—it distresses me to see you washing your hands all the time—but I'm not as confident as you that just because Alan's brother doesn't seem to know about his past, his wife won't either.

Love,

Dad

X X X

eighteen

My last port of call that day was a small 1930s semi in Isleworth with pebble-dashed walls and lattice-style windows. It was too far to walk so I took a taxi from Richmond station and asked the driver to wait in case there was no one at home or the occupants refused to speak to me. I heard a dog bark as I rang the bell, then the door was flung open by a small curly haired boy, and a Great Dane came bounding out to circle 'round me, growling. "Mu-mmy!" the child screamed. "Satan's going to bite a lady. Mu-mmy!"

A plump blonde in a baggy T-shirt and leggings appeared behind him and sent the dog back inside with a click of her fingers. "Don't worry," she said comfortably. "His bark's worse than his bite."

I smiled weakly. "How do you know?"

"I'm sorry?"

"How many people has he bitten?"

"Oh, I see!" She giggled. "None. *Yet* . . . No, I'm joking. Actually, he's a big a softy. Mind you"—she ruffled her son's hair—"how many times do I have to tell you not to open the door, Jason? Not everyone's as easy 'round dogs as this lady and if Satan did bite someone we'd have the police here in no time flat." She turned him 'round and steered him toward a door to her right. "Go and watch Tansy for me. I don't want her sticking her fingers in the sockets again." The corners of her mouth lifted in a questioning smile. "So what can I do for you? If you're a Je-

234

hovah's Witness you'll be wasting your time. That's why Satan's called Satan . . . to scare off the God squad."

She was like a gust of fresh air after the watchful suspicion of Maureen Slater, and I wasn't remotely surprised that Danny preferred her company to his mother's. "That would be Alan," I said.

"That's right."

"And you're Beth?"

She nodded.

"Alan knew me as Mrs. Ranelagh," I said, holding out my hand. "My husband and I used to live down the other end of Graham Road from his parents when he was a child. I was one of his teachers."

She looked surprised as she returned my handshake. "Are you the lady Danny was on about? He phoned a couple of nights ago and said he'd met someone who used to teach Al."

"Yes."

She glanced past me toward the taxi. "He said you were in Dorset."

"We're renting a farmhouse there for the summer. It's about ten miles from where Danny's staying. I'm in London today because there were some people I needed to see"—I didn't think she'd accept that I'd dropped in on a whim—"one of whom was Alan."

A look of uncertainty crossed her face. "He went really quiet when Danny mentioned your name . . . almost like you were Jack the Ripper or something."

"Did he?" I asked in surprise. "He always told me I was his favorite teacher. I wouldn't have dreamed of dropping in otherwise."

She looked embarrassed. "He's not here. He's working on a site out Chertsey way." A frown developed. "I'm surprised Danny didn't tell you. It's one of these executive-type estates . . . you know, houses with fancy stonework and porches on pillars—and he's been pestering Al for weeks to put his name up for the decorative bits. They're behind with the contract so my poor old boy's working overtime. . . . most evenings he doesn't get back till 'round 10." The frown deepened. "Anyway, how come you *needed* to see him? Most of his teachers were glad to be shot of him."

"Me, too," I said honestly. "Most of the time he couldn't be bothered to turn up, and when he did he was so disruptive that I wished he hadn't." I smiled to take the sting from my words. "Then I'd take a deep breath, remind myself of what his father was like, and try again. I couldn't bear to think he'd end up like Derek. And he obviously hasn't if everything Danny's told me about you and the children is true."

Curiosity won out, as I hoped it would, because my excuse for being there wasn't enough to persuade her to invite me in. "I never met his dad," she said, a gleam of interest sparkling in her eyes. "He was long gone before I met Al, but everyone says he was a bastard. Did you know him well?"

"Oh, yes. He threatened to rearrange my face once, so I tried to have him arrested." I turned irresolutely toward the taxi. "I asked the driver to wait in case you weren't at home, but I think he's left the clock running."

"Fuck that for a load of bananas," she said cheerfully. "They're all rip-off merchants . . . charge you an arm 'n' a bloody leg just to look you. Excuse my French. How about I give you a cup of tea and we'll call for a minicab later? If you're lucky, Al might get home early for once. I mean, it's not every day one of his teachers turns up"—she canted her head to one side—"though you don't look much like any of the old bats who taught me, and that's a fact."

With a grateful smile for the offer of tea and the compliment—and a silent, earnest prayer that *nothing* would induce Alan to come home early—I paid off the cab and followed her inside. As I might have predicted, the interior was a reflection of Beth's down-to-earth character. Colors were simple and direct—terra-cotta and straw being her obvious favorites. Floor coverings were practical—sanded floorboards in the hall and cork in the kitchen—and all her furniture was arranged to maximize space and minimize accidents for her children. It worked, and it was attractive, and when I told her so she was pleased but not surprised.

"It's what I want to do when the kids are both at school," she said, "take over someone's house and make it nice for them. I reckon I've got a talent for it, and it seems a shame to work in a factory if I can make money out of something I enjoy. I do it all myself—Al's too tired to be sanding floors when he gets home—and most of my mates go green when they come visiting. Half of them think women aren't made for this kind of caper, and the other half say they'd be too embarrassed to go to the hire shop for tools like sanding machines and wallpaper strippers because they wouldn't know what to ask for."

I skirted cautiously around the Great Dane, which had stretched itself full length on a fluffy rug in front of the cooker. "What did you do before you married Alan?" I asked, pulling out a kitchen chair and straddling it. The dog raised its head with a hostile look in its eyes, then, at a click from his mistress's fingers, yawned and went back to sleep.

"I was a hairdresser," Beth said with a laugh, "and I hated every minute of it. I was supposed to be a stylist but the only styling I ever did was blue rinses for miserable old women who had nothing better to do with their time than whinge about their husbands. And it didn't seem to make much difference whether the poor old bastards were dead or alive, they still got the treatment. Yackety . . . yackety . . . yack. He's mean. . . . He's stupid. . . . He dribbles on the toilet seat. . . . *Honestly!* It didn't half put me off getting old."

I laughed. "It sounds like my mother."

"Is she like that?"

"A bit."

"I never knew my mum," said Beth, pushing an armful of bangles up to her elbow as she carried the kettle to the sink and turned on the water. "Not the biological one anyway. She put me up for adoption when I was a baby. My adoptive mum's great . . . so is my dad . . . they love Al and they love the kids. They asked me once if I wanted to go looking for my real mum, and I said no chance. I mean, there's no guarantee I'm going to like her—half the people I know can't stand their parents . . . so why waste time looking for her?"

I didn't say anything.

"You think I'm wrong?"

"Not at all," I said with a smile. "I was thinking what a levelheaded woman you are and how lucky Alan is to have married you." I was also thinking of something that an educational psychologist had once written about Alan. . . . *He should be encouraged to form strong and positive bonds with adults. . . . He needs to feel valued. . . .* "You've obviously been good for Danny as well. . . . He certainly talks about you very fondly." It was sincerely meant and her cheeks flushed pink with pleasure. "What about their sisters?" I asked. "Do you see much of them?"

This must have been a thornier subject because her frown promptly returned. "The last time we saw them was at Tansy's christening and that's three years ago now. Al said we'd give it one more try, so we invited them, and they promptly lammed into me and Al as per usual . . . ruined poor little Tan's party . . . and we thought, to hell with it, life's too short for this kind of aggro." She swept some breadcrumbs from the table into her cupped hand and I watched in fascination as the bangles rattled down to her wrist. "Al says it's jealousy because we're doing okay and they're not—one of them's got four kids and no bloke because he buggered off when she fell pregnant the last time—the other's got five kids by different dads and two of them are in care."

"Where do they live?"

"A big estate near Heathrow."

"Together?"

"Neighboring blocks. The kids run around in a gang and terrorize the old people living there. I hate to think how many police cautions they've had. Someone told me the other day that the council's planning to take out injunctions to force Sally and Pauline to keep them inside . . . but I don't know if it's true. The worst thing is, they've been trying to get on the housing list here and I said to Al we'd have to move if it happened because there's no way I'm going to let Jason and Tansy get sucked into trouble by their cousins." She poured the tea and, like her mother-in-law, added milk automatically. "Al says it's not really his sisters' fault," she went on, passing me a cup, "not when you look at the kind of upbringing they had, but as I keep telling him, if that's true then he and Danny should be as bad."

She reminded me of Julia Charles, our neighbor in Graham Road, who had agonized in the same way about the terrible influence Alan Slater and Michael Percy would have on her children if she ever let them play in the street. They're such awful boys, she used to say, and it's not as though it's a "class" thing, or not really. It's their parents who're to blame. If their mothers spent more time with the kids and less time on their backs or on the bottle, then the kids would be better behaved. Everyone knew that.

"It sounds as if they've reversed their roles," I said slowly. "The two girls always seemed quite sensible when they were children. Either that or they were too terrified of their father to put a foot wrong. They used to follow in Alan's wake sometimes, but never further than the end of the road. They were both small and dark like their mother and Sally's the older of the two?" She nodded. "They were friendly with two other little girls of about the same age—Rosie and Bridget Spalding—and used to play hopscotch on the pavement. Bridget married Alan's friend, Michael Percy, and moved down to Bournemouth, but I've no idea what happened to Rosie." I raised a questioning eyebrow but Beth shook her head as she perched on the edge of a worktop and cradled her cup between her hands.

"Al hasn't kept up with anyone from Graham Road," she said. "He goes to see his mother once in a while, but never for very long because it makes him so depressed. Left to himself, he wouldn't go at all . . . but I keep saying, he has to set a good example to Jace and Tan . . . I mean, I'd die if they never came to see me after they were grown." She had pale lashes and pale eyebrows, which gave her face a bland look until she screwed one of her many expressions onto it. Now she made a grimace of irritation. "She doesn't make it easy, though. All she ever does is complain about how lonely she is and how miserable she is. It's a vicious circle. If she put herself out to be pleasant, he'd probably drop in more often. . . . Instead, he delays as long as he can, then goes out of guilt."

"Do you and the children visit her?"

More grimacing. "We did till Jason found her Prozac and ended up in the hospital. I was that mad with her. It's not as though she needs the stupid things. . . . Half the time she doesn't take them. . . . It's just a way of getting invalidity benefit so she can sit at home and watch the telly all day. I wouldn't mind so much if I hadn't asked her to keep them out of harm's way, but it's like talking to a brick wall. She smokes and drinks around Jace and Tan, takes no notice of what I might feel about it, then has the nerve to tell me she doesn't know what the fuss is about. 'It didn't do *my* kids any harm,' she says."

I laughed. "I used to get it about disposable nappies. I made the mistake of telling my mother what they cost and she lectured me for months about how I was wasting my money. 'What's wrong with terry toweling?' she kept saying. . . . 'If it was good enough for you, then it's good enough for your boys.'"

She sipped at her tea. "You don't like her much, do you?"

The directness of the question took me aback, if only because it was something I never asked myself. "Rather more than you like Maureen, I suspect."

"Yes, but Maureen's not my mum," she said despondently. "It doesn't half worry me. I don't like falling out with people, but the way Alan's lot behave we won't be talking to any of them soon. I have nightmares sometimes that it's in the genes, and that my kids'll storm off after a huge row, and me and Al will never see them again."

"I'm sure that won't happen," I consoled her. "If behavior was inherited my two would have upped stumps and left long ago. But they're so laid-back it'll take a stick of dynamite to shift them. Either that or a stunning blonde with a Ferrari."

She eyed me thoughtfully. "Maybe they got their genes from their father," she suggested.

More likely their grandfather, I thought, while thinking it was hardly a good time to remind Beth of the genetic link between her children and Derek. "Except I agree with Alan that upbringing has more to do with it," I answered. "Jason and Tansy are the sum of their genes and experiences, not the sum of their genes alone, otherwise they'd be virtually indistinguishable from each other. You made the point yourself when you said how different Alan and Danny are from their sisters." *And how different Alan seemed now from the boy I once knew,* I thought wryly.

"They're also very different from each other," she said. "Danny's a bit of a goer, but Al behaves like he was born middle-aged." She giggled and her face lit up immediately. "Jace said 'fuck' the other day because he heard it at nursery school and Al spent the next two hours worrying about whether it was his fault. I said, 'Don't be so fucking stupid. . . .' Excuse my French. . . . And he said, 'It's all very well for you to laugh but the only time my dad showed me any attention was when he said, "Fuck off, bastard."' And now he's hoping he *is* a bastard and Derek isn't his dad."

"I'd probably feel the same in his shoes," I said. "It's a bit like owning up to having Ivan the Terrible for a father."

She was agog with curiosity. "You said he threatened you. Why? What happened to make him angry?"

I was tempted to be honest, and not just because I liked her and felt guilty about using her. She was one of those rare people, irrespective of age, sex or background, whose straightforward, open personality demanded, and deserved, a reciprocal trust. Indeed, if I had any sadness at deceiving her, it was because I knew that in different circumstances I would be only too pleased to have her as an ally.

"We had a row in the street about the way he was treating Alan and he pushed my arm up behind my back and said if I ever interfered again he'd wipe the smile off my face." *It's not a complete lie,* I thought. The place was wrong, and the threat—which had nothing to do with my smile—was inflicted anyway, but Derek had certainly told me never to interfere again. "So I did what any sensible person would do and reported him to the police," I told her, "but they didn't believe me and repeated what I'd said to Derek."

If I were telling it as it really was, I would have added that I was betrayed twice in as many days by the same policeman and reaped a double dose of Derek's anger in consequence. But I wanted to woo Beth with amused indifference, not frighten her off with evidence of her father-in-law's savagery.

Her eyes widened. "What did he do?"

"Nothing much," I lied. "He was a typical bully—bluster on the outside and blancmange inside." I paused. "Danny told me he disappeared after Alan gave him a thrashing with a baseball bat?" I put an upward inflection into my voice, and Beth nodded. "So where did he go? Does anyone know?"

"Al doesn't talk about him much, except to say he doesn't want him anywhere near our kids. I know he went to prison because Sally got his address off a con who'd done time with him. It was before Tan's christening and she kept pestering us to invite him. She said he was back in London and wanted to meet up with his family again"—she shrugged— "but Al said if he showed his face here he'd get another thrashing, and that's what caused most of the aggro at the party. Sally and Pauline said Derek was skint and needed help, and Al said he could die of starvation before he'd lift a finger for him."

"Weren't you worried he'd come anyway?"

She glanced at the dog. "That's why Al got Satan. He wanted a Rottweiler but I said it'd be too dangerous with kids. Mind, I thought it was money down the drain at the time." She flexed the muscles in her right arm. "I reckon I'd be able to deal with Derek . . . no trouble . . . if he dared push his way in here, but Satan's sort of grown on us and I wouldn't be without him now."

I wanted to warn her against complacency, but instead I murmured, "Still . . . it's not surprising Alan was worried, particularly if Derek was close."

"Not *that* close. Sally said he was shacked up with some bird out Whitechapel way."

"He was lucky to find someone."

"Too right. I said the bird needed her bloody head examined—unless, of course, he hadn't bothered to tell her he was a wife-beater—and Sally got miffed and said I shouldn't spread rumors about people I'd never met. So I said, 'I'll remind you of that when he clobbers this one.'"

I smiled. "What did Maureen say?"

Beth grinned back. "Said it was a pity Derek hadn't died of drink years ago and that the two girls deserved everything they got if they let him swan back into their lives just because he was family. She got well worked up, said he'd done his best to ruin their lives when they were children and if they had any sense they'd keep well away from him now."

"Better late than never, I suppose," I said dryly. "She didn't do much to protect them when they were living with him."

A thoughtful expression creased Beth's forehead and I wondered if I'd displayed my prejudice a little too blatantly. "Except I reckon she was just as bad. It was her who bought the baseball bat, you know . . . not to use against Derek . . . but to beat her kids about the head whenever they annoyed her."

"How do you know?"

"Danny was teasing Al one day about being slow on the uptake. He said it was because his mum had addled his brains with the bat."

"Was she strong enough?" I asked doubtfully.

"According to Danny she was. He said she was like a wild animal when she was in a temper, and you either scarpered or locked yourself in the toilet till she calmed down." She watched my frown of disbelief and gave a small shrug. "I couldn't swear on oath that it's true—Danny's always telling fibs—but it was pretty convincing at the time. Let's put it this way, Al didn't deny it—just told me never to lift a finger against Jace and Tan or I'd be answering to him. So I said, 'You've gotta be joking! Since when have I ever raised my hand in anger to anyone?'" She grinned suddenly. "And I told him straight, it's fucking rich coming from a bloke who calls his dog Satan and reckons the only way to discipline him is to take a rolled-up newspaper to his backside." She blew an air kiss toward the animal, which raised its head immediately and thumped its tail on the floor. "I mean, what kind of way is that to train a dog when he'll do anything as long as you give him a biscuit?"

Satan and I examined each other cautiously. "He's a good guard dog," I murmured. "I wouldn't fancy my chances much if I were Derek."

"He'd rip his throat out soon as look at him," said Beth. "I used to tie Satan to the pram outside shops when the kids were smaller. He growled at anyone who came closer than six yards, which meant I could do my shopping in peace without worrying about someone stealing my babies."

"Amazing! And he does all that for a biscuit?"

Her grin broadened. "Don't knock it," she said. "It's a damn sight more effective than beating the poor brute with a newspaper. That just made him vicious."

"Mm." Ripping throats out seemed fairly vicious to me, and I wondered how he'd react if I stood up unexpectedly. I glanced at my watch. "I really ought to be going," I said, putting reluctance into my voice. "It's a long journey back to Dorchester and Sam will be wondering where I am."

"Al'll be sorry to have missed you."

I nodded. "It's a shame. I'll phone first another time." I finished my tea and stood up. "Can I say good-bye to the children?"

"You surely can. They're in the sitting room. I'd be interested what you think of it." She pointed to the floor as a growl rose in Satan's throat and he subsided immediately.

"So when does he get the biscuit?" I asked, following her into the hall.

"When I feel like it. That's why he does what I tell him. He's never too sure when the moment will come."

"Does it work with husbands and children as well?"

She flattened her palm and made a rocking gesture. "It depends what the treat is. Biscuits don't work so well on Al. He likes basques and black stockings better." She grinned as I gave a splutter of laughter. "The kids are in here," she said, opening a door. "You'd better like it because it took me two months to finish. I'll phone for a cab while you're looking."

I did like it, although it was totally out of keeping with a 1930s semi. It can't have been bigger than five meters square, but it was decorated in Mexican style with an arched ceiling, tessellated floor, roughly stuccoed walls and an ornate bronze candelabra hanging from the ceiling. French windows opened out onto a tiny patio, and a huge rococo mirror, with a myriad of tilted facets in a scrolled gilt frame, reflected the light in indiscriminate dazzling shafts across every available surface. Even the fireplace had been transformed into something that would have been more at home on a ranch than in a back street in Isleworth, with a brass artillery shell laden with silk flowers standing in the hearth. I wondered why she'd done this room so differently from the rest.

"It's all fake," said Jason from the corner where he and his sister were watching television. "Mum just painted it to make it look real."

I tapped my foot on the tessellated floor and listened to the hollow ring of wood. "She's a clever lady," I said, touching a hand to the rough stucco and feeling the smoothness of plaster. "Did she make the mirror as well?"

"Yup. And the candy-laber."

"What about the picture?" I asked, gazing at the Quetzalcoatl mosaic on the wall.

"That's Dad's."

"The sofa and chairs?"

"Ten quid, job lot, from a junk shop," said Beth proudly behind me. "And five quid for the patchwork throws. I begged, borrowed and stole material . . . dresses . . . old curtains . . . tablecloths . . . whatever . . . from everyone I knew. The five quid went on the reels of cotton to do the sewing. What do you think?"

"Brilliant," I said honestly.

"But a bit OTT for Isleworth?"

"A bit," I agreed.

"That's what Al thinks, but all I'm doing is setting out my stall. I can create any image you want, and I can do it for peanuts. This whole room cost under three hundred quid. Okay, it doesn't count my time, but you wouldn't believe how many of my friends say they'd pay me a tenner an hour to do it in their houses."

"I bet they would," I said dryly. "They're probably paying their cleaners as much just to Hoover their floors."

She looked crestfallen. "Al doesn't want me to do it at all, says he won't even think about it unless I ask a hundred per hour minimum."

"He's right."

"Except none of my friends can pay a hundred quid per hour."

I gave her hand a quick squeeze. "It's a bad mistake to work for friends," I said. "You should photograph each room and put a portfolio together, then go out and sell yourself. . . . Get some fliers printed . . . Take out ads in the local newspaper. You're way too good to work for £10 an hour." I patted my rucksack. "If you like, I'll take some photographs now and send them to you. I've got my camera with me, and I'd love my husband to see what you've done. We're toying with buying the farmhouse we're renting, and you never know"—*How can you be such a bitch?* I asked myself—"maybe I can persuade Sam that you're the interior decorator we need."

Her face flushed pink with pleasure again. "If you're sure."

"Of course I'm sure." I squatted down beside Jason and Tansy. "Would you two like to be in the pictures?" They nodded solemnly. "Then how about we turn off the telly and you sit on Mum's sofa, one at each end? It might be better if you stood behind me," I told Beth as I sat cross-legged in front of the windows and lined up the shot. "You're blocking the mirror."

She scurried onto the patio. "I hate having my picture taken. I always look so fat."

"It depends how they're done," I said, as I snapped off half a dozen shots of the sofa-side of the room before zooming in on the Quetzl-coatl. "Why don't you sit on one of the chairs with the kids on your lap, and I'll see if I can get a view of the fireplace with the three of you to the left?"

I should have choked on my own duplicity, instead I marveled at how easy it was to cajole her into letting me make a record of every-thing in the room, including the bangles on her wrist and a collection of small china cats at one end of the mantelpiece. "Who's the cat lover?" I asked, as I tucked my camera back into my rucksack, when the doorbell rang to announce the arrival of the minicab.

"Al. He bought them at a jumble sale years ago." She jumped the children off her lap and stood up. "You never said why you needed to see him," she reminded me, as we went back into the hall.

"I wanted to talk to him about Michael Percy," I lied, dredging up the only excuse I'd been able to come up with. "But you've already told me they lost touch"—I gave a rueful shrug—"so he wouldn't have been able to help me anyway."

"What did you want to talk about?"

"Whether Michael's as bad as he was painted in the newspapers," I said, pulling open the front door and nodding to the cab driver to say I was coming. "I'm thinking of visiting him in prison—he's just down the road from us on Portland—but I'm not sure if it's a sensible thing to do. I rather hoped Alan could give me some advice."

It sounded so weak to my ears that I expected suspicion to bristle out of her like hackles, but she seemed to find it reasonable. "Well, if it's any help, Al said it was well out of character for him to hit that woman. He reckons Michael was a lot less violent than he was when they used to hang out together. They had a fight before they fell out, and Al said Michael took a beating because he wouldn't defend him-self."

"What were they fighting about?"

"That girl you mentioned—Bridget. It was when they were in their late teens. Al was so crazy about her he wanted to marry her, then he walked in one day and found her in bed with Michael. He went berserk . . . broke Michael's jaw and God knows what else . . . even attacked the policemen who arrived to break it up. It was mayhem, apparently. Bridget was screaming in the hall, Michael was half out the window and it took four policemen to get Al off him. He ended up in juvenile detention for it."

"Goodness!"

"He's been straight ever since," she assured me.

"I should hope so."

Beth laughed. "It all worked out for the best. He wouldn't be married to me if he'd stuck with her." A wistful note entered her voice. "But he's never broken anyone's jaw for me . . . so I guess I'm not as attractive as Bridget."

I gave her an impulsive hug before heading for the cab. "Just don't test him," I warned over my shoulder. "I have a nasty feeling he'd break more than jaws if he found you in bed with someone else."

I spoke lightly, but the warning was sincere.

Letter from Dr. Joseph Elias, psychiatrist
at the Queen Victoria Hospital, Hong Kong—dated 1985

QUEEN VICTORIA HOSPITAL

Hong Kong

Dept. of Psychiatry

Mrs. M. Ranelagh
12 Greenhough Lane,
Pokfulam

June 12, 1985

Dear Mrs. Ranelagh,

I am sad to hear you're leaving Hong Kong. I
have enjoyed your letters and those all-too-rare
occasions when you have consented to talk to me in
person! You will like Sydney. I spent two years
there from '72 to '74 and it was a delightful
experience. Australia has the enthusiasm and vigor
that comes from a mix of different cultures and I'm
confident you will enjoy a polygeny where class
divides are nonexistent and success depends on
merit and not labels. You see, I have come to
understand you.

You mentioned in your last letter that you and
Sam have reached a fine understanding where the past
remains buried in England. You also tell me he's an
excellent father. You do not, however, say you love
him. Am I supposed (like Sam?) to take that for
granted? My friend the rabbi would say that nothing
thrives in a desert. He would also say that

whatever lies buried in England will resurface the minute you go home. But perhaps that's the plan? If so, you are a patient woman, my dear, and a little cruel, too, I think.

With best wishes for your future wherever it may be.

Yours affectionately,

J. Elias

Dr. J. Elias

nineteen

Sam was sitting in the car outside Dorchester South station when I finally reached it at ten o'clock that evening. I wondered how long he'd been waiting because I hadn't phoned to say which train I was catching, and I feared it couldn't have done his temper much good if he'd been there any length of time. My intention had been to take a taxi home and face the inevitable row behind closed doors but, if his bleak expression when he got out of the car at my approach was anything to go by, he planned to have it in public.

"Jock phoned," he said tersely.

"I thought he might," I murmured, opening the back door and dumping my rucksack on the seat.

"He told me you left him at about four o'clock. What the hell have you been doing? Why the hell didn't you phone? I've been worried sick."

I showed my surprise. "I said I'd make my own way home."

"I didn't even know if you were *coming* home." He stalked angrily round the bonnet to open the passenger door for me, but it was so out of character that I stepped back automatically, assuming he was opening it for himself. "I'm not going to hit you," he snapped, gripping me by the arm and pressing me clumsily into my seat. "I'm not a *complete* bastard."

He slid in behind the steering wheel and we sat for several minutes in silence. The tension in the confined space was palpable, although I had no idea if it was due to anger over my perfidy or concern at my late return. The station was virtually empty at that time of night, but one or two people peered curiously through our windows as they passed, presumably wondering why the two dimly seen occupants were sitting so stiffly and refusing to look at each other.

"Aren't you going to say anything?" he asked at last.

"Like what?"

"Explain?" he suggested. "I still can't believe you'd talk to Jock, and not to me. Why didn't you tell me Annie was beaten up? You know I'd have come clean if I'd realized how serious it all was."

"When?"

"What do you mean, when?"

"When would you have come clean?" I asked evenly. "I told you at the time what PC Quentin said about the bruising—but you just said we were talking bollocks. As I recall your comment was, 'Since when did a neurotic bitch and a disgruntled policeman know the first damn thing about pathology?' You could have told me the truth then and given me and Andrew Quentin a fighting chance against Drury . . . but you didn't."

He dropped his head into his hands. "I thought you were wrong," he muttered. "I was pretty stressed out at the time, and you didn't make it easy for me."

"Fine. Then you've nothing to feel guilty about. You were saving me from myself. No one's going to blame you for that." I looked impatiently at my watch. "Can we go now? I'm hungry."

"You're not making this very easy for me," he said. "You must know how awful I feel."

"Actually, I don't," I said honestly. "You've never felt awful before. That year, 1978, was one of those little unpleasantnesses—like where the cutlery drawer is and how to boil eggs—that you manage to erase so successfully from your memory. I've always envied you for it, and if you're troubled now it's probably just a reaction to knowing you've been rumbled. It'll pass. It usually does."

He tried a different tack. "The boys are twitched as hell," he said. "They keep asking me what I've done that's so bad you'd want to run away."

"Oh, for Christ's sake!" I said bluntly. "If you want to make me angry, then hiding behind your children is the surest way to do it. Luke and Tom know damn well I don't run away from things. They also know I wouldn't abandon them unless I was on a life-support machine somewhere. In any case, I told them I wouldn't be home until late so I imagine they're lying in front of the telly, as per normal, wondering why their father has suddenly gone 'round the bend."

"We had a row," he admitted. "I told them they were unfeeling bastards."

I didn't bother to comment because I wasn't in the mood to massage his bruised ego. "Look," I said, tapping my watch, "I haven't had anything to eat all day and I'm starving, so can we either go home or get a takeaway? Have you and the boys eaten?"

"Tom made some spag bol for him and Luke, but I wasn't hungry."

"Good, then we'll have a curry."

"Why didn't you eat on the train?"

"Because it was trolley service," I said crossly, "and the only thing left to eat by the time it reached me was a packet of dry biscuits. So I had some wine instead . . . and now I'm fighting mad and in no mood to play silly buggers with you or anyone else."

"I don't blame you," he began self-pityingly as he fired the engine. "I just wish there was something I could do or say—"

I cut him off. "Don't even think of apologizing," I said. "As far as I'm concerned you can grovel to me for the rest of your life. And it won't make a blind bit of difference. It'll make a difference to Jock, though. The sorrier you are the happier he'll be, and you'll be back in each other's pockets before you know it."

He mulled this over quietly as we turned on to the main road. "I've already apologized to Jock."

"I assumed you would."

"He calmed down pretty quickly as a matter of fact, once I'd explained what a mistake the whole damn thing had been."

"Okay."

"It didn't mean Jack shit, you know . . . just something that happened while you were away. The trouble is, Libby took it more seriously than I did. She and Jock weren't getting on too well at the time and it sort of ran out of control." He paused, inviting me to say something. When I didn't he went on, "Jock understands that. He's been there himself, knows what it's like to be caught between a rock and a hard place."

"Okay."

"Does that mean you understand?"

"Of course."

He flicked me an uneasy glance as he turned left at a pelican crossing. "You don't sound as if you do."

I sighed. "I'm your wife, Sam, and I've known you since I was twenty. If I don't understand you by now then I doubt I ever will."

"I didn't mean, do you understand *me*. I meant, do you understand how the thing with Libby happened? What a fucking disaster it was? How sorry I was afterward?"

I gave a small laugh. "The thing? Do you mean your *affair?* The time you rogered your best friend's wife because your own wife was away and you hadn't had sex for twenty-four hours?"

"It wasn't like that," he protested.

"Of course it wasn't," I agreed. "It was Libby's fault. She caught you at a low ebb, plied you with drink, then persuaded you into a quickie on the kitchen floor. Afterward, you found yourself in an impossible position. *You* regretted it intensely and hoped it was a one-off. *She* loved every minute of it and looked on it as the beginning of a great love affair." I watched him for a moment. "I should imagine Libby's version is a little different—*you* seduced *her* in other words—but the truth probably lies somewhere in the middle."

"I knew you'd be angry," he said unhappily. "That's why I never told you."

"Now you're flattering yourself," I said. "It's probably a huge disappointment but the only emotion I have ever experienced re you and Libby is indifference." Of course I was lying . . . but he *owed* me . . . *I* had honored my promises . . . and *he* hadn't. "If I'd been able to work up the energy to feel angry, I think you'd have realized something was wrong. Certainly Libby would, but then she's a woman and women are better at picking up vibes."

He pulled up in front of the Indian restaurant. "Wasn't it her who told you about us?"

"No. I suspect she's even more embarrassed than you are. We're hardly talking Abelard and Heloise in all conscience."

He clamped down on his anger. "Who then?"

"You." I smiled at his expression. "One night in Hong Kong. Not in so many words. . . . You weren't that drunk . . . but you said enough for me to put two and two together. It was quite a relief, actually. I remember thinking, *So that's what this has all been about—a grubby little affair with Libby Williams.* I even laughed about it afterward. I kept picturing you and her working up a sweat in Jock's bed while he was out getting blow jobs off the Graham Road tart. There was such a sweet irony about it—you being piggy in the middle of a couple of predators. It explained everything. Your unpleasantness . . . your lies . . . your dash to leave England. I even felt sorry for you in a funny kind of way because it seemed so obvious you'd sold your soul to the devil for something you hadn't enjoyed very much."

He shook his head in bewilderment. "Why didn't you say something?"

"I couldn't see the point. We were on the other side of the world. All I'd have been doing was closing the stable door after the horse had bolted."

Sam wasn't designed to remain humble for long. "Do you know what this feels like? It feels like I'm married to a stranger. I don't even know who you are anymore." He propped his elbows on the steering wheel and ground his knuckles into his eyes. "You always tell people what a great marriage we have . . . what great kids we have . . . what a great father I am. But it's all just crap . . . one huge pretense at happy families when the truth is you hate my guts. How could you *do* that? How could you be so bloody devious?"

I reached for the door handle. "The same way you did," I said lightly. "Closed my eyes to what a bastard you'd been and pretended none of it had ever happened."

He agonized over my indifference while we waited for the curry, almost as if I'd thrown doubt on his manhood by refusing to take his infidelity seriously. For myself, I was wondering when he was going to realize that the bone of contention was Annie, not Libby, and how he would explain that when he did. We took seats in a corner and he muttered away in an undertone, afraid of being overheard, although my refusal to lighten his burden with sympathetic comments meant his tone became increasingly—*and to my ears sweetly*—strident.

He didn't want me to get the wrong impression. . . . It wasn't true that he'd tried to pretend nothing had happened . . . more that he'd been terrified of losing me. . . . Of course he'd have admitted to it if I'd asked but it seemed more sensible to let sleeping dogs lie. . . . He knew I probably wouldn't believe him, but he *was* drunk the night Libby seduced him and the whole thing *did* turn into a total nightmare. . . . It was absolutely correct to describe Libby as a predator. . . . She was one of those women who thought the grass was always greener on the other side. . . . He remembered how shocked he'd been when he realized how jealous she was of me and how determined she was to bring me down to her size. . . .

"When I told her I wanted to end it, she said she was going to tell you what a rat you'd married," he said grimly. "I know it's not much of an excuse but I honestly think I'd have killed her if she'd actually done it. I loathed her so much by then I couldn't be in the same room with her without wanting to strangle her."

I believed him, not just because I wanted to but because he'd never been able to mention Libby's name without prefacing it with "that bitch Jock married." There was a brief period when I wondered if he said it out of regret because he, too, had been rejected but I soon realized that the antipathy was real and that Libby was as irrelevant to him as the women he'd slept with before we married. That's not to say I wouldn't have clawed his eyes out if I'd known about the affair at the time—objectivity needs time and distance to develop—but to come across it when the ashes were cold was a reason for private grief only, and not for a fanning of the embers.

"You don't need to do this," I said, glancing toward a nearby customer who had one ear cocked to everything he was saying. "Not unless you insist on washing your dirty linen in public. Libby's a dead issue as far as I'm concerned." I lifted one shoulder in a careless shrug. "I've always assumed that if you'd loved her you'd still be with her."

He brooded for a moment in offended silence, his gaze fixing abstractedly on the eavesdropper. "Then why tell Jock about it? Why get everyone worked up if it's all so unimportant to you?"

"Not all of it, Sam. Just Libby. I couldn't give a shit what you did to her . . . but I *do* give a shit what you did to Annie. You left her to die in the gutter then labeled her a drunk in case anyone accused you of neglect. That's the issue. And, as usual, you're busting a gut to avoid it." I paused. "I know you saw her there—and not just because Jock confirmed it this afternoon—but because you always get so angry every time her name's mentioned."

He wouldn't meet my eyes. "I thought she was drunk."

"What if she was? It was freezing cold and pouring with rain and she needed help, whatever state she was in."

"I wasn't the only one," he muttered. "Jock and that woman ignored her, too."

It was hardly an answer but I let it go. "They never got as close as you did," I said. "I was watching them."

"How do you know how close I got?"

"Jock said you told him Annie was reeking of drink, but I didn't smell anything until I stooped down to rock her shoulder." I watched him curiously for a moment. "And it wasn't drink I smelled either, it was urine, and I don't understand how you could mistake that for alcohol."

"I didn't. All I told Jock was that she reeked to high heaven. He assumed it was alcohol."

"Did you recognize it as urine?"

"Yes."

"Oh, my God!" I slammed my palms on to the table. "Do you know that every time I told Drury to question why her coat was reeking of piss he told me her neighbors said it was *normal* . . . that she was filthy and disgusting and *always* stank."

Abruptly he dropped his head into his hands. "I thought it was funny," he said wretchedly. "Your good cause for the year . . . Mad bloody Annie . . . wetting herself on your doorstep because she was too drunk to control her bladder. I went into the house and spent the next ten minutes laughing about it until I realized you were the most likely person to find her. Then I knew you'd bring her inside and clean her up and I thought, this is the day my marriage goes down the drain."

"Why?"

He breathed hard through his nose. "She knew about Libby—I think she must have seen us together at some point because she kept sneaking up behind me in the road and calling me 'dirty man.'" He forced out the words as if his life depended on it. "'Have you been fucking the tart today, dirty man.' 'Is that the tart I can smell on you, dirty man?' 'What do you want with trash, dirty man, when you've got a pretty lady at home?' I loathed her for it because I knew she was right and when I smelled her in the gutter"—he faltered painfully—"when I smelled her in the gutter, I kicked her and said, 'Who's dirty now?'"

I watched a tear drip through his fingers onto the table.

"And I've been in hell ever since because I so much wanted to take it back, and I've never been able to."

I watched a waiter come out of the kitchen and hold up a shopping bag to signal that our curry was ready, and I remember thinking that fate was all about timing. If I hadn't been at a parents' evening that night . . . if Jock had abandoned the pub at 8:30 when Sharon didn't show . . . if food didn't arrive at inopportune moments . . .

"Let's go home," I said.

Two days later, Maureen Slater phoned. She was angry and suspicious because Alan had told her I'd taken photographs of his house, and she demanded to know what my side of the trade was going to be. I repeated what I'd told her on Monday, that if she wasn't prepared to tell me what she knew, I would pass the Chiswick jeweler's affidavit to Richmond Police . . . and, for good measure, the shots of the Mexican artifacts in Alan's sitting room. "No one would doubt they were thieves," I said. The only question would be, were they murderers, too?

She told me some of what I wanted to know, but rather more interesting was what she chose to leave out.

Letter to Sergeant James Drury—dated 1999

Leavenham Farm

Leavenham

Nr Dorchester

Dorset DT2 XXY

4:30 A.M.—Friday, August 13, 1999

Dear Mr. Drury,

One of the downsides of finding Annie dying was that my sleep patterns were shot to pieces, and I count myself lucky now if I manage a four-hour stretch without waking. I've always hoped that an uneasy conscience has kept you similarly awake over the years, but I suspect it's misplaced optimism. To have a conscience at all means a man must question himself occasionally, and even in my wildest dreams I've never been able to picture you doing that.

I already know you will be absent when I leave this letter and enclosures at the Sailor's Rest, but it seems only fair you should have time to consider your response to the outstanding issue between us. I have, after all, had twenty years to consider mine.

Yours sincerely,

M. Ranelagh

twenty

Drury was watching for me when I came through the door of the Sailor's Rest at half past ten that evening. Being a Friday night in summer, the pub was crowded with holidaymakers and yachtsmen from the boats in the marina, and I felt a small satisfaction when I saw the flicker of apprehension in his eyes as I approached.

He came out from behind the bar before I could reach it. "We'll go through to the back," he said curtly, jerking his head toward a door in the corner. "I'm damned if I'll have this conversation in public."

"Why not?" I asked. "Are you afraid of witnesses?"

He made an angry movement as if to grab my arm and manhandle me in the direction he wanted me to go, but the curious glances of his other customers persuaded him to change his mind. "I don't want a scene," he muttered, "not in here and not on a Friday night. You said you wanted to be fair . . . so *be* fair. This is my livelihood, remember."

I smiled slightly. "You could have me arrested for making a nuisance of myself, then tell your customers I'm mad," I suggested. "That's what you did last time."

He resolved the problem by heading toward the door and leaving me to follow or not as I chose. I followed. The "back" was a scruffy office full of dusty filing cabinets and a gray metal desk, covered in used polystyrene coffee cups and piles of paper. It was a smaller, dirtier version of Jock's office and, as Drury motioned me toward the typist's chair in front of the desk and perched himself on a stack of boxes in the corner, I wondered why men always seemed more comfortable when surrounded by the trappings of "work."

He watched me closely, waiting for me to speak. "What do you want?" he demanded abruptly. "An apology?"

I dropped my rucksack to the floor and used the tip of my finger to push a half-filled cup of congealed coffee away from me. "What for?"

"Whatever you like," he said curtly, "just as long as it gets you off my back."

"There'd be no point. I wouldn't accept it."

"What then?"

"Justice," I said. "That's all I've ever been interested in."

"You won't get it . . . not this long afterward."

"For Annie or for myself?" I asked curiously.

He placed the flat of his hand on the opened brown envelope, which was sitting to one side of the desk. "Neither," he said confidently.

I wondered if he was aware of what he was saying because his words suggested he knew there was justice to be had. For Annie *and* me. "That envelope contains twenty-one years of patient research, showing Annie was murdered," I said lightly.

"And it's a bunch of crap." He leaned forward aggressively. "For every pathologist you produce, saying the bruises were inflicted hours before Annie's death, the Crown Prosecution Service will produce five who agree with the original postmortem finding. It's a budgeting exercise—always has been. Prosecutions are expensive and taxpayers get stroppy about funding failures. You're going to need a damn sight more than that to get the case reopened."

He was uncomfortably close and I sat back to get away from him, repelled by the energy that flowed out of him in waves. It was a far cry from twenty years ago when the same energy—authoritative, capable, comforting—had given me the confidence to talk more freely than I might otherwise have done. It's one of the great truisms that we only learn from our mistakes and, like Annie, I had since developed an abiding distrust of men in uniform.

"The climate's changed since the Stephen Lawrence inquiry," I said mildly. "I think you'll find the murder of a black woman will be at the top of the CPS's agenda, however long ago it happened . . . particularly when it's supported by evidence that the sergeant in charge of the case was a racist."

He pummeled and squeezed one fist inside the other, exploding the joints like tiny firecrackers. "A letter from a WPC claiming sexual and racial harassment, which wasn't upheld at the time?" he sneered. "That won't stand. And neither will Andy Quentin's log. The guy's dead, for Christ's sake, and he had an ax to grind because he blamed me for his career going nowhere."

"With reason," I said. "You never had a good word for him."

"He was a creep."

"Yes, well, he didn't have much time for you either." I opened the envelope and removed Andy's log of Drury's stop-and-search arrests of Afro-Caribbeans and Asians between 1987 and 1989, giving details of the derogatory language Drury had habitually used. "What difference does it make if he did have an ax to grind?" I asked curiously. "It's a straightforward account, which you're perfectly entitled to challenge if it contains errors."

"He hasn't logged the names of the whites I stopped and searched."

"He's given comparative figures. Your ratio of black to white was way higher than anyone else's in Richmond at the time." I shrugged. "But it's all on record so it's easily proved. If Andy's figures are wrong then you'll be vindicated. If they aren't, his conclusion that you used your stop-and-search powers as a form of racist sport will carry weight."

"Not true," he snapped. "I was doing my job like everyone else. You can twist figures to fit any conclusion you like. I can just as easily demonstrate that his motive in producing that list was vindictive. There was a known history between us."

"What about the seventeen-year-old Asian boy whose cheek you fractured?"

His jaw worked angrily. "It was an accident."

"The police paid undisclosed damages."

"Standard procedure."

"So standard," I murmured sarcastically, "that you were put on sick leave for the duration of the internal inquiry, then took early retirement immediately afterward." I unzipped the front pocket of my rucksack and removed a folded piece of paper. "I left this out of the envelope. It was the last thing Andy sent me. It's the confidential assessment made of you by your superior officer. Among other things, he describes you as 'a violent individual with extreme racist views who has no place in the Metropolitan Police Force.'"

He snatched the paper from my grasp and shredded it to pieces, the muscles of his face working furiously. He was the opposite temperament to Sam. A man who brooded over long-held grudges. A man who saw loss of face as weakness.

I stirred the pieces with my toe, thinking I'd be safer poking a viper's nest. "Is that how you always deal with evidence you don't like? Tear it up?"

"It's inadmissible. The slate was wiped clean as part of my retirement package. You'd be prosecuted just for having it in your possession. Quentin, too, if he were still alive."

"Well, maybe I think a prosecution's worth it," I murmured, "just to get it into the public domain. I can fire off a thousand copies tomorrow and throw so much mud at you that there'll be no one left who won't question your motive for wanting Annie's death ruled accidental."

"You'll be seen for what you are," he warned, "a bitter woman with a personal vendetta against the police."

"One policeman, possibly," I agreed, "but not the police in general. I was given too much help by Andy for anyone to think I tar you all with the same brush. In any case, who's going to tell them it's a personal vendetta? *You?*" I smiled at his expression. "How do you plan to explain why I'd want to pursue one?"

He screwed his forefinger into his temple. "It's all in your statements," he said. "You were a head case . . . persecution complex . . . mother complex . . . anorexia . . . agoraphobia . . . sexual fantasy . . . What was I supposed to do? Sit beside your bed and hold your hand while you bawled your eyes out?"

"You might have questioned your own judgment," I suggested.

"You've only yourself to blame for that," he retorted sharply. "Maybe if you'd backed off once in a while, I'd have taken you more seriously. I don't like people in my face all the time." As if to prove the point, he slammed his back against the wall and stared at me through half-closed eyes.

I looked away. "Then why didn't you let someone else take over? Why wasn't I allowed to talk to Andy? Why did you get him pushed off the case?"

"He was more trouble than he was worth. He believed everything you told him."

We both knew that wasn't the real reason, but I let it go. "Because everything I said was true."

"You mean like this." He jerked his chin at the brown envelope. "There's no evidence of murder in there. Just different opinions."

"That's only a fraction of what I've got," I said. "You didn't think I'd show my whole hand, did you?" I took the photographs of Beth and Alan Slater's house from my rucksack. "There's plenty of evidence that Annie was robbed." I passed the pictures across to him. "Maureen Slater admits most of this stuff was sitting in her house for months after Annie died . . . claims you saw it and even went back on one occasion, offering to buy the Quetzalcoatl mosaic. Which means you should have treated Annie's house as a scene of crime, if only because it must have been obvious to you that the Slaters had robbed her."

He gave the pictures a perfunctory glance. "Maureen said she bought it in a junk shop," he said dismissively. "I had no reason to think otherwise."

"She couldn't afford to go to the laundrette. How could she afford to buy paintings?"

"Not my problem. None of the stuff had been reported stolen."

"You must have recalled the Quetzalcoatl when Dr. Arnold started asking questions about Annie's possessions."

"No," he said bluntly. "It was four years later. How many houses do you think I'd entered in that time? I couldn't describe a picture I'd seen a week before, let alone one from way back."

"You offered Maureen twenty quid for it," I reminded him, "so it obviously made an impression on you."

He shrugged. "I don't remember."

"I didn't think you would," I said with a small laugh. "Any more than you'll remember Maureen giving you a gold statuette with emeralds for eyes and rubies for lips. She said you had no intention of buying the Quetzalcoatl. . . . All you wanted was something valuable as a quid pro quo for not asking awkward questions. What did you do with it? Keep it? Sell it? Melt it down? It must have scared you rigid when Sheila Arnold described it as one of the artifacts Annie had on her mantelpiece."

"Maureen's lying," he said bluntly.

"She's prepared to make a statement about it."

A glint of amusement sparked in his eyes. "You think anyone's going to believe her about something that happened twenty years ago? And why wouldn't I want to ask awkward questions of the Slaters? I had a reputation for being tough on the whole damn family."

"Not just tough," I said casually. "According to Danny, you were quite happy to frame them as well. He says you planted some cannabis in Alan's pocket and got him sent down for dealing."

Drury shook his head pityingly. "And you believe him, of course."

"Not necessarily. No one seems to know what Alan actually did. Danny says dealing, but Alan told his wife he was sent down for assaulting Michael Percy."

"Why am I not surprised?" he said with irony.

"Well?" I prompted when he didn't go on.

"She wouldn't have married him if she'd known the truth."

"Why is it such a secret?"

He pointed an accusing finger at me, as if Alan's crime were my responsibility. "He was always going to get off lightly. He was fifteen and couldn't be named, and neither could his victim. It's a bloody stupid rule in my book. All a kid has to do is see out his sentence, lie through his teeth, put a bit of distance between himself and what he did and he gets off virtually scot-free." He started popping his knuckles again. "Maureen kept it quiet because she was scared stiff of what people would say."

"What did he do?"

"Work it out for yourself. The victim was a woman."

"Rape," I suggested.

He nodded. "Took himself off to the other side of London where he thought he could get away with it. Dragged the woman into a car park behind some houses and proceeded to beat her up. But she managed to scream and one of the occupants called the police. Alan was caught in the act, pleaded guilty and did four years before he was let out."

"Anyone could have predicted it," I said unemotionally. "He was appallingly abused as a child, both physically and mentally."

But Drury wasn't interested in bleeding-heart excuses. "On that basis Danny would have become a rapist as well."

I stared at my hands. "Danny has no memories of his childhood. He was so young when his father left that he can't even remember what he looked like . . . and if he heard his mother being thrashed in the bedroom, he wouldn't have understood the connection between sex and violence." I raised my head to look at him. "It makes a difference. All poor Alan ever learned from his parents was that reducing a woman to a shivering wreck would result in an orgasm."

twenty-one

Drury's gaze veered away from mine but not before I saw the quickly veiled flash of intelligence that told me he knew what I was talking about. It was a powerful revelation because, despite everything, I had never been certain of how much knowledge he had. For the moment I let it go. "Did Alan get into trouble again after the rape conviction?" I asked then.

"Not that I know of. He moved into a bedsit out Twickenham way and took laboring jobs. We kept an eye on him but he was wary of coming into Richmond or seeing anyone he knew."

I had no reason to disbelieve him. "So why did Danny tell me Alan received £5,000 compensation for being beaten up by the police?"

Amusement brought a gleam to Drury's eyes. "Because the guys who arrested him didn't much like what he'd done to the woman. His solicitor bellyached about police brutality until he saw the state of the victim, then settled on five thousand and told Alan to be grateful they hadn't killed him. I'd say it was cheap at the price."

I nodded. "Did Derek ever get done for rape?"

"That would suit you, wouldn't it?"

"Why?" I asked mildly. "I never accused him of rape."

"All but. You said he shoved his penis between your legs."

"I said he put something between my legs which I *thought* was his penis, and as a result I *thought* he was going to rape me. I also told you that's exactly what he wanted me to believe. He was giving me a demonstration of how bad things would get if I didn't keep my nigger-loving mouth shut. It was your choice to tell him I'd accused him of attempted rape . . . your choice to put me in danger . . . even though you'd already agreed with Andy's assessment that the worst Derek could be charged with was threatening behavior."

"We couldn't charge him with anything," he said dismissively. "He had an alibi. In any case, I thought the guy had a right to know what the latest accusation was. You weren't exactly stinting yourself on the Derek Slater front . . . and sexual assault was a damn sight more serious than heavy breathing on the end of a phone."

"His alibi was a joke," I said. "You didn't follow it up until three days later."

"It makes no difference. It was watertight."

"Oh, come on!" I said impatiently. "A Kempton Park ticket stub which he could have picked out of the gutter the next day? The course is only a few miles outside Richmond in all conscience. And a telephone conversation with one of his friends? You didn't even bother to check on the remaining two."

"*You* didn't bother to report the incident until the day after it happened," he countered sarcastically.

I fingered my lip to quell the tic that was leaping and jumping beneath the skin. I couldn't stand the idea that he might interpret it as fear. "It took me twenty-four hours to pluck up the courage," I said matter-of-factly. "Half of me wanted to let the whole thing drop, the other half recognized that Derek wouldn't be terrorizing me if I wasn't right in what I was saying. I was very naïve, of course. It never occurred to me you'd bend over backward to protect a man you described as scum . . . just because he was white."

"That's not true, and you know it."

"Then why have you consistently protected the Slaters from questioning about Annie's death?"

"I haven't."

"Why didn't you follow through when Dr. Arnold told you Annie had been robbed? You must have realized then where the Quetzalcoatl mosaic came from."

"I didn't. I remember some bits of rubbish in the Slaters' sitting room, but I couldn't describe it now and I certainly didn't link it with anything Dr. Arnold said later."

I could almost believe him, if only because the death of a black woman had meant so little to him. "The children had been stealing from Annie for months," I said, "but they weren't very good at hiding what they were taking, and Maureen beat the truth out of Bridget Spalding when she spotted her wearing a ring that obviously hadn't come from Woolworth's. That's when she began to realize Annie might be sitting on a gold mine."

Drury flicked his hand dismissively. "The police can't act if a crime isn't reported."

I went on as if he hadn't spoken. "Annie was such an easy target. She wouldn't let people into her house, she distrusted anyone who spoke to her neighbors, thought council officials and men in uniform were against her, made an enemy of her bank manager. In fact the only person who came close to being a friend was her GP." I watched his face for a reaction, but it remained impassive. "Annie was fairly safe while Sheila was making regular visits because even Derek wasn't stupid enough to make a move while her doctor was taking an interest. Then Sheila left for America and everything changed."

"You can't blame me for that."

"More to the point, after Sheila's departure there was no one who could say what Annie did or didn't have." I held his gaze. "And you never bothered to ask because it suited you to believe a black woman would live in a slum."

"You're forgetting how many empty bottles we found. The conditions inside the house had nothing to do with the color of her skin, they were the result of a drink habit."

"They were vodka bottles," I said.

There was a tiny flicker of doubt in his eyes. "So?"

"She didn't drink vodka." I took a sheaf of papers from my ruck-sack. "Andy sent me a list of every landlord and off-license manager in Richmond in 1978. My father managed to locate just over half of them. Two of the off-license managers remember Annie well. They both say she was a regular and that she only bought Jamaican rum. And the landlord of the Green Man says he kept a stock of it just for Annie Butts because she used to get agitated if he ran out." I thrust the pages into his hand.

Drury frowned as he flicked through them. "It doesn't prove she wasn't buying vodka from a supermarket," he said.

"No," I agreed.

"Then it's not evidence."

"Not on its own, perhaps, but if you look at the last two pages you'll see that several off-license managers remember Maureen Slater as a vodka drinker. One of them describes how she used to come in after picking up her benefit money and buy half a dozen bottles at a time. He says he refused to serve her after she slapped one of her children—probably Alan—when he said he needed new shoes."

"So? All that proves is Maureen bought vodka; it doesn't prove An-nie didn't. What are you trying to say, anyway? That the Slaters put their bottles in Annie's kitchen?"

"Yes."

"When?"

"After she was dead."

"Why?"

"To make you think what you did: that she was a chronic drunk who lived in a tip and neglected herself. That's why they turned off the main supplies and took away all the food that she'd bought for the cats."

"Oh, come on," he growled impatiently. "*Everyone* said she was drunk, not just the Slaters." He smacked the paper with the back of his hand. "In any case, Derek was as thick as two short planks. He couldn't have followed through on a plan like that. He'd have given himself away the minute we started asking questions."

"Not Derek, maybe, but Maureen certainly could. All she had to do was play on your prejudices." I quoted his own words at him. "You'd never believe a 'downtrodden slut' could outmaneuver you, and 'a miserable black who couldn't hold her drink' was bound to soil her own floor and piss on herself. And why would you question the kind of bottles you found in Annie's house when the mere fact of their existence confirmed everything Maureen wanted you to believe?"

"There was no reason to question them. No one told us she didn't drink vodka."

I handed him another piece of paper.

"What's this?"

"A copy of Sharon Percy's statement. Your name's at the top as the interviewing officer. The first half deals with where she was during the evening—none of which is true as a matter of interest—the second half is her description of what Annie was like. Somewhere in the last paragraph it says: 'She used to get drunk on rum and start insulting everyone. She took swipes at the kids with the empty bottles. I kept reporting it but nothing was done.'"

Impatiently, he tore this page, too, into shreds and dropped it to the floor. "You're clutching at straws," he said. "You can muddy the waters as much as you like, it doesn't alter the fact that there was no reason to question anyone's statement at the time . . . and that includes your husband's. The pathologist's findings were unambiguous—Ann Butts died because she walked in front of a truck."

"Which is what you told him to say."

"You can't prove it. If Hanley's files are missing, there's nothing to show which of us said what first."

I gave a small laugh. "He didn't do you any favors by getting rid of them. At the moment, the only document supporting your accident theory is the one-page report Hanley submitted to the coroner, and that has so many mistakes it's a joke. He spelled Annie's name wrong, referred to bruising on her left arm instead of her right, and completely ignored the lividity in her thighs, which is very pronounced in the photographs."

I was amazed to see him run a nervous tongue across his lips. "I don't think that's right."

"It is," I assured him. "Hanley was so incompetent by that time he was taking dictation from whichever police officer presented a body for inspection. I assume you got muddled over the arms because I told you she was lying left side uppermost with her back to the lamppost."

He had to think about his answer. "Not my responsibility. He had his job. . . . I had mine. Let him take the flak."

I reached for my rucksack and zipped up the pockets. "Reporters don't hound dead people," I told him. "Only the living. And there's more human interest in a racist policeman who refused to investigate a black woman's murder than a troubled pathologist who killed himself with drink because he couldn't stand the unnecessary mutilation of corpses. Radley's won't keep you on," I went on dispassionately, "not once you're plastered across the front of the newspapers. All your decent trade will vanish overnight to be supplanted by thugs from the National Front."

Small beads of sweat dampened his forehead. "Tell me what you came for," he said, "because we both know this has nothing to do with Annie."

Was he right? I honestly didn't know anymore. "It was two years before I learned to trust myself again," I said slowly, "and another two before I dared trust anyone else. I still have nightmares . . . still run to the basin to wash myself . . . still check the bolts on the door . . . still jump out of my skin every time I hear a sound I don't recognize." I pushed back my chair and stood up, hooking my rucksack over my shoulder. "I'd say this has everything to do with Annie. The only difference between us is that she had the courage to stand and fight . . . and I ran away." I moved to the door. "Which is why she's dead and I'm alive."

Letter from Dr. Joseph Elias, psychiatrist
at the Queen Victoria Hospital, Hong Kong—dated 1999

QUEEN VICTORIA HOSPITAL

Hong Kong
Dept. of Psychiatry

Mrs. M. Ranelagh
Jacaranda
Hightor Road
Cape Town
South Africa

February 17, 1999

Dear Mrs. Ranelagh,

Goodness me! So it's home to England at last. I
shall await your news with bated breath. Yes,
despite my incredibly advanced years, I still have
a small consultancy in the hospital, but only
because my patients seem to prefer the devil they
know to the devil they don't.

And what of your devils, my dear? Somehow I
doubt that justice for Annie will be enough for
you. But who am I to criticize when my friend the
rabbi would say: To win the peace you must first
fight the war?

As requested, I enclose the notes I made in 1979.
Yours fondly,

J. Elias

twenty-two

Drury couldn't leave it alone, as I knew he wouldn't. For all his protestations about hating having people in his face, he disliked it even more when they walked away. I turned, left the pub and went about fifty yards toward the trawler moorings before I heard his footsteps behind me. Lights from the buildings along the quay shone a quiet glow across the cobblestones and, far ahead, tiny beacons bobbed upon the water like multicolored jewels, showing safe navigation for incoming yachtsmen. I had a moment to wish I could enjoy the scene for what it was—something beautiful—before his fingers closed about my arm.

"This is crazy," he said, jerking me 'round to face him. "You say you want to get even. Well, how? Destroying me isn't going to produce justice for you or for Annie. Are you asking me to deliver Derek Slater on a plate? Is that what this is about?"

I tried to pull away. "People are watching," I said.

"Let them watch," he growled. "I want this sorted."

"Fine. So when I decide to scream—which I certainly will if you don't let go—there'll be a hundred witnesses to confirm your superintendent's assessment that you're a violent man."

He released me immediately.

I smiled cynically as I rubbed my arm. "It's not so much fun when the boot's on the other foot, is it? The way things are at the moment, you'd crawl on your belly over these cobbles in exchange for a promise to burn what's in my rucksack. Am I right?"

"Don't push your luck," he said in an undertone. "I'm in no mood for games. All you'll achieve by going public is to make me a scapegoat, and that's not going to put Derek behind bars . . . not after all this time. Is that the kind of justice you want?"

"It's better than nothing."

He grasped one writhing fist inside the other as if afraid he wouldn't be able to control them. "If it was me you wanted, you wouldn't have put me on my guard," he said reasonably.

"Perhaps I like watching you sweat," I murmured.

"How about I break your fucking neck?" he said through gritted teeth.

"You wouldn't get very far. My two sons are standing right behind you."

The words made no sense to him—he didn't associate me with children—and he stared at me in baffled fury like a tired bull trying to work out how to defeat a matador. "What the hell are you talking about now?"

"Protection." I nodded to Luke and Tom. "I come better prepared these days."

It took a second or two for his brain to catch on, but he spun 'round eventually to discover I was telling the truth. Perhaps he was expecting something younger—*or smaller?*—but whichever, he was suitably impressed. "Shit!" he said. "What the fuck's going on?"

"Sam's waiting for us in the car," I explained. "I'd like him to hear what you're going to say next."

Drury glanced nervously at the boys. "Which is what?"

I made him the same offer I'd made Maureen. "A trade?" I suggested. "You see you're right about one thing. The kind of justice I'm looking for is a little more"—I sought for a word—"basic than making you take the blame for everything that happened."

I didn't think he'd follow me, particularly as the boys returned to the pub as soon as I moved away. But perhaps he misunderstood what I wanted Sam to hear . . . or what I meant by basic justice . . .

———

The car was parked beyond the trawler moorings, facing out over the water, and as we approached Sam opened the door and climbed out. In a spirit of mischief, I introduced them to each other as I lowered my rucksack onto the bonnet. "Mr. Ranelagh. Mr. Drury." They nodded to each other like a couple of wary Rottweilers, but didn't shake hands. "You asked me if I was expecting you to deliver Derek on a plate," I reminded Drury, "but I don't see how you can do that unless you suppressed evidence at the time."

He looked tight-lipped at Sam, aware that anything he said now would be heard by a witness. "There was no suppression of evidence," he said sharply, "merely question marks over where Derek was at nine o'clock. He claimed he was having a drink with the local tart who'd been touting for custom since the place opened."

"Sharon Percy?"

He nodded. "It was straightforward stuff—the two of them were regulars—and the publican agreed they were both in there that night although he disputed the timing when we first questioned him. He remembered seeing Sharon at nine o'clock but he didn't think Derek came in until later." He shrugged. "He backed off when we asked for a statement . . . said one day was much like another, and he couldn't swear he wasn't confusing two different occasions."

"This being the William of Orange," I said. "The pub Annie was banned from because she was black."

He gave an impatient shake of his head. "She was banned because she couldn't hold her drink and swore at the other customers. The publican was within his rights to refuse to serve her."

I looked questioningly at Sam.

"It was known locally as the Orange Free State," he told Drury. "There was a sign on the door saying 'no dogs' and the 'd' had been crossed out and changed to a 'w.' It was a popular pub—a fair number of policemen used it—but you never saw any blacks in there."

"If it offended you, you should have reported it."

"It didn't," said Sam honestly. "I never even questioned it."

"Then why expect me to?"

"Because it was your job. I'm not saying I'd have given you any medals for it—hell, the last thing I wanted was to have Mad Annie swearing at me over a pint—but the laws on discrimination were clear and anyone who put 'no wogs' on their front door ought to have been prosecuted." He paused to exchange a glance with me, clearly wondering how far he should or could go. "The landlord was cock-a-hoop after the accident," he went on abruptly. "Kept telling anyone who cared to listen that we had a truck driver to thank for making the streets cleaner."

"Not in front of me he didn't," said Drury so quickly that I guessed he'd had to answer that question before, probably at the time of his "retirement."

"So did you bother to challenge Derek about his alibi?" I said dryly. "Or was that when you decided to take him aside and tell him that *I* was the problem, and the best solution for everyone would be to shut me up? And how did you put it exactly? Do us all a favor, Derek, and teach that nigger-loving bitch a lesson because your alibi stinks and you'll be in trouble if you don't. Or did you drop hints to Maureen when you were looking at the bits of junk in her sitting room?"

I watched him flick a wary glance at Sam, but he took confidence from Sam's obvious ignorance of what I was talking about. "Of course I challenged him," he said bullishly. "He stuck to his story . . . so did Sharon. They both said they'd been there all evening. We didn't believe them, but there was nothing we could do if no one was willing to contradict them."

"Did you ever find out what they were really doing?"

He shrugged. "Our best guess was that Sharon had been on her back somewhere and Derek was out thieving. They both had convictions— Sharon for prostitution; Derek for assault and theft."

"Sharon was with Geoffrey Spalding," I said. "He lived at number 27 and used to meet her at a hotel once a month because he didn't want his wife and daughters finding out what he was doing. He's the one who said he saw Annie in the street around a quarter past eight and tried to persuade her to go home."

"I remember him."

"I think he was lying about the time," I went on. "According to Jock Williams, Sharon arrived in a taxi at the William of Orange shortly after nine. He said she was high as a kite and had obviously been with another client, and I'm betting the client was Geoffrey and the same taxi dropped him off at the top of Graham Road before taking Sharon on to the pub. Which means, if Geoffrey talked to Annie at all, it must have been an hour later than he said it was."

He refused to accept it. "I spoke to him in front of his wife and she didn't question that he was home by 8:30."

"She wouldn't have known. She was on chemotherapy for breast cancer and would have been asleep whatever time he came in. Where did he say he'd been?"

Drury thought back. "Late at work. Nothing to raise any eyebrows over."

I turned to Sam. "I've always thought he must have passed the Williams' house as you came out . . . otherwise you and Libby wouldn't have needed an alibi."

"Someone did," he admitted, "but I've no idea who it was. To be honest, I can't even be sure it was a man. It could have been a total stranger taking a shortcut, but Libby went apeshit and said tongues would start wagging—" He pressed his thumb and forefinger to the bridge of his nose. "I'm sorry," he said after a moment. "Is this the man you think killed Annie?"

"I don't know," I answered slowly, "but I've never understood why he said he spoke to Annie unless it actually happened. It was an unnecessary lie. He could have done what you and Jock did and said he saw her on the other side of the road."

"People embroider all the time," said Drury. "It makes them feel important."

I shook my head. "She was seen by two different couples at around nine o'clock. The Pardoes at number 8 who watched her from their bedroom window, and the couple in the car who say she lurched out in front of them. They all said she was on her feet . . . but by the time Sam passed her at 9:15 she was collapsed in the gutter."

"That's not what Mr. Ranelagh said at the time."

"His revised statement was in the envelope," I said impatiently, "so I know you've read it. The question is, was Annie on her feet when Geoffrey Spalding passed her? And if she was, did she speak to him? I think she was—and did—and that whatever she said made him so angry that he pushed her into the road. It would explain why he advanced the time by an hour . . . it would also explain why Sharon was prepared to give Derek an alibi. If she told you she'd been with a customer—and you found out who it was—you'd have worked out PDQ that Geoffrey was the last person to speak to Annie."

Drury frowned. "And?"

"You'd have come to the same conclusion he did . . . that he killed her."

He gave a grunt of irritation. "Half an hour ago you were producing pathology reports saying she was beaten up several hours in advance of her death, now you're saying Geoffrey Spalding murdered her. When are you going to make up your mind, Mrs. Ranelagh?"

Sam roused himself. "She's not saying Spalding killed her," he said reasonably, "just that he *thought* he did. If it comes to that, I've spent twenty years worrying that I did the same. And maybe I did. Maybe that fifteen minutes I left her to lie in the gutter was the difference between life and death."

"Then you should have cleared your conscience by telling us the truth at the time," said Drury with a far from friendly smile, "instead of contaminating the investigation because you couldn't keep your hands off your friend's wife."

He would have been wiser not to mention Libby, I thought with private amusement as I watched an angry flush stain Sam's cheeks. Guilt was the one thing guaranteed to fire my husband's temper.

"You told us there wasn't going to be an investigation," he snapped. "I remember it very distinctly. You came to the house the next day to explain the postmortem findings. Unequivocal, you said . . . a clear-cut accident . . . no hint of foul play. I also remember you saying that if there had been any question marks over the death, the whole matter would have been turned over to the CID."

"There *were* no question marks, Mr. Ranelagh. It might have been different if you hadn't lied, but we could only work with the information we had."

Sam smoothed a hand across his bald patch, staring past Drury to the lights on the other side of the water. "Jock and I didn't offer any information until the Thursday evening when we were asked to make voluntary statements in support of what Libby had told you the day before, namely that Jock was in my house."

"So now you're blaming Mrs. Williams?"

"No, merely pointing out that you'd made up your mind it was an accident a good twenty-four hours before Jock or I said anything." He stared thoughtfully at Drury as if he were fundamentally reassessing some previous judgment. "Would it have made any difference if we *had* told the truth? Wouldn't you just have claimed she was hit by a truck between the couple in the car seeing her and my finding her?"

Drury's silence was an answer in itself.

"You telephoned me several times at work," Sam went on, "telling me that my wife was suffering a classic response to stress and needed psychiatric help. You said you'd seen that sort of reaction before and it always led to more and more wild accusations."

"You agreed with every word, Mr. Ranelagh, including the necessity for an official caution."

My husband folded his arms and stared fixedly at the cobbles as if certainty lay within their uneven surface. "Did I have any choice?" he asked. "You read out a catalog of complaints against her . . . wasting police time . . . making false accusations against Derek Slater . . . reporting imaginary sex attacks to win sympathy . . . plaguing you with telephone calls and visits because she had an unhealthy obsession with you." He lifted his head. "You were a policeman. I had to accept you were telling me the truth."

"It must have tallied with your own opinion," said Drury persuasively, "otherwise you'd have argued your wife's case."

Sam made a troubled gesture with his hand. "I was in no position to argue. I hadn't seen her for nearly three weeks, and on the one occasion she phoned she was hysterical. I couldn't make head or tail of what she was saying so I called her parents and asked them to help her." He paused, trying to marshal facts in his head. "But you'd already persuaded my mother-in-law that an official caution in front of her family was the best way to deal with the situation. 'She needs shaming to stop her wasting any more police time,' was the way you put it."

There was a short silence.

"It worked then," I said lightly. "I'd have slit my throat rather than say another word to Mr. Drury . . . or to you and Ma, Sam. You both stood by and watched this bastard bully me into keeping my mouth shut"—I jerked my chin at Drury—"and then shook his hand at the end as if he'd done something fine. The only person who refused to go along with the charade was my father, yet he knew no more at that stage than you did. He just had faith in the woman he knew me to be rather than a pathetic, disturbed creature who was resorting to sexual fantasy to prolong her fifteen minutes of fame."

"You were never described in those terms or treated with anything other than courtesy," said Drury curtly. "Your husband knows that. That's why I asked him to be present, so that you wouldn't be able to rewrite the history afterward."

"You could be as courteous as you liked," I said, "because you knew I wouldn't argue with you. Not after the *unofficial* caution you arranged for me the night before. You should have joined the party," I told him.

"I imagine it was a great deal more exciting than hammering a needle into a twelve-year-old's arm or pounding at a black face until the cheekbone snapped."

The muscles along the man's jawline tightened. "Now you're slandering me in front of a witness."

"Then sue me. Give me my day in court. It's all I've ever wanted. But you'll be on thin ice . . . I've another copy of your assessment in my rucksack."

He took an abrupt step forward, swinging his fists at his sides. I thought he was going to hit me and dodged away 'round the bonnet of the car, but he snatched up the rucksack instead and tossed it into the water beyond the harbor wall. There was a second of silence before it hit with a splash, and Drury stared after it with a look of satisfaction on his lean face.

He flung off the nervous hand that Sam laid on his arm. "Leave it," he warned. "This is between me and your wife."

"You always were a shithead," I hissed angrily as I thought of my wallet and credit cards sinking into the sludge at the bottom of the river. "That's the only solution you've ever had to anything. Get rid of the evidence before your crimes find you out."

He laughed at my anger. "It's not so much fun when the boot's on the other foot, is it?" he taunted, resting his palms on one side of the bonnet and staring me down.

I did the same from my side, thrusting my face toward his and raking him with furious eyes. "Do you know what pisses me off the most? Not what you did to me"—I lifted a finger and stabbed it at his chest— "I learned to deal with that. It's the fact that you had the nerve to underestimate me . . . and still *fucking well* do." I could feel the stridency roaring in my voice and, for once, didn't give a damn how it sounded. If the truth be told, I'd always been closer to loudmouthed fishwives than effete Victorian ladies who gave way to the vapors. "How *dare* you think I'm so stupid as to carry a master file with me? How *dare* you think I'd give you an opportunity to outflank me?"

"You talked about a trade," said Drury aggressively.

"I want justice first," I flung at him. "*Then* I'll trade."

"What sort of justice?"

"The eye-for-an-eye kind. The same kind you believe in. You pumped a Neanderthal full of lies, then told him I'd be gagged the next day. What did you think he was going to do? Send me a bunch of flowers?"

He looked edgily toward Sam. "I don't know what you're talking about."

"Yes, you do. You got more and more angry every time I accused you of racism. That's why you made my official caution so public . . . so that even a moron like Derek Slater knew he could have a free run at the nigger-lover without any fear of my reporting it."

"You're inventing things again, Mrs. Ranelagh. If a crime was committed you had a perfect opportunity to give us the details the next morning."

"You mean in the middle of an official caution for wasting police time? In front of a husband and mother who didn't believe a word I said because they had more faith in a corrupt policeman than they had in me?" I flung out my arms and caught him across the chest with the backs of my hands. "How *dare* you suggest I had an unhealthy fixation on you? How dare you imagine for one minute that I'd be interested in someone who thought a woman's place was under a man . . . preferably bound and muzzled so that he wouldn't have to listen to her criticizing his performance."

He retreated warily but didn't say anything.

"I had nothing but contempt for you," I said. "I saw you as a *little* man . . . a pygmy in uniform . . . someone who was allowed to strut his stage because his superiors were too inept to see how incompetent he was . . . and the only reason I spoke to you at all was because I wanted justice for Annie. But I never thought of you as anything other than a reptile." I looked deep into the dead black of his eyes. "And that was my mistake, wasn't it? If I hadn't made it so obvious that the mere sight of you made my flesh crawl, you wouldn't have set Derek on me. Because it wasn't me who fancied you, you bastard, but *you* who fancied *me*."

I felt Sam move behind me.

"You're crazy," said Drury.

"You'd better believe it," I agreed, slithering 'round the bonnet of the car. "I haven't been sane since Derek did your dirty work for you. He knew I'd never let him into my house, so he sent Alan in first, blubbing about how his father had been hitting his mother again. The child was twice as big as me, and I was stupid enough to put an arm 'round him while I turned to shut the door." I gave a hollow laugh. "He had me flat on my back before I knew what was happening, and used his weight to hold me down while his filthy great hands yanked my hair out by the roots every time I moved my head." I halted in front of the offside headlight so that he wouldn't retreat any further. "They couldn't mark me," I went on, "because you'd told Derek I'd be at the police station the next morning. And they couldn't rape me because they didn't want to leave any incriminating evidence inside me." I tapped two fingers against my mouth. "So I got a mouthful of Derek Slater's urine instead."

I caught a glimpse of Sam's strained, white face out of the corner of my eye. "He pissed over my mouth and nose while his son held me down"—I glanced at the harbor's edge—"and it's like drowning. You can't breathe—so you drink. And the legacy is that you wash your mouth out every hour of every day as long as you live." I lifted my lips in a wolfish snarl. "They swapped places while I was choking to give Alan his turn—but he was too excited and couldn't control himself. . . ." I fell silent as Sam moved 'round behind the car.

Drury made a half-turn so he could keep an eye on Sam as well. "No one's going to believe you," he said, "not if there's no record of such a crime being committed. And why focus your anger on me, anyway? Why not blame your husband for abandoning you? If he'd had any guts he'd have stood by you instead of protecting his tart."

I had time to think that Drury was a shocking judge of character before—with one galvanizing charge—Sam launched at him, head down, and shunted him into the estuary after my rucksack.

twenty-three

Sam doubled up and backed away from the edge, roaring obscenities from an overdose of adrenaline, but I stayed to watch Drury rise. Luke had assured me that the westerly tidal stream in Weymouth harbor would carry a floating body toward the pontoons, but I had a small twinge of concern about how good a swimmer Drury was. When his face bobbed to the surface, we stared at each other for a moment before I gave him a one-fingered salute and turned away. *Gotcha!*

"We ought to call the police," said Sam, taking deep breaths to calm himself while he watched the man swim to safety.

"He can do it himself if he wants to. He knows our address." I walked back to the car. "But he won't. He'll bury his head in the sand and hope this counts as an eye for an eye."

"And does it?" he asked, following me.

"No chance," I said cheerfully, opening the passenger door. "He still has to answer for Annie, and he'll only do that when his name's plastered across every newspaper in this country with 'racist' attached to it." I slid on to the seat. "Come on," I called, buckling my seat belt, "let's shift. He'll be after your blood if I know anything about anything. Not reporting you to the police doesn't mean he won't break your jaw at the first opportunity."

Sam scrambled in beside me and fired the engine, twisting 'round to reverse the car out on the road. "I should have seen to him twenty years ago," he said as he spun the wheel. "I would have done, too, if I hadn't believed him."

"About Annie?"

"No," he growled, "about you stalking him. I know it sounds absurd now but at the time it seemed to make sense. The way you went off me after Annie died . . . the hours you spent at the police station . . . the fact that you were prepared to talk to him and not me." He eased the car forward and pulled out onto the road. "I started to think he was more your type than I was."

"That figures," I said sarcastically, reaching across him to buckle his belt. "I mean he had everything I wanted in a man: *hair,* a uniform, not to mention an enormous dick, which he kept permanently erect for the purposes of rogering every bit of totty that crossed his tracks."

He gave me a sheepish grin. "Actually, I'm being serious. I was incredibly jealous but I didn't think I had much of a leg to stand on after Libby. Then you got pregnant, and I thought, *Shit, is the baby mine or Drury's?* . . . and I was so bloody churned up that when you agreed to try to make a go of it, all I could think about was getting away, burying the whole bloody saga and starting again."

I was so surprised that I felt as if my jaw had just hit the floor. "You thought Luke was Drury's?"

He nodded.

"Good God! What on earth gave you that idea?"

He took his foot off the pedal and the car slowed to a crawl. "Because the only time we had sex throughout that whole miserable period," he said with a sigh, "was when I forced myself on you and you told me you never wanted to see me again. You really hated me that night . . . and I couldn't believe that something that was done with so much viciousness could produce something so grand."

I shook my head in amazement. "Why didn't you say something?"

"Because it didn't matter," he said simply. "I always thought of Luke as mine whether he was or not."

I was humbled. If our roles were reversed—if Libby had given birth to Sam's child—I could never have been that generous. "But of course he's yours," I said, touching the back of my hand to his cheek. "You should never have doubted it for a minute."

He leaned his head to one side, trapping my hand against his shoulder. "I haven't for a long time . . . not since Tom was born, anyway, because they looked so alike." He gave an abrupt laugh. "Then you insisted on bringing me here for lunch so that Drury could leer at you, and I thought, *Is this the first step to telling the sod that my son is really his?*"

I snatched my hand away. "You said you didn't recognize him."

He speeded up again. "I never forget the faces of men who make me jealous."

"There haven't been any."

"That's what you think." He leaned forward to wipe mist from the screen. "Where are we picking up the boys?"

"Beyond the swing bridge."

"Well, be prepared for some embarrassed silences," he warned matter-of-factly. "I spotted them creeping in behind one of the other cars, so I think the chances are they heard every word."

"Damn!" I said with sudden weariness, leaning my head against the seat. "I told them to make themselves scarce."

"Mm, well, I suspect curiosity won out. You can't blame them. We've both been behaving very oddly lately. It could makes things difficult with Danny," he warned again. "And I'll have to come clean about Libby . . . why I lied . . . why I ignored Annie. It's only right they should hear the truth from me."

"It's not what I wanted, Sam," I said with a sigh. "It was supposed to be just you who heard it because I didn't think you'd believe it if I told it to you cold."

"You should have trusted me," he said lightly. "I stopped being a bastard twenty years ago."

"I know." I felt tears prick behind my eyes. "But I could never find the right time to tell you. I'm sorry."

"Well, I'm not," he declared with sudden boisterous good humor.

"You've got more balls than an entire rugby team, my girl, and it's about time the boys found out what an amazing mother they have." He slapped his hands against the steering wheel. "I keep thinking of this Chinese proverb Jock quoted to me the other day. It's a variation on the theme of 'everything comes to him who waits'"—he turned to me with another grin—"and it's peculiarly apt in the present circumstances."

"How does it go?"

"'If you sit by the river long enough the bodies of all your enemies float by.'"

I thought I knew the man I married before that night, but now I know I could live to be a hundred and still not understand the twists and turns of human nature. I don't know what he said to the boys but whatever it was made them treat me like a valuable antique for twenty-four hours, until I started effing and blinding out of pure frustration, and normal service was resumed. They carefully avoided any reference to the Slaters, all of them understanding that it is one thing to reveal the presence of a scar, quite another to have it split open under the pressure of constant examination.

Nevertheless, it wasn't a subject that could be avoided for ever and, after much shuffling of feet on Saturday night, Tom confessed they were supposed to be meeting Danny Slater for a drink but weren't sure whether they should. Sam and I said in unison that Danny bore no responsibility for what his father and brother had done and that it wouldn't be fair to tell him. Leave him in ignorance was our advice.

"Has Dad told you he's thinking of letting Danny use the barn as a studio?" Tom asked me. "Assuming we buy the place, of course."

"It's just an idea at the moment," said Sam, "but I'd like him to know that we aren't just fair-weather friends."

"He'd have to slum it," put in Luke, "because Dad won't let him smoke dope in the house. But he can clean out the tack room and make it reasonably habitable. There's electricity down there and the loose boxes are big enough to work in. All he'd need to do then is beg some stone off one of the quarries, and he could have a bash at being a sculptor without having to bankrupt himself in the process."

Three eager faces turned toward me. What did I think?

I nodded and smiled and said it was a grand idea. But I knew it wouldn't happen. Danny would never forgive me for what I was about to do to his family.

The following Monday I visited Michael Percy in prison on Portland. It was a troubling experience because I was constantly reminded that his life was in limbo. Perhaps the extraordinary setting of the Verne, built inside an old citadel overlooking the harbor and standing alone at the end of a series of hairpin bends, added to my sense of unfulfilled promise and waste. Certainly, I felt its isolation very strongly and wondered if the same feeling was shared by the inmates.

The weather had turned blustery again and the wind plucked at my hair and clothes as I scurried from my car to the main entrance in the wake of a huddle of similarly windblown visitors. I hung behind them, following their lead, unwilling to show my ignorance in front of older hands who, by their relaxed expressions, had queued at reception a hundred times to present their visiting orders.

I thought of Bridget repeating this process month after month, year after year, and wondered if it was a cause for depression or happiness that at the end of it she would see her husband. For myself, I was overcome by a frightening regression to the agoraphobia of twenty years ago when I hadn't been able to leave my house for fear of being watched. Perhaps it had something to do with the officers' uniforms—or being touched during the searches—or having to sit at a table, twiddling my thumbs until Michael was brought to me—certain that everyone's gaze was upon me, even more certain that their gazes were hostile.

Whichever the case, his arrival was a relief, and I watched him walk toward me with an intense—and pleasurable—recognition. *There is no accounting for taste,* I thought. He was as bad—*if not worse*—than Alan, but, like Wendy and Bridget and every other woman he'd ever met, I imagine, he had won a place in my affections. He gave me a shy smile as he shook my hand. "I wasn't sure you'd come."

"I said I would."

"Yeah, but not everyone does what they say." He dropped into the chair on the other side of the table and scrutinized my face. "I wouldn't have recognized you if they hadn't said it was Mrs. Ranelagh."

"I've changed a bit."

"That's for sure." He tilted his head to one side to examine me, and I became very aware suddenly that the fourteen-year-old didn't exist anymore and this was a thirty-five-year-old man with a troubled back-ground and a history of violence. "Any reason why?"

"I didn't much like that person," I said honestly.

"What was wrong with her?"

"Too complacent by half." I smiled slightly. "I decided to try lean and hungry instead."

He grinned. "I bet it made your husband sit up and take notice."

I wondered if he'd known about Sam and Libby, or if his intelligence was even more acute now than when I'd known him in school. "It helped," I agreed, scrutinizing him in return. "You haven't changed a bit, although Mrs. Stanhope, the vicar's wife, claims not to have recognized you from the photograph in the newspaper. She's still hoping it was a different Michael Percy who robbed the post office."

He ran the flat of a hand across his closely cropped hair. "Did you tell her?"

"I didn't need to. I'm sure she knows."

He sighed. "She was pretty decent to me when I was a kid. I bet she was wrecked to find out I got done for pistol-whipping a lady."

"I doubt it. She has no illusions about you."

"She offered to adopt me one time, you know, and I said, 'You've gotta be joking.' It'd be like going from the ridiculous to the gorblimey. On the one hand there was Mum who couldn't give a shit if I never came home . . . on the other there was the vicar who kept giving me lectures about how Jesus could change my life. The only one who was halfway sensible was Mrs. S. . . . but she kept wanting to hug me, and I didn't much fancy that." He leaned forward to create an enclosed space for us among the intrusive hubbub of conversation around us. "I wouldn't have minded *you* giving me a hug," he said with an amused up-from-under look, "but you never showed much inclination."

"I'd have been sacked on the spot."

"You weren't sacked when you gave Alan Slater a hug."

"When did I give Alan a hug?"

"When he bawled his eyes out because the nurse found lice in his hair again. You put your arm 'round his shoulder and said you'd give him some shampoo to get rid of them. You never did that for me."

I had no recollection of it—as far as I knew I'd only put my arm 'round Alan once—and I wondered if Michael was confusing me with another teacher. "Did you ever have lice? You always looked so spick and span while, most days, poor Alan smelled as if he'd emerged from a sewer."

"He was a slob," said Michael dismissively. "I used to nick Prioderm out the chemist for him but he never bothered to use it until the nurse spotted eggs in his hair." He favored me with a crooked smile. "It bugged me that everyone thought I was a neat little kid with clean clothes and felt sorry for Alan because he came from a shit background. I started washing my own stuff myself when I was six years old, but it was only ever Mum who got credit for it."

I wondered fleetingly if the hug I gave Alan, and the hug I hadn't given Michael, had resulted in one settling down and the other doing fifteen years. "Most people thought she was a better mother than Maureen," I told him, "but it wasn't much of an endorsement. On a scale of one to ten, Maureen scored nought."

"At least she wasn't a prostitute," he said bitterly. "It does your head in to have a slag for a mother. Did you know that's what she was at the time?"

"I didn't know anything, Michael. I was very naïve and very stupid, and if I had my life over again I'd do things differently." I watched him for a moment. "You were too sexually aware," I said gently. "I never felt threatened by Alan in the way I felt threatened by you. I didn't think you'd be content with a hug."

His smile became even more crooked. "Maybe not, but I'd have been too scared to do anything about it."

"That's not how I saw you," I said with a small laugh. "You had a knack of singling out women who were vulnerable . . . like Wendy Stanhope. She becomes very wistful when she talks about you, so I doubt her feelings were entirely maternal."

"What about yours?"

"I don't know. I never tested them."

"But you *did* like me?"

I wondered why that was important. "Oh yes."

"What about Alan? Did you like him?"

"No," I said flatly, wondering how much he knew.

"He had a crush on you," he said. "Used to talk about how you couldn't keep your hands off him and how the only reason you refused to get the police involved when you caught him nicking from your handbag was because you were afraid he'd spill the beans about the sex he'd had with you." He examined my face closely and seemed to find the reassurance he wanted. "I knew it was a load of crap but it used to bug me the way you put yourself out to be nice to him."

I didn't say anything.

"And you're wrong about him not being sexually aware," he went on. "He was so damn big he had tackle the size of an elephant's by the time he was ten. Sex was the only thing he thought about. He used to nick porno mags and wank himself stupid over the pictures. It was pretty funny till he started doing it for real. He got hold of Rosie, Bridget's sister, and said he wanted to do it with her, and when she told him to fuck off he pushed her to the ground and said he was going to do it anyway. Poor little kid, she was only twelve and she didn't stop bleeding for weeks." His mouth thinned angrily at the memory. "But she was too frightened to tell anyone except me. Her Mum was ill and her dad was never around. So it was down to me to do the business. I beat the shit out of Alan and said if he ever did something like that again, I'd rip his head off."

"How old were you?"

"Fifteen. It wasn't long after you left."

"Did he do it again?"

Michael shrugged. "If he did, I never got to hear about it. He turned on his dad with a baseball bat a week or so later . . . almost as if his brain caught up with his size and a bubble came out of his head saying, 'I'm big enough to take on guys.' After that, he didn't seem so interested in sex."

I tried to get a grip of the timing. "His wife told me you and he came to blows over Bridget."

He shook his head. "We only fought the once, and that was over Rosie."

"She told me Alan was besotted with Bridget until he found her in bed with you . . . then he beat you half to death and spent time in juvenile prison for it."

"In his dreams maybe." He pulled a puzzled frown. "Bridget never gave him a second look after what he did to her sister, so why pretend otherwise? Who's he trying to con?"

"Beth?" I suggested. "His wife."

"Why?"

It was my turn to shrug.

"Stupid bugger. It's always better to be honest"—he smiled as he listened to himself—"*after* you've been caught anyway. Nothing remains secret very long in this kind of environment."

I looked around the room, which was packed with prisoners and their families—all talking, all listening, all under observation from prison officers—and I thought I could easily believe it. There was no privacy in a goldfish bowl. And I wondered what sort of control Maureen Slater exercised over her family that no hint of Alan's viciousness had ever leaked out.

Letter from John Howlett—RSPCA inspector who entered Ann Butts's house on the morning after her death— now resident in Lancashire—dated 1999

White Cottage
Littlehampton
Nr Preston
Lancashire

Ms. M. Ranelagh
Leavenham Farm
Leavenham
Nr Dorchester
Dorset DT2 XXY

August 11, 1999

Dear Ms. Ranelagh,

May I say first how heartened I am by what you wrote. I have always been troubled by what we found in Miss Butts's house, and I feel so much happier to be asked to view it from a different perspective. As you so rightly suggest, I never had any reason to believe Annie was cruel until after she was dead.

Dr. Arnold was of the opinion that Annie had been robbed in the days before her death and suggested this was the cause of the rapid decline in her circumstances which we found on 15.11.78. While I had some sympathy with that view, I never felt it adequately explained the number and/or condition of the cats. The police "take" on the matter was that Annie was a difficult and disturbed woman who was clearly unable to look after herself and whose behavior had given rise to numerous complaints. What we found in her house, therefore, merely confirmed this belief. It's worth mentioning here that PS Drury told me an hour in advance of entering the house that there were in excess of twenty cats on the premises in order to ensure I brought enough cages to accommodate them. When I questioned this figure, saying that in my experience there had never been more than seven, he said it was based on information received from neighbors.

I blame myself now for not asking how her neighbors could be so exact about numbers, but it's easy to be wise with hindsight. At the time, my colleague and I were so shocked by what was there that all our efforts went into assessing and rescuing the animals. It would have been different had Annie still been alive because we would certainly have sought to prosecute on the grounds of cruelty, but her death meant that we effectively handed the responsibility for asking questions to Sergeant Drury. I know that Dr. Arnold had severe reservations about his handling of the case—and it would seem from your letter that you do, too—but in fairness I should stress that he was as shocked as we were by the conditions in the house and said several times, "I should have believed them." By this I assume he was referring to her neighbors, whom he described constantly as "low-life." I say this only to remind you that he, and we, were dealing with a situation that, even if it was unexpected, did in fact bear out every- thing that had been said about Annie for the last twelve months.

With respect to your specific questions: Annie said her "marmalade" cat had died of "heart failure." She was extremely distraught about it and asked me several times if I thought cats felt pain in the same way we did. I said I didn't know.

Most of the live cats were malnourished—except the six I was able to identify as hers. Several of the strays had bald patches 'round their muzzles, but in almost every instance the fur was beginning to grow back. I'm afraid there was no evidence that "efforts had been made to help them." Rather the reverse, sadly, as the only sensible help would have been a visit to the vet. However, if your premise that the cats' mouths were taped by someone other than Annie, then clearly the removal of the tape and the purchase of chicken and milk, etc., were an indication of "efforts to help." Her own cats were in noticeably better health than the rest.

I'm afraid it's impossible to say how much time had elapsed since the tomcats' mouths were taped, simply because their condition when we found them was so appalling. However, I take on board your suggestion that Annie was unlikely to render them helpless only to release them again.

If I accept your premise that it wasn't Annie who brutalized the animals, then I can also accept your premise that the reason we found sick cats shut into the back bedroom was because she wanted to protect the vulnerable cats from the rest. However, and sadly, I can recall no evidence from the postmortems to prove this, as we had no way of telling if the cats were confined after being bitten and scratched, or before.

Assuming the above premises to be true, then it is certainly possible that the healthy cats killed the sick ones and that the ones with broken necks were the result of "mercy killings." However, if Annie confined the sick toms to protect them from the others, they may well have turned on each other within the confines of the room. I agree that Annie may have chosen to confine the cats inside the house—despite their fouling the floors—in order to protect them from a greater danger outside.

In conclusion, I am a great deal happier with the suggestion that Annie was a savior of cats rather than a tormentor of them, though I fear you will have difficulty proving it.

With best wishes for a successful campaign,

John Howlett

twenty-four

I asked Michael when he last saw Alan. "We stopped hanging around together after he hurt Rosie," he said, stroking his jaw in thoughtful reminiscence. "If I remember right, I didn't see hide nor hair of him from about '80 on . . . but I was in and out of the nick myself on a pretty constant basis which probably accounts for it." He shook his head. "It's pretty bad when you think about it."

"What?"

"That there were only two families in that whole road that couldn't keep out of trouble. The Percys and the Slaters. We had the same chances as everyone else, but never used them. Do you realize we must have done over twenty years in prison between us—what with Derek and me, and whatever it was Alan did?"

"Habits are hard to break," I said.

"Yeah, like Rosie's."

"What happened to her?"

"OD'd on smack in a squat in Manchester about five years ago," he said bitterly. "Some idiot dealer was selling it uncut around that time so it was probably accidental and not deliberate. Bailiffs found her body under a mattress the day after her mates vacated the place. The police reckoned she'd been dead three days, but no one did a thing about it . . . just left her there while they packed their bags and scarpered."

"I'm sorry."

He nodded. "It was pretty sad. Bridget kept trying to get treatment for her, but Rosie couldn't hack life without it. She always said she'd die of an overdose, so I guess she wouldn't have minded too much if she knew what was happening to her."

"What did her father say?"

"Zilch. I'm not sure he even knows she's dead. The girls stopped talking to him after he shacked up with Mum."

"Couldn't you have told him?"

"No way. He kicked me out when he moved in. That's when I started living with Rosie and Bridget." He jammed his hands between his knees, shoulders hunched in sudden anger. "He really hates me . . . persuaded Mum I was no good," he said resentfully, "even though I was the one that looked out for her when it mattered."

"When was that?"

He turned away so that I couldn't see his expression. "It's not important."

I was sure it was, but couldn't see the point of pursuing it as he clearly didn't want to tell me. "What did you do to make Geoffrey dislike you so much?"

"Told Rosie and Bridget he was one of Mum's clients. He was a two-faced bastard . . . kept making out what a saint he was to have given up his job to look after his dying wife . . . while all the time he was 'round at our place. It was the girls who did everything for their ma. Geoff did sod all except complain when his dinner was late. Vivienne was a nice lady. I used to sit with her most afternoons, and it pissed me off to hear her talking about Geoff as if he'd been good to her."

"Did she ever find out about your mother?"

"I don't think so. She died with a smile on her face, so I reckon he fooled her to the end. Me and the girls never told her anyway. It didn't seem kind."

A small silence fell while I wondered what to say next and immediately unwanted sounds crowded in on us—raucous seagull cries from the skylights above our heads, laughter, a baby's cry from the children's play area—and I found myself blurting out the one question I had been determined to avoid: "What on earth are you doing here, Michael? How can a man who's kind enough not to tell a dying woman that her husband's cheating on her attack an innocent stranger in a post office? It doesn't make sense."

"I needed the cash," he said simply, "and it seemed like a good idea at the time."

"And now?"

He gave a mirthless laugh. "Now I reckon it's the dumbest thing I ever did. I was only planning to frighten her . . . hold the pistol to her head . . . but she started screaming and shouting . . . and I went crazy." He fell silent, contemplating some private darkness. "She reminded me of Alan's mum," he said abruptly, "so I smashed her ugly face in. I really hated that bitch. It was her who used to get everyone worked up."

"How?"

"Just stuff," he said before lapsing into another longer silence.

I changed the subject by asking him what he'd meant in one of his letters when he said Bridget had posted her hair through my letter box as a "sacrifice." "Sacrifice for what?" I asked.

He was more comfortable talking about Bridget. "All the bad things that were happening to you," he said. "You told her once that you wished you had hair like hers, so she thought if she gave it to you the bad stuff would stop." He smiled at my expression. "Okay, it was a bit wacky but she always did have weird ideas. She put a load of raw onions into her mother's room one time because she read somewhere that onions absorb disease, but the smell was so bad that Vivienne couldn't sleep."

"I think they're supposed to work on colds," I said abstractedly, while pondering the rest of what he'd said. "What made Bridget think bad things were happening to me?"

"You looked so scared all the time," he said matter-of-factly. "It stood to reason there was some lousy shit in your life."

"Did you know what it was?"

A flicker of emotion crossed his face. "We guessed they were doing to you what they did to Annie."

"Who?"

"The Slaters. I saw Alan's dad try to barge you off the pavement one day . . . and his mum used to call you a nigger-lover. She said you'd be lynched for the things you were saying if we lived in America."

"What about *your* mother? Did she agree with Maureen?"

He looked away again, as if the subject of his mother was something he found hard to deal with. "I don't know," he said curtly. "We never talked about it."

"Did you talk about Annie's death?"

"No." Even more curt.

"Why not?"

"What was to talk about? Hell, we were glad to see the back of her. It meant Mum could take in more clients without having abuse bellowed at them through the wall. And that's all she was interested in," he finished bitterly, "making money out of saps."

"It was a vicious circle," I told him. "Every time you or the Slaters ratcheted up your aggression, Annie got worse. She might have been able to control her language if you'd left her alone, but she hadn't a hope in hell's chance once you started invading her space and making her afraid."

He shrugged. "Mum always said she should be in a loony bin."

"Only to give herself something to feel superior about," I murmured. "She didn't like being called a 'whore' . . . because that's what she was. The Slaters didn't like being called 'trash' . . . because that's what they were."

He gave a surprised whistle as if the comfortable image he had of me had suddenly been shattered. "That's a bit harsh."

"Do you think so?" I asked mildly. "I've always thought how generous Annie was. Had I been her, I'd have come up with something far stronger to describe low-grade scum who got their rocks off torturing cats."

He flinched perceptibly.

"Was it you and Alan who did it?" I asked. "It's the kind of brutality I can imagine you enjoying . . . inflicting pain on something smaller and weaker . . . then pushing the sad little remains on to Annie to see how she'd react. Was it Derek killing the marmalade cat that gave you the idea or was Maureen lying about that to protect Alan?"

"Jesus!" he said with a spurt of anger. "And you wonder why I hate the bitch? Talk about fucking twisted. Alan used to say her brains were shot because his dad knocked the sense out of her, but I'd say it was the other way 'round. The bitch was born twisted and that's the reason the poor sap went for her." He leaned forward aggressively. "It was Maureen killed the cat, and she did it because it made her feel good. She got Alan to hold it down on the kitchen table while she beat its brains out with a baseball bat, and when Alan started blubbing because he really liked animals, she took the bat to him instead and said, if he ever told on her, she'd nail the next one to the fence and make him watch it while it died."

It was like a floodgate opening. Once Michael started on his hatred of Maureen he couldn't stop. He talked about her lousy parenting, her drinking, her vilification of him and his mother. "It makes me sick what she's got away with," he finished angrily. "It makes me even sicker that she's on the out and me and Derek are stuck inside."

"What would she have been charged with?"

"Assault and battery of her kids . . . drunk and disorderly . . . you name it."

"Killing Annie?"

He didn't answer immediately. "All I know," he said then, "is what I told you in my letter. That I came home from the arcade to hear that the stupid cow had died in the street from some sort of accident."

I nodded as if I believed him. "Did you know the Slaters went into the house later and robbed it?"

"Rosie sussed it when the police described old Annie as living in poverty," he admitted. "She reckoned we ought to say something but I didn't want have to explain how any of us knew what was in there."

"Did Alan not mention it?" I asked curiously. "You were inseparable at the time. I'd have expected him to boast about how clever they'd been."

"No."

"Because it *was* clever, Michael," I said idly. "Way too clever for Derek and Alan alone. It was the odd little extras like turning off the mains water . . . and soiling the floors to give the impression of self-neglect and poor hygiene. I've always wondered why that was necessary. Unless the smell of human urine was stronger than cats' urine and needed explaining."

He shook his head, but whether in denial that he knew what I was talking about or in refusal to answer the question, I couldn't tell. From the way he started to look for an officer to rescue him from me, it was clear the whole subject made him as uncomfortable as talk of his mother.

I plowed on determinedly. "You said it makes you sick that Derek's in prison," I reminded him. "Does that mean he's in at the moment?"

"He got two years in February '98. A guy on my wing shared a cell with him in Pentonville before he got shipped down here. He reckons Derek's dying. His liver's packed up with the drinking, and the one brain cell he has left can just about remember his name . . . and fuck all else."

"When's he due for release?"

He made a quick calculation in his head. "He'll have served half so he'll be out by now . . . assuming he's not dead already."

"What was he convicted of?"

"Burglary," said Michael dispassionately. "It's what he gets done for every time."

"Why does that make you sick?"

He gave an unexpected sigh. "Because he needs an education, not endless bloody punishment. Him and me were on the same landing in the Scrubs when I was on remand for this one. He's completely illiterate . . . just about manages a 'd' and 'e' for his signature but can't get to grips with the 'r' or the 'k.' I wrote some letters for him to his kids, but the only one who ever answered was Sally, and then only because she thought he might have some dosh hidden away somewhere. It pissed me off, it really did. The poor sod was only trying to tell them he loved them, but as far as they were concerned he didn't exist."

I was surprised. "You used to hate him when you were a child."

Michael shrugged. "It doesn't mean I can't feel sorry for him. I got to realizing how limited a guy's life is if he can't read and write. It's pretty mind-blowing when you think about it. I mean, you can't apply for a job if you can't sign your name to a form . . . and people sure as hell look down on you if they think you're an ignorant jerk. I reckon it's what made Derek violent. The only way he could get people to respect him was to slap 'em about and make 'em afraid of him."

"Is that his excuse?"

"No. He's not into excuses. Maybe that's why I feel sorry for him. He told me a bit about his childhood . . . how he got dumped in institutions because his mum didn't want him, then legged it to live on the streets till he was nicked for shoplifting and sent to Borstal. That's why he's illiterate, never stayed in school long enough to learn basic skills. It makes you realize how important love is to a kid. If his mum had wanted him"—he pulled a rueful face—"maybe he'd have been one of the good guys."

I guessed he was talking as much about himself as he was about Derek. "Everyone has to deal with rejection at some point in their lives," I said.

"Worse when you're a child, though," he said bleakly. "There has to be something wrong with you if even your mum doesn't like you." He fell silent, squeezing his fists in an echo of Drury. "Derek reckoned he only married Maureen because she reminded him of his mum," he said suddenly. "He had this black and white photo of her, and it was the spitting image of Maureen . . . skinny and slitty-eyed . . . called her a sidewinder."

"As in snake?"

He nodded.

"Why?"

"Because she never looked him in the face . . . just stabbed him in the back. It sounded halfway reasonable till I realized he feels like that about all women. 'They're all snakes,' he said, and snakes have shapes. If you can't recognize the poisonous ones you're a dead man."

"How did Maureen stab him in the back?"

"Gee-ed up Alan to take him on. It was like a war zone in there, went on for months. If we had our windows open we could hear the fights all the way past Annie's empty house . . . the screaming and yelling . . . bodies being slammed against walls. It was like the minute Annie died all hell let loose."

"Why? What changed?"

Michael shook his head. "Mum reckoned they reverted to type. They were bullies and bullies need someone to hit on . . . so while Annie was alive they hit on her and when she was dead they hit on each other."

It made sense, I thought. People never pull together so well as when they have a common enemy. "How many times did Maureen end up in the hospital?"

"Two or three. But it wasn't Derek who put her there, it was Alan. He was well out of control. It was around the time he raped little Rosie. Derek kept him in check for as long as he could but by the time Alan got to fifteen he was two inches taller than his dad and twice as heavy, and there wasn't much Derek could do to stop him."

"Did they know about Rosie's rape?"

He shook his head. "Not unless Alan told them. Rosie was paranoid about her mum finding out—thought it'd kill her quicker than the cancer—so we kept quiet."

I tried to make sense of the chronology. "And this all happened in '79?"

He nodded.

"Was it Alan who attacked Maureen while I was still living there?" I thought back. "Sometime during the February of '79?"

Another nod. "She was drunk one day and started slapping him about when he answered her back. He went for her like a maniac."

"Who called the ambulance?"

"Derek. He came in about an hour later and found her on the floor with little Danny trying to clean up the blood. Alan was blubbing in the garden because he thought he'd killed her. Derek had to run to the nearest phone box."

I eyed him curiously. "Did you know this at the time, or did Derek tell you about it afterward?"

"Derek told me," he admitted, "but it made sense when I thought about what Alan did to Rosie."

"Except Maureen said Derek did it," I murmured.

"Yeah, well, she's a liar. She snapped little Danny's arm across her knee one time, then swore to the doctors he'd fallen off his bike. Us kids knew it wasn't true because she did it in front of us." His lips thinned to threads. "She was a scary woman, and if we hadn't been such fucking cowards—" He broke off to stare at the table. "Derek was right pissed off when I told him about it. That's why he wanted to write letters to his kids. He really cared about them." He lifted his eyes to mine. "I know what you're thinking. Michael's not as bright as I thought. He spends a couple of months talking to a man he despises and ends up getting conned by him. Well, that might be true—I wouldn't go to the wall for it—but the one thing I *do* know is that Derek's so damn stupid even a moron could run rings around him. Sure, he was a bully and, sure, he used his fists, but he had to be *told* to do it. He was like a guided missile. Point him in the right direction and give him an instruction and—*wham!*—he did the business."

M. R.

From: Sarah Pyang (spyang@victorhos.com)

Sent: 15 August 1999 14:19

To: mranelagh@jetscape.com

Sent as from: Dr. Elias

Such are the wonders of modern technology! My secretary tells me she received your e-mail yesterday (Saturday) and you wish me to reply by return. Well, I'm happy to do so but I wonder if answers given in haste are wise.

You pepper me with questions. Who is more to blame: the architect of a crime or the one who carries it out? Should a whole police force be smeared because of one bad apple? Can justice be selective? Can the damage done by a mother to her child be mended? Can rapists be cured? Can children be evil? Is any crime excusable? Should the sins of a father be visited on his family? Should the sins of a mother?

In a poor attempt at wisdom might I suggest that, if you are honestly seeking justice for your friend, then you arrogate too much authority merely by thinking such things? These are not your decisions to make, my dear. Justice is impartial. Only revenge is prejudiced.

But isn't prejudice what you've been fighting all these years?

All best wishes,

Joseph

twenty-five

It was three o'clock by the time I drove down to the main road with my brain worrying away at what Michael had said like a tongue at a sore tooth. Each time I negotiated a hairpin bend the panoramic view of Weymouth Bay and Chesil Beach was spread out below me, but I was too absorbed in thoughts on motherhood to notice it. I wondered sometimes if my rush to judgment of the Sharon Percys and Maureen Slaters of this world was a way of punishing my own mother—and by extension myself. For everything I did as a parent was either in mimicry of her—or in defiance—and I had no idea which was right and which was wrong.

I had few feelings for Sharon beyond contempt for abandoning her son out of embarrassment the minute she acquired a modicum of respectability after Geoffrey moved in with her. Yet I couldn't understand why Michael had seemed so worried every time her name was mentioned when anger would have been a more normal reaction. He'd been angry enough with Maureen. Did Sharon's shying away from society's censure of her son's violence really make her ipso facto incapable of murder? And did Maureen's willingness to keep Alan's violence under wraps, together with my absolute certainty that she was the instigator of the hate campaigns against Annie and myself, make her ipso facto capable?

I was tired, and a little depressed, and I hadn't intended to see Danny that afternoon, but when I reached the T-junction at the bottom of

Verne Common Road I took an abrupt decision to turn left toward Tout Quarry. He was still at work on Gandhi when I turned into the gulley fifteen minutes later. "How's it going?" I asked.

He dropped his hands to his sides, resting the chisel and hammer against his thighs. "Okay," he said with a pleased smile. "How about you?"

"I've been to see Michael Percy. He sends his regards, says if you're bored he'll be happy to entertain you for an hour in the visitors' room."

Danny grinned. "A bit of a comedian, eh?"

"He has his moments," I agreed.

Danny laid his tools on the ground and brushed dust from his arms. "What would we talk about? I was just a snotty-nosed kid to him." He took his cigarettes from his pocket and perched on a rock beside Gandhi. "He gave me a lecture once when he caught me sniffing glue behind the church."

I sat next to him. "Did it do any good?"

"It did as a matter of fact. He was pretty decent about it, said he understood why I was doing it, then gave me a graphic description of what it's like to die of suffocation. He told me I had more going for me than to peg it in a graveyard with a nose full of glue fumes." He flicked me a sideways glance full of amused self-deprecation. "So I tried heroin instead."

My disillusionment must have shown. "Meaning Mr. Drury's terror tactics were more effective than Michael's lecture?"

Danny's smile widened. "I never liked glue-sniffing anyway . . . and as for heroin"—he gave a sudden laugh—"I'd been sitting on the bog for half an hour trying to pluck up courage to stick the bloody needle in before Mr. Drury caught me. I'd always hated the damn things."

I eyed him affectionately. "You were going to give up anyway?"

"Sure . . . injecting at least. I went on smoking it for a while, then I thought, to hell with it. I don't need this. I prefer cannabis. You keep a better grip on things with dope."

"Why didn't you tell your mother that at the time instead of letting Drury take the credit?"

"Because she wouldn't have believed me." He turned his cigarette in his fingers. "You wouldn't either. I was a pretty wild kid and it's not easy getting people to change their opinion of you when all you do is let them down."

I nodded. I'd seen it myself many times during my teaching career. Give a dog a bad name and he was hanged forever afterward. It was the sort of unforgiving prejudice I hated—as Dr. Elias had so pointedly reminded me. "What did Michael mean when he said he understood why you were sniffing glue?"

"He knew what it was like for me at home. There was only me and Mum and we loathed each other's guts. Most of the time she was passed out drunk"—he shook his head—"and when she wasn't, she'd lam into the first person she saw—usually me. It was pretty depressing. She's got real problems but she won't do anything about them . . . just locks the door and sinks into a stupor."

"Has she ever said what her problems are?"

"You mean apart from the physical dependency?"

I nodded.

"The same as any other addict I guess," he said with a shrug. "Fear of living . . . fear of pain . . . fear of having to look at yourself too closely in case you don't like what you see."

I wondered if he was right. "She seemed all right when I saw her."

"Only because she knew you were coming," he said dismissively, "but you can bet she was back in front of the telly with her fags and her booze within five minutes of you leaving. She can put on an act for a while . . . but she's too lazy to want to make it permanent. It makes me sick."

"Do you ever see her?"

"No. Last time was at Tansy's christening. I phone her once in a while just to let her know I'm still alive but the only one of her kids she wants to hear from is Alan. He's always been her favorite. She'd forgive him anything . . . but not me or my sisters."

I nodded. "What stopped you from being wild?"

He thought about it. "Getting sent down at sixteen for nicking and driving cars," he said with a grin. "Remember I told you I spent time in prison? It was the best thing that ever happened to me. Got me out of Graham Road. Made me think about what I wanted in life." He tilted the tip of his cigarette toward Gandhi. "There was an art teacher who showed me I had a talent for this kind of thing . . . he was a good bloke . . . got me a place at art school . . . even let me live with him and his wife for a while till I found somewhere of my own."

Perhaps I'd been wrong to tell Maureen that Beth had worked a change in Danny when it seemed to have been an unknown art teacher who had influenced his life. "Prison can work then?"

"Only if you want it to."

"Did Alan want it to work? Is that how he turned himself 'round?"

He shrugged. "He had a bad time . . . got bullied because he wasn't too bright . . . made him scared to go back. Then he met Beth and reckoned he had a future even though she strung him along for ages before she agreed to marry him." Another shrug—more dismissive this time. "Prison doesn't seem to have done Michael much good."

"Or your dad," I said slowly, thinking about Alan being bullied and the truism that most bullies are cowards. "Michael told me he and your dad were in the Scrubs together five years ago."

"Lucky Michael," said Danny sarcastically.

"He said your dad's illiterate . . . can't even manage his own name. So Michael wrote some letters for him. He said there was one to you which you didn't answer."

"He's lying," said Danny bluntly. "I could be dead for all that bastard cares."

"I don't think so."

"Where did he send it?"

"To your mum's house."

"She'd have torn up anything with a prison logo on it. What did it say?"

"That he cared about you."

Danny gave a snort of derision. "He doesn't even know what I look like."

"Mm," I agreed.

"I expect he was feeling guilty about abandoning us."

"Mm," I said again.

Danny frowned. "What else did Michael say?"

"That you had a broken arm when you were a child. Do you remember that?"

He cast an involuntary glance at his right hand. "Sort of. I know I was in plaster once, but I thought it was something to do with my wrist. It aches sometimes."

"Do you know how it happened?"

"I fell off my bike."

"Is that something you remember or something you've been told?"

A difference in my tone—too much curiosity perhaps—made his brows draw together in a puzzled frown. "Why so interested? All kids break bones at some time or another." I didn't answer and he seemed irritated by my silence. "Probably something I was told," he said curtly. "I don't remember much before I was six or seven."

"Neither do I," I said equably. "It's odd. Some people have very clear memories of their early childhood, but I have none at all. I used to think the stories my parents told me were real memories, but I've come to the conclusion now that if something is repeated often enough it acquires a reality." I paused to watch one of the student sculptors chip nervously at a small block of stone which had so little shape I wondered why he was bothering. "Michael said he doesn't remember seeing Alan after your dad left," I said next. "Is that the time he went to prison for dealing?"

Danny appeared to be on safer ground with this question. "Sure. It's the only sentence he's done. He told me about it once, said it did his head in something chronic." He leaned forward to pick a stone from the ground. "He didn't come home afterward. I think they reckoned he was a bad influence on the rest of us, or vice versa." He polished the stone with the ball of his thumb. "I only found out what he looked like when I skived off school one day to go wandering 'round Twickenham. It was when I was about thirteen, and this big guy stops me in the street and says, 'Hi, I'm Alan, how you doing?' He'd have been about twenty-four by then"—he gave a hollow laugh—"and I hadn't a clue who he was. I knew I had a brother somewhere but it was a bit of a shock to find he was only four miles away. He said he'd been keeping an eye on me from a distance."

"Did you tell your mother you'd seen him?"

"No chance. She used to get really wound up every time his name was mentioned, then she'd hit the bottle and start breaking furniture. I always thought she blamed Al for making my dad leave until Al turned up out of the blue a year later and she wept all over him and said how much she'd missed him."

"Why did he come?"

"Wanted to see her, I guess."

"No, I meant, why *then*? Why wait so long?"

He looked interested, as if it were something he'd never considered before. "It was after Mr. Drury retired," he said. "I remember Mum saying there was no one left who'd recognize him—" He broke off abruptly. "She probably just meant he wouldn't be picked on anymore."

"Is Alan fond of her?" I asked, remembering what Beth had said about Alan's depression every time he visited Maureen.

"Maybe. He's the only one who bothers to see her."

"But?" I prompted when he didn't go on.

He stretched his right arm and dropped the stone, staring at his hand in absorbed fascination as he flexed his fingers. "He's scared of her," he answered abruptly. "That's the only reason he goes . . . to keep her from turning on him."

We went for a walk through the sculpture park, diving down little al-leyways between craggy walls of stone. We squeezed through a cleft into a cave where a pink blanket and a pile of empty cans suggested someone had taken up residence or a couple of lovers had found a private retreat.

"Maybe I should take it over," said Danny, "and sneak out at night to carve the stones by moonlight."

"Do you enjoy it that much?"

He made a rocking motion with a hand. "Not all the time—it can be bloody frustrating when it doesn't go right—but it's what I want to do."

"Sam's willing to let you work in the barn at the bottom of our garden," I said, leading the way back out again. "It'll mean slumming it in the tack room and working with the doors open if you want any light"—I shrugged—"but it won't cost you anything. If you can scrounge some stone and don't mind sleeping rough for a bit . . . it's free and available."

He was less than appreciative. "I'd freeze to death in the winter."

"Mm," I agreed, "and Sam'll have your hide if he catches you smoking cannabis."

"What about you?"

"I never argue with my husband in public so if you come . . . and he catches you . . . you're on your own." I turned to look at him. "Think about it, anyway. You won't get a better offer today."

He became very quiet as we approached the car. "Why would you want to help me?" he asked, taking the keys from my hand to unlock the door.

"Think of it as an investment in the future."

He held the door open. "You'd never make a penny," he said gloomily. "I haven't that much talent."

I gave him a quick hug. "We'll see." I lowered myself on to the seat. "But it's not a financial investment, Danny, more a loan of goodwill that you can repay with interest to someone who deserves a similar chance at another time."

He wouldn't meet my eyes. "What do you want in return?"

"Nothing," I said honestly, reaching for the door. "There are no strings attached. The barn's there if you want to take us up on it. If you don't, no hard feelings."

He shuffled his feet on the gravel. "Alan's phoned a few times wanting to know what you've been saying about him," he said abruptly. "He's really twitched even though I keep telling him you're only interested in what happened to the black lady."

I didn't answer.

"What did he do to you?" he asked me.

"What makes you think he did anything?"

"Your face goes blank every time his name's mentioned." He put his hand on the door to stop me closing it. "I'd never go against him," he said painfully. "He's my brother."

"I wouldn't expect you to," I said as I started the engine. "But the offer of the barn has nothing to do with Alan, Danny. If you're happy to come, we're happy to have you. I hope you'll remember that . . . whatever happens . . ."

My last visit that day was a prearranged one to Sheila Arnold in her office. She and Larry had been away the previous week on a whistlestop visit to the Florida condo—"keeping Larry happy" had been her wry description over the telephone—and this was my first opportunity to show her the photographs of Beth and Alan's house. She had agreed to see me at the end of afternoon surgery and was updating some patients' notes on her computer when I dropped into the chair beside her desk. She gave me a quick smile, then pushed her keyboard away and turned to face me.

"Well?"

I'd had more copies made from the negatives after Drury's fit of pique with my rucksack, and I produced these from my pocket and spread them across her desk.

"My God!" she declared in amazement. "I thought you were exaggerating when you said you'd found the mother lode."

I tapped the bangle on her wrist, then pointed to a close-up of Beth Slater's forearm. "Snap?" I suggested. "She has four of them, and I think she wears them all the time because she pushes them up her arm every time she goes near the sink. I doubt she has any idea they're valuable or even that they're jade. She probably thinks they're plastic or resin."

Sheila studied a picture of Beth with her children. "She has a nice face."

"Yes," I agreed.

"You liked her."

"Very much," I said with a sigh, "which makes it difficult to know what to do next. I don't think she has any idea these things were stolen. She told me Alan bought the Quetzalcoatl in a junk shop then started collecting other Mexican pieces because he believes the Aztecs were an alien civilization. Her children were full of it while I was taking the photographs—they think their dad's a genius because he knows more about aliens than anyone else—and it seems rather pointless to make them unhappy just for the sake of proving he was a thief twenty years ago."

Sheila lifted each picture in turn and studied it closely. "I remember some of these things," she said finally, "but I couldn't swear to all of them. Also, apart from the bangles and the mosaic, there doesn't seem to be much of any value. What happened to the gold and silver pieces, for example?"

"Alan's mother sold them to buy her house," I said, "but I've very little proof to back that up." I showed her the Chiswick jeweller's affidavit. "The description of the woman fits Maureen—along with half a million others who can manage a Birmingham accent—but it's only five items and accounts for less than £1,000."

"How much did the house cost her?"

"About £15,000 in total. She claims it all came from a win on the football pools which is why she didn't have to declare it." I lifted an amused eyebrow. "The house is now worth upwards of £200,000 and increasing every day as the housing boom takes off."

"My God!" said Sheila in disgust. "We didn't get much more than that for our four-bedroom job seven years ago."

"I know. It's sickening." I isolated a wide-angled shot of the sitting room. "Maureen stuffed most of this into the cupboard under her stairs because she didn't think it had any value"—I smiled ironically—"and it was still there when you were trying to persuade Drury Annie had been burgled. In fact, as Alan didn't retrieve it until a good ten years later Drury could have found it if he'd bothered to investigate."

She looked annoyed. "And I would have been vindicated?" I nodded. "I'll never forgive Peter Stanhope for accusing me of neglecting her, you know. He said I'd only invented her wealth to make myself look better."

"I know." It obviously still rankled with her, I thought, and decided to keep to myself that Drury had known about the Quetzalcoatl long before Sheila had reported it stolen. I wanted an objective opinion, not one given in anger. "The worst of it is," I said, showing her the picture, "that poor Beth did all this decorating herself to make a Mexican setting for the artifacts . . . and it seems cruel to take them away just to prove a point. No one else is going to appreciate them as much as she and Alan do."

Sheila propped her chin in her hands and regarded me solemnly. "Is this a way of asking me to forget that I ever said Annie was robbed?"

"I don't know," I sighed. "I keep wondering if it's right to destroy innocent children's lives over a crime that was committed twenty years ago."

"Except I seem to remember you telling me that if you found Annie's thief you'd also find her murderer. Were you wrong?"

I studied a close-up of the brass artillery shell that stood in Beth's fireplace with colorful silk flowers fanning out of it like peacock feathers. "Does it matter?" I asked her. "Doesn't the same principle apply whatever the crime? Wouldn't I be choosing the lesser of two evils if I left Annie's death as an accident?"

She eyed me thoughtfully. "It depends how two-faced you want to be," she said bluntly. "That was probably Sergeant Drury's excuse as well . . . yet you've spent twenty years trying to prove him wrong."

Correspondence re: a meeting on 20.08.99

Leavenham Farm

Leavenham

Nr Dorchester

Dorset DT2 XXY

Alan Slater

12 Peasmont Road

Isleworth

Surrey

Tuesday, August 17, 1999

Dear Alan,

I shall be at your mother's house at midday on Friday, August 20. Please ensure that you and she are both there, otherwise I shall carry out my threat to go to the police despite the pain this will cause your wife, children and brother. You should be aware that I am writing to Sharon Percy and Geoffrey Spalding to insist that they, too, attend.

Yours sincerely,

M. Ranelagh

From: Mrs. Wendy Stanhope, The Vicarage,
Chanters Lane, St. David's, Exeter

Wednesday, August 18

I can certainly be outside Richmond station by 11.30 a.m., which, as you say, should give us ample time to reach Graham Road by midday. I can't imagine why you think I might be reluctant to support you against the Slaters. I'm not easily intimidated! Also, I've always regretted that Annie didn't think of me as a friend while she was alive. So thank you for asking me, my dear.

With love,

Wendy

twenty-six

It wasn't until we approached the Kew Road intersection on the outskirts of Richmond that Sam asked me if I knew what I was doing. The drive from Dorchester had taken over three hours and he was remarkably restrained throughout with only the odd bout of swearing at other drivers to betray his anxiety. We had discussed tactics the previous day while sitting over a glass of wine in the sunshine, and the plan had seemed reasonable then—perhaps plans always do under the influence of alcohol—but the friendly, rolling hills of Dorset were a far cry from the congested rat-runs of London's link roads, and the idea of taking on four potentially violent people in the most anonymous city in the world began to seem dangerously flawed.

Even then, I might have abandoned the whole project if Sam hadn't agreed with Sheila's view. The story wasn't mine to control anymore. And it wasn't a question of the lesser of two evils, he said. More of a Pandora's box. I'd opened the lid and the secrets were out. Danny for one—Michael Percy for another—would start asking questions: of Alan, of their mothers, even of Derek if they could find him. And it wasn't fair for the innocent to be tarred with the same brush as the guilty.

I laid an affectionate hand on his arm as he drew up at the traffic lights. "Thank you," I said.

"For what?"

"Holding back. I know how worried you are, but it has to be more sensible to take an open-minded woman with me than an angry husband who's likely to lose his temper."

"We can still go to the police."

I shook my head. We'd been through this a dozen times. "They wouldn't do anything . . . certainly not today . . . probably never. It took Stephen Lawrence's parents seven years to win an inquiry, so I can't see myself walking into Richmond Police Station out of the blue and being believed." I sighed. "I tried that twenty years ago and all it achieved was to persuade everyone I was a head case."

He nodded.

"In any case I really do want the truth this time, and Wendy was the only person I could think of. Sheila's too conservative to work outside the rules—and Larry wouldn't have let her come, anyway."

"Could he have stopped her?" asked Sam in surprise.

"She'd have insisted on it," I said cynically. "She uses him as her get-out card whenever her involvement becomes too onerous." I recalled Sheila's horrified refusal when I invited her to confront the Slaters—*Good God, I couldn't possibly. Larry would never allow it for a minute*—and I thought how wrong I had been to think that Annie's doctor would be the best support I could have. If I'd had any sense I'd have realized how passive she was when she admitted abandoning Annie's cause at the first sign of irritation from Larry, but I'd been seduced by her sympathetic report on Annie to the coroner and her gutsy defense of herself against accusations of negligence. The real irony, of course, was that I need never have upset my mother by moving the family to Dorchester if only I'd known in advance that an eccentric vicar's wife in Devon had more courage and crusading spirit in her little finger than Sheila Arnold would ever have. "And, apart from my ma," I went on with a sigh, "I couldn't think of anyone other than Wendy who had the guts to come with me."

Sam gave an abrupt laugh. "Did I hear right? Did you seriously consider asking your mother? Is this progress . . . or what?"

"Actually, she was the first person I thought of," I said with a wry smile, "until I realized she'd handbag the lot of them and leave me worse off than when I started." I gave an indecisive shrug. "But it *is* odd . . . maybe it's true that blood's thicker than water."

He sobered rapidly as we approached the station. "Well, just keep that in mind when you're talking to Alan Slater," he advised. "Unless he's a complete idiot, he's bound to realize that the best way to keep his children in ignorance is to stand by his mother. . . ."

We were fifteen minutes early but I refused to let Sam hang around to meet Wendy. I was afraid he'd be shocked by her age and her thinness—in his mind I believe he thought of her as a larger-than-life person, a mighty Valkyrie come to conduct me through a battlefield—and I had visions of him putting his foot down about the whole enterprise when he was presented with the reality. It was worse than I feared. Wendy's early start and long journey from Exeter had exhausted her and, away from the secure confines of the vicarage, the impressive vulture had given way to something with about as much substance and solidity as a stick insect.

"Oh dear," she said cheerfully as she crossed between the taxis on the forecourt in response to my wave, "do I look that bad?"

"No," I lied, giving her a warm hug, "but are you sure you want to go through with it? There'll be four of them and two of us," I warned, "and it could get very rough."

She nodded. "Nothing's changed then. You made that all very clear on the phone the other day. But don't forget I have the advantage of knowing a few of their secrets"—she gave a little chuckle—"so if all else fails I ought to be able to shame them into behaving well."

Or fire them up even worse, I thought worriedly. "It just seems more real now," I said lamely.

She tucked her hand through my arm and turned me firmly in the direction of Graham Road. "If you'd wanted someone to tan their hides, you'd have invited your husband and your sons to go with you," she pointed out. "Instead you invited me. Now, I can't promise not to let you down—I may fold at the first huff and puff—but I have no intention of giving up before we've even tried."

"Yes, but—"

She rapped me sharply over the knuckles. "You haven't come this far to walk away at the last hurdle, so let's have no more argument about it."

Sharon and Geoffrey were standing in their open doorway when we came abreast of their house, but they made no move to come out. "This is pure bloody blackmail," snapped Geoffrey angrily. "And what's *she* doing here?" he demanded, catching sight of Wendy at my side. "What the hell business is it of hers? She was always poking her long nose in where it wasn't wanted."

"Hello, Geoffrey," said Wendy with an amiable nod. "I see your temper hasn't improved much since I left. You really ought to have your blood pressure checked, my dear." She switched her attention to the woman. "And how are you these days, Sharon? You're looking well."

A tight little smile thinned Sharon's lips, as if she suspected the compliment was insincere, although as she'd taken so much trouble with her appearance—*Intent on putting Maureen in the shade,* I thought—Wendy had spoken only the truth. "We're not coming," she said. "You can't make us."

I shrugged. "Then the Slaters can say whatever they like about you and I'll have to accept it because this is the only opportunity you'll have to set the record straight before I go public."

They stared at me with fear in their eyes.

"Look, I know you were together that night until nine o'clock and that because of it Geoffrey was the last person to speak to Annie," I said bluntly. "And I'm guessing that if I could work that out then so could Maureen." I watched their fear increase. "So what did she do? Demand money?" I shook my head impatiently as I saw from their expressions that I was right. "And you have the nerve to accuse *me* of blackmail?"

"You're no different," said Geoffrey, clenching his fists. "Sending us threatening letters . . . on our backs all the time . . . trying to ruin our lives."

"If you'd been honest at the time," I said wearily, "I wouldn't have had to write any letters at all. You weren't responsible for Annie's death, Geoffrey, any more than my husband was. He passed her *after* you—also thought she was drunk—and also did nothing to help her. You were both guilty of unkindness but neither of you killed her." I watched his eyes widen in shock and smiled unkindly. "But I'm glad you've spent so long thinking you did. You deserve to pay some sort of penalty for lashing out when she begged you for help. That's what you did, isn't it? Knocked her down, then panicked when you thought you must have pushed her into the path of the traffic?"

He put a nervous hand on the door, but whether to steady himself or slam it in my face it was hard to say. Whatever his intention, Sharon thrust him away and wedged her foot against the bottom of the door. "Go on," she told me tightly.

"Whoever killed Annie attacked her in her house three or four hours before Geoffrey passed her in the street and those are the injuries she died of. She was beaten so savagely that she passed out . . . but she came to some time later and found the strength to stagger out into the street to look for help. The most likely time for the assault was around six o'clock but, as far as I've been able to discover, neither of you was in Graham Road at that time, so I can't see what you have to fear by telling the truth."

Geoffrey wasn't easily convinced. "How do we know you're not lying?" he asked.

"To what purpose?"

"To catch us out . . . make us say what you want."

"Oh, for heaven's sake!" said Wendy in sudden exasperation. "I had no idea you were such a stupid man, Geoffrey. Is the truth really so frightening that you must keep Sharon a prisoner to it?" Her eyes sparkled angrily. "Mrs. Ranelagh's trying to help you—though, goodness me, I'm not sure you deserve it—but you'll be tying her hands if you can't find the courage to stand up to Alan and Maureen."

"It's not just them though, is it?" he said unhappily. "They've got Derek in there as well."

I felt like a rag doll that had just lost all the sawdust out of its knees, and, from the way Wendy clutched at the gatepost, I clearly wasn't the only one.

I should have considered the size of Maureen's sitting room before I picked her house as the meeting place. Barely ten feet square, it was too small to allow each of us the amount of space we wanted, and we grouped ourselves in uncomfortable proximity according to our fragile alliances. This meant the Slaters sat rigidly on a sofa against the internal wall while Wendy, Sharon, Geoffrey and I faced them on hard-backed chairs in front of the window. It was reminiscent of trench warfare during the First World War—and I began to wonder if the outcome would be as futile.

I had been swept with nausea from the moment I saw Derek, and I struggled to contain it as the sour smell of him—more remembered, I think, than real—filled my nostrils. I kept asking myself why it hadn't occurred to me that Maureen would confront me with him, when instilling fear was what she was best at. I tried to speak and found I couldn't.

"Go on then," she said, gloating over my discomfort. "Say what you have to say, then get out."

It was a strange moment. The anger and bitterness inside me had been through a number of evolutions over the years—from a savage desire to kill, through apathy and a wish to forget—to this, my final position. Most of the time I could delude myself that I was pursuing justice for Annie—indeed I believe that most of the time that's what I was doing. But every so often I recognized that Dr. Elias and Peter Stanhope were right and my motives were based on revenge. If Maureen had kept her mouth shut, I might have been able to persuade myself forever that it was justice I was seeking . . . but such a surge of hatred shot through me in that moment that I was back where I started.

If Derek was dying, as Michael had suggested, it wasn't immediately obvious. He was thinner than I remembered, and his hands had the permanent tremor of alcoholism, but he still held his head like a boxer, watching for any opening, and he still radiated an illiterate's aggression. As for Alan, he was just an older, broader version of his brother and I couldn't look at him without thinking of Danny. I had pictured him for half my life as a muscular giant with a child's brain, but the reality was a nervous man with grimy fingernails and a beer gut who strove to keep as much distance from his parents as a three-seater sofa would allow.

In the end it was Derek who spoke first. His voice had changed very little—hard vowels and glottal stops—and it grated on my ears as it had twenty years ago. "You can't blame the boy," he muttered, putting a cigarette between his lips and lighting it. "He only did what I told him to do."

"I know." I looked at Alan's bent head. "I've never blamed him."

"Then you'll drop the rest of the stuff if I admit to it? That's what you've come for, isn't it? My head in a noose."

"Not just yours."

His eyes glinted dangerously. "You brought it on your own head," he ground out. "You shouldn't have set Drury on me . . . shouldn't have accused me of murdering the nigger."

I swallowed bile. "I didn't," I answered, forcing my voice to remain steady. "Mr. Drury asked me to give him the names of anyone I thought might have a grudge against Annie, so I named Maureen, Sharon and you. But he was only interested in you—probably because you had convictions for assault—and asked me what your grudge was. I said you were a drunken bully who made no secret of your racist views, that you had low self-esteem, a negligible IQ and a 'poor white' mentality. I also told him you were in the habit of punching and kicking anyone who annoyed you, and cited the time you thrashed Michael

Percy because he stood up to you after your own son ran away. At no point did I accuse you of murdering Annie." I held his gaze for a moment. "In fact the only accusation I ever made was that you threatened me with what might happen if I didn't keep my mouth shut."

He stabbed a trembling finger at me. "You lied about that."

I shook my head. "If you'd read my statement you'd have known what I said. But you couldn't read, so you accepted Mr. Drury's interpretation." I smiled slightly. "The funny thing is, I don't even blame *you* very much either. It's your nature to piss on anything you don't understand, so to condemn you for doing it is about as senseless as blaming a rat for spreading disease"—I looked at Maureen—"or a snake for being venomous."

The woman's eyes narrowed immediately. "Don't drag me into this," she snapped. "It was none of my doing."

There was a short silence while she and I stared at each other with our mutual hatred written strong on our faces. "But at least you know what Derek and I are talking about," I said evenly. "Which no one else does"—I gestured to right and left—"except Alan of course. You see, I've always wanted to know who planned it. It was too"—I sought for a word—"*subtle* for either of these morons to work out alone."

"Whatever they did, they did off their own bat. Ask them if you don't believe me."

"There'd be no point," I said with an indifferent shrug. "You've already persuaded Derek to take the blame. Just as you always did."

"And how would I do that, Miss High-and-Mighty?" she demanded with a sneer. "He's a man, isn't he? He does what he wants."

It was interesting to watch Alan's reactions. He sat between his parents, leaning forward, elbows on knees, staring at the floor, but every time his mother spoke his body leaned perceptibly closer to his father's.

"I don't know," I said honestly. "Probably by frightening Alan into paying him off. It has to be worth a try. Alan's got so much to lose. A wife and children who love him . . . a home . . . happiness."

Alan's knuckles squeezed into white knots as I spoke. "You said you didn't blame me," he muttered.

"I don't," I answered, "but I will if you insist on supporting your mother's lies. I came for explanations, Alan, not to have your father made the scapegoat. Why did I have to be threatened, anyway? Drury had lost interest in the whole subject by that time. . . . All he wanted was to shut me up because I kept accusing him of racism. . . . That's the only reason he got Derek fired up."

Maureen's lip curled in a sneer. "You were no better than the nigger," she said. "You called my man a 'poor white' and types like him don't take kindly to insults. Particularly not from a jumped-up schoolteacher who fancied herself way above us. Why wouldn't he want to shut you up?"

The depressing part was, I was sure she was telling the truth, at least where Derek was concerned. A woman's sneer was the only motivation he would ever need to assault her. I looked at him. "Did you piss on Annie, too?" I asked him. "Is that why she reeked of urine?"

He stared at me through unintelligent eyes.

"When did you do it?" I went on. "Before or after she lost consciousness?"

He turned irresolutely to his wife, looking for an answer.

"None of us touched her," she snapped angrily. "She was in the morgue by the time we thieved her stuff. I've already told you that."

It was such an open admission—and so unrepentant—that you could have heard a pin drop in the silence that followed. And I remember thinking to myself, *This would all be so much easier if I didn't believe her.*

twenty-seven

Alan stirred unhappily to life. "Mum's telling the truth," he said doggedly. "Okay, I'm not saying we're perfect—and I'm not saying we didn't go into Annie's house after we heard she was dead—but we're not murderers."

"Then why was her coat stinking of urine when I found her?" I asked him.

"She always smelled," flashed Maureen sharply. "And how do you know it was on her coat, anyway? Maybe she pissed her pants after she was hit."

"The smell was too strong and she was curled up in a ball to protect herself. In any case, she must have been saturated in it otherwise the rain would have washed it away." I turned back to Alan. "I think it was a practice run for what you did to me two months later . . . just as *I* was a practice run . . ." I hesitated, all too aware that Rosie Spalding's father was sitting next to me—"for the cause of your bust up with Michael Percy."

His eyes flickered involuntarily toward Geoffrey before he dropped his forehead into his hands to mask his expression.

"That was Michael's doing," retorted Maureen so fast that my blood ran cold. *My God! Had she known about Rosie's rape and done nothing about it? She didn't stop bleeding for weeks, Michael had said. . . .* "Michael lost his temper for no good reason and went berserk. He's always been danger-ous . . . look at what he's in prison for now." She flicked a spiteful

330

glance at Sharon. "If it's a murderer you want, then concentrate on him—even better, his mother's fancy man. Try asking who was the last person to speak to Annie. That'll give you the answers you want."

Geoffrey half rose from his seat, his face purpling with anger, but Wendy laid a restraining hand on his arm and held him back. "Don't let Maureen set the agenda, my dear. Can't you see she's trying to start a fight by provoking that peppery temper of yours? It's really most interesting. She doesn't want Derek and Alan to answer Mrs. Ranelagh's questions and I'm intrigued to know why."

Maureen's mean little eyes slid across to look at her. "What's it got to do with you?"

"Quite a lot considering I was one of your victims. You admit to theft so casually, Maureen, as if it's something to be proud of but your children broke my heart when they stole my mother's brooch. It was quite irreplaceable—the only thing I had of hers—but completely worthless, of course, as you must have discovered the minute you tried to sell it."

"Nothing to do with us. It was Michael who took that."

Wendy shook her head. "No," she said firmly. "I know exactly when it went. You came seeking shelter, as usual, and kept me talking in the kitchen while your children looked for what they could steal. I blamed myself, of course, as you knew I would. I should have locked all the doors the minute you came into the house. It wasn't as though I had any illusions about you."

The woman smiled unpleasantly. "Too right. You treated us like dirt."

"Not at all," said Wendy firmly. "I made a point of extending the same courtesy to you and your family as I did to everyone else."

"Yeah, well maybe you made that a bit obvious. You never liked us, that's for sure."

Wendy nodded immediately. "Yes, that is certainly true," she confessed. "In fact, it was a lot worse. I couldn't *bear* you . . . couldn't bear your children . . . couldn't bear to have you in my house. My heart used to sink every time you came knocking on our door because I knew I'd face a struggle between the complete revulsion you all inspired in me and my duty as a Christian."

The directness of this response took Maureen aback, as if she believed vicar's wives should deal only in euphemism. "There you are then," she said doubtfully. "That proves you treated us like dirt."

"Oh, I don't think so," murmured Wendy, "otherwise you wouldn't be so surprised to hear me agree with you. I said I *struggled* with my revulsion, not that I gave into it. Our door was never closed to you, Maureen, not even after the theft of my brooch. We gave you and your children every assistance even though you were quite the most unpleasant family we'd ever had dealings with."

I watched Alan's head sink deeper into his hands.

"What about Michael Percy?" demanded Maureen belligerently. "He was a thief same as mine, but you couldn't do enough for him . . . always turning out to hold his hand while the tart"—she jerked her chin at Sharon—"was otherwise engaged. But your pet ends up pistol-whipping old ladies and my lad comes good. So how did that happen, eh? Explain that."

Wendy shook her head. "I don't claim to know the answers, Maureen. All I can do is tell the truth as I see it." She, too, looked at Alan. "In any case, it's Alan you should be asking, not me. He's the only one who knows his story."

"Yeah, well, maybe I was a better mother than you thought I was," said Maureen triumphantly. "How do you like that for an explanation?"

"You were no better than me," said Sharon in a tight little voice. "The only difference between us was that yours were frightened of you, and mine wasn't."

"More fool you then," retorted Maureen, her eyes glinting to have lured the woman into the open. "Look where it's got you. Your Michael's such an embarrassment to you, you haven't spoken to him in years . . . or that bitch of a wife who shopped him." She gave a harsh laugh. "Not that I blame you. He was a wrong 'un through and through. Do you think my kids would have thieved if he hadn't shown them how? Do you think Annie would have been stinking of piss if he hadn't found her and done the honors?" She pointed her cigarette at Sharon's heart. "That makes you sit up and take notice, doesn't it? You didn't even know he was in her house that night, let alone used her as a piss pot."

I glanced irresolutely at Sharon and was shocked by her terrible pallor. "Are you suggesting Michael killed her?" I asked Maureen.

"Helped her on her way maybe. He told Alan he got home about 8:30, saw that her door wasn't properly shut and went in to see if he could nick something. He found her lying on the rug in her sitting room, reckoned she was drunk and thought it'd be funny to piss on her." She broke off on a laugh. "The place stank of cats so he didn't reckon she'd notice when she came 'round."

"What happened?"

She gave a careless shrug. "He said she started moaning so he got the hell out in case she went for him. But the chances are he's lying through his teeth, and he gave her a kicking as well. It's what he liked doing."

I glanced at Alan's bent head. "Was Alan with him?"

"'Course he wasn't," snapped Maureen. "He's already told you he never touched her. But you'd rather believe it of him than Michael, wouldn't you? You're like *her*"—she cast a baleful look at Wendy— "always think well of one and ill of the other."

Wendy leaned forward, propping her elbows on her knees and examining Maureen curiously. "Why is it so important that Alan wasn't there?" she asked.

A ferocious frown gathered on Maureen's face. "What's that supposed to mean?"

"You seem so determined to push the blame on to Sharon's son but, if I've understood correctly, it was *your* son who performed the same disgusting act on Mrs. Ranelagh a few weeks later. Yet none of you seems too worried about that."

"So?"

"It suggests that something worse happened to Annie than happened to Mrs. Ranelagh . . . something you don't want Alan associated with."

Was it my imagination or was Maureen scared? Certainly Alan was—if his head dropped any lower, I thought, it would be touching his knees.

"Michael told us about it afterward . . . gave us the idea," said Derek suddenly. "Seemed only fair to do to the nigger-lover what was done to the nigger. They both thought they could badmouth us and get away with it."

"That's right," said Maureen. "But it was Michael did it first, just like always. He was a bad influence, that boy. Everything evil in this street started with him and his mother, but it was always us got pilloried for it."

"What about rape?" I said cynically. "Whose idea was that? Because it certainly wasn't Michael's. He thrashed Alan within an inch of his life when he did it to Rosie. Doesn't that count as something evil?"

It was a form of words—spoken in angry defense of someone who wasn't there to defend himself—yet time stood still as soon as I'd uttered them. No one moved on the sofa. It was as if they believed that stillness could somehow freeze us all in time and space and leave my knowledge forever unspoken. My first reaction was surprise that Derek seemed to understand what I was talking about until I remembered Michael saying that Alan hadn't come to blows with him until after Rosie's rape.

My second reaction was entirely physical as the reason for their petrified expressions dawned on me. *Alan had raped Annie, too.* . . . Oh, dear God! Forget control. Forget justice. Forget *revenge.* Twenty years of reasoned evolution were overturned in a second, and I regressed to a primeval desire to kill.

I leaped on Alan like a tigress—my revulsion—my fear—my hatred—*everything*—racing in a torrent through my blood. "You *FUCKING* little *SHIT!*" I roared, slamming his head against the wall. "She was *DY-ING,* for Christ's sake. How *DARE* you violate a dying woman?"

He cringed away from me. "I never . . . only in her mouth . . ."

Out of the corner of my eye I saw Maureen's claws reach out to scratch my face. And with every ounce of hatred that I had I planted my fist between her teeth.

It would have turned into a free-for-all if Geoffrey hadn't been a pacifist at heart. He pulled me off Maureen by seizing me by the arms and spinning me 'round behind him. "Enough," he said sharply, standing between me and the sofa. "Control your mother," he ordered Alan, "or I'll ask Mrs. Stanhope to call the police."

It was an unnecessary instruction because Alan was already holding her back with an arm hooked 'round her neck, but mention of the police at least persuaded her to sink back into her seat. She eyed Geoffrey balefully. "You're in no position to play God," she spat. "Your hands are as dirty as ours."

He lowered his head like a terrier after a ferret, and stared fixedly at her. "Mrs. Ranelagh says Annie was beaten up in her house two or three hours before I passed her—and those are the injuries she died of—so don't accuse me of having dirty hands. You're the only one 'round here got free with a baseball bat."

Maureen's narrowed gaze focused on me. "You're being fed a pack of lies. A week ago this bitch was saying it was Derek gave Annie a thrashing before dumping her in the street. . . . Now she's trying to put the blame on me. Well, how could I have got the fat cow through her front door? Tell me that."

"She got herself out," I said, breathing deeply through my nose to try to quell the shudders that were jolting my body with electric shocks. "She had a fractured skull . . . a broken arm . . . she'd been unconscious for God knows how long with your filthy son all over her . . . but she still had enough will to live to stagger out into the street and look for help." I made another lunge forward, only to be blocked by

Geoffrey. "And no one gave it to her because they thought she was drunk."

"Your husband being one," she snarled.

I pressed a finger to the tic of hate that throbbed beneath my lip. "I think she came to my end of the street because she knew I was the only person who would help her. I even think she may have knocked on my door—and I feel so damn guilty I wasn't there, because I was sitting at school waiting for parasites like you and Derek to come and talk to me about your children's progress." I dropped abruptly on to my chair again, energy spent. "Some joke, eh? We all knew the only direction your children were ever going was toward prison."

"Don't you call us para—" began Derek.

But Geoffrey cut him short. "What did you do to Rosie?" he demanded of Alan.

"Don't answer him, son," snapped Maureen, spitting blood. "Just because that bitch of a teacher tells lies about us, it doesn't mean we have to start explaining ourselves."

"It damn well does," said Geoffrey belligerently. "If he raped my Rosie I want to know about it. He ought to be locked up."

"*Your* Rosie?" demanded Maureen, dashing the blood from her mouth with the cuff of her sleeve. "That's rich, that is. How come she's yours all of a sudden when you couldn't get shot of her quick enough to move in with the tart?"

"More to the point, Maureen," said Wendy forcefully, "when did Alan tell you about his part in all of this? And why did you do nothing to stop it getting any worse?"

She shrank into the back of the sofa. "You should be asking Derek that," she said mutinously. "He's already said it was him told Alan what to do. What could I have done except take a beating myself . . . which is what happened every time Derek reckoned I was interfering."

But Derek gave an angry shake of his head. "I said I'd take the blame for the schoolteacher," he muttered. "Nothing else."

"There *is* nothing else," she snapped angrily. "All we ever did was thieve a few things off the nigger and teach Miss High-and-Mighty here a lesson in manners. All the rest is lies."

I looked up. "What about the cats?" I asked coldly. "Were they a lesson in manners, too?"

She dropped her eyes immediately and fumbled for a cigarette.

"You were too precise about the numbers inside Annie's house. It's not a figure you'd have known if you hadn't notched up each sad little stray as you tortured it."

Why should this be the key that unlocked Alan? Was a cat's death more dreadful than a woman's? A cat's humiliation harder to forget? A cat's cries more poignant? *Apparently so.* Annie could die. . . . I could be humbled. . . . Rosie could weep . . . but an animal must be loved. His anguish was frightening for, as I watched him battle with tears for those long-dead creatures, I found myself wondering if he was still as dissociated from human pain as he so obviously had been then. If so, I had little hope for Beth and her children.

It would be impossible to relate what he said in the way he said it. Once released, his emotions were a river in spate, sweeping aside everyone's sensibilities but his own and given in stuttered sentences which were barely comprehensible at times. We became party to his mother's hatred of sex, his father's brutal taking of her whenever he wanted it, their drunkenness, their violence toward each other and their children. But, more than anything, he dwelt on Maureen's slaughter of the marmalade cat, repeating over and over that when he tried to stop her she turned the baseball bat on him.

I asked him why she'd done it and, like Michael, the only explanation he could offer was that it made her feel "good." She laughed when its brains went everywhere, he said, and she wished it had been the nigger's head she'd smashed.

"What about the other cats?" I asked him. "Why did she go on with it?"

"Because it sent Annie 'round the bend to have them put through her flap. She took to wailing and hollering all the time and behaving like a crazy woman, and Mum reckoned if she didn't pack up and go of her own accord, it was a dead cert she'd be taken out in a straitjacket."

"But if hurting animals upset you so much, why did you help?"

"I wasn't the only one," he muttered. "We all did it—the girls, Mike, Rosie, Bridget. We used to go out looking for strays and bring them home in boxes."

I wondered sadly if that was the real explanation for Bridget's sacrifice of her hair. "But why, if you knew what was going to happen to them?"

"It wasn't as bad as having their heads split open."

"Only if you believe a quick death is worse than a slow one."

"They didn't all die. . . . Annie saved most of them . . . and that's what we reckoned would happen." He pressed his forehead into his hands. "It was better than having Mum kill them straight off, which is what she wanted to do. It was them dying that got Annie worked up."

"The ones you put under my floorboards died," I said, "because I didn't know they were there."

He raised his head with a look of bafflement in his eyes, but didn't say anything.

"And if you'd refused your mother," I pointed out, "none of the cats need have died. Surely Michael was bright enough to work that out even if you couldn't."

"Us kids wanted rid of Annie, too," he said sullenly. "It wasn't right to make us live next door to a nigger."

I don't know what was going through Maureen's mind while he spoke. She made one or two halfhearted attempts to stop him but I think she realized it was too late. The odd thing is I believe she was genuinely ashamed of her cruelty—perhaps because it had been the one crime she committed herself. More interestingly, she had eyes only for Sharon when Alan admitted that he and Michael had entered Annie's house together around 8:30 on the night she died.

"It was Mike spotted the door was ajar," he said. "We were going into his place to watch telly because we knew his mum was out, and he says to me, 'The coon's left her door open.' The place was black as the ace of spades . . . no lights . . . nothing . . . and he says, 'Let's do a prowl before she gets back.' So we creep into the front room and damn near fall over her. It was Mike started it," he insisted. "He turns on the lamp on the table . . . reckons she's drunk as a skunk and pulls out his dick—" He broke off, refusing to go any further.

"Did she speak to you?"

He raised his eyes briefly to Sharon's. "Kept saying the tart had hit her . . . so Mike goes apeshit and kicks her till she shuts up. After that we went down the arcade, and Mike says he'll kill me if I ever breathe a word about his mum . . . and I say, 'Who cares? It's good riddance, whoever did it. . . .'"

"I told you it wasn't us," jeered Maureen with a gloating smile on her face. "'Look to the tart,' I said. It was her and her son did it between them." She jabbed two fingers in the air at Geoffrey. "That's why you shoved the mad cow in the gutter—because she told you who'd hit her."

I felt physically sick. Even though I'd suspected Michael had known how Annie had died, I'd always hoped he hadn't been involved. *But could a "kicking" at 8:30 have caused the sort of blood-seepage into Annie's thighs that was so obvious in the photographs?* I looked at Sharon. "*Stand up for your son,*" I wanted to shout at her. *Tell them how small he was for his age . . . and how murderous kicks like that must have come earlier . . . from someone who was stronger . . .*

"Is that true, Geoffrey?" asked Wendy in shocked tones.

"No," he muttered, looking at Sharon in sudden disbelief. "She didn't say anything . . . just kept grabbing at my sleeve, trying to hold herself up . . . so I pushed her away . . ." His voice petered into silence as he began to question how many lies Sharon had fed him. "No wonder you let me think it was my fault," he said resentfully. "Who were you protecting? Yourself or that bloody son of yours?"

But Sharon's only response was a tiny gesture of denial as the last vestiges of color fled from her face.

"If she faints she'll hurt herself," I warned.

"Let her," said Maureen spitefully. "It's no more than she deserves."

"Oh, for God's sake," I sighed wearily, standing up to help Wendy support the limp body. "If you believed that then why didn't you tell Mr. Drury the truth at the time?"

But it was a stupid question, which she didn't bother to answer. She had no regrets over Annie's death. Indeed her only goal had been to steer retribution well away from herself so that she could indulge her spoils to good advantage. And if that meant exploiting men's baser instincts to instill terror in women, then so be it. In a bizarre sort of way I could even admire her for it, for hers was a vicious world, where greed—be it material or sexual—was a way of life, and by her own standards she had made a success of it. Certainly she was the only person in that room who owned her house through the quickness of her mind.

I touched a hand to Sharon's peroxide hair and it felt dry and dusty beneath my fingers. "The worst thing this lady ever did to Annie was pour a bucket of water over her head and make a few complaints to the council," I told Geoffrey, "but if you can't believe that then you should bugger off and give her a chance to get her son back. Wendy's right. All you've ever done is make her a prisoner to the truth."

"But—"

"But what?" I snapped. "Would you rather trust Maureen's version of events? Mine come free, remember, and hers come at a price." I grabbed his elbow and forced him to look at Sharon. "This woman has stood by you for over twenty years—how much longer do you need to know her before you trust her? Or must she always be judged by the rotten standards that you"—I gestured toward the sofa—"and this vermin over here choose to live by?" I spoke as much for myself as I did for Sharon, for I knew all too well the pain of living in an atmosphere of disbelief and distrust. You sink or swim . . . fight or give in . . . and whichever route you choose, you take it alone.

Geoffrey gave an uncertain shake of his head.

I knelt down abruptly in front of Sharon and took her hands in mine. "Sell your house and move," I urged her. "Cut this man out of your life and start again. Make friends with Bridget . . . help Michael go straight. He needs his mother's love just as much as he needs his wife's . . . and you owe him that much. He thought you were a murderer, Sharon . . . but he protected you . . . and he doesn't understand why you were so quick to abandon him. Fight for him. Be the mother he wants you to be."

She was too dazed to grasp what I was talking about and stared helplessly from me to Geoffrey, her subservience to men so ingrained that she would do whatever he told her to do.

Maureen's triumphant voice came at me from the sofa. "There's only ever been one tart in this street, and she's gone down like a sack of potatoes because she's been found out. So go tell that to the police and see if they care about the few bits of trash we pilfered."

I wanted to kill her. I wanted to squeeze her scrawny throat between my fingers and choke the venom out of her. Instead, I stood up with a sigh and reached for my rucksack. "Annie never called Sharon a 'tart,' Maureen, she called her a 'whore.' You told me that yourself."

Her mouth dropped open, for once unable to find words, because she knew I was right. I longed to be strident . . . to scream and yell . . . to stamp my feet . . . to roar my frustration to the winds. I had hoped for the miracle that would prove me wrong, but instead I just felt desperately sad and desperately weary.

"And I wouldn't rely on the police letting you get away scot-free if I were you," I went on with commendable steadiness, exercising the sort of ladylike control that would have brought a smile of approval to my mother's face. "The only protection you've ever had was other people's silence. As long as they had secrets to hide you were safe." I shrugged. "But there aren't any secrets anymore, Maureen. So where does that leave you?"

Derek gave an unexpected laugh. "I told her you'd never give up," he said, "but she wouldn't listen. Said schoolteachers were too prissy to get up off their knees and fight." Maureen pursued Wendy and me to the door, demanding answers, which I refused to give. Who did it if it wasn't Sharon? How much was I going to tell the police? What proof had I of anything? Her lip had fattened from the punch I'd delivered and she caught at my sleeve to hold me back, threatening me with prosecution if I didn't give her some *"fucking* explanations."

I pulled away from her. "Go ahead," I urged. "I'll even tell you where I'm going—I'll be with Mr. Jock Williams at 7 Alveston Road, Richmond—so by all means send the police 'round to arrest me. It'll save me having to call them. And, as for giving you answers"—I shook my head—"no chance. What you don't know can't help you, and I'm damned if I'll be party to Derek and Alan telling any more lies for you." I raised my eyes to where Alan was standing in the shadows of the hall. "I have every reason to hate and despise you," I told him, "but I think your wife is the one woman in a million who can rescue you from your mother. So my best advice is, go home now and take your father with you. If Beth hears the truth about you from Derek, then she may understand and forgive. If she hears it from your mother, she won't."

"Goodness me!" Wendy gasped, patting her fluttering heart as we walked away. "That's the first time I've seen her afraid."

"Are you all right?" I asked in concern, reaching out to support her under the elbow.

"Absolutely not. I've never had so many shocks in my life." She lowered her bottom on to the garden wall of number 18. "Just let me get my breath back." She took some deep breaths, then wagged a finger at me as she began to recover. "Peter would counsel you strongly against this obsession with revenge, my dear. He'd say the only path to heaven is through forgiveness."

"Mm," I agreed. "That's the advice he gave me when I told him about Derek and Alan."

She tut-tutted crossly. "Is that the time he let you down?"

I watched a car negotiate the speed bumps in the road. "He didn't do it on purpose," I demurred. "He was like everyone else. . . . He thought I was hysterical." I looked toward Maureen, who still hovered by her gate. "I think I know why now. I never remained objective long enough to keep my voice under control. And that worries people."

"But why Peter?" she asked curiously. "Didn't you have anyone else to talk to?"

Only Libby . . . "It was the church more than Peter," I said non-committally. "I couldn't think of anywhere else to go."

"Oh, my dear, I'm so sorry. You really *were* let down then."

I shook my head. "Rather the opposite actually. I went in weepy and pathetic, looking for sympathy, and came out like an avenging angel." I gave an abrupt laugh. "I kept thinking, if I *ever* forgive, it'll be on my terms and not on the say-so of a fat, sweaty bloke in a dress who thinks I'm lying." I sobered just as suddenly. "I'm sorry. I didn't mean to be rude."

Wendy squared her thin shoulders and stood up. "It's a good description of Peter," she said tartly. "He's an actor at heart so he's only really happy when he's in costume. He thinks it lends authority to what he's saying."

"I was pretty peculiar at the time," I said by way of apology, "and he did try to be kind."

"He's got no fire in his belly, that's his problem. I keep telling him his sermons are ridiculously PC. He's supposed to be addressing evil, not offering a policy statement on behalf of liberals."

I chuckled. "You'd be a thunderbolts-and-lightning vicar then?"

"It's the only kind to be," she agreed cheerfully. "A whiff of brimstone and sulphur puts sin to flight quicker than anything. *And* it's more dramatic. The fires of hell and damnation are a great deal more exciting than the bliss and majesty of heaven."

I adored her . . . for her openness . . . her steadfastness . . . *God save me, her similarity to my mother* . . . but I could see she was too exhausted to take another step. I persuaded her to sit back down while I fished in my rucksack for the mobile I'd borrowed off Luke that morning for the purpose of calling a minicab. A car drew up beside us before I could find it.

"Do you want a lift?" asked Alan gruffly through the open passenger window as he leaned across to fasten his father's seatbelt. "We'll be passing Alveston Road."

I was too startled to answer, and looked at Wendy.

"Thank you, my dears," she said, rising graciously to her feet. "That's most generous of you."

Nothing more was said until Alan stopped his car in front of Jock's house. Derek and Wendy were content to appreciate the silence, while Alan kept darting me worried glances in the rearview mirror, his mouth working to frame a form of words that would be acceptable to me.

But it was only when he drew to a halt in Alveston Road that he found the courage to take a chance. He turned 'round. "It's probably a bit late"—he faltered—"and I wouldn't blame you if said no—but I wish I'd never— Did Danny tell you I've been straight these fifteen years?"

I stared him down. "If you want to say sorry, Alan, then say it. Don't spoil it by making excuses."

He ducked his head in a scared nod, an echo of the schoolboy I had caught thieving from my purse. "I'm sorry."

"Me, too." I held out my hand to him. "I didn't help you when I had the chance and I've always regretted it."

His hand was warm and sweaty in mine—and I can't say my flesh didn't crawl at the contact—but it felt like closure. For both of us. I toyed with warning him against interpreting it as a reason not to be honest with Beth, but Derek's presence was an optimistic sign and I held my peace. In the event I was glad I did.

"Just so you know," he said, as I assisted Wendy out of the car, "it wasn't us who put cats under your floorboards."

I frowned. "Does that mean there were no cats? Or someone else put them there?"

He jerked his head at Jock's front door. "There was nothing Mr. Williams didn't know. . . . He used to watch everything us kids did from Sharon's window . . . and the only reason he kept quiet was because the nigger called him a 'faggot.' He hated her for it 'bout as much as we did for being called 'trash.'"

I closed my eyes for a moment. "I *will* be going to the police, Alan," I said sadly. "You do understand that, don't you?"

"Yeah."

"Then do yourself a favor," I said with a heartfelt sigh, "and drop 'nigger' from your vocabulary because I will take you apart piece by piece if you ever refer to Annie in that way again."

He nodded obediently as he engaged his gears. "Whatever you say, Mrs. Ranelagh."

Wendy rapped sharply on Derek's window. "What about you?" she asked. "Are you going to apologize, too?"

But he looked at her as if at an irrelevance before gesturing to his son to drive on.

We stood on the pavement, looking after them until they turned on to the main road. "I think you've just been suckered," said Wendy with a small laugh. "What's the betting they head straight for the nearest cash-point so that Alan can drop Derek a hundred quid to vanish off the face of the earth?"

"Oh, ye of little faith," I said, escorting her between our car and a mud-splattered Renault Espace that was parked beside it in Jock's drive. I wondered briefly where the elderly Mercedes was before it occurred to me that Jock, forever a prisoner to truth, would have hidden it away in order to continue his pretense that he had an XK8 in a lockup garage.

M. R.

From: Libby Garth (liga@netcomuk.co)

Sent: 17 August 1999 20:17

To: M. Ranelagh

Subject: Re Meeting on Friday at Jock's house

Dear M—written in haste before I rush out to collect Amy from her
friend's house. You say it's water under the bridge and that none of us
needs be embarrassed after so long, but I am MORTIFIED! How can I
look any of you in the face, particularly you and Jock? I know you've
asked me not to explain or apologize, but I do feel badly about it. AND
I AM SORRY. Please believe me, whatever Sam and I had going all
those years ago—it was dead as a dodo before you left England.

I know you say this meeting on Friday is important, but I truly can't
face it. You and Jock must feel very raw to have Sam confess after
twenty years—you, in particular, must hate me for my hypocrisy. You
probably think I was only pretending friendship by helping you over
Annie, but it honestly wasn't like that. I was pleased to help, even
more pleased that we went on being friends in spite of everything.
The truth is I let myself believe that Sam would never tell—more
because he remained so close to Jock, I think, than because he
thought you wouldn't be able to take it—and it wasn't as if it was
terribly important where he was that night, just so long as he and
Jock admitted they didn't see Annie at 7:45. In all these years, the
only lies I have ever told you were to do with that wretched alibi—God

knows, I wish we'd been honest at the time—but it seemed so unimportant compared with the hurt you'd feel to learn about the affair. Of course, it was wrong, but I couldn't see any harm in it. Sam and Jock obviously had nothing to do with Annie's death—as I kept telling you—and I didn't want you thinking badly of me.

Anyway, the upshot of all this is that I have written out a statement, with precise times and details of all movements in and out of number 21 that night—insofar as I remember them—which I am sending as an attachment. I think you'll find they agree with what Jock and Sam say. I will, of course, do it formally when the time comes. Meanwhile, I will end with love, and pray you can still accept it.

Love,

L

PS: Apart from anything else, I can't just abandon the girls to their own devices for the day, and poor old Jim would be deeply alarmed if I told him I was about to have a reunion with my ex-husband! He'd want to know why . . . and then I'd have to tell him about Sam . . . and how I'd wronged my best friend. I'm sorry, m'dear. I hope you understand.

Libby Garth

From: M.R. (mranelagh@jetscape.com)
Sent: 18 August 1999 12:42
To: Libby Garth
Subject: Re Friday

My dear Libby, attachment received and understood and love accepted in the spirit it was given! Believe me, I've always valued the help you've given me re Annie's "cause"—I wouldn't have known half as much as I do about her hateful neighbors if it hadn't been for you! Unfortunately, there are one or two discrepancies between your statement and Sam's—i.e., he says you were doing the laundry when he arrived, while you say you were watching TV. Also, he says you'd had a bath before he arrived, and you say you'd been cooking. I know they're only small things—but I really do need the accounts to match before I hand them to the police. You know I wouldn't ask if it wasn't important. And there really is nothing to worry about. Jock and Sam are reconciled—if a little cool—while Sam and I are like Darby and Joan. We've been together so long we're tied at the hip and can only walk in step these days. However, if you can't manage to come down here because of leaving the girls and worrying about Jim, the three of us can—and will—come to Leicester.

Love,

M

twenty-eight

I had asked Jock to leave his front door ajar so that Wendy and I could let ourselves in when we arrived, and as we walked through the hall toward the kitchen I saw Libby before she saw me. She was sitting on a hard-backed chair, her face in profile, and I had a second or two to take stock before the sound of our footsteps alerted her to our presence. *Oh, sweet revenge!* Gone was the startling brunette in her mid-twenties who had flaunted her looks and figure to good advantage, and in her place was a scrawny, beak-nosed woman with a sagging chin and newly dyed hair that was too dark for her complexion.

My strongest memories of her were the impatient gestures and petulant expression that had spoken volumes about her frustration with her life in 1978, and I was amused to see she still had them. Indeed, the impression she gave was that all the water that should have passed beneath her bridge had merely piled behind a fragile dam . . . which was on the point of bursting.

"I've had enough of this," she was saying, stabbing angrily at her watch as Wendy and I approached. "She told me 12:30, and if she doesn't come in the next five minutes—"

She broke off as Sam and Jock looked up in relief to see us in the doorway.

"Hello, Libby," I said with a bright smile. "You're looking well."

She took similar stock of me but there was no answering smile. "You're late," she snapped.

Perhaps I should have been surprised by her lack of cordiality after the numerous letters, faxes and e-mails she'd sent over the years professing support, friendship and . . . *love* . . . but I wasn't. Her saccharine sweetness had been conditional on my continued ignorance of her affair with Sam because that made me a fool. But Sam and Jock had obviously told her, as I had asked them to do, that I'd known about it since before my first letter to her—which made *her* the fool. And that was the one thing she had never been able to tolerate . . . being a laughing stock.

"I know and I'm sorry," I said cheerfully. "It took longer than I thought. Do you remember Wendy Stanhope, the vicar's wife? Wendy . . . Libby . . . Jock . . . Sam." I raised inquiring eyebrows at the men as they stood up to shake Wendy's hand. "Did you get the sandwiches? Because *we—are—starving!*"

Jock pulled open his fridge door with a flourish. "All here," he said, removing plates to the table, and handing a bottle of chilled Chardonnay to Sam.

"We were reliably informed this was your favorite," said Sam, filling a glass and handing it to Wendy. "I should think you've earned it, haven't you?"

She chuckled happily as she took a huge swig. "Goodness me, no! I was just the chorus to your wife's dazzling *coloratura*. You must be very proud of her, Sam."

"Oh, I am," he said, handing me a glass before shepherding Wendy to a chair. "She's a bit of a cracker, too, don't you think?" He dropped me a sly wink. "Just as beautiful as the day we married."

I watched Libby's mouth turn down as she rejected the glass Sam tried to offer her and wondered how much of this she would be able to take before she sunk her talons into my cheeks. "I'm driving," she said curtly.

"What do you think of Jock's beard?" I asked, stationing my back against a worktop from where I could look at her. "It suits him, don't you think?"

"She hates it," said Jock, giving it a stroke. "Says it makes me look seedy."

Libby gave an irritated smile. "We've been there, done it. Also Sam's baldness . . . Dorchester . . . Leicester . . . the weather . . ." She drummed her fingers impatiently on the table. "You *promised* me 12:30 so that I could be back on the motorway before the Friday rush hour begins," she said sharply. "You *knew* I wanted to be home before Jim."

"Call him and tell him you're going to be late," I said reasonably.

"That's what we've been suggesting," murmured Jock.

"I can't. I don't want him knowing I've left the girls on their own."

"Couldn't they have gone to friends?"

"Not without questions being asked," she snapped, "and I really didn't want to go into long explanations about why this ridiculous meeting was necessary. Can we just get on with it?"

I ignored the request. "You should have let us come to Leicester," I said disingenuously.

Ah, me! If looks could kill . . .

"It's not as though Jock's about to stake a prior claim or anything," I went on, reaching for his hand and swinging it lightly at my side, ce-menting alliances, ranging my troops. "He prefers them younger and blonder these days."

Jock gave a snort of laughter. "Too bloody right," he agreed un-kindly. "And *never* with marriage in mind. That's one mistake I don't plan to repeat."

It was cruel but I have no conscience about it. If I'd known of the affair at the time, I'd have slapped the smile off her face before nailing my husband's bollocks to the wall. But a slow revenge is just as satisfy-ing. I was sure it would drive her to distraction if she was forced to make banal small talk with her ex-lovers—her nature was too impatient and too self-centered for anything else—and neither Sam nor Jock was equipped to deal with a frustrated woman. They had failed dismally in the past, and I couldn't believe much had changed in the meantime.

Her lips thinned. "It's got nothing to do with Jock," she said tightly. "Jim thinks Amy's too young to look after her sisters. But she's not. She's almost fourteen."

"It's only natural," said Wendy idly, protruding long fingers like forceps to select a tuna and cucumber sandwich. "An untended nest and a hungry brood suggests to the male that his partner has flown." She smiled at Libby. "I suppose he's found it empty before, has he?"

There was a minor hiatus while Libby looked daggers at her and Wendy bit into her sandwich. The rest of us buried our noses in our wine glasses. To be honest, I wasn't remotely surprised that she was still a player but it was a shock to the men who both assumed, naïvely, that her passionate nature could be tamed by motherhood and a career. They lowered their heads to stare at their feet, and it was so perfect an example of the double standards that operate between men and women that I couldn't help smiling to myself.

Of course Libby saw it. I was her only real enemy so I was bound to be the focus of her attention. She bridled immediately. "You think you know it all, don't you?" she flashed.

"No," I murmured. "I was completely wrong about you. I thought you had more dignity than to go sniffing after other people's husbands."

"Oh, *please!*" she said scathingly. "Any sniffing that was done was done by Sam. He couldn't get unzipped quick enough when the opportunity arose. Or is that forgiven and forgotten because he's served twenty years of your downcast looks and injured pride?"

Sam stepped forward angrily but I shook my head at him. This was my fight and I'd waited a long time for it. "If you want a slanging match, Libby, then I'm happy to oblige . . . Sam and Jock, too, I should imagine. But if you're as desperate to get away as you say then I suggest we sort these statements."

She hated her position of weakness, but she had the sense to force a smile. "All right. What do you want to know?"

"Which is correct? That you'd had a bath and were doing the laundry when Sam arrived? Or that you'd done the cooking and were watching television?"

She shook her head in convincing perplexity. "I honestly don't know," she said slowly. "It's so long ago I've forgotten most of the details. I just wrote down what I normally did at that time—cooking then catching the news—but if Sam's positive—?" She broke off to look at him. "Do you remember it that well?"

"Yes."

She was disconcerted by the bluntness of his answer. "I don't see how you can. It's not as if it was the only time you came to the house looking for sex."

"No," he agreed, "but it was the *last* time . . . and I'd told you it was going to be the last time over the phone that afternoon. I said I wanted to talk to you about ending the affair without destroying everyone in the process. And I was furious when you draped yourself all over me the minute I came through the door, saying you'd had a bath in my honor and were washing sheets so you'd be able to replace our dirty ones on the bed before Jock came home. You can't have forgotten that, Libby. You told me I was frightening you because I said I'd do you some damage if you didn't take your hands off me immediately."

She gave a small laugh. "Oh, well . . . if that's how you want to play it . . . it's no skin off my nose. What does it matter what I was doing, anyway?" She shifted her gaze back to me. "We'll go with Sam's version. Does that make you happy?"

I nodded.

"Then you're a fool."

"Maybe." I crossed my arms and studied the point of my shoe, in no hurry to go on.

"Is that all there is?" she said indignantly. "Did you make me come all this way just so you could feel better about your husband's cheat-ing?"

"Not quite," I said without rancor. "There's a major question-mark over the time of Sam's arrival. He says 7:45, you say 6:30."

She frowned, as if trying to remember. "Okay, split the difference," she said helpfully. "Make it 7. Neither of us can be that precise after twenty years."

"Sam can," I countered mildly. "He's worked out his timing rather more accurately than you have . . . and there's no way he could have reached you before a quarter to eight. If you calculate his walk from the office to the tube, the average time of the train journey, plus the walk from Richmond station to Graham Road, it's impossible for him to have done that trip in under an hour and a quarter. Which means 7:45 has to be the agreed time because he didn't leave work until 6:30."

Her hands moved impatiently in her lap. "How do you know that? Why should Sam's memory of the time he left his office be any better than mine of the time he arrived?"

"Because I'm not going by Sam's memory," I told her. "I was so sus-picious of him after he and Jock made their statements that I checked with his office. I hoped I could get some proof that he was lying about the time he reached Graham Road because I knew the security guard clocked everyone out at the end of the day to make sure the building was empty before he locked up. I persuaded him to let me have a pho-tocopy of the register for 14.11.78." I nodded toward the rucksack at my feet. "It's in there with 18:30 against Sam's name."

Her eyes dropped immediately to the bag but she didn't say any-thing.

"So we're agreed that 7:45 was the time Sam arrived?" I repeated.

She made a dismissive gesture with her hand. "I can't see what dif-ference it makes. All we did was talk."

"Yes, that's what you both say. Your version is that you talked for two and a half hours. His is that you talked for an hour."

She shrugged. "I didn't keep track."

"But you disagree over how the conversation went. Sam says he gave you an ultimatum—either the affair had to end or he'd come clean with me that night. You say it was you who delivered the ultimatum."

She cast a malicious glance in Sam's direction. "He can't say anything else," she said, "not if he wants you to believe I draped myself all over him when he came through the door."

I smiled slightly. "But that's the whole point, Libby. After the show you put on when he arrived, Sam expected you to be difficult . . . but you weren't. You said you'd leave him alone . . . no more hanging around outside his office . . . no more demands on his time . . . and the only quid pro quo was that he keep his mouth shut so that Jock wouldn't have an excuse to divorce you."

"Which suggests it was me who delivered the ultimatum, doesn't it?"

"If that were true, why was Sam so keen to accept it?"

Her eyes narrowed warily as she tried to see the point I was making. "What makes you think he was?"

I shrugged. "Because he couldn't sign up to your fabricated alibi quick enough. He was even happy to rope Jock into the lie if it meant he could distance himself from you. Not that your husband minded," I said with an ironic glance in Jock's direction, "because he didn't want his Tuesday evenings with Sharon made public. But why would *Sam* go along with it unless he had something to gain? There were any number of reasons he could have given for being in your house that night— none of which were remotely suspicious. Looking for Jock, being one."

"Why ask me?" she demanded. "Sam's the one who lied. All I did was tell the truth, which was that I'd been at home all evening, waiting for my husband. And I didn't have to pretend I was alone either because the police made that assumption themselves. It's not my responsibility if Sam decided to sign a statement saying he was at your place when he wasn't."

"Except he says you didn't give him any choice. According to him, you phoned him at his office the next morning to say the police were asking about people's movements the previous night because they were looking for anyone who'd seen Annie. You then told him you'd dug him out of a hole by saying he and Jock had been at our house from 7:45 and it was down to him to persuade Jock to support the story. You said I'd never suspect he'd been with you if it was your husband who gave him an alibi. And you were right, I didn't."

"This is Sam's version, presumably?" she murmured sarcastically.

"Yes."

She glanced at my rucksack again. "And there's no statement from an earwigging telephone operator to back it up?"

"No."

"Then *you* can believe what *you* like, and the police can believe what *they* like," she said indifferently. "Sam's always going to put his own gloss on it—he wouldn't be human if he didn't—but he's the one who lied and I'm the one who told the truth. And I'm damned if I'll let him put the blame for his perjury on to me."

I nodded as if I agreed with her. "Fair enough, but you'll need to be ready for police questions about who proposed what and when because Sam's revised statement says the ideas came from you—in particular his and Jock's alleged sighting of Annie at 7:45." I paused. "According to Sam, that was your suggestion. You told him the police wanted proof that she was staggering about in the road earlier in the evening, and if he gave it to them they'd call it an accident and the whole bloody mess would go away."

I was lying, of course—Sam had never denied that the reason he mentioned Annie was to get himself out of the hole he'd dug with me when he told me she was drunk—but Libby didn't have a monopoly on invention, and it was fascinating to see how rapidly her control deserted her when she was accused of something she hadn't done. In a horrible sort of way, she reminded me of Maureen as she hissed and spat her furious denials. We were all shits . . . ganging up on her because we didn't like her . . . making Sam out to be the victim . . . trying to shove responsibility on to her . . .

"Why would I have suggested anything so bloody stupid?" she finished. "Supposing the police hadn't believed Sam and Jock? Supposing we'd all had to admit what we'd really been doing that night? Why would I tell him to say he'd seen Annie just before the one period in the whole evening when we both had a cast-iron alibi? It's ridiculous. They'd think we were in collusion to cast suspicion away from ourselves. I'd never saddle myself with anything so unnecessary."

I studied her for a moment. "But why would you even worry about collusion?" I asked curiously. "Surely all you knew when you phoned Sam the next morning was that Annie had died outside our house at 9:30? How does that make mention of her stupid and unnecessary?"

She sobered rapidly. "Sam told me you were saying it was murder."

"Not true," Sam countered fiercely. "I was so ashamed of leaving the poor woman in the gutter that I steered clear of the whole blasted subject. All you and I discussed that morning was how to avoid saying that I'd been with you."

She gave an angry smile. "Then maybe I'm talking with hindsight, but it's hardly the point at issue. You're accusing me of inventing an absurd lie when anyone who focused attention on themselves by saying they'd seen Annie that night was a fool . . . particularly if they were trying to hide an affair. *You* may be that kind of fool, Sam, but *I'm* certainly not."

"That's very true," I said before Sam could fire off again. "I've always thought how clever you were to keep your story simple, claim absolute ignorance and offer no alibi at all. All you had to say was: '*I can't help you . . . I was home alone from five o'clock . . . didn't hear anything . . . didn't see anything . . . didn't go anywhere.*' You could repeat that till you were blue in the face because there was no one to contradict you except Sam. And once you'd muzzled him, you were safe as houses, because if the police *had* caught you out in a lie, you'd have shrugged and said, you were only trying to keep the affair secret."

"I didn't need an alibi," she said.

"No," I agreed, "but only because no one saw you with Annie at

6:30. I presume you bumped into each other in the road, and she started calling you a 'dirty tart' again. But why the hell did you have to go out at all, Libby? What was it for? To buy some booze in the hopes of putting Sam in a better mood? Or maybe you needed it yourself because you were boiling mad about being given the elbow? Is that why you lost your temper with Annie so quickly? Because you were angry that Sam had made it clear he'd rather stay with his wife than play stud to a bored tart who hadn't got the gumption to get up off her backside and find an identity for herself that didn't involve exploiting men? Why couldn't you stay in your sordid little bed and weep for your own inadequacies instead of killing Annie because she dared to point them out to you?"

Caution smoothed the planes of her face turning it into a practiced mask. "Don't be ridiculous," she said. "What's 6:30 got to do with anything?"

I took a printout of her e-mailed statement from my pocket. "It's the time you gave in here, so presumably it's important."

She made another dismissive gesture. "I've already said I'll go with Sam's version, not mine. Are you going to crucify me for making a mistake?"

"Your worst mistake was to have a bath and start washing your clothes," I said, "but I suppose you had her blood on you. The postmortem photographs prove you went for her like a madwoman."

"Oh, for God's sake!" she said wearily. "I assumed Sam and I were going to make love, so of course I had a bath. And it wasn't my clothes I was washing—it was sheets."

I tapped the e-mail. "Then why didn't you put that in here? Why pretend otherwise?"

She managed a creditable laugh. "Because I forgot. In any case, I wouldn't have let Sam in at all if I'd had anything to hide."

"You couldn't afford not to. He'd already told you over the phone that he was going to confess everything to me that evening if you didn't agree to end it."

"It was over anyway. Why should I care?"

I looked at Sam. "Because you were afraid he'd tell me Annie knew about the affair. He says she was always accosting you in the street calling you a 'dirty tart.'" I touched my toe to the rucksack. "There's a letter in here from Michael Percy, describing how you lashed out at her with your shopping bag and ended up on the ground, arse over tit. And you wouldn't want me adding you to the list of people with grudges against Annie," I finished, "not if you'd just left her for dead in her house."

"I never set foot in that tip," she said in a remarkably steady voice, "then, or at any other time."

"Oh, yes, you did," I told her. "You pushed in behind her as she unlocked her door because she'd had the bloody nerve to call you what you were—a cheap tart." I took the photograph of the brass artillery shell in Beth Slater's sitting room from my pocket. "Is this what you used?" I asked, showing it to her. "It's the first thing that would have come to hand because Annie kept it in her hallway. What did you do? Yank out the peacock feathers and bring it down on the back of her head with two hands so that she collapsed on her sitting-room floor? Then what? You lost your rag completely and beat her and kicked her until she lost consciousness? Do you dream about that, Libby? Do you wake up in a sweat every time you remember it?"

She stood up abruptly, sending her chair flying. "I don't have to listen to this," she said, reaching for her handbag.

Sam raised his head. "I'm afraid you do," he said in a surprisingly gentle voice, "because it won't go away, Libby. Not this time. No one's prepared to support your lies anymore."

She turned to look at him. "I haven't told any, Sam, or not deliberately anyway. You know that . . . and so does Jock."

He watched her for a moment. "You primed Jock to tell me Sergeant Drury was getting his leg over in my house. Wasn't that a lie?"

She flicked a triumphant glance in my direction. "Of course it wasn't. Anyone with an ounce of sense could see what was going on.

Your trouble is you're so full of guilt yourself, you assume everything this sanctimonious little bitch says must be true. But why should she be any more faithful than you were?"

There was a short silence before my husband answered. I felt his hand creep into mine, and I felt it tremble, but whether from hatred of Libby or hatred of himself I couldn't tell. "She believes in keeping her promises," he said simply. "Unlike you and me, Libby, who broke ours the minute it suited us."

My one-time friend flicked me another glance, this time full of loathing. "You're such a child, Sam," she said scathingly. "Don't you know by now how vindictive she is? She was always going to pay me back for stealing you . . . even if it meant accusing me of murder . . ."

Official correspondence with the Metropolitan Police—
dated 1999

From the office of the Commissioner
Metropolitan Police
New Scotland Yard

Mrs. M. Ranelagh

Leavenham Farm

Leavenham

Nr Dorchester

Dorset DT2 XXY

October 5, 1999

Dear Mrs. Ranelagh,

Re The death of Ann Butts, 30 Graham Road, Richmond—14.11.78

The Commissioner has asked me to keep you informed on matters relating to the above. I can now confirm that a full series of interviews has been conducted, with the exception of Mr. Derek Slater, whose present whereabouts are unknown.

I can also confirm that the following charges have resulted from these interviews. Mr. Alan Slater—burglary at 30 Graham Road at or around 02:00 on 15.11.78. Mr. Alan Slater and Mr. Michael Percy— indecent assault and actual bodily harm of Miss Butts at or around 20:30 on 14.11.78. Mrs. Maureen Slater—obtaining money by deception from Smith Alder, Jewelers, Chiswick, between 06.06.79 and 10.11.79. In addition, RSPCA officers are looking at the issue of animal cruelty, although as Miss Butts almost certainly contributed to the cats' distress and deaths by failing to report incidents and/or seek veterinary advice, a prosecution is unlikely.

The commissioner is aware that these charges may fall short of your expectations. However, he asks me to remind you that the burden of proof in criminal cases is an onerous one, which is not made easier with the passage of time. Indeed, the only reason any charges have been brought is because Mr. Alan Slater, Mr. Michael Percy and Mrs. Bridget Percy have cooperated fully with the investigators. No such cooperation has been forthcoming from Mrs. Maureen Slater, Mr. James Drury or Mrs. Libby Garth, all of whom vigorously deny the allegations made against them.

Mr. Drury refutes your allegation that he saw stolen articles in Mrs. Slater's house following Miss Butts's death. He also refutes any suggestion that he accepted a bribe from Mrs. Slater to "turn a blind eye." Without confirmation from Mrs. Slater that these allegations are true, there is no evidence that Mr. Drury was negligent in failing to treat Miss Butts's house as a "scene of crime." Mrs. Slater categorically denies that she ever suggested to you that Mr. Drury had accepted a bribe and further denies any collusion with him, either at the time of the original investigation or more recently.

Mrs. Slater also denies that she had any advance knowledge of the crimes her husband and son committed. She admits being told about the burglary afterward, but claims the articles were taken away by her husband and son and subsequently displayed in Mr. Alan Slater's house where you photographed them. She further denies being the woman who sold the rings in Chiswick. Nor is it likely that Mr. Alan Slater's assertion that it was his mother who "ordered" the burglary will stand up to cross-examination as he was adjudged during a trial in 1980 to "be seeking to lay the blame for his worst excesses on his mother." This is a matter of public record, and Mrs. Slater has quoted it several times in her defense during interviews. Investigations continue into how she was able to afford the premises at 32 Graham Road. To date there is no evidence to disprove her statement that she won the money on the football pools as records are regularly destroyed.

Mrs. Libby Garth has been interviewed on a number of occasions and refutes all suggestions of having any involvement in the death of Miss Butts or trying to persecute you through the making of telephone calls to your house, the writing of poison-pen letters and inflicting cruelty on animals. She denies that the various "supportive" conversations she had with you following Miss Butts's death were "fishing expeditions" to discover how much you knew and whether your husband was beginning to waver over his alibi. She further denies any knowledge of the Slaters' harassment of Miss Butts in the months prior to her death, refuting absolutely any allegation that she similarly harassed you in order: 1) to focus your suspicions on the Slaters; and 2) to drive a wedge between you and your husband.

In conclusion, the commissioner has asked me to tell you that the file on the death of Miss Butts remains open, even though, on the evidence to date, it is doubtful that the Crown Prosecution Service will agree to prosecute Mrs. Garth for Miss Butts's murder.

Yours sincerely,

Alisdair Fielding

For: the commissioner, Metropolitan Police

Leavenham Farm

Leavenham

Nr Dorchester

Dorset DT2 XXY

Alisdair Fielding

The Office of the Commissioner

London Metropolitan Police

New Scotland Yard

October 7, 1999

Dear Alisdair Fielding,

Please inform the Commissioner that, not only do the charges mentioned in your letter fall short of my expectations, but I had already foreseen three of them when I encouraged Alan Slater and Michael Percy to be honest with the police. Both men were fourteen years old in 1978, therefore any charges now amount to little more than a technicality unless you intend to try them as adults in a juvenile court. The charge against Maureen Slater is equally valueless, as it will depend on the jeweler's identification of her after twenty years.

I presume the commissioner is offering these charges by way of a sop to keep me quiet for another few months while his officers continue the pretense of investigating Ann Butts's murder. If so, he has dangerously underestimated my commitment to justice for my friend. I repeat what I wrote at the beginning of the report I submitted in September: *Ann Butts was murdered because a regime of racial hatred and contempt for handicap was allowed to fester unchecked in Graham Road.*

I have no intention of letting this rest. Unless you come back to me within a week with more positive news, I will approach the press.

Yours sincerely,

M. Ranelagh

epilogue

It was an unsettled autumn in Dorset with southwesterly winds piling in from the channel and whipping the trees into a frenzied dance around the farmhouse. Sam and I spent days raking the leaves into russet piles, only for them to be blown away again as soon as the wind returned, but it didn't seem to matter. It was so long since we'd enjoyed the glorious turning colors of an English autumn that just being outside brought contentment.

The boys settled into local college life in order to prepare for university the following year. They were older than their contemporaries, particularly Luke, but they preferred the idea of a year's adjustment to diving in at the deep end. Sam and I appreciated it, too. None of us was quite ready to see them go their separate ways when we were still trying to put down roots. I had one or two anxieties as we signed away our fortune to buy the farmhouse. Would the roof blow off before we had time to repair it? Was the wet rot under the floorboards as bad as it looked? But Sam was indomitable and gave us all confidence.

My father took the boys to the highlands of Scotland during the half-term break to give them a taste of the true Ranelagh homeland, and in return Sam and I had my mother to stay. My father's somewhat Machiavellian intention was that we should all get to know each other a little better—and in a way we did—because Mother had a fine old time interfering with Sam's renovation work and telling me how frightful my taste in curtain material was.

It would be an exaggeration to say our relationship improved. The dynamics of competitiveness and mutual criticism had existed too long between us to vanish overnight. I was still a poor wife to Sam, ignoring his coronary, encouraging him to do too much, not cooking his meals on time . . . and the boys, though absent, were still too free and easy in their manners and still needed haircuts. As for her . . . well . . . she would always be a control freak, offering advice that wasn't wanted and dominating everyone while pretending to play the role of martyred slave. But the sparks flew a little less regularly, so perhaps we were making progress.

She had a residual jealousy of Wendy Stanhope, whose visits had been rather more frequent than hers. I introduced them on one occasion but it was a mistake. They were too alike, both of them strong-minded women with decided views, though with little prospect of their minds ever meeting. Wendy admired youth and longed to give it space, while my mother wanted only to corral and discipline it. Wendy would never be so rude as to pass a comment afterward, but Mother, with no such restraints, told me it didn't surprise her at all that the silly woman was in the habit of screaming from clifftops. "Why?" I asked. "Because she was unable to make friends with her own age group," was the barbed answer.

One of the reasons for Wendy's frequent trips was to visit Michael in prison and drive on to Bournemouth to see Bridget. Wendy and I made the round journey together the first time, but on subsequent occasions she went alone. In between whiles I visited Michael myself. I asked him once if he thought Wendy still wanted to adopt him. He grinned and said she only ever gave him lectures these days because she'd transferred her affections to Bridget and was acting like his mother-in-law. Was that a good thing or a bad thing? Good, he told me. It would be harder to let his wife down in the future if he had a fire-breathing dragon on his back. He added somewhat wistfully that it was a pity Mrs. S. hadn't taken that tack before. And, by implication, me too.

For myself, I wondered why my more intelligent pupil had to struggle with the concept of good behavior being its own reward, while Alan, the Neanderthal, had put it into practice and accepted it. In the end I accepted Sam's analysis—a strong-minded woman is a man's best friend.

I had an angry letter from Beth Slater midway through September in response to one from me, which had set out to explain how committed I was to Annie's cause and why it was necessary to involve Alan. But she couldn't be persuaded, and her anger saddened me. She hated people who pretended one thing and did another. She hated the police, who had stripped their house of everything, even the things Alan could prove he'd bought himself. She hated Derek, who was a bastard, and Maureen, who was a bitch. And was it surprising Alan had gone off the rails when he had been so abused as a child? But nothing could excuse what I had done. Did I not realize that by destroying Alan I'd destroyed Danny as well?

She ended by saying she never wanted to hear from me again. However, I remained optimistic because I'd learned a great deal about the healing powers of time—and I was sure she knew how much I admired her.

To my relief, Danny turned up like a bad penny toward the end of October. He had a filthy hangover. He was irritable and tetchy, and laid down rules and regulations about his private space and what he was allowed to do in it. "Like what?" asked Sam.

"Chill out . . . smoke a joint now and then . . ." He needed peace and quiet to get his head straight, and we owed him that much for setting his family at each other's throats.

Sam, equally relieved, backed him against a wall. "What about my wife's head?" he demanded. Didn't his family owe me something for what his father and brother had done to me? Danny was scornful. How could the Slaters compensate his missus? What did they have that she wanted? Hell, she was in a different league. That's why he'd come. He reckoned she could teach him a thing or two . . . about internalized pain . . . and how he could use it to exploit his genius.

Sheila Arnold and I remained friends, but at a distance. We greeted each other warmly when we met in the street but recognized we had little in common. In the end I preferred the anarchy of clifftop scream- ing to the elegant conformity of matching panama hats. She agreed grudgingly to allow me to use parts of her correspondence in press re- leases, but insisted that I make it clear she was unavailable for inter- views. "Larry would never approve," she said.

Jock arrived for a long weekend in November and helped us re-felt and re-tile the western end of the roof above the attic. He and I did most of the heaving of materials while Sam straddled the gable and shouted orders. Then, come the evenings, we dropped into armchairs and threw cushions at Sam until he agreed to pour us enormous glasses of wine and make our supper. I came to wonder why I had ever dis- liked Jock, and what had persuaded me that Sam might choose his friends unwisely.

Jock disappeared into the barn every so often to share spliffs with Danny and give him the benefit of his wisdom on money and women but, fortunately, most of it went in one ear and out the other. More sensibly, he bought the first, and rather fine, sculpture that Danny carved at Leavenham Farm. It was a folded figure of a woman with her head resting on her knees, entitled *Contemplation,* and was a huge leap forward from the *Gandhi* on my terrace. But I wouldn't have swapped *Gandhi* for the world.

On his first evening, Jock produced a copy of Richmond's local newspaper, featuring an article on Annie's death with the headline: "Accident or murder?" He asked us if we'd seen it, and showered me with new respect when Sam laughed and said I'd written it. Of course it had been heavily edited, but I'd tried to re-create the atmosphere in London during 1978's winter of discontent when society was at war with itself in the months leading up to a vote of no confidence in Par- liament and the dramatic fall of the Labor government. I asked how in such a climate there could be any certainty that the death of a black woman had been properly investigated. I went on to describe the racial hatred that had been allowed to flourish in Graham Road, citing the catalogue of unsubstantiated complaints against Annie by "benefit scroungers" which went unchallenged by the authorities, and the vicious bullying and harassment of a vulnerable woman by a "hate group" that was never questioned by the white policeman in charge of the investigation. They allowed his name to stand, Sergeant James Drury, together with his subsequent "forced retirement" for a racist assault on an Asian youth. Publish and be damned, they said! But, for me, the most satisfying part of the article was an unflattering photograph of Maureen Slater, caught in the act of closing her front door, with the caption: "Benefit recipient denies orchestrating hate campaign." *They've done me proud,* I thought.

I made Sam swear he wouldn't mention Libby. There was too much pain involved. Jock had lingering sympathies for her because he felt himself partly to blame. . . . Sam had lingering guilt for the same reason . . . while I swung between a sense of triumph at my vindication, and an ongoing sadness for what I was doing to her children. But somewhere along the line I was outvoted and, at Sam's instigation, Jock brought me up to date over the dinner table on the last night of his stay.

The word from "mutual friends," he told me, was that Libby's husband had kicked her out and imposed a restraining order to prevent her having access to her children. Apparently her fuse was so short these days—"too many police asking too many questions"—that she'd taken a steel rod to her eldest daughter and the child had ended up in hospital. More disturbingly, the girls had revealed that beatings had been commonplace whenever Libby's frustrations had reached the boiling point, and now she faced prosecution for child abuse and the inevitable loss of her teaching job.

Jock said she was showing her true colors and he wouldn't blame me for crowing. But Sam just reached for my hand under the table and held it companionably while I pictured myself beside a river . . . watching the bodies of Annie's enemies float by . . .

Note from Ann Butts, which was pushed through the Ranelaghs' letterbox at number 5 Graham Road the day before she died. It was addressed to the "Pretty Lady."

30 Graham Road
Richmond
Surrey
November 13, 1978

Dear Pretty Lady (I'm afraid I don't know your name),

I am sorry for calling you honky. I get troubled sometimes and say things I shouldn't. People think it means I'm not a nice person, but the doctor would tell you I can't help myself. I only have cats for friends because they know I don't mean to be rude.

I have tried to talk to you but my tongue gets twisted when I'm nervous. If you come to my house I will let you in, but please forgive me in advance if I call you honky again. It will just mean I'm troubled. (I'm troubled quite a lot at the moment.) I would like a friend very much.

Yours hopefully,

Annie